LEO'S REDEMPTION

BY

OTIS L. SCARBARY

Thanks for reading

Otis Scarbary

ACKNOWLEDGMENTS

I want to thank you dear reader for taking time to read my first novel. It has been a wonderful journey that began as a dream thirty years ago. Your support is truly appreciated in making that dream come true.

Many thanks are owed to family and friends lending their assistance and encouraging me in these efforts. A special thank you goes to the following people for reading the manuscript and offering feedback: Cindy Adams, Darryl Bollinger, and Nancy Scott Malcor. Darryl especially deserves recognition for offering his insights into the writing and publishing process.

My three favorite women provided additional critiquing: my mother, Shirley; my wife, Donna; and my daughter, Mandy. They are lights in my life, and I could have never accomplished what I have without them.

Any mistakes remaining are mine.

DEDICATION

For my family who has provided all the inspiration, and
especially my parents, who insisted hard work was
required to get what you wanted in life.

PROLOGUE

The old man was still in his bed after two weeks of faltering health. Father Time was coming for him, and there wasn't a damned thing he could do about it. He couldn't even sit up by himself if he wanted to.

There was a constant hiss from the oxygen tank that could be discerned from the ceiling fan's tick. Stale air circulated in the dimly lit room. Wisps of dust floated like translucent button jellyfish inside a few strands of light peeping through partially closed blinds.

A single table lamp illuminated his desk containing the journal. No one had ever been allowed to read any of the entries. Secrets were there. His life in his words was to be seen by one person and no one else.

If I just had a few more days to write it down in my book...Maybe I could make 'em understand.

Fleeting thoughts were all he had now. Regrets and guilt occupied what was left of the once strong mind.

The bedroom door cracked open slightly, and a smallish head peeked in. "Mr. Leo, you wanted to see me?"

"Come in and close the door," croaked the dying man.

Creeping inside as if the occupant was asleep, the tiny female tiptoed to the side of the bed nearest the door. She appeared ready to bolt any second.

"No need to be scared, girl. I couldn't get you now if I had a mind to. I wanted to see you one last time so I could ask a favor."

The man was aware he sounded like he had been gargling gravel, and some was stuck in his throat. His mouth was as dry as the desert in summertime.

"Yes sir, but I don't know what I could ever do for you."

Looking toward the nightstand the man nodded slightly. "Just a little sip of water first."

The impish girl, who reminded him of her grandmother, picked up a topped Styrofoam cup and adjusted the straw. She placed it evenly to the old man's mouth, and he sipped until the dryness was gone.

He smiled at her, and the tired wrinkles around the well-worn face crinkled. She responded with a concerned look that he knew was genuine.

"Thank you, child." His voice was less scratchy now. "Time is short. This is what I want you to do when I'm gone…"

CHAPTER 1

Dark rain clouds hung low in the sky. Any minute a deluge matching Biblical proportions threatened the small crowd gathered to say their goodbyes to the deceased. The cemetery scene was as bleak as the weather. Most of the surrounding headstones appeared battered and bruised by years of other storms and neglect.

The few attendees huddled under the green tent protecting themselves and a plain wooden casket. The flag draping the top that signified the man's service to his country looked damp already.

This is just too damned dreary, thought Leo Oscar Berry, III. *I wonder if Papa planned his service as a final way to say 'screw you all' after his ninety-one years on the planet. There must be a life lesson involved.*

The preacher appeared nervous about the weather or maybe just having to say words over someone who had never been inside his church. He spoke haltingly.

"Dear family and friends of Mr. Leo. We are gathered for this solemn occasion to bid farewell to a loving husband, father, and grandfather."

Well, maybe part of that is true, Leo was thinking. *He always treated me okay even though I hated being known as Little Leo. I just can't believe he's gone.*

"In keeping with Mr. Leo's wishes, I will make this service short. As the family knows, he did not care for a lot of formality. Leo didn't say much, but when he did we all listened."

As the service droned for the next few minutes, Leo's mind drifted back to his childhood. Papa had been a giant to him during those early years. A self-made man was how he described himself. Nothing was more important than having a strong work ethic and not counting on anybody else for a handout. Nobody approached his toughness. He had been a legend to everyone who knew him.

Mr. Leo to most folks, Big Leo to the family, demanded respect without saying. He had come from humble beginnings, and had grown up on a farm in rural Georgia. Formal schooling had not been part of his life although he had been taught to read, write and do math by someone Little Leo could never find out about. Papa always said it was most important to learn the basics of anything you wanted to do in life the best way you could. Never stop learning was his mantra.

The earliest memory of his grandfather involved a trip into one of the cornfields closest to the farmhouse. Leo was only a few years old and for some unknown reason alone with Papa and his Border collie mix, Rusty.

They were walking down a long line of stalks that appeared ten feet tall to Leo. However, Papa's head was right up there with the tops of the plants. The sun was falling out of the sky and kept peeking through the corn and bouncing off Papa's felt hat. It almost felt magical as a breeze blew through the field, and the fresh smells along with the rustling sounds hung in the air.

Rusty was trotting slightly ahead and occasionally would look back and grin at Leo. *I really did love that dog,* remembered Leo. *He could run faster than anything and jump over the old wooden gate leading to the field without ever getting a splinter.*

Suddenly, Rusty stopped in his tracks. The dog turned around and his gaze was transfixed causing the grandfather to come to a halt.

Papa looked down on Little Leo and whispered, "Be still. Don't even breathe."

In the distance a crow cawed. There was a much more sinister sound, too. A rattle, but not a toy. Definitely not a thing to be played with.

Shifting his eyes without moving his head toward where the noise was coming from, a mere two feet to his left, coiled and poised ready to strike, was a huge rattlesnake. A fear that would remain the rest of Little Leo's life paralyzed the boy. The paralysis did not keep pee from running down his left leg into his tennis shoe or tears from welling in his eyes.

Without warning, Papa spoke with authority. "Sic him, Rusty!"

Just as it appeared the evil monster would launch an attack on the boy, a black and white furry blur grabbed it in his mouth and began furiously shaking the demon from side to side. Slobber and blood splattered on the frozen child as he watched wide-eyed.

It was over in less than a minute. Rusty dropped the snake and Papa immediately came down on its head with a size eleven work boot heel. Without batting an eye, Big Leo whipped out his Case pocketknife that was always honed to razor sharpness and sliced off the head while grinding it into the dirt. This was followed by him unceremoniously cutting off the rattles at the other end and slipping them into his pocket.

Big Leo squatted down beside his grandson who had begun to shake uncontrollably. "Leo, look at me son." The big man's eyes glinted in the sunlight and looked like blue ice to the boy.

"I want you to always remember that life teaches you lessons everyday, if you listen and pay attention. This is only one lesson today, but it's an important one." He looked over at Rusty, patted him on the head and smiled.

Staring back into the boy's eyes, he continued, "You can be havin' a real nice day. Feelin' fine. Not a care in the world except maybe what's for supper."

Big Leo glanced over at the snake's remains and spit out a nasty looking glob. He continued talking in his southern drawl without ever pronouncing the letter g on the end of a word.

"When you least expect it, life can change and throw somethin' in your way. How you face whatever comes at 'cha will make you into the man you'll be. Do you understand?"

"I'm not sure, Papa. All I know right now is how scared I was when I saw that snake. You don't ever seem scared of anything," Leo whimpered.

Big Leo slowly shook his head and took off his hat. "See these white hairs? Every damned one of them came from somethin' I've had to deal with durin' my life. I've been scared plenty of times. Healthy fear is normal. Lettin' it rule your life will ruin you."

"You did fine just then by keepin' the devil lookin' at you so Rusty could take care of the threat," continued the grandfather.

Pulling the rattlers from his pocket and putting them in the boy's hand, he said, "Keep these as a reminder to listen for warnings in your life."

At that moment a jagged lightning bolt flashed in the not-so-far distance followed by a huge thunderclap. Leo was jarred from his memories and once again heard the preacher.

"Dear family, I think somebody wants us to wrap this memorial up right away!" Glancing around at the ominous weather he finished, "And I wouldn't be surprised if Mr. Leo has something to do with that."

Nervous laughter followed, and somebody behind Leo added a hearty, "Amen!" As a few rain dollops began to fall, Leo Oscar Berry, Sr. was then lowered into his grave and the mourners scattered to their cars.

Yeah. Papa's trying to teach another of his lessons. Get your ass inside when a storm is comin', remembered Leo.

Little Leo always listened to Papa.

CHAPTER 2

Leo slammed the door to his car as water started splattering the windshield. Other cars had started their engines, cut on their lights and began leaving the cemetery. Within minutes all of them had departed except for an older model Chevy parked to the right of his vehicle. Prior to that moment, he had not noticed the other car that reminded him of days gone by.

As he was squinting to try and get a better look, the passenger side door was jerked open and a soaked miniature female plopped down on the seat next to Leo. In her hand was an old box that somehow had stayed dry. Startled, Leo didn't have a chance to speak before the teenaged-looking girl began to talk.

"I know you, but you probably don't know me. My name is Michelle Thomas, but everybody calls me Mickie," she paused. "I knew your granddaddy."

Leo struggled to place her as he eyed the young face. She had dark features and was not unattractive. *Couldn't weigh a hundred pounds,* he thought. She seemed familiar and maybe he had seen her before, but he had no immediate memory to confirm that.

"Well, most people from around here knew Papa, I mean Mr. Leo," he stammered.

The girl had started mopping water off her face with the sleeve of her blouse, but was not having much success since it was almost as soaked as her skin. Leo opened the console between them and pulled out a folded golf towel his wife kept in the car for emergencies.

"Here, see if this works better," he said as he handed the towel to her. "That's about the best I can do on such short notice."

She remained quiet as she dried her face and then started patting her long dark hair. "Thanks, I really didn't mean to get your car wet. I just needed to give you something."

"It's okay about the car. I usually drive the older one, and my wife Dee drives the newer one. We would've been in that one together if the weather had not looked so bad. She's got a thing for storms," he replied.

He continued, "You've got me totally befuddled. I've usually got a pretty good memory, and you do have some familiarity, but I'm sorry I don't remember you. I can't imagine what a stranger might have to give me."

Mickie smiled for the first time, and the gloominess seemed to disappear for a moment. "I don't think I've ever heard anybody use the word befuddled except for Mr. Leo. Kinda old-fashioned. It's a funny word to me. It sounded funnier when he said it."

It was Leo's turn to smile, and then it became a big grin. "You're right. I think the first time I heard him say that he was talking about my late uncle who drank himself to an early grave. When I asked Papa what the word meant, he told me to look it up in the dictionary. He did that to me more than once."

"The first time I heard him use that term he was talking about the chickens. They were running around their coop acting crazy, and that's how he described them. He later spied a chicken hawk in a nearby tree and said that was why the chickens were scared and befuddled. When he shot that hawk I remember the chickens all calmed down," said Mickie.

"Did he tell you there was a lesson to be learned?"

She smiled again. "Yeah. Some things that confuse aren't always apparent. As you said, he did those kinds of things more than once."

Leo looked back toward where the two gravediggers still labored under the tent. Rain continued to drum on the car as he watched them work. They had to be getting wet. He wondered if they should wait until the ground dried out or at least until the rain stopped.

"Papa was a hell of a man. Bigger than life in so many ways. It's been hard trying to live up to the name, even more so the man."

"Mr. Leo was proud of you. He told me so several times. He said you always learned your lessons even when you made mistakes," said Mickie.

She paused a few seconds, "Mr. Leo preached that you should never make the same mistake twice because that made you fatuous."

Leo laughed upon hearing another word Papa had used that caused Leo a look-up in Webster's. "It's obvious you knew my grandfather pretty well. You've heard some of the same things he taught me. When was the last time you talked to him?"

"The last time I saw him was the night he died. Mr. Leo sent word for me to go to his house. I didn't want to because I was afraid he was dying, but I couldn't turn down a request from him. He was always good to me and my mom." She shivered at the memory.

Leo was blown away by Mickie's statement. He had known Papa was in poor health, but had been so busy at work the last few weeks and put off a visit until it was too late. The feeling of guilt occurring after first learning of his grandfather's passing flooded over him again. There really was no excuse for him not making an effort.

It was almost as if Mickie could read Leo's inner turmoil as she reached over and lightly touched his arm lying on the console. "No need to beat yourself up over what's done. That's another one of Mr. Leo's lessons he taught me."

Leo offered a weak smile and spoke softly, "I got that lesson, too. I guess I figured he would be fine until I got over to see him. He always seemed too tough to die."

"Anyway, Mr. Leo insisted that I give you this box after he was 'in the ground' and made me promise on my mother's grave." Mickie looked down at the box she had laid in the floorboard. "That's one promise I could never break."

Leo wondered about that, and he wanted to question her why Papa would put such a trip on her. Losing your mother had to be hard, and he was glad not to have faced such a loss. Losing his dad a few years before had been awful, but Leo had always been a "Mama's boy" and couldn't imagine that grief.

"What's in it?" asked Leo as he glanced at the box. "I don't think I've ever seen it before."

"I don't know exactly, but it must be a journal of some sort. Mr. Leo said you should have it because 'if anyone was able to decipher his words, it would be Little Leo.' He told me to use a key to his desk that he had taped to the back and get this box and contents. His instructions were clear. No one was to look at it but you."

The rain was letting up although it was still coming down at a steady rate. It looked like the guys might be finishing up at the gravesite. He made a mental note to check back on the grave in a few days to make sure it was okay.

"So, you didn't look inside the box?"

"No! I promised Mr. Leo."

"Okay, okay. I'm sorry. Let me see it."

Almost reverently, Mickie picked up the box and gave it to Leo. Taking control of the item he could tell there was something inside as it slid slightly to one end. It was cloth bound and slightly tattered at the edges. Old sewing box maybe? There didn't appear to be a lock, but there was a tarnished copper clasp holding the top on.

"Well, let's see what mysteries are inside," said Leo as he fumbled with the latched top. Glancing over at Mickie, who appeared horrified, made him stop.

"Please wait until I'm gone. You don't understand. I don't want to see. This was a dying man's request and I swore, too." Mickie began to shake.

Leo put the box down in his lap. He could tell he had almost gone too far with someone he had just met and who was only trying to fulfill the wishes of a man they had both respected. A dying man's wish seemed too much like a cliché to Leo, but he would honor it.

"Alright, alright. I didn't mean to be insensitive. I really appreciate you bringing it to me, Mickie. My curiosity can wait until later." Leo sighed and looked out the windshield. "Maybe we can talk about it some more another day."

Mickie seemed relieved and also let out a sigh. "You're welcome. I'm glad to finally meet you although it seems I know you already."

Leo opened the console again and fumbled around until he found a business card. "Here's my card. If you need me for anything, give me a call."

Taking the card without reading it, Mickie opened the car door and said with a smile, "You can never tell what might come along. That's what Mr. Leo always said."

"Ain't it the truth?" Leo replied.

Before he could say more, the girl jumped out. Mickie Thomas was in the Chevy and fired it up while Leo sat with his mouth open. He could only watch as the old car snaked down the narrow road leading out of Woodland Hills Cemetery.

Shaking his head from side to side Leo spoke aloud, "Now that was strange."

Part of him wanted to open the box lying in his lap, but the mystery would have to wait for a little while longer. He needed to get home and check on his family. The weather continued to be less than ideal, and Dee would be scared. Sliding the box behind his car seat on the rear floor, he started the car and began the drive home.

CHAPTER 3

It was as if the storm was stalking Leo with some malevolent purpose. Tree limbs cluttered the road and more than a few cars had found shelter under overpasses. Several low-lying areas were flooded which caused his wheels to throw up a wake resembling a powerboat on a lake at low speed.

The drive back to Leo's home was taking longer than normal because of the inclement weather. The cemetery was in an adjacent county from where he and his family lived, so it was only about thirty miles away. If it were not so nasty, forty-five minutes would have been plenty enough time to make the journey. As it was, Leo had been maneuvering his mid-size Toyota for over an hour trying to get back. Tension in his hands went up his arms into his neck and shoulders from grasping the steering wheel.

Leo couldn't afford to think too much of the funeral because of the drive, but he was glad Dee and Mindy had decided not to attend the service. His wife truly feared storms to the point Leo thought she might need professional help to cope with what might be a phobia. Mindy was more like Leo and not so scared. If anything she didn't respect the forces of nature enough. Although not quite a teen, she would be keeping an eye on her mom until Leo made it back.

What a helluva way to spend a Saturday! Leo couldn't help but feel a little guilty the moment he had the thought. He really had deep feelings for his grandfather although they had lost contact in the last few years. Maybe even longer than that if Leo was honest with himself. Sure, they saw one another on most major holidays and Papa would even call him once in a while if Leo hadn't seen him, but there always seemed to be something more pressing to do than visit. At least that's what he told himself to help assuage the guilt.

Assuage. That's another of Papa's words, remembered Leo.

He didn't know what to think about Mickie and what she had said. It seemed overly dramatic not wanting to know what was in the box or in the methods Papa had used to ensure Leo would be in control of the contents. While Leo had always felt the elders of his family had secrets that he knew nothing about, he had pretty much blocked any feelings about any significance to himself. Could this have anything to do with what was in the box?

Or, maybe the box contained Papa's will. It had only been a few days since his passing, but come to think of it, he had not heard from any of the family about Papa's desires on disposing of his estate. But then again, why should he? There was an uncle and an aunt who still lived nearby and lots of cousins and other relatives who might be in charge of those issues.

But, at least Leo had gone to law school while nobody else in the near family had even gone to college. So, why wouldn't it be logical for Leo to review Papa's papers?

These thoughts were still swirling in his head as Leo turned onto the street containing three cul-de-sacs where he lived. There were only twenty houses in the neighborhood and all seemed eerily dark as he drove past. Even though it was daytime, it took Leo a minute to realize the power must be off again. Anytime a major storm moved through the area there seemed to be a good chance Georgia Power would have to be called out to restore electricity. Leo knew Dee would be freaking out.

The garage door was down so Leo knew he would have to enter through the front door. Parking the car near the closed garage, he jumped right into a puddle as he exited. Water filled both Johnston & Murphy loafers.

"Shit!" exclaimed Leo. Those were his best shoes and cost him more money than he normally liked to spend on such things.

Momentarily forgetting his usual routine, Leo didn't take time to retrieve the box from the back nor to lock the car doors. His main thoughts were to get inside without getting soaked and to check on his family.

Down the street someone in a nondescript new model sedan watched as Leo took his keys from his front pocket and entered the house. It was impossible to see the cigarette smoke escaping the slightly cracked open driver's side window or the two figures slouched in the front seat.

"He don't look like much of a problem to me," said the figure on the right.

"Nah, he don't," replied the driver. "Alright, let's get outta here before the power comes back on. We need to let the boss know."

CHAPTER 4

Upon entering his home Leo saw two flickering candles in the foyer and the soft glow of a battery operated lantern coming from the kitchen. There was no other immediate sign that indicated anyone was home.

"Wink," called out Leo.

Wink, or Winkie was the pet name Leo used for his wife. It was short for Rip Van Winkle and stuck because Dee Berry could seemingly fall asleep anywhere and anytime she got still. Leo wished he could sleep so soundly.

Leo proceeded through the kitchen into the master bedroom. Not seeing his wife, daughter or dog, he then walked back through the kitchen and went into the family room. This large room in the middle of the house was the normal gathering place for the family when everybody was home.

"Dino," Leo called out a little louder as he walked through the empty room toward the other side of the house.

Dino was Mindy's nickname and was posted on her bedroom door that was uncharacteristically shut. Leo paused as he reached for the doorknob. He usually respected his daughter's privacy, but he was getting concerned.

Just as he began turning the knob all sorts of commotion started throughout the house. Gunshots rang out from the great room, music blared from behind his daughter's door, and all the lights blazed brilliantly.

"What the hell?" exclaimed Leo.

The door was snatched open out of Leo's grasp. There stood Dee and Mindy with huge smiles on their faces. Their little Jack Russell, Tiki, was poised between the two of them snarling and ready to attack the intruder. When he saw Leo, he also seemed to grin and immediately relaxed to a sitting position.

More gunfire erupted, but Leo now realized it was only the television that was playing some bang-bang shoot-em-up action flick. His heart felt like it skipped more than a few beats from the turn of events and Leo felt light-headed as he stared at his family.

Everybody converged into a group hug after the initial surprise. This activity always occurred as a response to either happy or sorrowful family experiences.

While the human family embraced, Tiki bounced up and down like a yo-yo. He was a jealous dog when not included. After going unnoticed for a few seconds, he jumped into Mindy's bed and assumed the Sphinx position. He watched the others with his head turned sideways as if puzzled by their huddle.

Mindy stepped from the love fest first and admonished Leo. "Daddy, we thought you would never get here. The lights went out and Mama was scared to death!"

"I'm sorry. The drive back was awful," replied Leo. "I really could've used a boat. Hey, how about cutting down the stereo so I don't have to yell?"

As Mindy lowered the music, Leo looked at Dee who slightly shook her head. "I can't believe anybody would have a funeral in this kind of mess. Did anybody say anything about Mindy and me not coming?"

"Not a word. But really, I hardly spoke to anyone at the service. I didn't even see Mama or my brothers. I think everybody was ready to get the hell out of there as quickly as possible."

"Daddy, you said a bad word again." Mindy placed her hands on her hips and was frowning as she continued. "You told me to remind you when you used 'inappropriate language.'"

She used the index and middle fingers of both hands to emphasize the last two words as a quotation. Both Leo and Dee figured her dramatics might lead her to acting one day.

"Okay, Dino. I forgot momentarily. You are the 'inappropriate language' police for this family and I will deposit my $1.00 fine in the kitty."

Leo took out his wallet and gave a dollar bill to Mindy. She promptly scurried off to put the money in the canister where imposed penalties were kept. Leo and Dee had started the practice several years before as a way to keep their use of foul vocabulary to a minimum and hopefully keep their daughter from picking up bad habits. It seemed to be working pretty well so far. Since she would be a teen in a couple of more years, Leo secretly doubted the plan would be successful for much longer.

Dee embraced her husband and he returned her hug. "I'm sorry, babe. You know I would've been with you for your grandfather's funeral if the storm were not so bad. I know how you felt about him and I cared about him, too."

"Really, it's okay. Thankfully the service was pretty short. I didn't want to leave y'all here, but I think it was for the best. Maybe in a couple of weeks we'll go to the gravesite and pay our respects in a more personal way. Papa would've understood and that's all that matters."

The two of them separated and smiled affectionately at one another. Much could be said between them without any words spoken.

Leo whispered, "I love me, and you, too." It was a joke Leo and Dee had been using with one another since they fell in love eighteen years ago.

"Me, too. You, too." Dee displayed her dimples. "Hold that thought until later tonight," she added with a slight wink.

"I recognize that look," he said. "And you can count on me to remember."

Mindy entered the room as her parents were gazing into each other's eyes. Placing her hands over her eyes she said, "Do you think we can have pizza before y'all start getting cozy?"

Dee's porcelain skin turned pink and Leo started to laugh as Mindy used their secret term for being amorous. It might be a good idea to come up with another term since their daughter had figured out at least some of the significance thought Leo.

"Pizza sounds perfect to me," Leo said. "Home made or take-out?"

"Nobody makes it better than us, Daddy. Not even up for discussion."

"Okay, chefs. Everybody take your places in the kitchen and let's fix a big 'Very Berry' special before the power goes off again," said Leo.

As Mindy ran from the room, Leo turned to follow. He whispered in Dee's direction, "Pizza first, we'll get cozy later."

Dee watched them both leave and realized how fortunate they all were. She offered up a little prayer that they all could stay that way forever.

CHAPTER 5

Sundays are great, Leo was thinking as Dee lay sleeping beside him. They could sleep in later than any other morning although it never seemed to work out that way for Leo. Weekdays were always hectic getting ready for work and school. Saturdays were always busy, too, as he tried to visit his mother on that day. Since the family rarely attended church services, each of them used the time to do things they didn't have time for during the week. They always saved time for family activities after lunch, though.

Glancing to the left, the LED display on the clock showed it was 5:25. Well, at least he had gotten almost an extra thirty minutes sleep than normal. Since the girls would sleep until 7:00, Leo figured he would have time to get in a run, read the paper and maybe look at the mysterious contents of Papa's box.

Leo slid from underneath the covers and was a little surprised at the coolness of the air in the bedroom. Maybe autumn, now a couple of weeks away, had started to settle in. Or maybe they had just left the air conditioner setting too low.

He slipped his bare feet into his well-worn moccasins and quietly left the room. Closing the door he glanced back at Dee still snuggled in the warmth of the bed. It had been a great night from Leo's perspective and he thought Dee had enjoyed their cozy time, too. *I'm a lucky man,* he thought.

Once in the hallway Leo could definitely tell the temperature was a good fifteen degrees cooler than when they went to sleep the night before. Studying the thermostat, which looked like sixty degrees in the dim light, Leo realized he had left his glasses on the nightstand again. They were a necessity when not wearing his contacts.

"Damn it," he hissed.

He couldn't decide if he was more irritated at having forgotten his glasses or needing them in the first place. The latter he decided as he cracked open the bedroom door and eased back inside.

Creeping over to his side of the bed, Leo stepped on a loose board causing a muffled creak underneath the carpeted floor. He stopped in his tracks and looked in the direction of the still form of his wife. Deciding she was asleep, he continued his journey before stumping his big toe on the corner of the bed while picking up and promptly dropping his glasses.

Dee's voice was raspy from sleep, "You make the most noise trying to be quiet. Why don't you turn on the lights before you hurt yourself?"

"Oh shit," Leo whined, "I think I broke my damned toe this time." Sitting down on the edge of the bed, he began massaging his toe with both hands.

Reaching out with her right hand, Dee began patting her husband on the back and murmured, "It'll be okay. Just lay back down for a few minutes. The paper probably hasn't come yet anyway."

Leo did as he was told on his left side while Dee lifted the sheets allowing him to scrunch against her front with his backside. They remained in this spoon position for several minutes without making conversation before Leo said, "We still fit just right, no matter which way we lay together."

"Um hum. You still want to get up though, I can tell."

"How's that?" replied Leo.

"By the way you're breathing," Dee answered. "You're dying to get the coffee going."

Leo remained still thinking of an appropriate response. She was right, of course. Nobody knew Leo Berry better than this warm person wrapped around him.

"I'm sorry, but I can't get back to sleep once I wake up," he finally replied in what he thought was his sexy voice, "unless you want to get cozy again."

Dee reacted by slapping his butt as he once again left the warm confines of their bed. "Go run it off, crazy man, and let me sleep." She was giggling as he left.

"I really do wish I could sleep more like you, Wink," said Leo as he shut the door to the bedroom.

Leo thought of his lifetime of limited sleep as he walked into the kitchen and turned on the coffee maker. It had started in childhood when he liked to stay up and watch television. It continued through college and law school when it was necessary to find study time. For those seven years he had worked practically full-time to help pay the bills while attending school. He often wondered how he had ever finished. At any rate, now it seemed little sleep was ingrained in his psyche.

As the whir and drip began Leo peaked through the custom blinds on the door leading into the double garage. Momentarily he was confused when he saw only Dee's newer model sedan parked there.

I'm a dumb ass, he thought.

Remembering he had left his car outside the garage, he opened the door located in the kitchen. The suction caused by the weather stripping around the door in turn made the blinds rattle. Leo chuckled to himself over his wife's comment earlier about how noisy he was. He pressed the button to lift the garage door and watched as the light inside slowly illuminated the car outside the door. While still dark, it almost looked like he had left a light on in the car.

"Uh, oh," he muttered to himself.

Easing down the two stairs so as not to aggravate his aching toe, Leo shuffled to his car. Although the rain had stopped during the night, the big puddle next to the driver's door remained. Sure enough an overhead light in the car was on and he could tell the door was not fully shut.

Leaning over the puddle Leo opened the car door and then slammed it shut. The light went off and he hoped the battery had not run down. Since he didn't have his keys with him he decided he would wait until later to check it out.

Moving to the back door on the driver's side, Leo opened it so he could retrieve Papa's box. His initial glance into the floorboard caused panic. He did not see the box, but then again it was dark.

Although the puddle was not as big in front of that car door, Leo had to straddle accumulated water and squatted awkwardly to get a closer look. Balancing with his right hand, he began feeling inside the car with his left.

Just as he was about to reach full panic mode, Leo's hand felt the box underneath the driver's seat. He slid it out and let out a large, "Whew!"

Holding the box under his arm like it was a football, Leo looked toward the end of the driveway. Muted light from a streetlamp across the street cast an eerie glow in his cul-de-sac. Generally speaking, Leo was not easily spooked, but the scene and the early morning coolness caused him to briefly shiver.

Leo walked toward the mailbox to check if the morning paper had arrived. Just as he approached the brick structure at the end of the driveway, an older model pickup truck screeched around the corner and headed in Leo's direction at a rapid rate of speed.

Startled, Leo ducked behind the mailbox. The truck came to an abrupt stop only a few feet away from the crouching Leo. Hearty laughter could be heard coming from the vehicle.

"Good morning, counselor. Did ya think I was gonna run ya ovah?"

Leo stood up and saw the familiar face of the paper deliveryman sitting behind the steering wheel of a truck he had not seen before. The huge grin showed the glint of a silver crown right in front.

"Crap, Leroy. Yeah, I thought for a minute you were some disgruntled defendant ready to get even for me sending him to jail."

"I'm tryin' out this truck on the route this mornin' since my car's in the shop." The jovial guy made Leo think of the E Street band and the late-great sax player Clarence Clemmons.

"Well, it's not going to last long if you keep cutting corners like you just did, Leroy. Besides that, you might end up needing a lawyer if the cop down the street sees you driving that way."

"I'm sorry, Mr. Berry. If I evah do, I'm sho going to call you. I still remember what you did for my boy last year. He's doin' good now. No more troubles since you helped him out. I'm just a little bee-hind right now, so I got to run. Here's ya papuh," Leroy said with the smile still creasing his face.

Leo remembered getting his deliveryman's son into a drug rehab program after a drug arrest and was glad to hear the young man was doing well. "I'm happy I could help a little, Leroy. And,

I appreciate the prompt delivery, Mr. Haugabrook," Leo paused for effect, "even if you almost caused me to soil my shorts."

The truck took off around the circle with the sound of laughter cutting through the quietness of the early morning. Leo shook his head as he watched the truck continue the rounds through the neighborhood.

Let me get my butt in the house before something else scares the shit out of me, thought Leo.

CHAPTER 6

After pouring a mug of steaming coffee and adding a little half-and-half, Leo took it, the newspaper and Papa's box to the little room set up as a study in the front of the house. The compact room contained a functional desk with a computer on one side, with a love seat and matching chair catty-cornered on the other side. There was a small bookcase located next to the desk containing several law books and a few novels Leo liked enough to keep. Although a voracious reader, he didn't keep books unless they spoke to him in some way. Leo particularly liked Pat Conroy, John Grisham, Ken Follett and Stephen King for different reasons, and several of their works could be seen on the shelves.

Inspecting the box more closely in the well-lit room revealed little of its origins. It was maybe six by nine inches and about two inches deep. The cloth covering the box except for the brass hardware was worn in several places. Leo knew very little about antiques, but this appeared to his untrained eyes to be over fifty years old.

Leo lifted the clasp that held the top of the box and slowly opened it as if it were a Christmas present to be savored. Inside laid a brown leather book with the simple inscription JOURNAL on the cover. The only other contents immediately observable were two medals that appeared to be connected to military service. Leo cursorily inspected those and thought they must have belonged to Papa when he had served. Since Papa never spoke very much to Leo about that time of his life, Leo guessed he would have to research them later.

Opening the book for the first time caused Leo to pause. This book had belonged to his grandfather, a man who was a legend to many. So much of his life had been a mystery to Leo, but Papa had inspired him in ways others might not realize or understand. And now, it had been handed to him, Little Leo. Did he really deserve to have the honor of reading private thoughts of the man?

Yes, he decided. The book had been delivered to him at Papa's specific instructions. It was time. He opened the yellowed pages.

Leo read an inscription and recognized Papa's precise script:

I don't know if anyone will ever see the words I write in this book. However, a doctor has told me it will help heal my soul if I can be honest with myself. As long as I think it helps, I will do just that here. If I feel it does not help, or if I find myself being dishonest, I promise to all those I love I will throw this in the fireplace and watch it burn.

The first page was not signed nor dated. It had Leo's attention, though. He flipped to the next page and kept reading.

Looking back, I was no more than a kid when I joined the Army. I did so without hesitation because it was expected. Everybody had to do their part and I was no different.

I didn't mind the structure and I had no problem with authority. I thought basic training was an adventure. None of it really gave me a problem and once my superiors noticed my shooting abilities, I got even better treatment. It also helped that I could read and write.

When I was picked to be part of a special group that jumped out of airplanes, I was excited. Imagine me, a farm boy from Georgia who hadn't ever been on a plane, being selected to do such a thing. I was very naïve, but I was full of piss and vinegar and eager to try anything new.

But, war has a way of changing a man's mind. It damned sure changed mine. The things I saw, the things I did during that time, left images in my head that I pretty much try not to think about now.

There is no sense in me writing about all my wartime experiences because others who have been through those things have done it much better than I ever could or would. I'm sure mine are no worse than others. Most I try to forget.

However, I have to talk about one of the things that happened because that's the whole point of this exercise. I guess you could say it was a watershed event in my life.

I had gotten separated from the other men in my company after my first jump. This was partly because I was an advance scout and also because everything was a little confused after we jumped behind enemy lines during nighttime.

The next morning as I was trying to find my guys I stumbled upon horror. Funny, it didn't seem that way when I first saw the farmhouse. It even reminded me of home.

I approached thinking I could seek shelter and maybe some information about the location of my unit. I never realized the Germans were seeking the same things.

After knocking on the front door, I could hear no sounds from inside. Peeking in the window, everything looked homey and peaceful.

I walked to the back of the house and saw a small barn located maybe fifty yards away. I hiked around a garden to the building's opening and at first couldn't comprehend the sight.

A young girl was tied to a post near the middle of the barn. Her dress had been ripped to the waist and her dark hair hung to her breasts. She was sobbing. An older man and woman lay crumpled a few feet away unmoving.

Three enemy soldiers surrounded her. One held a knife, one held a Lugar and the other held a rifle. None of them looked my way when I entered the barn.

As I stood there trying to understand the scene, I didn't even remember taking my .45 out of the holster. I didn't think about I had never taken a life before. I didn't even think about being in a goddamn war. All I could see was an innocent girl being violated.

A calm came over me like I experienced when I used to go hunting back home. Shooting accurately requires that calmness. I squeezed the trigger twice while under that feeling and the soldiers with guns immediately fell.

Before I could take aim again, the one holding the knife quickly moved to the girl and held the weapon to her throat. I couldn't understand much of the German language he screamed at me, but I could tell he meant to harm her if I didn't stop.

I laid the pistol on the floor of the barn and put my hands in the air. I didn't know what else to do without putting the girl's life in further jeopardy. For a few moments neither of us moved. The girl looked at me with such fear in her beautiful eyes.

He then said something and indicated with his foot he wanted me to kick my gun away. I did and my pistol skidded across the floor.

The soldier looked at his fallen comrades and he shifted to the other side of the girl continuing to hold the knife at her throat. I could tell he intended to get the pistol lying next to one of the dead soldiers. I knew I couldn't let him do that.

When he made his move to grab the pistol, I dropped to one knee and swung my rifle from behind my back to my shoulder. We fired simultaneously.

His bullet whistled by my ear and mine hit his forehead causing it to explode blood and bone. My first combat experience was over.

I was still a teenager and had killed three men. Life lessons were all around me.

With my ears still ringing from the gunfire, I approached the girl. I cut the ropes and she fell into my arms. She was crying and kept saying, "Merci, merci," over and over.

After several minutes of consolation, she modestly pulled her dress over her upper torso and ran to the older couple lying on the floor. "Mama. Papa," she cried with despair in her voice.

A good part of the rest of that day was spent burying the dead. I did most of the digging and the heavy lifting, but the girl also helped. She showed me where to dig the graves.

She knew very little English and I knew less French. But even with our limited communications, I learned the older couple was her parents.

I also learned other things from her. Her name was Georgine and she was the first girl I ever loved.

This was where the first entry in the journal ended. Leo looked around the room and then back down at the book.

My God, he thought. To his knowledge all of what he had just read had never been spoken to anyone. If this was the only time Papa had let this out, no one knew his grandfather.

Leo flipped through the remaining pages to see if the book had been filled. Sure enough, with the exception of about a half-dozen pages toward the end, the journal contained line after line of Papa's writing. Although he didn't take time to completely read any more of the entries, Leo could tell Papa must have been writing for many years since the pages closer to the end contained written scratches more difficult to decipher. Leo attributed the latter entries to his grandfather's aging.

Lost in deep thought, Leo didn't notice that Tiki had stationed himself next to the desk. It was if the dog knew his master was busy and shouldn't be bothered. That condition wouldn't keep Tiki still for long though and he suddenly yipped.

Leo almost jumped out of his chair and looked down at the Jack Russell. "Damn it, Tiki! What's with everybody and everything wanting to scare me this morning?"

Realizing he had not yet seen to the family pet's needs, Leo slipped the book back into the box and then placed it in the bottom drawer of the desk. Leo hated to stop just when the journal had whetted his appetite, but knew he had chores and other things to take care of before he could continue.

"Alright, buddy. Let's get your leash and go outside for some exercise. You ready?"

Tiki dashed to the front door and dutifully waited while Leo changed into the Nike running shoes located under a small rack by the door. The dog was grinning with his tongue hanging out as Leo slipped the retractable leash on the dog's collar. This had become a daily routine since Tiki's rescue from the pound on Mindy's sixth birthday. Although Leo didn't know exactly how old the pet was, he figured it must be six or seven. Leo only wished he had half the dog's energy.

Out into the early morning hours, man and companion went running. Other stuff would have to wait.

CHAPTER 7

Leo arrived early to work on Monday. The weekend had been even quicker than usual with the funeral taking up time he would have normally spent with his mother.

Routine. That was important to Leo. When something threw a monkey wrench into his routine, Leo felt out of sorts and it often meant he might forget something. It suddenly occurred to him he had not even phoned Mama all weekend. He made a mental note to do it later in the day.

He couldn't tell if any of the other employees of the Solicitor's Office had gotten there before him. It was a busy office most of the time, but everyone seemed to arrive and leave promptly at the designated office hours, eight to five. That was just one of the reasons Leo loved his job and he felt pretty secure he would have at least thirty minutes before most of the others made their entrance.

For the last seven years the office had served as home away from home. Looking back now, it was hard for Leo to believe he had ever wanted to do anything related to the law other than prosecute criminal cases.

At first, he had enjoyed being his own boss and the unexpected cases encountered in private practice. Leo had taken all sorts of cases and endeavored to do his best no matter if it was a divorce, closing a loan, drafting a will, handling a personal injury claim, or defending someone charged with a criminal offense. After a few years of riding that roller coaster, it was not so fun. Leo had gained a reputation as a criminal defense attorney unafraid to try a case, but it was not as lucrative as the general public thought, and he had soured on representing clients who for the most part were unsavory and not folks he would like to hang out with.

After reaching the conclusion that criminal law was his forte just not as a defense lawyer, Leo made inquiries with local elected prosecutors and had snagged a job with the State Court prosecutor's office. He thought the fact it was called the Solicitor's Office was humorous since they were so busy and didn't solicit a thing.

Leo had made friends with the staff while in private practice and had done battle with the other lawyers many times. Leo knew the work backwards and forwards and discovered the niche he had longed for since graduating from law school. He was a fair negotiator when dealing with members of the bar and had probably tried more cases than most. Leo was liked and respected by just about all of them. Time had flown by since starting as a prosecutor.

Because weekend chores and family time had occupied the day before, Leo had brought the box and journal to the office thinking he would have some spare time to read more. The thought had occurred to him he was being way too secretive about the journal, but for some reason Leo felt it would be better to finish reading Papa's private writings before letting Dee or anyone else know about it. Leo rarely kept anything from his wife and he wouldn't this time either. However, the circumstances surrounding obtaining the journal from Mickey were unique and he believed Dee would understand in the long run.

Leo closed the door to his small office and set the box on the desk. He wondered if Papa would reveal more secrets as he opened it and took out the journal. Flipping to the point where he had stopped the day before, he started to read again.

I probably should not have stayed with Georgine after the events described. She was devastated and alone. A profound sorrow consumed me, too.

For the rest of that eventful first day and night, she clung to me and eventually I clung back. In hindsight it is easy to predict two young kids thrown into such a situation would react to the grimness that way. I think we had just seen how short life is and how unpredictable it can be.

Between the tears of innocence lost and the need for love in a world gone crazy, we lost ourselves in each other that night. What started awkwardly ended beautifully. I think somehow hope was restored for both of us that night.

I could have spent the rest of my life there. As it was, I knew my unit was nearby and needed me. I had obligations to them and my country that transcended what I wanted at that moment. I found out that war is like that.

The next day I packed up and said goodbye to Georgine. She cried and begged me to stay, but I knew I couldn't. There didn't seem to be any alternatives available at that moment.

Although her English was not very good, it was much better than my French. I promised I would come back as soon as I could. She promised to wait for me at a nearby relative's home. We both meant what we said.

Little did I know I would never see her again.

The telephone on Leo's desk began ringing and he was transported back to the 21st century. From the caller ID Leo saw it came from the District Attorney's Office. *What in the hell do they want with me this early in the morning?* He thought.

Leo got one of his business cards from the holder on his desk and used it as a bookmark in the journal. He answered the phone on the third ring, "This is Leo."

"Hey, dingle berry. Did you leave any hanging on your ass this morning?"

Leo couldn't help but smile at the crude attempt at humor from Chief Assistant District Attorney, Jessica Lynn Mooney. Smart and a great prosecutor, she was irreverent and known as much for her wisecracks as her courtroom skills. She was also known for wearing the highest heels in the courthouse.

"Mornin', JLM. If I do, it's a hazard of having a hairy ass. And really, you should keep your smartass comments to yourself. With a name like Moon—ey, I could ask you the same thing."

The sounds of snorting could be heard coming from the other end of the line. Leo waited for the laughter to subside. Sometimes the exchanges from the two of them could go on for a few minutes before getting down to real business.

"Truce, Leo. It's too early to get cranked off laughing. I really need your help with something."

"Well of course you do. Why else do you keep me on speed dial?" Leo paused for only a second and continued, "Let me guess. Hmmm, You want us to handle a knife fight as a misdemeanor because the victim only needed six stitches to close his wound."

Jessica was getting tickled again but at least didn't sound piggish at the moment. "Now Leo, those kinds of reduced charges don't happen any more since I became chief, do they?"

"Or how about letting a burglar go for criminal trespass because he only took a lawnmower and string trimmer from the locked garage? Maybe a wife-beater who broke his spouse's jaw, but is remorseful? You know, I could go on and on," Leo continued.

"Really, you've gotten those kinds of cases lately?"

"Jess, you know I wouldn't kid a kidder. You don't review everything sent over from your office, right?"

"Well, maybe I should if y'all are getting those cases."

"Okay, JLM. If you want I can start sending everything back to your attention when we have a question. Or, if you could just ask your peeps to take time and write down a reason for the transfer, that might help."

"Alright, Leo. I'll do that if you'll agree to help me with a little conflict we have over here."

Leo thought the tone of the ADA sounded like she was slightly begging. Conflict cases happened from time to time for various reasons. Maybe a defendant was related to a member of the DA's Office. That had happened a couple of years ago in a theft charge and Leo's office handled the felony as a favor to avoid the conflict of interest that might have been perceived by the public.

"What do you say, Leo?"

"I say I need to hear about the case and what the 'little conflict' is. I'm not blindly accepting prosecuting a felony without a lot more information."

Leo could hear the sound of shuffling papers and Jessica clearing her throat. Already the mood had changed from jovial to serious without her saying anything.

"The case involves the homicide of a guy who chased down a robber. It's not a very complicated case, but the facts are kinda screwy. Lonnel, aka, Nelly Murphy was downtown a little after midnight and spotted a purse inside an unlocked car. He grabbed it and the victim's boyfriend who just happened to be carrying a gun gave chase. They ended up in an alley and somehow Murphy ended up with the weapon. The victim was shot and killed. Murphy was arrested later that morning."

Leo sat a moment absentmindedly stroking his close-cropped beard. All kinds of questions popped into his head. However, at least on the face of it he agreed with the ADA that it didn't seem overly complicated.

"What's the conflict, Jess? Why can't your office handle it?"

"Well, we started it without any conflict--that we knew of anyway. In fact, two of our younger assistants started trying the case a couple of weeks ago. You'll have to ask them about the details, but it seems that everything went to hell with the second state's witness. Right in the middle of the testimony the defendant nutted up at his table and started making all kinds of allegations in open court. He started ranting about the DA and the judge conspiring to put an innocent man in prison for the rest of his life. Murphy also allowed that it was all about racial injustice because he was black and the victim was white. Judge Smith was unable to get the situation calmed down quickly enough and some of the victim's family and/or friends chimed in with their thoughts on Murphy. The 'n' word was thrown about more than in a rap song. As usual, not enough bailiff beef was in the courtroom and a real cluster fuck ensued. By the time it was all said and done a mistrial had been declared."

"And that was enough for y'all to need a special prosecutor? We deal with people acting out on a regular basis and I don't remember us ever conflicting out under those circumstances," replied Leo.

"We just got a motion filed last week by the defense asking that the judge and our office be recused. Long story short, the circuit judges agreed with the motion and now we need help. I guess they were just being abundantly cautious. Of course, we'll have to notify the Attorney General about the appointment, but the boss and I agree you would be perfect to handle this for us."

"Geez, thanks to the both of you. I can't say for sure without running it by my boss and I would want to review the entire file with your other assigned assistants, but I think I could manage it."

Jessica sighed and said, "Leo, you really are a damned good guy even though you didn't go to UGA."

Leo laughed and replied, "That's the very reason why I am. Otherwise, I would look rode hard and put away wet like other alums from that establishment who I won't name in polite company."

Jessica started snorting again. She really was a bawdy chick and loved such dialogue way too much. Leo smiled as he knew his colleague on the third floor was going to get the last word and could only wait to hear what it was.

"Wouldn't you like to know dingle berry? Too bad you'll never find out! I'll get you the file in a day or two after we let the Attorney General know. Really, thanks again."

Leo hung up the phone and glanced at the journal on his desk. He thought about surprises. They always seemed to happen when you least expected them. What could you say except it's another Monday?

He could hear voices coming from outside his door, so Leo knew the staff had begun to arrive to start the day. Placing the journal inside the bottom drawer on the right side of his desk, Leo locked it with a key on his Toyota key ring. Somehow he needed to find time to read the book through to the end before other responsibilities took over. Right now, Leo felt like young Papa leaving Georgine so he could do battle against evil.

Papa, at least my obligations didn't involve winning a war, Leo thought. *Well, at least not to such a grand scale.*

CHAPTER 8

Even though it was not quite fall the weather in middle Georgia was still muggy. This was much more like middle Georgia weather than had been the coolness of yesterday morning. Remnants of the storm that had passed through over the weekend lingered north of Macon causing many to think summer would last until mid-October at the least.

Leo was on his lunchtime run through the streets of town from his local health club all the way to Mercer University, his alma mater. The routine he had started several years ago kept him in reasonably good shape. Leo still weighed a solid 175 that was only a few pounds heavier than he was when he graduated from college.

Typically, it took him about 32-35 minutes to complete the four mile loop. That was enough time to contemplate anything going on in his life and served as a stress reliever if the morning had been extremely busy. Leo loved the shower afterward as much as the runner's high he got from pounding the pavement. He felt it broke up the day perfectly and helped him feel fresh for the afternoon ahead.

There were several items bouncing around in his head today. Papa occupied his thoughts when he started out. Leo had only read a couple of entries in the journal, but he had to admit that his grandfather was more complex than Leo had ever imagined. Leo decided he must hurry and finish reading the book even if it meant letting other stuff slide. Also, he decided Uncle James should be called in order to ask him some discreet questions about Papa's past. He was the only living son and was something of a know-it-all anyway.

Leo's thoughts jumped to his immediate family. He needed to call his mother since he had not talked with her in over a week. She rarely called him unless she had an urgent need. Leo decided she might know something more about Papa's past, too. Although Leo and she had always been close and maybe even closer since his dad's death, Mama had been a Berry for almost forty years and Berrys knew how to keep their mouths shut about anything negative concerning the clan. He felt that Shelly Berry would tell Leo, if she knew something though.

I better think about dinner, thought Leo. Though Dee could cook very well, Leo usually undertook the chore of cooking for his family. Many times he would place something in the crockpot before leaving for work so it would be done when everyone got home. Since he had left a little earlier this morning,

Leo had not done that today. However, he knew he had some ground chuck defrosted in the fridge and all the other ingredients he needed to make spaghetti. Everybody loved his version including himself, so that would work, he decided.

Just as Leo was changing his thoughts back to work and some of the cases he had on the horizon, an unmarked sedan slowed down in the lane beside the sidewalk where Leo was running. As was the case many times while doing this routine, Leo could not see into the vehicle because of the tint on the windows. He assumed the car had some of his friends or acquaintances from local law enforcement since it was not unusual for someone in that position to blow their horn, wave a hand or to give an occasional obscene gesture.

This time the car maintained Leo's pace without giving any indication who was in the vehicle. After a few seconds and several glances in that direction, Leo slowed his pace and placed both his hands to his sides' palms facing upward.

"Whassup?" Leo yelled.

The car maintained its pace and no window rolled down. The sinister feel of the encounter was building when the PA system from within the car blared.

"Woo-woo! Where you going, hot legs? Want a ride?"

The car veered in front of Leo with the front right wheel stopping on top of the curb. Out jumped Detective Fletcher Richards from the passenger side showing a Cheshire Cat grin punctuated with a wooden toothpick. Leo and Fletcher had worked together on cases in the past, and Leo was always glad when they were concluded.

"You're a dick, Fletch," said Leo.

"That's what all the women tell me. Specially your wife," cackled the detective.

"If she told you that, I promise she was not flattering you, ass-lick."

Richards was a large man with a protruding stomach. He began rubbing his ample belly and belched.

"You should be working on your tool shed at lunch rather than risking skin cancer, Strawberry."

"What in the hell are you talking about, Fletch?"

The detective kept rubbing his stomach and grinning. "Get it? This is my tool shed." More laughter erupted from the other occupants of the car.

"Looks like you're building a shed for a Cadillac, but I'm guessing you drive a VW," replied Leo.

The others in the car were hooting with laughter. The toothy grin never left the detective's face.

"It ain't the size of the motor, it's how you drive it!"

"Whatever you say, Fletch. Do you have some real reason for sexually harassing me?"

Richards' grin changed to a grimace. "I was talking to Bitch Mooney before lunch, and she said you were going to take over the Murphy case. Is that right?"

"Maybe," Leo paused for a second and continued. "What's it to you?"

"Not only was the victim, Johnny Thomas, a friend of mine, I helped work the case. That little Negro ought to get the death penalty, but those a-holes in the DA's office are scared of their shadows. At least I know you got some balls, Berry. Or at least you used to, if you ain't become a pussy, too."

Leo crossed his arms and shifted his weight. Richards' name-calling was perturbing him almost as much as having his run interrupted. Locker room talk was not overly offensive to Leo, but it always seemed to be more offensive when it came up in a public setting or with this particular detective. Ten years ago Leo would have laced a few profanities at this guy, but now he continued to pause before replying.

"Look, Fletcher. I'll take you at your word that the victim was a friend of yours, and that's enough to upset you. But, you should know me by now. We've been handling cases together for awhile. I don't appreciate your characterizations unless I ask for them and I damn sure don't appreciate you stopping me while I'm trying to enjoy my lunch time activities."

Leo unfolded his arms and glanced at his watch. He really was getting off schedule and didn't like it. Richards hung his head slightly, but looked Leo in the eye as the prosecutor continued.

"I should know in a few days if I'm going to be handling that case, and then I'll call you to set up a meeting. We can go over the evidence, and you can count on me to do what I think is best. Until then I don't have an opinion about it, okay?"

The detective took the toothpick out of his mouth and shook his head as if he were trying to clear it. "Okay, Leo. I'm sorry man. It's just shitty that Johnny had to die like he did. You've always been straight with me, and we've worked okay together. I really hope you get the case."

Richards got back into the unmarked cruiser and closed the door. The car then made a U-turn heading back toward town.

Leo watched as the car traveled away. He couldn't swear to it because of the dark tint, but it looked like somebody was giving him the finger..

Leo thought, *Great. I've agreed to handle a racially charged murder case with one of the most biased and opinionated police officers I know. Probably not a great career move, Leo.*

Oh well, just something else to think about as he ran off.

CHAPTER 9

The door to Leo's office had been shut and all his calls had been held from 1:00 to 4:30. He had come back from his workout and began to read Papa's journal while nibbling on the turkey sandwich he had packed for lunch.

The entries were fascinating and covered a wide range of Leo's grandfather's life. Many of them seemed mundane at first blush and gave insight into Papa's business acumen. For example, Leo learned that Papa had tried other ventures besides farming and had evidently been somewhat successful in buying and selling tracts of land. He had also bought timber rights and had an interest in a sawmill for awhile.

Although Leo had not heard about most of these ventures before now, they all seemed to make perfect sense. They were extensions of his life-long love of the land. What was unclear to Leo was how Papa had financed these ventures.

The only two names that were mentioned in connection with the entries concerning his business were Simon Katz who evidently had known Big Leo during the war and Gene Thomas who had been a partner in the timber and lumber deals. Neither was mentioned in great detail although Katz's name surfaced in an earlier entry.

The war took on a different tone for me after leaving Georgine. Killing did that as much as finding love. I knew I wanted to live for her and dreamed of starting a new life when the fighting was done. I tried not to take unnecessary chances with my life as a result, but sometimes it could not be helped.

One such time occurred with my friend, Simon Katz. Some of the guys had nicknamed him Kitty, but I thought of him more as a lion. He came from a well-to-do Jewish family in Atlanta and probably could've gotten out of the Army if he had wanted to. He caught some crap during our basic training because of his religious beliefs and of being a rich kid. Kitty weathered all of it and was as tough as anybody I've ever known.

Anyway, Kitty and I were scouting an area when we came across an enemy outpost. We radioed it in and were told to keep out of sight and wait for our unit. We didn't intend to engage anyway, so we fell back and found shelter.

We talked about our dreams of the future while we waited. Kitty wanted to become an accountant and told me he understood investments. He had already completed a couple of years of college at Emory and he said he would finish that and use his contacts to parlay financial success. Kitty promised to help me if we made it out of the war alive.

The firefight came out of nowhere. I don't know if the Germans were looking for us or if it was an accident that they found us. All I know is the two of us started taking fire. Both of us were wounded, but his was more serious. I was able to help get a tourniquet around his right leg while we kept firing our weapons. I am sure we both saved each other a few times that day. When our guys finally got to the location and took out the enemy soldiers, they numbered over a dozen.

For Kitty it was the end of the war. His wound caused permanent damage to his leg. He told me I would make it out alive, too. The last thing he said to me before his evacuation was that he would see me back home and that he would make my dreams come true.

He couldn't help me with my number one dream of getting back to Georgine, but he did help me become successful.

Leo read in a couple of other entries that Katz had provided help, so he assumed Kitty had fulfilled his promise financially. There was a mention of some Coca Cola stock, so Leo thought that could have been part of Papa's financing. That was at least a possibility since Katz was from Atlanta and evidently connected. Leo made a mental note to see if he could find out more about Papa's wartime buddy.

The most emotional entries involved Papa's efforts to find Georgine after the war was over. Throughout the journal were references to love lost. Even after years of not knowing what had happened to his first love and even after Big Leo had married and had kids, Leo read the agonizing writing like this:

I've never been a religious man. I believe in a greater power, so don't get me wrong. Otherwise, none of this makes sense. I can only hope when my days are over on this earth, my spirit will find Georgine's. I mean no disrespect or lack of love for the rest of my family. Maybe these thoughts are misguided, but I think God is pure love and all love eventually returns to Him. And corny as it may sound, I believe that love can conquer all, even the death of the physical body. True love endures and I'll find you, my love. We will be together again.

Leo remembered conversations with Papa throughout his reading of the journal. It was amazing to him how seeing the most intimate thoughts of his grandfather triggered those memories many of which had been forgotten.

One particular vivid memory came flooding back when Leo had been about the current age of his daughter. Big Leo had asked Little Leo if he wanted to learn how to shoot a pistol. While he had never really cared about guns, Leo told Papa that he would take some lessons if Papa thought he should.

They had gone to some remote area of Papa's land near the beginning of a tree line. Papa had brought along with him a knapsack containing some old tin cans, his vintage Colt .45, a S&W .38 and a .22 with a longer barrel.

On the walk to the area Papa kept talking about safety. He reiterated several times that guns when used properly were nothing more than tools. The major problem with guns according to Papa was that too many idiots owned them and didn't use them as they were intended. Part of the conversation Leo could hear in his brain.

My daddy taught me how to shoot when I was younger than you are. Back then we would go huntin' together and we didn't kill anything we wouldn't eat. He taught me that all life was sacred and should only be taken when necessary to survive.

Leo, I'm goin' to teach you how to shoot today. The main reason I'm doin' this is to make sure that one day you'll know how to protect yourself and your family if you ever need to. Don't ever forget the main lesson, though. A gun is a powerful tool that can make you sorry you ever learned to use. Believe me, boy.

That day, Little Leo learned how to shoot and was pretty good at it. Papa started him with the .22 and then got Leo to fire the .38 with accuracy. While he never shot the big .45, Leo marveled when Papa took it out and hit everything dead center.

Leo came back to the present holding the journal in his hands. There was so much to digest and things he needed to figure out. He had just read the last entry and it shook him to the core.

The handwriting was not nearly as neat as the earlier entries. It was short and contained on a single page. He read it again.

As my time on this earth is almost over, I have to make a confession. It is hard for me to do. I can only hope it will bring some closure to my life.

I guess you now know I killed men during the war. It was awful, but I came to some amount of peace because I guess some good came out of it.

What you don't know and what's not been written about to this point is I killed again when the war was over. I'm not proud of it and maybe I could've handled it differently. I don't know.

Leo, I am leaving this journal for you. Somehow, some way, I am counting on you to redeem me for the mistakes I made.

I hope you can figure out what needs to be done to make it all right. I tried to teach you some lessons during your life that should help you. I only wish I knew what else to do to ease this pain I feel.

Just do the best you can to help. I love you, grandson.

Leo closed the book and laid it down on his desk. He pinched the bridge of his nose and shook his head.

I need a plan, he thought.

CHAPTER 10

Leo got home before Dee and Mindy to begin preparing dinner. He never minded cooking for the family, and they all enjoyed the evening meal when they could catch up on the day's activities. Leo took pride in making his relatively simple and favorite dishes. Many he had learned from watching his mother cook when he was a kid.

After taking off his jacket and tie, Leo petted Tiki who was waiting for the first arrival. He always appreciated the first person home to give him attention after spending the day alone in the house. When that was done he trotted back to the other side of the residence where he usually stayed.

Leo browned the ground chuck while chopping a bell pepper and onion on a small cutting board kept handily nearby. He removed a metal colander from the cabinet and placed it in the sink. Running the hot water until steam was rising, he first placed the hot meat onto a couple of paper towels sitting on a plate and then dumped the meat into the colander to rinse any remaining grease.

After wiping it out with another paper towel, Leo placed the nonstick pan back onto the burner and added some virgin olive oil. The onion and bell pepper were added to the oil and began to cook. After those ingredients softened, Leo added the meat and stirred. Reducing the heat from medium to low medium, Leo went to the pantry and grabbed a jar of spaghetti sauce containing fire-roasted tomatoes. He added this to the pan along with another can of diced tomatoes, a small can of black olives, a jar of sliced mushrooms and a tablespoon of minced garlic. The final touch was a good dose of Italian seasoning he got from the spice rack near the stove.

As Leo stirred the sauce, he couldn't help but think more about Papa's revealing journal. He wanted to talk to someone else about what he had read, but he felt the burden of what it might mean to the family. Was this something he needed to figure out on his own?

Secrets. Everybody had them, right? Shouldn't he keep Papa's to himself? Big Leo sure as hell did and took them with him to his grave. Maybe they needed to stay right there.

The door from the garage opened and Mindy was the first to enter. "Dad, it smells so yummy in here. I was just telling Mom how much I love your spaghetti."

"Great. And I love the way you make the garlic bread, so would you take care of that while I finish the skitty?"

"No prob, Diddy. I'm pretty good with bustin' a rhyme, too," she said with a big smile.

Mindy got a loaf of Italian bread from the bread box, a baking sheet from underneath the oven, garlic spread from the refrigerator, a butter knife from the silverware drawer and went to work. Leo and Dee always encouraged their daughter's participation in dinner prep whenever possible and thought she was pretty advanced for her age in cooking as well as everything she tried to do.

Dee trudged into the kitchen carrying her work satchel, pocketbook and a plastic bag full of grocery items. She didn't look happy as she set all of the items on the floor.

"Hey, Sweetie. I'm guessing your day was less than stellar," said Leo.

"I don't know why you would say that. Let's just say it was a Monday."

"It could have something to do with that Kevin face you have on," replied Leo.

Dee frowned even bigger and looked away from her husband. Kevin was Dee's dad and was known for having the frowny face setting the standard for such. For a moment, Leo was afraid he had hurt his wife's feelings.

"Why don't you go change into your soft clothes and I'll pour you a glass of wine before dinner?"

Dee smiled slightly so that her dimples were barely noticeable. Leo was sure she really didn't understand how much he loved her smile.

"You do love me," she said.

"I'm glad you finally believe me."

Mindy stopped working on the bread and looked from Leo back to Dee. She was grinning as she said, "Are y'all both going to drink some wine? Are y'all going to get happy?"

'Getting happy' was the phrase that had been used in the past when the grownups had a little extra adult beverage in the presence of their kid. It had only happened on very rare occasions and was nowhere near the over indulgence that the term might imply to others who didn't know the family.

"No, we are not getting happy tonight. A glass of wine is not going to bring about such a celebration, Dino," said Leo.

Leo grabbed a bottle of pinot grigio from the small wine rack in the corner of the eat-in-kitchen near the table. He placed it in the freezer so it would chill just a bit before opening.

"That's right, young lady," chimed in Dee. Looking at Leo she continued, "You've got a deal, Lil' Leo."

She grinned and the dimples were fully displayed. There was already a spring in her step as she left the kitchen headed toward their bedroom.

Leo turned his attention back to the stove. He filled a large pot with water and placed it on one of the electric eyes. The pot was usually used for pasta or his signature soups and stews. Leo poured a little olive oil into the water as he turned up the heat.

The sauce had started bubbling and smelled good. He stirred the pan again and added a little more spices. The pan was covered and the heat was turned down to low.

Mindy finished the bread and it was ready for the oven. Without any prompting she got the bagged salad from the fridge and started putting everyone a serving on the table. While Leo dropped the pasta into the now boiling water, Mindy finished setting the table.

When the pasta finished cooking, Leo drained it in the colander that had remained in the sink and added it to the sauce. He had always mixed his spaghetti with the sauce rather than ladle it on pasta because he thought it more flavorful, and it seemed to be better as leftovers. Leo loved having it for lunch a time or two during the week after it was made.

Dee arrived back in the kitchen just as the finishing touches were being completed. Leo retrieved the bottle of wine from the freezer and uncorked it. He poured himself and Dee a healthy glass.

Everyone sat down and joined hands. They all bowed as they had done many times before and Mindy said, "Thanks God for this food and my family."

They ate the meal with gusto while each of them told of their days. Mindy dominated much of the conversation as she often did.

"I'm going to be the moderator in the next school play. Mrs. Adams said I am a natural."

"You'll get no disagreement from us," said Dee.

"That's for sure," said Leo.

"Yeah, she said I have no problems talking in front of others."

"I seem to remember you've always been that way since you first started talking," Dee said.

"I also remember your first grade teacher's comment on a report card that 'Mindy is very social,'" continued Leo.

"I told Mrs. Adams it was probably in my genes since Dad is a lawyer."

Leo started laughing. "Maybe that's so, but what do you know about genetics?"

"Really, Dad? We've been studying about genes this year in our science class. I've been paying attention to characteristics people inherit. Like, I get my looks from Mom and my ability to speak from you."

"She got you there," Dee piped in.

"Okay, smarty britches. Genes can play a big role in your life, but remember environment can have a huge influence, too," said Leo.

"Dad, do you think you got some of Big Papa's genes?"

Leo was momentarily stunned. Mindy had always called his grandfather that name, but they had not discussed his passing very much. Also, it was a pretty good question that Leo had not really thought about.

"Hmmm, I'm not sure. I've never thought about it, but I guess if pressed I would say that Papa always kept learning and I try to do the same. Maybe that's genetic."

"Yeah, maybe. I also think you've got principles, Diddy. Just like Big Papa."

Leo could only sit there thinking about what he had learned about Papa in the last couple of days. He had always thought that Big Leo was the most principled person he had ever known, but now he was not sure of that at all. This topic was just too much to digest right now. Time to change the subject.

"Well, as Papa always told me, 'Things aren't always as they seem.' I'll take your comment as a compliment, Dino. We'll talk about this more when I have more time to think about it. Now, lets finish eating so you can do your homework."

The rest of the night was uneventful. Leo wondered how long that would last, though.

CHAPTER 11

Over the course of the next couple of days, Leo went back to the journal several times, re-read and made notes. Questions arose over several entries that Papa had written and Leo knew he would have to seek answers to those before he could make any effort to solve the mysteries. Since he never used all of his accrued vacation, he decided to ask his boss for a few days off.

'The Colonel' was Clay Johnson's nickname. Like Leo, he had family ties to the community that spanned nearly two hundred years. They were even distantly related on his mother's side three generations removed. He was a respected leader in government and had served as Solicitor for nearly forty years. Leo liked working for him, and knew he could stick his head in Colonel's office any time.

Leo peaked inside the corner office and saw his boss reading the paper with his right foot propped up on the desk. *Pretty typical look,* thought Leo.

"Colonel, I've got a favor to ask."

"Come in and sit down, J.R.," replied Colonel. "We really haven't talked since your granddaddy died." Colonel referred to Leo often as J.R. that stood for the Jolly Rancher candy Leo enjoyed sucking on. Leo always kept a jar of the confection on his desk and too often found himself with a piece of it in his mouth. Sometimes, more than one. Sweets were a weakness he just couldn't shake.

"Yes sir, it's been a crazy week since Papa died. I know it's been busy up here, but I'm pretty much caught up with everything. Since Rob and Sandy are going to be around for at least the next couple of weeks, so I was hoping I could take off next week to do a few things."

Colonel closed and folded his newspaper and took his foot off the desk. He turned around his chair so that he was facing Leo. His full head of white hair and the long matching eyebrows cemented the image of a southern gentleman.

"How are you feeling, J.R.?"

"I feel good, Colonel. Why, do I look bad?

"You look a little tired to me. Your eyes look puffy. You sleeping enough these days?"

Leo and Colonel had talked about this before. It was not unusual for Leo to get by on less sleep than a lot of people he knew. He was not nearly as bothered by that fact as others, but

Leo knew sleep deprivation could make him grouchy and less attentive on occasion.

"I think I'm getting enough, Colonel. I've had some things on my mind since Papa died, and maybe it's affected my sleep a little more than usual."

"Maybe you need to take a few days off. Rest a little. Have some fun. You work and worry way too much about this job. By the way, how many days do you have to retirement?" Colonel smiled as he asked the question.

This was a running joke around the office about Leo's "pending" retirement. Leo was always able to tell the express time left before he would be eligible.

Without batting an eye, Leo answered, "22 years, 6 months, 5 days, 7 hours and 21 minutes."

They both laughed.

"Seriously, Leo. I just got a call from the DA a few minutes ago asking if you had mentioned to me about handling a murder case for them. Don't you think there's enough on your plate right now?"

"I'm sorry I forgot to ask you about that, Colonel. No excuses, but I guess my mind has been a little cluttered. Really, I'm okay to take over the case for them. I don't think it will be overly complicated. However, it's funny you mentioned me taking off a few days. That's the favor I came to ask for."

"Great minds work alike, right? You take off as much as you like. And, I'm okay with you helping the DA if you want to. Get with the other assistants and y'all work out the details."

"Thanks, Colonel. I won't let you down."

Leo left his boss's office and went immediately into the one next door. Rob was the senior assistant solicitor with a reputation as being a hard-nosed prosecutor. His tough ex-military persona provided the perfect opposite side of the coin to Leo's more amiable approach to the job. It was a version of good cop/bad cop the two prosecutors used often when dealing with certain defense lawyers. While the end results were usually the same, some attorneys responded to Leo's subtle approach better than the tougher one used by Rob.

The other assistant, Sandy, was also in Rob's office. Sandy was the youngest prosecutor of the three, but the smartest. She was a small woman who took many defense lawyers by surprise the first time she came against them in the courtroom. She was also the only one of them to have been on law review while in school. Together, the three of them were a formidable group of prosecutors, thought Leo.

They were discussing a pending DUI case over a cup of coffee. Leo always appreciated that the three of them could bounce ideas off each other when there were issues a little out of the ordinary. Leo listened to the conversation from the doorway.

"It's a crying damned shame the way some lawyers waste their client's money," said Rob.

"There are only four or five of them who persist on using so-called experts," responded Sandy. "We all know who they are, and why they like to do the dog and pony shows."

"I don't know why they keep calling these idiots to testify. Like that fat guy from Florida. Has a single jury bought his bullshit yet?" Rob was in his incensed mode.

"Well at least he only charges the defense a couple of grand to offer up his crap. Some of them are charging a lot more like Dr. What's His Name talking about the flora in the lungs," Sandy said while shaking her head.

"I guess it fools some people some of the time, but I think it's borderline incompetence of counsel to use those guys," said Rob with a frown.

"The only one who is somewhat effective is the former cop who used to train officers on the proper techniques for field sobriety testing," piped in Leo. "But, how many times have we told the lawyers we would not use tests improperly done if they would just take the time to point out the defects?"

"Hell, yeah!" said Rob.

"A couple of the lawyers get it, save their clients money and get as good if not better results," said Sandy.

Leo walked into the office and sat down in the empty chair beside Sandy. These impromptu meetings happened regularly and often occurred in any of the other's office.

"I don't know who called this meeting of the bored, but I need to ask y'all something," started Leo.

"Who said we were bored?" replied Sandy.

"Yeah, what's on your mind to cause you to interrupt such an important meeting?" said Rob.

"A couple of things. First, I just asked the Colonel if I could take off a few days and he approved. I thought it would be okay with y'all since court looks to be manageable the next week. Okay with y'all?"

"We'll make it somehow, Leo. It'll cost you though," Sandy said showing a slight smirk.

"How many pens?" responded Leo. Everyone knew Sandy had a thing for collecting ink pens. Good ones, bad ones, nice ones, crappy ones, it didn't matter. You could always get a favor by bringing her one. Leo figured she had at least a couple of hundred squirreled away.

"I got an interesting one from the funeral home last week that I'll let you have," said Leo. "I think the saying on the pen is, 'Grief is good and we use the best wood.'"

Sandy laughed, "You're kidding, right?"

"Of course."

"You know it's fine, Leo," said Rob. "What's the other thing?"

"Jessica wants me to handle a case for them and I said I would. I was also hoping y'all are okay with that and maybe even want to help."

"Damn, Leo! Don't you know that's why all of us like working misdemeanors? Why do we want to add any more stress? We already prosecute thousands of more cases than them with a whole lot less help and less money, too." Rob looked like his blood pressure might be going up.

"I'll help," Sandy was barely audible.

"Thanks, friend-girl. I know, Rob. We're unappreciated by most folks including a lot of them in the DA's office, but I think I should help when I can. It's maybe a little hokey, but I think I owe it as an officer of the court to aid the function even when I don't have to or really don't want to. I won't let it interfere with my job here, I promise. Besides, like Kay used to say, I'm trying to make a name for myself."

That got Rob laughing. Kay had been a secretary with the office for a long time before finally retiring. Known for her strange wardrobe, squared-off orange hair, ruby red lipstick and old-fashioned ways, she had said many times that Leo was only trying to make a name for himself whenever he had earned a praise for a job well done.

"I just had a flashback to that fitted leopard print dress and three-inch heels," said Leo. "I never could understand how she could walk in those things, not that she ever got in a hurry. No wonder everybody called her Lightning."

All of them were snickering. Colonel suddenly slammed his door shut, as he was known to do when things got loud in the outer offices. They all tried to stifle their laughter that of course was impossible now.

"I guess he couldn't concentrate on his newspaper," deadpanned Sandy.

"Okay, Leo. You do the case for those a-holes and Sandy can help. Now, let's try to get some work done that won't give the Colonel apoplexy."

Leo retreated to his office and sat behind his desk. There was a red light blinking on his phone meaning he had a message or ten. He punched in the code so he could check it.

"Leo, this is Tim Hines. If you have a moment, please call me. It's about your grandfather's will."

This was a development. Tim Hines was an older very respected lawyer in town. Leo knew him more by reputation than personally. Maybe, just maybe, he would have some answers to questions Leo had.

CHAPTER 12

After confirming the lawyer was available to meet, Leo walked across the street from the courthouse to the tallest building in Macon. It had once contained a private hospital management company where Dee had worked several years ago. That company had gone bust due to unfortunate mistakes and now the building housed various offices. In particular a couple of the largest and most prestigious law firms occupied a major part where the previous owners held their executive offices. Tim Hines was a partner in one of those firms.

Upon arrival at the receptionist desk Leo was asked to have a seat in the plush waiting area. Expensive leather chairs and inviting couches occupied the spacious area. Leo couldn't help but think that the waiting area was larger than probably all the offices combined where he worked. There were also several paintings on the walls that appeared to be original works. Upon closer inspection Leo was able to recognize local artists' signatures on the paintings.

After only a couple of minutes, Leo was asked to come through the door adjacent to the receptionist's desk and was escorted down a hallway with more art on the walls. He passed by three progressively larger offices until at the end of the hall he came upon a heavy-looking ornately carved wooden door with a gold plate etched in fancy lettering, "Timothy H. Hines."

Impressive, thought Leo.

Immediately, the lawyer greeted Leo. He was dressed in a suit costing a month's salary for Leo. Leo felt under-dressed in the distinguished attorney's presence. Hoping that he looked more comfortable than he felt, Leo stuck out his right hand to take the older lawyer's hand that was already positioned.

"Leo, long time no see. How have you been?"

"I'm good, Mr. Hines. Thanks for asking. Yes sir, I don't think I've seen you in a few years. I think it was at some bar function, as I recall."

"Probably so, I haven't been to anything the local bar has put on lately. I used to attend them all, though. Things change as you get older. Come over and make yourself at home."

Leo was led to the rear area of the huge office away from Hines' ample desk. Leo looked around in amazement at the tastefully decorated palace. He was asked to sit in a comfortable leather chair facing the skyline. There was a small table between them as Hines sat down opposite of Leo. A silver service coffee pot and china cups were already arranged on a white linen cloth.

"Mr. Hines, excuse me for sounding like a member of the Beverly Hillbillies, but all I can think of is, 'Woo, doggies!'"

Hines threw back his impeccably coiffed head and laughed heartily. Just that quickly Leo felt less intimidated. He knew a lot of these trappings were for effect and could disarm opponents or impress potential clients. Leo was determined not to be either until he could find out more about the purpose of the meeting. Come to think of it, that was a lesson Papa had taught him at some point. It seemed he was realizing more and more how many lessons Leo had learned from his grandfather.

"Leo, I haven't thought about that show in years. I can see your point, though. I honestly don't see all this as that impressive after being here for awhile," he said as he gestured with his right hand around the office. "At least I don't have a 'fancy eating table' like the Clampetts had."

Leo couldn't help but chuckle at the reference to the pool table from the show. It made him relax even more.

"They just don't make television shows like that anymore. I'm just thankful there are a couple of networks that still play the old stuff," replied Leo.

"No, they don't. At least I don't think they do. I really don't know since I rarely watch TV these days," said Hines.

"Believe me, sir. It's basically too crazy to watch now. If I see one more so-called reality program perpetuating some stereotype, I'm going to have the cable disconnected. At least I'd save over a hundred bucks a month."

"Some might say the Hillbillies were perpetuating stereotypes, too," said Hines.

"Maybe, sir. But at least Jed, Granny and the rest looked smart compared to some of the clans people watch now."

"Fair enough, Leo. Anyway, we've got some important things to discuss this morning rather than the state of television. Do you mind?"

"Not at all. I'm more than a little curious."

"How about a cup of coffee while I give you a little history lesson?" Hines bent at the waist and reached for the pot.

"If you saw the dirty-looking coffee maker we use at work, you would probably cringe, Mr. Hines. Sure, I would love a cup."

He poured each some coffee and handed the saucer containing a cup to Leo. Leo hoped he wouldn't spill a drop on the expensive carpet.

"Help yourself to cream and sugar, if you like."

Leo added a little cream from another silver piece and stirred with a silver spoon. This really was different than he was accustomed. His usual stained college mug looked as if it needed a good scrubbing. Otherwise he often drank the morning fuel out of a Styrofoam cup. Hines watched with a slight smile.

"I've actually followed your career with a great deal of interest, Leo. You probably don't know this, but I was charged with doing just that by your grandfather."

"You've got to be kidding me. I didn't even know you knew Papa, I mean my grandfather."

"My relationship with Big Leo began right after I started practicing law almost 40 years ago. When I graduated I had a small office on Mulberry Street. I always wanted to be my own boss, so I never looked for a job. I didn't really have a clue what I was doing at first, but I was full of ambition."

Hines paused for a minute and gazed out of the window. His eyes softened slightly, and it appeared to Leo that Hines was looking through time.

Hines turned back to Leo and continued, "It was quite the happenstance when I met him. I was at the counter of the old Young's Drug Store right across from the courthouse. Since my office was right up the street, I spent a lot of time there because the coffee was good and you could get an inexpensive meal."

"When Big Leo entered the store that day, I swear everybody in the place got quiet and looked at him. I'm sure you remember how he commanded such attention."

"Yes sir, I do. But, he always seemed not to notice."

"Yes, you're right. It wasn't like he required the attention. It just seemed to happen because of the air he projected. It also didn't hurt that he was a war hero and he had those blue eyes that seemed to pierce through whatever he was looking at."

"Anyway, he sat right down beside me. I swear, I thought I'd piss myself!"

Leo laughed and could picture the scene. "I can relate, Mr. Hines," he said.

"I was only trying to be respectful like my parents had taught me to be, so I greeted him with, 'Hello, Mr. Berry. I'm Timmy Hines. How are you today?'"

"He looked at me with those eyes and said, 'I'm good, son. Thanks for asking.'"

Hines stopped momentarily, blinked a couple of times and Leo thought the older lawyer was going to get emotional at the memory.

"Sorry, it still gets to me when I think of the significance of that first meeting. The upshot was we ended up connecting as a result. He had a way of getting you to think about things. For whatever reason, he found a way to believe in me over a cheap blt and a cup of coffee. Before I knew it, I was hired to search a few titles for him. That led to me drawing a few contracts, incorporating a couple of businesses and then doing all kinds of legal work for Leo Oscar Berry, Sr. You can't imagine what that did for my reputation, my bank account, but more importantly for me personally. I came to love that man, Leo."

Leo was taking in what Hines was saying. Once again he found himself learning something else about Papa. He was sure his grandfather's lawyer could answer some of the questions that had arisen while reading the journal. The only reason Hines might not was because of lawyer-client privilege.

"I never knew, Mr. Hines. I've been finding out a lot about Papa since he died. I would love to hear anything you could tell me about him. Of course, I would never want you to violate the Code of Ethics. I certainly respect our limitations as attorneys."

Both lawyers sat for a moment without speaking. Leo sipped on his coffee. It really was delicious and full-bodied. He could get used to drinking that.

"I appreciate that, Leo. It's true what Big Leo told me about you quite a few years ago. You're perceptive."

"You and Papa talked about me?"

"Yes, like I said, he told me to watch over you in any way I could. He didn't want me to interfere with your career or anything like that. Just to watch and report to him. I did just as he asked. I also referred a few clients back in the early days of your practice, as did Big Leo. We were careful though, because we could tell you didn't want a handout and let's say your younger fiery personality might not have been so understanding."

Leo shook his head and thought about that. Yeah, it made sense now. It seemed magical at the time when a new client showed up and could actually afford to pay a fee. Now he understood why. Good clients had been funneled to him without his knowledge.

"Big Leo was so proud of you. When you decided to go into prosecution, I thought it was a mistake and told him. I was prepared to recruit you for my firm, but he was insistent that I let you make your own decisions. He told me while he knew you wouldn't make the money you could in private practice, you would be happier doing the people's work."

"He was right about that, Mr. Hines. While all this is really nice, I don't think I could ever be very comfortable in this setting although I could get used to this coffee. I really do like what I'm doing...at least most the time."

"I guess maybe I feel like I know you a lot better because of Big Leo. You are doing a good job by all accounts, and I think you will have opportunities to further your career in a short time. You can count on my support when those arise. However, right now I want to get back to the main purpose of this meeting," said Hines.

"Thank you, sir. I'll take you up on that offer if that ever happens. So, since your message was about Papa's will, I guess that's what this meeting is about," replied Leo.

"Yes. As your grandfather's attorney, I did draw his will. The last modification of it was done a few years ago. Obviously, all of the heirs at law will be notified and in fact that will be done later today if you wish. Since you are designated as the executor you may want to choose another lawyer to handle the estate; however, I should inform you that my client listed his non-binding preference in the document for me to do the legal work."

Leo sat perfectly still with his mouth open as he heard the news. He never thought for a minute that Papa would have chosen him to be his executor. He really did not know enough about Papa's affairs to feel competent to handle such a responsibility. What would his surviving son and daughter think? Family issues were swirling in his head.

"Mr. Hines, I'm floored," stammered Leo.

"I understand. I really did encourage my client to divulge this to you when he amended the will for the last time making this important change. He promised me he would think about it, but he did not want to burden you at that time. Your daughter was only a few years old then and he was afraid you would insist that he not make the change because of your other responsibilities. I see by your reaction that he never told you. Honestly, I waited for a few days before calling because I thought you knew and would contact me," Hines related.

Leo was searching his brain for a memory where Papa may have hinted of this. Since Papa often spoke with him using various techniques to make Leo use his head, Leo figured there had to be some reference in a past conversation. Damned if he could remember anything right now.

"Well, it goes without saying I'll carry out his wishes. I mean, I'm honored he wanted me to do this for him. Certainly, if he trusted you all these years to represent him and his interests, I'd be foolish not to have you represent the estate during probate. Thank you, Mr. Hines."

"I appreciate your confidence, Leo. I hope we can be more than lawyer and client. I already feel that way. It would help me if you would start by calling me Tim."

"Sure, Mr. Hines, uh I mean, Tim. It's just the way I was raised."

The two lawyers smiled at one another. Leo knew he would probably still call him Mr. Hines at least for awhile. Hines was old enough to be his father and Leo remembered his own daddy drumming "respect your elders" into his very core. But, now Leo had a first-class lawyer as his own. Somehow this magical moment had come to pass like a lesson from Papa. It was as if Papa had arranged it and Leo thought in a way that was true.

"Okay, then. I have taken a few liberties before your arrival, Leo. I have made you a copy of the will and I have prepared a petition to admit the will for probate. I know you did some of this work when you were in private practice, so I'm sure you understand the procedures. I've also had letters prepared to all of the heirs at law asking for their consent of service. Since there are a couple of bequests in the will that some heirs including yourself may question, I need your input as to whether or not we should have a formal reading of the will. My suggestion is that we attach a copy of the document with the letter to each of the heirs. That way, if someone has a question or even chooses to contest the will, they have everything they might need to seek their own counsel."

"Would you please give me a synopsis of what is included in the will?"

"Of course. It's really not very complicated. There are several specific bequests of various amounts of money to grandchildren ranging from five thousand dollars to as much as twenty-five thousand dollars. You and your three brothers are included in those bequests," Hines began.

"Wow, that's pretty significant," said Leo.

"Well, your grandfather had substantial assets. I doubt many, if any, of the family realize the extent of his estate," replied Hines.

"I'm finding out more every day as to how many secrets he kept."

"Yes, he was a very private person and I know he hid things from me as well," said Hines.

"Please continue, I didn't mean to interrupt."

"Right. The bulk of his real property is to be divided between his surviving children, your Uncle James and your Aunt Lois, with two exceptions. The original home place and the property where it is located is bequeathed you, Leo. There is an adjacent tract of land that is left to Michelle Thomas."

Leo felt his mouth fall open again. The surprise was evident on his face.

"What? You mean he left me the farm? Why? I've never even thought about that possibility. That's got to be a mistake. And why leave anything to Michelle Thomas? I just met her after Papa's funeral. She seems nice enough, but I don't understand," said Leo.

"I asked Big Leo those very questions when he amended the will. As to you inheriting the home place, he said that you would come to respect it. He said he trusted you to do the right thing with the place, and he didn't want his surviving kids to fight over it. Since your daddy and your other uncle had recently died, he had obviously done some soul-searching over the matter and decided that the other children didn't really care about the place anyway."

"As to the bequest to Michelle Thomas, he was somewhat vague. He said he felt extremely close to the family, especially her. They had been renting the property for a number of years from Big Leo and for some reason he felt a responsibility to her. I do know at one time he had some business dealings with her father, Gene Thomas. I guess you'll have to talk with her about anything further since I don't know," relayed Hines.

"This is a lot of information for me to absorb," said Leo.

"I understand. I must also tell you there are some other aspects of the will that cover your daughter and the other great-grandchildren. Trusts are set up so that each will have money to further their educations. Big Leo was a firm believer in the power of learning."

"How incredibly like the man I remember," said Leo. "Okay, I think you're right on the money as to how we should proceed, Tim. I see how there could be an eye raised or some hurt feelings about Papa's will, but I really think everyone will be fine as they think about his wishes. In the end, I don't think any of the heirs will want to balk. One or two of them might be afraid he would come back to haunt them if they did."

"Well, unless you have any further questions at this time, we'll get the paperwork started and keep you abreast of any developments. I really have enjoyed seeing you again today, Leo. I know you will undertake this responsibility as your grandfather would want."

"Thanks, Tim. I will certainly try."

Leo was in a daze as he left the plush offices and waited for the elevator. He was glad he had a few days off from work to let all this sink in. He only hoped he wouldn't let Papa down.

CHAPTER 13

Leo went directly to his car parked in the county lot. He didn't see any need to go back to the office before leaving for a few days. Copies of the file Hines had prepared were under his right arm when his cell phone began vibrating and playing Buffett's version of "Brown-Eyed Girl." Leo knew his wife was calling since that was the ring tone associated with her. He had to shift the file to his other hand to retrieve the phone from his coat pocket. This took a few seconds longer than it should, and another court house employee laughed out loud as Leo struggled to free the device.

"Hello, my brown-eyed girl," said Leo when he finally got the phone to his ear.

"Did I catch you at a bad time, Babes," responded Dee.

"No, I just couldn't get the damned phone out of my coat. I had a file in my hand, and I'm sure I looked like a klutz trying to get it."

"Did you talk to the Colonel about taking a few days off?"

"Yeah, I did and he said okay. I've got some news to talk to you about, too."

"Okay, but can it wait? I've got a really busy day at work today, so I was calling to see if you could pick up Mindy from school later."

Dee worked as an executive assistant at a large insurance company and the pace could be rather hectic at times. Most of the time she was able to see to Mindy's safe return home after school because she had an understanding boss who let her be flexible with her time at work. Other times Leo would take care of that duty.

"No prob. Yeah, it can wait. We'll talk about it tonight at dinner. While I've got some free time today, I think I'll go to Mom's and visit. Maybe take her out to lunch."

"Sounds like a plan. Don't forget to pick up our diva," replied Dee as she hung up.

"Okay, I will," said Leo to the phone. He laughed to himself.

Before leaving the parking lot Leo gave his mother a call and told her he was coming over. She sounded cheerful and said she'd look forward to seeing her oldest son.

Leo then drove across town to his mother's house. He and his brothers had grown up here before the neighborhood had started to decline. Leo still felt a kinship to the area and knew Mom would never leave it no matter how rough it might become. She had said so in no uncertain terms many times to Leo and his brothers.

Upon entering the house Leo could smell the familiar aromas of a home-cooked meal. His mom, Shelly, had a reputation for being an outstanding cook. Leo's stomach began grumbling almost immediately. *Pavlov's dog*, thought Leo.

"Hey, Sugah. Did you think your old mama forgot how to cook?"

"Never, Mama. But I was going to take you out for lunch. Did you start cooking right after I called?"

"No. These are leftovers from a couple of days ago. I've got fresh butterbeans, a squash casserole, meatloaf and mashed potatoes heating up. All I've got to do is fry up some flat cornbread and we've got a meal. No need to spend your money on me. I bet you don't get enough vegetables anyway."

"Sounds delicious and it sure smells that way. I didn't realize how hungry I was until I got a whiff."

"Go ahead and get you a plate and sit up at the bar. I'll get you some tea."

Leo dished himself a healthy sized portion of the food and sat at the middle bar stool closest to the opening into the kitchen. From there he could look out the windows into the back yard. He could see the inviting pool his parents had built from this vantage point. Leo knew she would close it soon since the seasons were changing.

His mother fixed herself a plate with smaller portions and sat down next to Leo. She seemed to be glowing. Shelly always had a healthy tan even not in season. Because the weather was still warm enough to enjoy, she had not closed the swimming pool yet. Loving the sun and working in the yard led to her youthful look. It also didn't hurt that she walked three miles every day. Although she would turn sixty next year, Shelly could easily pass for ten years younger.

"So, what brings you to the house on a Thursday?" she asked.

"Well, of course I missed last Saturday because of Papa's funeral. And, I've been meaning to call you ever since. It's been really hectic for the last several days. I asked the boss if I could take off a few days, so I decided to come by and check on you when he said yes."

"You know I always love to see you, but I've told you not to worry about me. I can take care of myself."

Since Leo's dad died so young a few years ago, Leo had felt guilty if he didn't see his mom at least once a week. He had settled into a routine of going to the house on Saturdays. Initially, he had cut the grass. After a while though, she showed her independent streak and started doing it herself. At some point she said she would hire the work to be done, but after she retired a couple of years ago, Shelly always told others she had plenty of time to do it herself. Shelly Berry was the epitome of self-reliance.

"I know, Mama. I know."

As Leo dug into the home cooking the two were silent. Leo wanted to ask some questions about the past, but was a little wary. Leo felt his mother's instinct still wanted to protect him from some of the past. He certainly did not want her to feel uncomfortable about that or anything else.

When they finished eating, Leo cleared the two plates from the bar and placed them in one side of the double sink. As a holdover from being a kid, he started running water in the other sink and added some liquid dish washing detergent. All of the boys had been expected to help with such chores back in the day.

"Leo, you don't have to do that. Just leave them soaking and I'll do it after while. Come on in here and have a seat. I know something is on your mind and you might as well tell me what it is," said Shelly as she stood in the doorway between the kitchen and the den.

Not wanting to disobey his mother's directive, Leo cut off the water, left the dishes soaking and dried his hands. He went into the cozy den and took a seat in a chair across from her recliner. He was thinking she was pretty doggoned perceptive.

"I've been thinking a lot about the family over the course of the last week, Mama. I guess for the most part it's because of Papa's passing. I've learned more about him since then than I ever knew before. I know from past discussions and from some of my memories, you often didn't feel a part of the Berry clan.

I'm now more curious about all that, but I don't want to be disrespectful to you and don't want you to think I'm prying. I was hoping you could help me understand."

"Leo, I would've gone to the funeral if the weather had not looked so bad that day. I respected Big Leo although I never felt very close to him. I'm not sure if anybody was very close to him, especially all the daughters-in-law. I think he had issues with expressing love and maybe it was because of the woman he married. I hate to say bad things about the dead, but your grandmother was not a nice person."

"No, I know that. It really was a bad day for a funeral. And, I think I have some understanding about your feelings about Grandma. She was definitely a hard woman to like, and I was always scared of her. I don't remember her ever smiling."

Leo pictured Elanor Berry in his mind as they spoke. Although she had been dead for close to twenty years, he could still remember the time as a kid when he saw her switch his cousin for some offense he couldn't remember. No doubt about it, he had to agree with his mom.

"You just don't know the half of it, Leo. She intimidated me every time I went to the house. She never said it to me, but I don't think she thought I was a good match for your daddy. Always referred to me as a city girl. I think she finally gave me a little respect after you and your brothers started growing up, but she never told me directly to my face. I hope I never treat my daughters-in-law like she did."

"Do you think she loved Papa? Do you know how they met?"

"To tell you the truth, I never heard the whole story about how they got together. Your Aunt Constance and I have talked about it some over the years. What we always heard was your grandfather was a little shell-shocked after the war and she was a nurse who treated him for awhile afterward. It was like some kind of family secret that nobody ever talked about, though. Did they love each other? All I can say is I never saw any public shows of affection. They had five kids together. I guess that says something."

"Now that you mention it, I don't remember seeing them be affectionate toward one another either. I guess Grandma has been gone so long now, I don't have as many memories about her. It's kinda sad to me."

Shelly looked at her son. She could tell he was struggling with something, but didn't want to interfere. She had always thought he was more sensitive than her other boys. She knew sooner or later he would tell her what was really on his mind.

"Mama, I've got some news. I just found out this morning I'm Papa's executor. I really haven't processed it yet. I'm trying to figure out why he chose me. I'm finding out a lot of stuff about him I never knew. Is there anything you know about him that could help me to understand?"

Leo watched the expression on his mother's face cloud over. He could tell she was less than thrilled.

"I can't believe he would leave that on your shoulders. On second thought, maybe I can."

She got up from her chair and looked at photographs displayed on the bookshelves. There were pictures of all the family from days gone by to more recent times. She finally settled on one of Leo's father and took it from its location.

"You know, it was tough on your daddy being named after Big Leo. He talked about it on occasion. That's why I never could understand why he wanted you to be named after him as well, but he insisted. His only explanation was that you would have a chance to improve on it that he never could."

"Yeah, daddy told me that he didn't like being called 'Junior'. I went through something similar being known as 'Little Leo' as well. It's like you have to work extra hard to be your own person."

"At least you had an extra generation in between. Your daddy rebelled early on by leaving the family to seek his way in the world. Because of that, Big Leo didn't help him as much as some of the others. It was okay with your daddy and he felt good about making it in the world without anybody's help. It really took years for them to work through those issues. That, and when you came along taking over the namesake."

"It's funny having to differentiate your name because there are others with the same tag. I think about all the nicknames that come from such a process. I see it all the time in my job. At least Papa's and Daddy's first name wasn't Richard. Then I would've ended up being known as Little Richard or even worse, Little Dick."

They both laughed. The mood changed and Leo pressed a little more.

"So, do you know of anything else that could help?"

"Alright, you might have to talk to your Uncle Jim to find out more, but there is one relationship that Constance and I have discussed often. It involves a family who live near where Big Leo lived. Their last name is Thomas. I'm not sure what the connection is, but something is just not right about all that. There was a big fire out there years ago and a couple of people died."

"Was Gene Thomas one of them?"

"Yeah. There was something about him none of the family liked. I know he had some business dealings with Big Leo. Whenever I asked your daddy about him he would get mad and say he didn't want to talk about it. None of them would discuss Thomas, at least not to me."

"Well, I can tell you that Papa is leaving some property to a Thomas girl I met after the funeral. Her first name is Michelle, but she calls herself Mickie."

"I can't wait to tell that to Constance! That is news, Sugah."

"If you don't mind, please wait until I've had enough time to check more into all this. Y'all will have lots of time to speculate about Papa's motives. I've got to let all the heirs know and I don't want anything blowing up in my face before I even get the will probated. Okay, Mom?"

Shelly frowned. She could see the wisdom of her son's request, but she and Constance had been close friends since they both married Berry brothers. They confided with each other. That relationship was even stronger since both of their husbands were deceased.

"Alright, but you let me know as soon as I can tell her."

"I will, Mama. Now, I'm sorry, but I need to run. You can let my brothers know I'll be calling them. We all are going to get some money from Papa that should really help financially."

"That's nice. Leo, I know you'll do this, as you should. Thanks for coming over to tell me. Love you."

"Love you, too."

CHAPTER 14

Leo was distressed. He was shackled to a heavy iron radiator that looked to be a hundred years old. The ghostly light of the room played tricks, but he could see scurrying rodents in the corner across from him. Their squeaks were unnerving. He hated everything about the creepy little bastards.

How in hell did I end up here? Thought Leo.

Leo's mind was so foggy. Had he been drugged and dragged to this location? He couldn't remember. It only led to more of a panic.

Who would want to do this to him? Was it somebody he had prosecuted and felt he had wronged them in some way? Maybe it was a defendant he had represented in the old private practice days. He certainly had defended some bad people and had been threatened on more than one occasion.

Think, Leo. You've got to use your brains if you want to get out of here.

Leo studied the shackles. They looked as old-fashioned as the radiator. Whoever was responsible must be tied to the past.

The sudden explosion was deafening. Then he felt heat as flames licked under the door. Leo started pulling with all his might against the radiator, but it wouldn't budge.

Heeeeeeelp! He tried crying out. Could there be anyone close by who would help him.

Somehow he was able to free one of his hands from the cuffs. It must have been looser than he initially thought. Using the free hand Leo pulled against the other one still secured.

Yanking and struggling with all his might, Leo pulled the other hand free. *God, it is so hot in here. I've got to get away before I die. It can't be my time to go just yet.*

Flipping on his stomach while staying as close to the floor as possible, Leo took a couple of gulps of air. There was an old towel nearby that he threw over his head to offer what little protection he could find. Leo felt his strength starting to fade and knew loss of consciousness must be near. He kept trying to call out for help, but his voice was weak and muffled.

"Leo." Someone was shaking him, but he was too far-gone to respond.

"Leo, Babes!"

Impossible, Leo's fogged up mind thought. *Dee found me.*

"Leo, you're having a bad dream. Wake up, Sweetie," whispered Dee.

Leo raised his head slightly and his feather pillow shifted enough so he could breathe again. He was on his stomach in his and Dee's king-sized bed. The sheets were wrapped around his waist in a tangled knot and the comforter was thrown to Dee's side of the bed. The sound of the furnace could be heard in the background having come on for the first time this year. A single night-light in the far corner was just noticeable behind a chair.

"Frigging nightmare," was all he said.

Rolling to his side and facing his wife, Leo took in a deep breath. He could see the love and concern in her eyes.

"Are you okay?" She asked.

"Yeah, it seemed so real though. I haven't had one of those in a long time."

Dreams, sometimes nightmares, had been a part of Leo's life for as long as he could remember. He was fascinated by such occurrences and was convinced they had significance in people's lives. Leo was not totally convinced that they could foretell the future, but on several occasions things he dreamed did come true. More often than not when he had a bad dream, he took it as a sign of possible danger ahead. His mom shared the same phenomenon, and they discussed their dreams when they were particularly vivid.

"I woke up and you were fighting to get out from under the cover. You were mumbling and when you flipped on your belly and got under the pillow, I thought you would suffocate. You never get on your stomach, so I knew something was wrong," said Dee.

"I'm sorry. I guess my mind is trying to work through some stuff even when it should be resting."

That really was true in Leo's mind. After picking up Mindy from school they had gone home and practiced playing guitars for a little while. Mindy then showed Leo the latest school lessons. The quality father/daughter time helped to take his mind off the events of the morning.

By the time Dee arrived after work, dinner was ready to be served. Over pot roast cooked in the crock-pot, mashed potatoes and green beans, Leo had given a condensed version of what his responsibilities as executor entailed. Both listened intently to the explanation and agreed Leo was up to the task.

Evidently the day's news was playing out in his psyche more than Leo thought. No other explanation was attributable for having such a dream.

Come on, shackled to an old radiator? Surely this brain of mind can come up with a better metaphor, he thought.

"Do you want to talk about the dream, Babes?" asked Dee. She switched on a lamp beside her.

"It just seems silly to me now. I was trapped in some dump. Cuffed to an old radiator. There was fire and heat and rats—you know, things I don't like. Speaking of heat, did the furnace come on. I know if I'm hot, you've got to be burning up."

"Yep, I guess this first cold snap of the year triggered the thermostat. I'll get up and turn it down."

Before he could protest, Dee was out of the bed and headed toward the hallway where the controls were located. By the time she returned the heater shut down. The two fans they kept at the foot of their bed seemed to work better now. They both were hot natured, and they found the fans a way to help them stay cool. The two of them even kept the fans blowing after the weather turned a whole lot colder than the end of September.

Now wide-awake, Leo looked at the clock on his bed stand and saw it was 2:30. He padded to the bathroom and peed before returning to the bed. Dee had propped her head up on her pillow and was looking at him intently.

"Leo, have you told me everything going on with your grandfather's estate? I have this feeling you're holding back," she said.

Leo did not want to worry his wife with the details of Papa's life he had found out already. He had decided he would fill her in as needed.

Since she had only asked about the estate he answered, "Well, you're right that I've only given you a general description of what I've got to do as executor. And, it could get a little tricky with a bequest or two that Papa directed. Nothing for you to worry about though."

Dee kept looking into Leo's eyes as he spoke. She knew he was always honest with her, but he could keep a confidence as she also well knew. Having been his partner for an extended period of time, she trusted him to tell her if there were problems. Now she was somewhat conflicted because he had not indicated any real problems, but he rarely had bad nightmares unless something was going on. She decided to let it drop for the time being, but she would watch for other signs of stress.

"Okay, Leo. I'll take that for now. You know I'll help you with anything. Just don't lock me out of that head of yours."

They kissed. Dee turned off the light and was soon snoring. Leo's poor sleep habits kept him thinking.

CHAPTER *15*

I f you weren't looking for the driveway, you might miss it. Someone unfamiliar with rural settings wouldn't think anyone lived at the other end. The access was packed red Georgia clay sprinkled with bits of gravel on top. Other rocks were lodged into the hard ground as well. Wispy knee-high grass abounded and moved in waves when breezes made way into the area. Deep ditches were on both sides of a large metal pipe running underneath the entrance. A rickety wooden post with a beat up mailbox was located to one side. It had no number on it and only contained one word, "Thomas."

The few folks who got invitations onto the property were often hesitant to enter. It was heavily wooded with hardwoods and tall pines that seemed to envelope any occupant almost immediately upon leaving the old highway. More than one person had called it spooky.

The customized truck pulled into the driveway without problem even though it was a pitch-black night. Three red reflectors down the mailbox post helped the driver, but he had made the trip many times over the course of his life, and felt he could drive the long and winding driveway blind-folded.

Even so, the truck crept at a snail's pace and the driver looked around constantly as he drove. He wasn't scared, just cautious. As a reminder of that emotion, he touched the Glock 40 always on his right side.

After about a hundred yards, the truck came into a clearing. The driver saw the small mobile home located to his right where Mickie lived. The front porch light was turned on, but otherwise the place looked dark. This was the sign Mickie always left if everything was okay with her. If that porch light were off, the driver would've stopped. He always kept an eye on her.

He continued past the trailer and entered another wooded area. If anything, this area of the property was even more populated with trees and underbrush. After a couple of hundred more feet, the driver came upon a sturdy gate and had to stop the vehicle. It also contained the same series of red reflectors as on the mailbox.

The big man exited the truck and unlocked the gate that was illuminated by the vehicle's lights. He had to admit to himself it looked pretty eerie in the daytime, much less at dark-thirty. That alone kept away any potential troublemakers.

After driving through the gate, he stopped again and re-secured it. Some might think him paranoid, but he didn't. In his opinion you could never be too careful. In his experience he knew of others who chose not to be vigilant in their surroundings and were no longer in the land of the living. He had made a promise to himself many years ago that would not happen to him.

The familiar sight of the comfortable log cabin came into view as he drove into the next clearing. The big man didn't think of the home as small—it was cozy. Much of the construction had been done with his own hands.

He pulled right up to the front steps, turned off the truck and listened for a few moments before getting out. Nearby an owl hooted, but that was the only sound to be heard.

Adds to the ambiance, he thought.

He unlocked the front door with a key on his ring and entered the residence. The light switch was to his left, and he flipped that on while keeping his right hand on the holstered gun. His narrow eyes took in the surroundings.

The area was open and easily surveyed. The den space contained inviting well-worn leather furniture arranged near a stone fireplace and a modern flat screen television. The adjacent kitchen area was smaller but had all the conveniences and a heavy wooden table with four chairs. On the opposite side of the den was his bedroom. It was a more Spartan effect than the rest of the cabin, but there was a king-sized bed that provided comfort for his large frame.

Locking the door behind him, he walked into the kitchen and retrieved a cold Budweiser from the refrigerator. He sat down at the table and took a heavy pull from the bottle. When he set the bottle in front of him, half the beer was gone. It was good and relaxed some of the tension he felt from the long day's activities.

The man reached into his front right pocket of his blue jeans and pulled out a white letter sized envelope. He opened it, pulled out a wad of bills and started counting.

He finished and smiled to himself. He thought if he could just keep this pace up awhile longer, he would retire from his other job. He was smart enough to know his line of work put him in danger. Sooner or later, the law of averages would catch up. The trick was to get out before that happened. That's just what he intended.

God help anybody who gets in my way, he thought.

He got up from the table and went to the small secret vault hidden near the fireplace. The recent earnings were added to his stash of bills.

Glancing over the mantel he saw the oil painting and looked into the eyes of the woman shown. She was beautiful.

CHAPTER 16

Leo planned to spend most of the day by going to see his Uncle James and then by going to Papa's, now his, farm. He told himself this could provide more answers to his grandfather's secrets. Otherwise, Leo felt he might be running out of options to help him solve the mysteries from first-hand sources. He still planned to get on his computer and do searches of a couple of names and events, but nothing learned there would be as good as the horse's mouth.

First, he would cook breakfast, take Mindy to school and then maybe go on a short run. He hated going more than a day without exercise and since he missed out yesterday, Leo felt he needed to do that, too.

The smell of bacon frying filled the kitchen as Leo prepared breakfast. He didn't do this often because his family tried to avoid fried foods. When he did indulge by cooking bacon, it normally was wrapped in paper towels and nuked in the microwave oven. That process got rid of most of the grease and was a whole lot quicker than the old-fashioned method he was now using. At least Leo had spread several paper towels on the platter to absorb the lion's share of the remaining drippings, as he removed the crispy pork from the pan.

There was also a pot on the stove containing stone ground grits that he ordered online from a store near Callaway Gardens. They were the best grits he had ever eaten and he considered himself a connoisseur. The only final touches needed to finish them were to stir in a cup of shredded cheese and a half-cup of half-and-half.

After removing the last of the bacon from the pan and turning off the heat on the grits, Leo broke some fresh eggs in a bowl and started beating them. Out of nowhere Tiki showed up and started licking his chops. Anytime he heard the sound of scrambled eggs going down, he came running. Leo would add a little of the eggs to his food for a special treat this morning.

Just as the eggs reached the soft-scrambled readiness that all the family preferred, Leo spooned some onto three plates and added some to Tiki's bowl. He added a serving of the steaming grits and a couple slices of bacon. Mindy arrived just in time to place the plates of food on the table.

Dee walked into the room as Mindy and Leo were pouring a cup of coffee. "Yum, this smells delicious. I feel like I could eat a horse," she said.

"Mom just used a hyper-bowl, right?" asked Mindy.

Leo and Dee started laughing. "That's hyperbole, Dino. And where did you learn that word?" asked Leo.

"I was being funny, Diddy. I know how to pronounce it. I looked it up in my dictionary when I heard somebody say the word on TV. It means an exaggeration. I do know how to look things up, you know."

"Yeah, I know. I'm sorry. That's one of the things I learned from Papa when I was a kid and I passed on to you. I don't know why you still blow my mind sometimes," said Leo as he laughed again.

"Actually I think I'm pretty advanced for my age. I know a lot of stuff already, and I get to do things that most of my friends don't. Like drinking coffee, for instance."

Truth be told, Leo and Dee were still a little undecided about that activity. It had started when she was maybe four years old and Leo's daddy initiated her. Her "coffee" was half milk and had a fair amount of sugar, just like Leo, Jr. drank it all his life. She didn't show any side effects though and really only asked for it once in awhile, so the parents decided not to make a big deal out of it.

"Reading on a tenth grade level when you're in the sixth grade does mean you're advanced in some regards, Dino. That doesn't mean you're as advanced in other ways, young lady," admonished Dee.

"Yes, ma'am," Mindy said as she slurped her coffee and milk drink. "You know granddaddy taught me how to drink coffee."

"How could we forget? We still remember you saying that at your mom's work banquet when you were in kindergarten. Priceless." responded Leo.

"Yeah, we were afraid some of those people would call DFCS on us," said Dee.

The family devoured their breakfast, and Leo volunteered to clear the table as Dee and Mindy left to finish getting ready for their days. He decided to use the dishwasher rather than wash the dishes in the sink as he normally did. Just as he finished rinsing and loading, the two of them arrived back in the kitchen.

"Babes, I know you've got a busy off-day planned, so I'll take Dino to school," said Dee.

"Yeah, Diddy. We want you to enjoy your day off because you never do that."

"You two are awesome girls. I don't know how I got to be so lucky," said Leo.

"We're the lucky ones," Dee and Mindy said simultaneously.

"In stereo, too. All right, we're all lucky. Let's keep it that way. We'll meet up tonight, and maybe I'll fire up the grill."

CHAPTER 17

After going on a run around the neighborhood with Tiki, Leo showered and dressed in some jeans and a long-sleeved Margaritaville tee shirt. He preferred wearing casual duds any day than the mandatory coat and tie that was expected at work.

Leo was convinced that fashion was a lot of hooey contrived by that industry to make everyone spend way too much money on things that only lasted a season or two anyway. If he had his way, Leo would get rid of every cloth torture he had ever knotted around his neck and never buy another one. As it was, he had to use ridiculous amounts of his hard-earned pay to get at least one new tie every time he got a new suit or sports jacket. In the closet were testaments to the madness in every color and width imaginable. The only saving grace was eventually the older widths would be new again and he could recycle.

Leo made the drive across the county to his uncle's house via the interstate. I-75 saved a lot of time, but it always amazed Leo how much traffic flowed on those lanes. The Colonel cussed every time anyone mentioned the system and would question, "Where in the world do all those people come from?" Leo found himself agreeing with that sentiment more often than not. To him it was a convenience and a curse. Leo was able to get to his destination in twenty minutes, but cars sped and darted by him the whole way. It had not gotten as bad as Atlanta traffic yet, but he felt the day was coming when it would.

Since Leo knew Uncle Jim lived and breathed his work, Leo had not bothered to call before heading to the shop. For the most part, all of the Berry clan had a work ethic that bordered on fanatical. James Berry took it to the next level, though. He was known for working double shifts several times a week and even kept a cot in a back room of his business in case he needed a short nap. That way he wouldn't have to go home and sleep which he often thought a waste of time. He had worked hard to build his reputation as a master welder, and Uncle Jim didn't intend to lose that even if it killed him.

As he drove into the small parking lot, the only concern Leo had was that Uncle Jim would be too busy to stop and talk to him. Leo had only been to the business a couple of times with his dad and it was a hubbub of activity both times. This morning there were only a couple of pickup trucks in the lot and Leo felt hope for the opportunity to speak with his uncle unfettered.

Leo stepped into a time portal as he entered the shop area. There was an old fifty-something Ford Fairlane parked in one corner that looked to be going through some sort of restoration project. He spied an equally old welding machine that he remembered being there on his first visit as a kid. Littered all around were different jobs in various states of completion. The most interesting appeared to be a rather large jungle gym ready for a playground somewhere. It was painted a bright red color and had ladders and bars galore suitable for any kid to climb.

No one was visible as Leo scanned the shop. He walked around the floor admiring some of the work. It was much as he remembered from his other visits, but for some reason it seemed a lot smaller now. Leo thought that's how it always seemed when visiting sites you remembered only as a child--like going back to your grammar school.

Nostalgia swept over Leo while he looked around. Leo, Jr. had helped out his brother on occasion when they were both younger. Leo's dad was a year older than Jim and worked part-time there and other places when he wasn't doing double shifts at his regular job as a machinist. Daddy was good with his hands, and Jim liked having him around when the schedules allowed. They shared the same work ethic as most Berrys and could communicate without speaking while completing tasks.

Leo couldn't help feeling sadness at those days gone by. Although Leo had no such skills as his father and Uncle Jim, he still admired people like them who could make things or fix things with their own hands. Leo counted his own brothers in that same club. All three worked in skilled trades that Leo could never do.

Leo remembered other aspects of Uncle Jim's life as he continued exploring the shop. One time when Leo was a teen, his uncle had been involved in an explosion as he was working on a propane tank for a customer. Daddy had been upset and concerned when he heard the news. When his father returned from the hospital after visiting his brother Leo remembered being told that, "Jim was burned from head to toe." However, Uncle Jim fully recovered and was back at work in record time. Yep, he was Berry tough.

As the one surviving Berry male from his dad's generation, Uncle Jim was the only one who could give Leo the perspective he felt he needed most. Leo didn't feel especially close to his uncle, but he did admire him. He remembered when he was just a kid and his daddy, Jim and their other deceased brother, Billy, gathered on Papa's porch telling stories on each other and everybody laughing with great gusto. It seemed like a lifetime ago now.

The story that seemed typical of those times was the one Uncle Jim told on Leo, Jr. accidentally killing one of the chickens. Leo could still hear Jim relaying the story when Leo was just a child as he and all the other grandchildren listened raptly. By today's standards, some people might think his relatives were animal abusers or budding serial killers, but Leo didn't think so. He recalled Uncle Jim's story:

Everybody knew Jr. was the favorite. He could do no wrong in Mama's eyes. Well, the day Jr. knocked off the hen's head with a baseball bat, I got the blame, but it was him! True enough, we were taking turns batting around the yard with an old ball we had. Everything would've been okay except we lost the ball and got bored. Jr. started pretending that a chicken head would be a good substitute for the lost ball. He was swinging that Louisville Slugger like Hank Aaron when he made contact with that old hen. Billy and me were laughing like hell, but Jr. was mortified. He never meant to do it and it like to have scared him to death. All he could do was drop the bat and run off. Then Mama came out and saw the dead chicken, and she whipped Billy and me. I guess we shouldn't have been laughing. That was a life lesson for me that I didn't get from Papa! Never laugh at death, even a chicken and even if it is an accident.

There were several of those old stories, and Leo loved hearing them all. It somehow made his daddy and uncles more human. Back then Leo found it difficult to believe they had ever been kids. All three of them were strong men and seemed so serious at other times than when they were sitting out on the porch telling those stories.

They recounted details of their lives from their perspectives. Isn't that what life's about was what Leo thought. We all live our lives and remember what we remember. Is it true, or is it colored by other things out of our control? Leo didn't know. He only knew there were good times in the past and he chose only to try and remember those.

In Leo's mind his dad, Jim and Billy were frozen in that time. They were kids again and remembering their times in the continuum. Dad, Jim and Billy were kids again and screwed up as kids do. They weren't bad, and they weren't condemned to eternal damnation for screwing up. They were just kids. A single tear fell from Leo's eye as the moment passed.

Leo looked around the shop again as the memories faded. The memories were strong though and they lingered. He guessed he was more sentimental than he always thought.

"Well, look what the cat drug in," said Uncle Jim.

Leo turned to where the comment had come from. There stood the uncle he had been remembering. Uncle Jim was an older version of all the memories that had flooded his brain earlier. He seemed shorter with a bigger belly. Without warning, Leo remembered Grandma. Jim looked like her. He had never made that connection before now.

"Hey, Uncle Jim. Long time, no see."

"Yeah, Leo. Where you been so long?

"Just doing my thing, Uncle."

"I hope you're doing it like there is no tomorrow."

"Pretty much, Uncle Jim. Pretty much."

Leo's uncle turned around and started walking back to the office area of his shop. Leo followed without thinking there was no invitation to do so.

As they got back to the office, Jim sat down behind a small desk cluttered with paper. Leo took a chair on the opposite side. He glanced around and saw a couple of framed photographs on the walls. One was of a much younger Jim shaking hands with a former sheriff.

"What brings you out here, nephew?" said Jim.

"A couple of things, Uncle Jim. The first, I guess, is that I found out I've been named Papa's executor. I wanted you to hear from me first."

"Screw that. I already knew, boy."

Leo was momentarily taken aback. He should have known Uncle James would be ahead of him.

"I'm sorry, Uncle Jim. I didn't mean any disrespect. I just found out yesterday. You know, I wouldn't want to do anything to cause any problems."

Jim shifted in his chair and leaned back. He stared at his nephew and appeared to be sizing up the situation.

"I never quite understood why Papa thought you were all that special. Yeah, you went to school and that was a first, but you didn't know about family."

Leo didn't want to respond at first. Didn't know about family? What made him think such a thing?

"Uncle Jim, I don't know what to say. I hope I understand about family. I know I love mine."

James seemed to withdraw momentarily. Leo could tell he was thinking.

"Okay, Leo. That was unfair. I guess I'm feelin' a little less than myself."

"I understand, Uncle Jim. Me, too."

The two men looked at each other. Both sized the other before responding.

"Uncle Jim, let me say this. I've never said this before, but I think you're awesome. What you've done in your life is remarkable. I could never do what you've done. I know Daddy was proud of you. And, I appreciate what you did for him personally and us as a family. Letting him work with you was a good thing. He liked it and I knew it."

Water was welling in his uncle's eyes. He brushed it away immediately.

"It wadn't nothing."

"Yes, sir. It was. I know it if nobody else does."

Jim got out of his chair and started walking around the small office. Body language was enough to show his discomfort.

"Look. Anything I did was voluntary. Understand? Your daddy and me were tight, but he earned whatever he made here. I didn't give him anything. I always liked having Jr. around here. We could talk about things like only brothers can."

"I know, Uncle Jim."

James walked over to his chair and slumped down. He started rubbing his eyes with the heals of his hands. When he looked up at Leo he looked ten years older.

"I don't know where all the years have gone. You wake up one day and you're thirty. The next day you're forty. Now I wake up and I'm almost seventy. I never saw it coming, Leo."

"I can only imagine, Uncle Jim."

"No, you can't, Leo. When you're my age, maybe. It goes by so fast. You never think it's gonna happen to you."

Leo was thinking. It really was hard to put yourself in someone else's skin. Still, he had always tried to do that as long as he could remember. He had to try even harder if Uncle Jim was going to let him in.

"Uncle Jim, I know you've been through a lot. I don't think I'll ever have to do what you've done. I really want to understand. Do you mind talking about it?"

James put his head on his cluttered desk. For what seemed like a lifetime to Leo, Uncle Jim was frozen in that position.

When Jim finally looked up, his blue eyes were locked on Leo. Those blue eyes were all that looked like Papa. Come to think of it, all of the Berrys had those genetic similarities.

"Okay, boy. What do you want to know?"

To Leo the moment had arrived. If he was ever to find out secrets, it was now. Otherwise, whatever his uncle knew would stay a secret forever.

Leo blew out a breath. There was much he wanted to know.

"What do you know about Gene Thomas?"

Jim's eyes narrowed. Leo wasn't sure if Uncle Jim was mad or relieved.

"Gene Thomas only cared about himself and his bunch."

"But, who was he?" asked Leo.

"He was an asshole, Leo. The biggest conniving asshole I ever knew."

"I know he worked with Papa, I just don't know who he was. What can you tell me about him, Uncle Jim?"

James turned his head to the window. It was not difficult to tell his mind was in another time. There was a long pause before another word was spoken.

"It started in the early 70's. A little before you were born. A crazy time in more ways than one. Vietnam, mini-skirts, hippies and dope. Seemed like everybody I knew was a little crazy then," James said and shook his head.

He continued, "I guess us Berrys were no different than others during those times. Your daddy, Billy and I were all in our early 20's. As you know, Jr. had stomach problems that kept him out of the military, but Billy and me did a hitch. I joined the Navy to keep from getting drafted. Billy took his chances with the lottery and got drafted into the Army right after high school."

"Yeah, Daddy told me he tried to join the Marines, but couldn't pass the physical," said Leo.

"That surprised the whole family when he tried to do that. Your daddy was a tough one, but he always held things inside. I think that's why he had ulcers."

Leo had never thought of it in those terms. It sounded right, though.

"Anyway, while Billy and I were traveling the world on the government teat, your daddy was still at home helping run Papa's farm. There were some good years and some bad ones. Papa always seemed to keep it going one way or another. He was always dabbling in something. Lumber, buying and leasing property, stuff like that.

"So, I got out of the Navy a few months before Billy finished his stint. I had gone in a year and half before him and I was tired of all that shit. I couldn't wait to get back to the red clay of home although I had no intention of ever doing what the old man did. The best thing about the experience was I learned how to weld and I meant to use that to my benefit. I guess that turned out like I wanted."

Leo watched his uncle with great interest. It was almost as if he were the kid on the porch listening to the old stories again.

"I don't think Papa ever expected me to be a part of his businesses, but he did seem disappointed when I told him I wanted to start my own. But, he loaned me a little money to make a down payment on this very shop. All he said was to be the best welder around these parts and to try not to embarrass the family or myself.

"Well, there I go getting off the subject. By now you know us Berrys have a tendency to talk," said James.

Leo laughed. "Yeah, I do, Uncle Jim. It's a family trait for sure. Mama has always said Daddy could talk to a post for hours. I can remember her getting mad because Daddy would go to the store to get milk and bread and then stay gone an hour. When he finally got home, she would ask what took him so long. He would then recount everybody he had run into at the store and their conversations."

Uncle Jim chuckled as well. "We came by it natural." He paused again. "You asked about Gene Thomas. Why?"

"Papa's lawyer mentioned him, and I heard he did some business with Papa," replied Leo.

"Like I said before I got a little side-tracked, it started about the time I got back from the service. I thought the old man seemed different somehow. When he found out I wanted to go my own way, he only seemed more distracted than he did before I left home for the Navy. By then your daddy had also left the clutch, so to speak, and had married your mother. Billy was still a few months from getting out and he was in Vietnam, which was scary as hell to all of us. Lois had also gotten married and moved out, so the only child remaining at the house was Ollie. You never knew her, but she was a wild child of the biggest magnitude. Ollie rebelled in every way imaginable. So, I guess Papa was a little lonely. He and mama were just so cold around one another, it could not have been a happy time for him as I think back on those times," relayed Uncle Jim.

"Sometime between the time I went into the Navy and the time I got back, Gene Thomas showed up. He was a big man, almost as big as Papa. Spoke differently than anybody around here. Papa said he was from Canada, but I don't know if that was true or not. I asked Papa several times about the man and always got very little information in return. The times I was around him,

I don't know why, but I always felt a little uneasy. Like he knew something I didn't."

"So, Papa never told you more about him other than he was from Canada?" asked Leo.

"No, but there's more to the story," answered Uncle Jim. "They became business partners in a few ventures. Before you know it, he had rented a parcel of land beside the old home place from Papa. That was odd to me because Papa never liked having people who were not related in some way that close to him. That was one of the reasons he gave me for buying that piece of property years before. It was a "buffer" he called it. Since Papa owned property on the other side of the place as well as across the road, I believed him. I knew he wanted all of us to live close by, but none of us ever wanted to. Secretly, your daddy, Billy and I referred to all that land as the compound."

"I heard Daddy and Mama referring to Papa's place as the compound one time," responded Leo.

"Yeah, none of us meant it to be derogatory, I don't think. It's just that all of us wanted to be independent. Make our own way in the world. Papa was so intimidating in many ways, often times not meaning to be, but he just was. We felt like if we stayed nearby, we would lose ourselves and be another extension of him. Don't get me wrong, we all loved him. Some crosses are too heavy to bear, I guess."

James got out of his seat and walked around the room again. He walked over to a stained coffee pot and poured a portion in an equally stained mug. He didn't offer his nephew any and Leo was glad he didn't.

"There I go getting off point again, Leo. I've thought about these things many times over the years. When I analyze it, maybe I was jealous of Papa's relationship with Thomas. True enough, I didn't want to be in business with Papa because I felt in my heart he would run it. And in the end, that may have ultimately led to the downfall for Papa and Thomas. I don't know that for sure, mind you."

"You mean Papa and Gene Thomas had some falling out over their business together?" asked Leo.

"Yeah, about twenty years ago around the time of the fire. You might remember something about that since I guess you were a teenager by then. Let me ask you something. How far would you go to protect your family?"

Leo was taken aback by his uncle. He thought a moment before responding.

"Hmm, I remember there was a fire on some land of Papa's. I overheard Daddy and Mama talking about it, but I don't remember the details if I ever knew them in the first place. Maybe it didn't bother me back then because nobody I knew had been hurt. For some reason it didn't register with me. I didn't even remember that people died in the fire until Mama mentioned it. She did say you could probably provide more information. Now as to your question about how far I would go to protect my family, I would have to say I would do whatever necessary including giving my own life," said Leo.

James smiled but it resembled more of a grimace. "Your mother always has been a smart woman, Leo. I remember the first time Jr. brought her over to the house. She was a pretty one and Billy and I were a little jealous. Your grandma was not so nice to her though. The fact was, she was never real nice to anyone and your mama picked up on that quickly. I never heard Shelly respond in a fashion to take my mama's bait like a lot of people. I heard your grandma tear into others as long as she lived, but Shelly dodged it by killing her with kindness. Damn it, there I go off on a tangent again."

James continued, "The reason why I asked you the question was to get an idea of your thoughts on family. Protecting his family was number one priority for Papa. Your answer is a pretty good summary of what he believed, so it looks like you've picked up some of him along the way. Now, I'm going to tell you some things I've never told anyone. By you telling me what you've just said, I trust you to protect not only your immediate family, but your whole family. Understand?"

"I think I do," replied Leo.

"Okay. I'll pick up the story a few years after Billy got back from Nam. All of the Berrys had moved out of the home except Ollie and she was running with a wild bunch. Your grandma had developed some medical problems and became even more irritable. You and your brothers had been born and were like stepping stones keeping your parents busy. Your Uncle Billy was drinking way too much, but had a good trade and making a decent living. He married your Aunt Constance, and she helped ground him at least for awhile. My business was going well and I had plenty to do. Papa had his fingers in a lot of pies. With financial backing from an old war buddy, he had bought land in several middle Georgia counties, bought timber on others and was part owner of a sawmill. The farm was less important to him, but he still made a profit most years. He seemed to have a knack of growing quality crops people wanted."

"Was the old war buddy Simon Katz?" asked Leo.

"Yeah, Papa called him Kitty. I only met him once long time ago. Papa told me he was probably the best friend he ever had. Said the guy saved his life more than once although he never would tell me the stories. Papa didn't like talking about his time during the war. How do you know about Katz?"

"I guess I must've heard about him somewhere," answered Leo.

"Well anyway, getting back to what I was talking about before the interruption. Gene Thomas had woven his way into a lot of the things Papa was doing. He had a half interest in the mill. He leased some of the farmland Papa owned and grew crops of his own. He took up with a gal named Beverly and had a couple of boys with her. I don't know if they were ever legally married, but she went by his last name. He put a double-wide trailer on the property beside Papa's place where they lived until they died."

James got on a roll and spoke without looking at Leo. He stared out the window of the shop like he was watching a movie.

"This played on throughout the 70's even after Ollie died of an over-dose and everybody's families continued to grow. Everything seemed so much simpler back then. All in all, times were good. As you know, we would gather regularly at Papa's on Sundays," Uncle Jim said as he turned toward Leo. "I remember a wide-eyed kid listening to us tell stories."

"Those were the times I liked best going to Papa's and Grandma's. I was always fascinated when y'all would start telling stories. I've thought it would be good if I could get you to recount all those old tales on tape so we could share them with the younger kids," said Leo.

His uncle laughed and slapped his hand on the cluttered desk. Several items shifted and a couple of invoices fell to the floor.

"Yeah, that might be a hoot to do. Of course, some of those tales got taller over the years and some might be too risky to recount. We can talk about that later if you want, but now I need to get back on track while this old brain still works."

Uncle Jim continued, "The 80's got a little rougher for some of the family. I married your Aunt Mary who already had a couple of kids. That may have been the final straw for your Grandma because she died very shortly afterward. Your daddy and mama were working extra hard to raise you and your brothers. Your Aunt Lois lost her husband to cancer and had her hands full raising her kids by herself. Billy struggled with depression and at times would drink excessively. Your Aunt Constance, bless her heart, had all she could do to try and keep him straight and raise their kids at the same time. Papa became even more stoic during all those events. I know he helped Lois a lot financially and he probably helped some of the others as well. That didn't bother me any. He continued to do well in his business matters and he lived so much below his means, helping others in the family was easy for him to do. I never once heard him brag or complain, he just did what he had to do," James said and paused again.

"Uncle Jim, I was pretty young then and never thought much about the troubles some of the family was having. Thinking back to some of my conversations with Papa, he must've been trying to prepare me for life against all those troubles he was experiencing. At the same time, I wonder if he was internalizing those problems. I don't mean to sound like some kind of psychiatrist, but did you see any signs that he was depressed?" asked Leo.

Uncle Jim pondered the question for a moment and replied, "Could've been. I do know he saw an Army doctor on occasion up at the VA hospital in Dublin. He didn't say much about it other than periodically he would tell one of us he was going to Dublin to see his doctor. But you can believe Papa played everything close to the vest."

"I'm sorry for interrupting your recount of Berry history and I do appreciate you sharing it with me, but I'm still interested about Gene Thomas and his role in it," said Leo.

Uncle Jim started laughing. "Maybe I have attention deficit disorder. Okay, but I needed to set the stage."

Once again his uncle got out of the chair and went to the coffee pot. James topped off his mug and sat back down at the desk.

"Alright, where was I? Oh, so all during the 80's business was booming for Papa and Thomas. I don't know how much money was made, but I bet it was a lot. It all came to a screeching halt in the summer of '92. Or maybe I should say the the Big Leo/Gene Thomas business got so hot that it caught fire and burned to a crisp that summer."

"The fire that killed some people?" asked Leo.

"Yep, the fire that killed Gene Thomas and the mother of his baby named Mickie," replied Uncle Jim.

"Oh my God," said Leo barely audible.

"Yep. So I guess I need to tell you what I know about the fire," said Uncle Jim.

And so he did. It didn't answer all Leo's questions, though.

CHAPTER *18*

Leo made the drive from Uncle Jim's shop to Papa's place in a daze. Were some things destined to remain family secrets?

Throughout his adult life and particularly as a lawyer, Leo had learned that not everything was black or white, right or wrong, good or evil. If he was going to fulfill Papa's wishes for redemption and make some sense of what had been learned so far, it was going to take some doing. Leo was not sure if he was up to the task. He only knew he had to try.

A sense of deja vu filled his senses as Leo drove onto Papa's driveway, and the old house came into view. It was a structure holding memories from days gone by. He remembered as a child of a few years of age, and Leo was taken back there again.

Leo, Jr. and his mother got out of the front seat of the family Ford. Little Leo and his brothers, Eddie, Denny and

Tommy all piled out of the back of the car like puppies set free from a cage. The four of them from oldest to youngest were only separated by one year each. There were some shared characteristics so one could tell they were related, but only if you saw them all together. Otherwise, the four of them were different in looks as well as personalities. At this point in their young lives, they were curious about everything on the farm.

Leo's younger two brothers, Denny and Tommy, ran toward the back of the house where the chicken coop was located. They liked to get handfuls of feed that were gleefully thrown into the fenced-in area. The white hens would cluck, peck and scratch as the four and five year olds scattered the rewards. The boys laughed as the big red rooster caused the females to get out of the way so he could get more than a fair share.

Eddie ran toward the red barn located on the eastern side of the property. He wanted to climb aboard the green John Deere tractor that was inside. There he would spend a good bit of time acting as if he were navigating the fields. Papa had let Eddie ride with him on the machine during a recent visit and hold onto the steering wheel. Now all Eddie wanted was his own tractor.

Little Leo walked around the western side of the house toward the cornfield. He looked up as he passed the two-storied white home. The sky was blue with little puffy clouds dotting the view. He would always associate that skyline with going to Papa's house.

As he got to a huge oak shade tree near the gate, Leo found what he was looking for. His pal, Rusty, lay resting in the cool grass. Since the near fatal encounter with the big rattler last year, Little Leo always looked for the dog before doing anything else. This time the collie mix was curled up in the shade near the little house Papa had put under the tree for his partner to sleep in. It was painted the same red color as the barn and Rusty's name had been painted in white above the door opening.

Leo squatted down where the dog was laying and began to lightly stroke the long black and white hair. There were some mats that the boy took care to disentangle as he petted Rusty. Daddy had told Leo that Papa got Rusty when he was a puppy and right after Leo was born. Now they were both seven years old. Originally the dog was supposed to be his, but it was decided that Rusty needed more open space. Mama didn't really care for pets and money was tight, too. So, the dog became Papa's, but Little Leo also thought of Rusty as belonging to him. Leo loved him as much as anything.

As soon as Leo finished petting Rusty, the dog sat up and looked him squarely in the eye. When others were not around as now, Leo liked to pretend he would speak for the animal. He had made up a voice only used for such a purpose and invoked it now.

"Well, hey Little Leo. You don't mind me using your nick name, do you?"

"Not you, Rusty. You can call me whatever you want."

"What's been going on?"

"I started the second grade. My teacher, Mrs. Gordon, told Mama I'm gifted."

"Don't let it go to your head, kid," replied the dog in his modified Leo voice.

"I'm not, Rusty. I don't think I'm all that special. I just like learning new stuff."

"Good, good. Papa told me to never stop and you remember that, too."

"I won't, I promise. Hey, have you seen any more snakes?" asked Leo.

"Nah, I think they stay out of my way."

"They better! Rusty, the snake-killer should be your new name."

"I like that, Leo. Just keep it between us, okay?"

"Okay. I love you, Rusty."

"I love you, too, Little Leo. Now, let's go for a walk."

During their conversation Rusty continued to look into Leo's eyes and both felt calmness. It was a moment in time when Leo felt connected to some greater power.

Back to the present, Leo found himself in the same place where he once carried on imaginary conversations with Rusty. Sadness momentarily overtook Leo as he looked under that same old hardwood. The doghouse was long gone, and there was no buddy to talk with about the problems Leo now faced.

Leo was conflicted about keeping secrets from Dee, his mother and even other members of the family. He generally had no problems respecting confidences and people had trusted him when they told their innermost thoughts, feelings and circumstances. The major problem with secrets was they were no longer such when shared with someone else. In his experience, Leo knew of instances when a secret was shared with someone who shared it with someone else and so on until it was no longer a secret, and was often twisted to something only resembling the original thing told in confidence. It was a touchy subject to even think about the number of secrets he had heard during the last week and whether any should be breached by revealing to others, even his wife who he never kept out of the loop.

Leo looked across the field that at one time consisted of acres planted with corn, peas, butterbeans and other vegetables. Now it looked desolate and unattended. Why would Papa ever think he would know what to do with that land?

Looking to his right and behind the house, Leo saw that someone had removed the old chicken coop and the wire that surrounded it. He crossed the backyard and walked to the other side. The barn looked to be in bad shape and probably could not be salvaged. When Leo walked inside he only saw a broken down plow and a few hand tools way past their prime.

Leo headed back toward the house that still seemed to be in fairly good condition. A new coat of white paint would help, but the wrap around porch and the steps leading to it and the front door looked sturdy even after sixty years of use. The outdoor furniture was dated and worn, but still appeared functional. Leo pictured his dad and brothers sitting there telling their stories on a Sunday afternoon.

Leo admired the view across the road. It was still very much the rural setting he remembered. There were only a couple of homes visible in the distance, and what wasn't used as pecan groves or other farming purposes was heavily wooded.

He reached into his front pocket and removed a key ring containing only two keys. Leo slipped one into the keyhole on the deadbolt lock and it worked perfectly. The other one was for the doorknob lock that didn't work as well. He had to jiggle the key and twist the knob with just the right combination before the door opened.

It had been a few months since Leo last visited and nothing had changed inside. Family pictures were displayed around the living room as they had been as long as he could remember. Some of them were older than Leo. The ones that stood out were his uncles' service pictures. Both Uncle Jim and Uncle Billy were grinning wearing their dress uniforms. They were young and fresh-faced and ready to conquer the world.

An equally youthful Leo III appeared in his cap and gown as he graduated from college. Since he was the first Berry to achieve that honor, his daddy had insisted Leo get one for his grandfather. "Your grandson, Leo," was written on the bottom in his signature that remained essentially his same script.

Leo walked through the front living room into the large dining area. Many meals had been consumed over the years in that room. Most of the time the kids would eat on trays as the grownups ate at the sturdy wooden table that could seat up to ten. However, Leo had been allowed to eat with the grownups on occasion as he got older and was always in awe of how much food could be accommodated.

If there was one positive thing he remembered about his childhood visits around his grandmother, she was a great southern cook. Not as good as Mama, mind you, but good just the same. Leo could almost see and smell the large platters of fried pork chops, bowls of boiled cabbage, fresh peas, sliced tomatoes and cucumbers arranged on the table.

Most, if not all, the vegetables were grown right on the farm. Hogs were always raised and a few butchered by Papa, Daddy and his uncles after the first cold snap. Although it was not an activity Leo looked forward to, he would accept whatever chore he was assigned to do when hog-killin' happened. The homemade sausage that resulted afterward always made the process at least tolerable.

Leo continued through the main level of the house passing through the kitchen and past Papa's bedroom onto the back deck. The deck was an addition to the house, which allowed his grandfather the ability to look over the farm without leaving after he became too infirm to walk around the property. It was a nice view.

The fields to the east and the west extended to a small pond in the center of the property. Just beyond the water was a tree line that consisted of several varieties of hardwoods and Georgia pines. Yep, it was pretty impressive thought Leo.

After a few minutes of admiring the landscape, Leo walked back into the house and entered his grandfather's room. It had a musty smell as if it had been closed for a lengthy period without access to fresh air. Leo located the window nearest the bed and raised the blinds. He unlatched the window and attempted to raise it.

Damn, he thought. *Did somebody super-glue this shut?*

Leo used his hand to strike all along the top of the window. He was careful not to use too much force in fear of breaking the glass. A satisfying sound of paint cracking rewarded Leo with his next attempt in opening the window. He opened it fully and felt a cooling breeze enter the room. Leo could also smell the Japanese tea olives that were planted along that side of the house.

Leo looked around the room and his gaze settled on the old desk in the far corner. He sat down in the chair and rolled it forward. Leo studied the desk like he had never seen it before. It had character. No doubt it would have some value as an antique, but Leo decided he wanted it as a memento of his grandfather, if for no other reason.

He had seen Papa sit at that desk several times when Leo visited. Papa would be deep in thought about something, but would brighten as Little Leo entered the room. Leo smiled at the memory.

Leo began opening the drawers of the desk and looking at the contents. All were organized to a degree that implied perfectionism. Leo had always thought himself to be orderly, but nothing like Papa's desk.

As Leo systematically went through each drawer and glanced at the contents, he noted anything that might be important for administering the estate and took possession of those items. However, that was not all Leo was looking for. Specifically, he wanted to locate any reference to business dealings with Gene Thomas. He was disappointed when he could find nothing of the sort. Leo decided no such materials existed, and if they ever did, must have been destroyed long ago. Thomas had been dead for twenty years according to what Uncle Jim had told him earlier and there really were no reasons to keep such records.

Leo got up from the desk and strolled around the bedroom. It already smelled fresher. There were bookshelves that Leo also remembered as a child because that was where Papa kept his dictionary. It was on the lowest shelf easiest for somebody like Little Leo to access. Leo knew Papa often told others besides himself they should look up the definitions of words they heard and did not know.

He picked up the well-worn book and once again was transported to his childhood.

Papa was sitting at his desk and was writing checks to pay bills. Little Leo had slipped into the bedroom and walked over to the dictionary. He wanted to look up what vertigo meant because he heard Uncle Billy talk about having it, whatever that was. Leo was having difficulty finding the word and must have shown audible frustration that he didn't realize.

Are you havin' trouble, Leo"

I'm sorry, Papa. I didn't mean to disturb you. Yes sir, I was trying to find a word.

You're not disturbin' me, Leo. Besides, I'm the one who taught you to look up words you don't know, right?

Yes, sir.

Okay, what's the word you're tryin' to find?

Bertigo, I think it is some kind of sickness.

Papa got out of his chair and walked over to Leo. He leaned his tall frame over so he could see the page. He laughed.

You're on the wrong page, son. Or, as in that line from 'Cool Hand Luke','"What we have here is failure to communicate.

Papa flipped the pages to the V's and said, *The word you're tryin' to find is vertigo. You just heard the v as a b. Now see if you can find it.*

Leo spelled the word in his mind as he had previously learned to do. He found the word without further trouble and read the definition. Now it made sense what he had heard his uncle complain about. Leo had felt that before when he had climbed a big tree.

Papa, who is Cool Hand Luke?

Papa started laughing again. *He's a character in a movie by the same name. You're probably old enough to watch it some time, but you should ask your daddy and mama if you can. If you do, we can talk about what you thought. There's some good life lessons in that story.*

Leo was still thinking about the exchange when he heard a rapping at the front door of the house. He replaced the dictionary and got to the door just in time to see through the window as Mickie Thomas headed down the steps.

"Mickie, wait," Leo said while opening the door.

She turned toward him and Leo got a much better look at her than in his car during the previous encounter. Mickie appeared to be a little older than he had originally thought. She was probably in her early 20's, a shade over five feet tall with long dark hair tied in a ponytail and captivating blue eyes. Leo immediately thought Dee would love that combination of features as she had told him many times she wished her eyes were blue instead of brown. She was even cuter than he first thought.

"Oh, hi Mr. Berry. I was just headed home from school, and I recognized your car parked in front of the house. I thought you might not be inside when you didn't answer the door," Mickie said.

"I'm sorry. I don't guess I heard you at first. Momentarily stuck in the past."

"I understand. The house holds a few memories for me, too," she said.

"Do you want to come in? It would give us a chance to talk a little while. I'm not sure what refreshments might be in here since I haven't checked yet," said Leo.

"Sure, I've got a little while before I've got to go to work."

Leo held the door open as Mickie entered the house. He didn't know the fragrance she was wearing, but recognized it. But then again, Leo claimed all colognes were recycled from others in the past. Leo and Dee had discussed this several times and agreed no matter the names on the bottles, they were at best variations of old ones. Dee had even proven it one time when they were in a department store. She made him close his eyes and then held two bottles, one an older perfume and the other the latest rage, under Leo's nose one at a time after clearing his nasal passages with the coffee container kept on the counter. He was unable to tell the difference. At any rate, Mickie's smell was clean and fresh and fit her perfectly.

They walked to the kitchen and Leo looked in the refrigerator. There was not much inside, but he spied a couple of individual size plastic bottles of Diet Coke.

"How about a diet soda?" Leo asked. "I don't normally drink these things but about once a month, but that's all I see."

"That's fine. That's about how often I indulge, too."

"Let's go sit down in the living room, said Leo.

When they got back to the room, Leo waited for Mickie to sit in one of the stuffed cloth chairs and then he took a seat on the couch that was directly across from her. She took a swallow of her drink and set it on a coffee table beside her. Leo drank a healthy swig, screwed the top back on and placed it in his lap.

"You're going to school? Where? What are you studying?"

"I'm in my last semester at Macon State in the nurse's program. I'll be glad to finish and get a full-time job. I'm working part-time at the Medical Center now and my supervisor told me I won't have a problem as long as I pass my boards," replied Mickie.

"That's a noble calling. I've always admired health care professionals. I know I couldn't do what you do. Congratulations on being so close to achieving your goal."

"Thanks. It's something I've wanted to do as long as I can remember. I really like caring for patients. I might even want to go further and get a nurse practitioner's license or maybe even eventually go to medical school. Mr. Leo used to tell me to aim high and never stop learning. I need to make some money and get some experience first."

"Sounds like a plan to me," said Leo. "I felt the same way about becoming lawyer. Papa gave me that same speech, by the way. Speaking of school, you might just be able to seek your dreams faster than you think."

"What do you mean?"

"I don't know if you've gotten any information from Papa's lawyer yet, but Papa left you some property you could sell and there may be some other money with you named as beneficiary as well. I don't have all the details right now, but I can tell you Papa designated me as the executor of his estate and I'll be working hard to see that his wishes are fulfilled."

Mickey's mouth dropped open. The look of genuine surprise and maybe confusion filled her face.

"I don't understand. No, I haven't seen anything from a lawyer. The mail does run a little slow out here in the country sometimes, or maybe my brother picked up the letter and forgot to give it to me, yet. I mean, I don't understand why Mr. Leo would leave me anything."

"It's possible the mail hasn't gotten to you yet, but it should be coming soon. If you don't get anything by early next week, let me know and I'll make sure you are notified. I must admit, I was a little surprised when I heard you were mentioned in the will. I guess I was surprised because I didn't know you at all until the funeral."

"I don't remember ever meeting you until then, too. But, Mr. Leo talked about you a lot. He told me I would like you and that one day we would be friends."

She continued, "I knew him all my life. He would come see me at my house sometimes and other times I would visit him here. It's strange, but I don't remember ever meeting anybody else in the family except your Uncle Jim. That didn't seem so odd until the last few months after Mr. Leo got sick. His housekeeper, Mrs. Smith, would call and tell me Mr. Leo wanted to see me and I would come running. He would always be alone at those times."

"So, have you lived where you do now all your life?"

"As far as I know I've always lived on the next property over. I don't really remember my parents because they died when I was two. But, I remember living with my aunt over there when I was small and we never moved. My brother, Pete, lives in a cabin on the property, too."

"Does your aunt still live there?"

"No sir, my Aunt Vickie has dementia now and is in an assisted living facility. She's been there about two years. She was my mother's only sister and raised me as her own after my folks passed. My aunt is one of the best people I've ever known. Truth be told, I always thought she was a little sweet on Big Leo. They always looked at each other with affection anytime I saw them together," said Mickie.

"I'm sorry, Mickie. I don't mean to get too personal. And, you don't have to call me sir. It makes me feel old. Please call me Leo. I want us to be friends. Anybody who could get as close as you were to Papa has got to be special," replied Leo.

Mickie smiled. She was touched by Leo's acceptance and felt he could be trusted. Yes, she wouldn't mind being friends with this guy. In a way, she thought of him as a member of her family.

"It's okay, I don't think you're being too personal. I like having somebody to talk to besides my brother, Pete. I love him, but sometimes I don't think he realizes how lonely I can get. Since we're both so busy, I don't see him everyday because of crazy shifts. He looks after me, though. I feel safe because not only is Pete my brother, he's also a local deputy. He's been in law enforcement for quite a few years, but would like to quit. I think Pete might be a little burned out. You should meet him sometime since you two have a few things in common. He's a little older but in good shape like you are."

"Sure, I'd love to meet him. And, I'd like you to meet my wife and daughter, too. Maybe we can arrange dinner soon. I have lots of friends and acquaintances that work in law enforcement, so Pete and I may even know some of the same people. I don't normally come into contact with the sheriff's office over here. I appreciate the compliment about being in good shape. I try, but it keeps getting harder and harder."

"Believe me, when you work in health care you learn to notice the bad effects of not keeping active. I might be young, but I see it every day," said Mickie.

Leo thought Mickie was pretty sharp to recognize the benefits of exercise at such a young age. He certainly didn't think about it much when he was in his early 20's. In fact, as much as he enjoyed the runner's high he got nowadays, Leo hated to run back then unless he was playing some sport.

"If you don't mind, could I ask you a few questions? Like I said, I don't want to get personal or take up too much of your time. You might be able to help me understand some stuff that I didn't know that much about until Papa died.

"Fire away, lawyer guy," Mickey said with a grin. "I've never known a lawyer, but I've always heard y'all like to cross-examine folks."

Leo chuckled. "Lawyer guy, that's funny. Nobody has ever called me that. Almost sounds like it would make a good skit for Saturday Night Live. But, seriously. I don't want you to think of this as a cross-examination. Just tell me if I ask anything you don't want to answer and I'll 'withdraw the question' as we lawyer guys do sometimes in court."

Mickey only grinned more at Leo's response. She thought he was kinda funny. He thought someday she was going to break some guy's heart with that smile. They both felt at ease with the other.

"Okay. Since I was picked by Papa to execute his will, I've been trying to learn as much as I can about his past business dealings. I never knew it, but your father and my grandfather were evidently in business together. I realize this would have been before you could know anything personally about such activity, but I'm curious if you've ever heard anything from anybody about those dealings."

It appeared cogs were turning in Mickie's head. She pursed her lips and shook her head slightly.

"What little bit I've heard was from my brothers. Johnny was always more vocal and bitter about such things than Pete. Johnny used to say Big Leo didn't treat my father right. Stole from him. I never believed Johnny because I knew Big Leo a lot better than Johnny did. Big Leo wouldn't steal, no way," said Mickie.

"I guess I had forgotten Gene Thomas had two boys. So, Pete and Johnny are a good bit older than you. Your mother must've been very young when she married your father."

"Maybe I should explain my family situation because it's a little complicated. Of course, this was told to me because I really have very few memories about my early life. My Aunt Vickie would always answer my questions about my parents, but I felt detached to them and thought of Aunt Vickie as my mother. I never even called her Aunt Vickie, I called her Mom and it made us both happy."

She paused for a moment and continued, "Anyway, my mother and my mom were young teenaged girls still in high school when they first met my father. Mom said he was tall and handsome with long hair and would come into their family's store to buy supplies. They heard he was new to the county and had taken up residence near Big Leo's place. This was maybe around 1970. My mother started flirting with my father even though there was an age difference and before long she had left home to take up with him. Mom, or Aunt Vickie, that is, told me their parents did not approve because my father was about twenty-five and Beverly, my real mother, was only sixteen. Are you following me so far?" asked Mickie.

"I think so, but maybe it would be easier to refer to the people by their first names," replied Leo.

"Okay, good idea. So, Beverly and Gene started living together. Beverly got pregnant and dropped out of school. They had a trailer on the property where I still live. Not the same one I live in now, but I'll get to that. My oldest brother, Peter, was born followed by my brother, John, a year later. During those early years, some people called my parents hippies because they looked the part. I've got a couple of pictures of them back then, and they appeared like flower children with long hair and bell-bottom jeans. They never formally married, but Aunt Vickie said they performed some kind of ritual in the yard that only a few people attended and then declared themselves as husband and wife. As I understand it, common law marriages were recognized in Georgia back then."

She sighed and smiled at Leo. "I always thought that story was kinda weird."

"Yeah, before my time as well, but that part of history is interesting to me. I still listen to all the music from that period," said Leo.

"I guess it's a little bit interesting, but I try not dwelling in the past. Anyway, my parents settled in raising my brothers and living their lives. They were happy and successful as far as I know. Gene was working pretty hard and developed his relationship with Big Leo that went on for a long time. Nobody expected me to come along in '90. My mother had some female problems after John's birth, and Aunt Vickie told me Beverly didn't think she could get pregnant again. But, she was still young enough and the miracle me was born. I was a preemie and only weighed a little over four pounds."

"You're still relatively tiny," noted Leo.

"Yeah, it used to bother me more than it does now. Mom always told me I would be glad I was small when I got older. I see why she said that now, but I didn't believe it when she told me. Pete and Johnny were so big, and I wanted to be like them."

"When I was a kid I ate everything I could that I thought would make me bigger," said Leo. "I didn't realize I was burning those calories as fast as I ate them. I wish I could do that now."

"Never a problem for me. Oh well. Anyway, I was born and then, excuse my French, everything went to shit. I'm not sure why, but Big Leo and my father had some disagreement about something. According to what Johnny said, Gene cut his ties with Big Leo because Gene wanted to be his own man. Gene had ideas about crops to grow and Big Leo didn't agree. Johnny always said this is what caused our father's death. I think that's why Johnny was always so negative about your grandfather."

"Do you know what the crops were?" asked Leo.

"Johnny never said."

Mickie got a faraway look in her eyes. Leo thought she might start crying.

"Look, Mickie. I really don't want to pry. I appreciate the history lesson and it probably really doesn't matter anyway. All that may have happened is so far removed from the present day, it loses importance. I am curious though. Does Johnny still talk about any of that?"

Mickey stared at Leo. Did he see anger in those eyes or something else?

"You didn't know Johnny was killed last year? Murdered by a thieving little piece of shit? He's coming up for trial soon and I hope he fries!"

Leo fought not to show emotion. *Why didn't I make the connection? I'm right in the middle of a CF! I'm supposed to prosecute Mickie's brother's killer? Holy shit,* he thought before speaking.

"I'm so sorry, Mickie. I didn't know who your brother was. I don't know what to say. I do know a little about the case, but I didn't make the connection. Anything I say now seems inadequate and inappropriate. My only hope is that you and your family will find justice."

Mickie sunk into her chair. She looked frail and defeated.

"It's alright," she said. "I hope so, too. I'm not sure what justice looks or feels like. It seems like death has been around me all my life and it's all so unfair."

So much for continuing this conversation, thought Leo. "Look, this is enough for now. Let's talk about this another time, okay?" asked Leo.

"Yeah, I need to go home and get ready for my shift," said Mickie.

She got up from her chair and tried to smile, but failed. "Mr. Leo said I would like you and I do. I enjoyed talking with you, Leo. I'm sorry for ending today like this."

"I like you too, Mickie. I really am very sorry about your loss and my insensitivity. I'm sure we'll be talking again soon."

Mickie left the house and Leo remained with his thoughts. The odds of all the recent happenstance had to be astronomical. Sometimes life was stranger than fiction.

CHAPTER 19

Leo got to the office an hour early on Monday so he could check all forms of contact he had missed over the last few days. It was almost too much trouble to be off. There were over twenty voice messages, an equal number of emails and a stack of mail left by the US Postal Service. In addition, several incident reports had been left on his desk that needed his review before filing accusations in court. The most prominent item catching his attention was a different looking file than the ones used in the state court. He recognized it as one from the District Attorney's office.

There was a yellow sticky note on the front of the file that read, "Leo, Thanks for handling this case for us. I owe you one. Love ya', mean it. JLM." The tab contained the case number and the defendant's name, last name first. Murphy, Lonnel.

Leo opened the file and was surprised to see that it was relatively thin considering it was a homicide case. On top was the usual police incident report called a stat 5. Typically these were done by the arresting or reporting officer shortly after the incident occurred which required a police response. To Leo these reports were critical to successful prosecutions and officers were taught to detail them as much as possible. Unfortunately many times officers did a poor job of documenting these reports that led to all sorts of problems. Leo had seen officers made to look incompetent on the witness stand by defense lawyers when their reports were lacking.

A young blue coat named Sullivan had written the report. Leo recognized the name and was relieved. Ted Sullivan was an up-and-coming officer in the police department and showed lots of potential. Leo was fairly certain even without reading the report that it would be professional and answer all the questions of what, when, where, who and how much. However, as he skimmed Sullivan's work, Leo was more than a little disappointed.

Leo learned that Sullivan had been the first officer on the scene after the 911 call from Johnny Thomas's girlfriend, Janice Hill. Originally the call went out as a theft of her purse. Since Sullivan was only a few blocks from where that incident had taken place, he was able to arrive in less than five minutes of the call. The girlfriend was frantic when Sullivan arrived. She reported that her boyfriend had chased the perp into one of the alleys down Cherry Street near where their car was parked. She told the officer her boyfriend had a weapon on him, and she had heard a single gun shot shortly before the officer's arrival.

After a brief interview with the girlfriend, Sullivan tracked the route Janice Hill described that the suspect and Johnny Thomas took after the theft took place. He also called for backup and reported that at least one shot had been fired.

Sullivan found the still warm body of Johnny Thomas moments after entering the alley. He had a wound to the chest and no vital signs. Sullivan secured the scene and radioed the fatality. Sullivan's report indicated no weapon was found, and the suspect was not in the area either. There was a homeless person listed as a potential witness named Winton Stiles.

Backup arrived within minutes of the body being located. The crime scene was turned over to detectives. Lt. Fletcher Richards took command of the investigation as the ranking officer on duty that night.

A BOLO was issued based on the description given by Janice Hill. The suspect was described as a young black male teenager with close-cropped hair wearing a dark hoodie and baggie jeans.

Officers Will Little and Samantha Jones arrested the suspect less than two blocks from the shooting scene. There was a significant amount of blood on his clothing. In his possession was a nine-millimeter Glock handgun and $1250 cash contained in an envelope that was confiscated incident to arrest. The suspect was identified as eighteen-year-old Lonnel, aka, Nelly Murphy.

As Leo finished reading Sullivan's report, he thought it skimpy. It had the basics, but Leo felt it was not up to par with other reports he had read of the officer's work on much lesser crimes. In fact, Leo remembered reading a stat 5 done by Sullivan a few weeks ago on a DUI stop that was much more detailed than this effort. Leo knew he would need to interview Officer Sullivan soon to answer some questions.

Leo looked through the rest of the file that contained a copy of the indictment charging the defendant with murder and armed robbery. Leo immediately wondered about the armed robbery count, but let that slide for the time being.

There were also supplemental reports by Detective Richards and the arresting officers. Leo noted they were not written with enough details also. They were perfunctory at best, sloppy at worst. Leo couldn't help but question as to why the file was not more developed. Did the police simply think it was an open and shut case? Or, were they trying to hide the ball from the defense? Leo knew either could be a possibility. He did not want to think it was simply poor police work.

Leo decided a meeting with the lead detective was the first order of business. He also decided to meet with the other witnesses separately and try to find out more of the details. Leo wanted to make sure of the knowledge of each witness independently of the others. That would be crucial to his evaluation of the case. His initial review of the file now complete, Leo got to work on the other items on his plate.

Next, Leo methodically went through his emails answering those that needed immediate attention. He liked the flexibility this medium of communication afforded. Although Leo subscribed to the belief that he should always respond to folks who asked him some question, he found it easier to do on his own time sitting at his computer. Quite a few people he came into contact with had problems requiring delicate responses, and Leo liked doing this with the benefit of being able to edit or modify a reply, or even using the delete button when discretion was warranted.

An example of this phenomenon occurred as Leo hurried a reply to an unhappy friend of a recent witness in a noise ordinance violation. Why was it such minor cases in the grand scheme of prosecution many times gave him the most grief?

The email from one Mr. Simon Lasseter blasted Leo and everyone in the office for not taking their jobs seriously and by failing to treat his lady friend, Nell Grayson, with respect in her quest to rid her neighborhood of a barking collie known as King.

According to Mr. Lasseter, no less than three citations had been issued by the Sheriff's office for the heinous offense that threatened the sanctity of the otherwise peaceful Ms. Grayson's residence. He felt the need to blast Leo for not giving the matter sufficient redress.

Leo's blood started to boil when he read, *Your callous disregard for the rule of law, and the disrespect you have shown* *for Nell Grayson places you on a long list of other so-called public servants who only care about themselves and not the very tax payers who pay your inflated salaries. I plan to notify the media of your dereliction of duty and have them expose you for what you are, a **COWARD!***

Leo's fingers flew across the keyboard as he typed a response to the email message. He finished the message and read it over. Woah, way too much profanity and snarkiness were included. No way he could send that, so he deleted the response and started over. When he finished the edited version, Leo read it over to himself.

Dear Mr. Lasseter:

I have just received your email message from last week. I apologize for not getting back to you sooner, but I had some pressing personal business that kept me out of the office.

Let me assure you and Ms. Grayson that I take my job very seriously. I have always tried to follow the law and give all parties the respect they deserve in the process.

As you may know, I met with Ms. Grayson on several occasions about the complaints she made to the Sheriff's Office with respect to a barking dog. I went over the ordinance with her and made suggestions about how we should proceed when the case came to court. I specifically asked for her to check with other neighbors to see if they would be willing to testify. I also said it might be helpful if she could record the commotion she claimed was so disruptive.

When the case came to trial a couple of weeks ago, Ms. Grayson was the only witness who appeared. She informed me that none of her other neighbors would agree to testify. She also indicated she was not successful in recording the dog barking other than intermittently.

The deputy who wrote the citation testified he never heard the noise she complained about, and on cross-examination admitted he only issued the citation after his lieutenant instructed him to do so. He further testified, over my hearsay objection, that the lieutenant bowed to pressure by you and Ms. Grayson after many calls demanding action.

The Judge rendered his verdict of not guilty after hearing the evidence presented. Obviously, you and Ms. Grayson are upset by the Judge's verdict.

If you feel that my handling of this matter is worthy of some complaint, you certainly have the right to take whatever steps may be available. While I may disagree with your assessment, I will defend your right to make it.

Sincerely,

Leo Berry, III

Assistant Solicitor-General

For grins, Leo put a smiley face at the bottom of the document. After a moment, he deleted that emoticon and then hit the send key. Only after sending the message did Leo say out loud, "Asshole!"

Leo finished going through the rest of the work on his desk and opened the door to his office. Out front was a beehive of activity. Secretaries were answering phones and pounding their keyboards while the receptionist was dealing with a disgruntled customer at the front counter.

The oldest secretary employed in the Solicitor's Office looked up from her computer as Leo walked by in the direction of the coffee pot. She was a remarkable lady who had retired after thirty years in the banking business. Dorothy had only made it a month before getting bored and taking the job she now held. She was dressed in bright floral colors that were her signature. Leo thought of her as a cool older person very much like his mother. He poured coffee into his Mercer mug and added a little creamer before she spoke.

"Good morning, Leo," she said with a smile. "Get here early to catch up after a few days off?"

"Yes, ma'am. You pay for it around here if you take some time off. Crap just piles up," said Leo.

"Yeah, job security," Dorothy said. "Are you doing okay? I was very sorry to hear about your loss."

"I'm fine, but thanks for asking. Papa lived a long life. We should all be so lucky."

"I can relate, Leo. I'll be 75 on my birthday and I feel great! I want to work until I'm at least 80. I don't know what I would do with myself all day if I retired again. Speaking of which, how much time do you have left?"

"22 years, 6 months, 1 day and 7 hours," said Leo looking at his watch. "I won't be breaking your record, Dorothy."

"I wouldn't be so sure. Wait and see," replied Dorothy.

"I'll take your word on it. By chance, have you seen Shep this morning?" asked Leo.

"I think he went into Sandy's office awhile ago. Didn't see him leave."

Leo walked down the hall to Sandy's office and saw her talking to their investigator Albert "Shep" Shepard. Shep was an investigator's investigator. He had worked in law enforcement his entire adult life. A third generation cop, Shep worked as a MP while in the service and then thirty years climbing up the ranks of the police department. He looked much younger than his fifty-five years and ran with Leo on occasion. It was all Leo could do to stay up with him when they shared that activity.

"Morning, guys. Mind if I join y'all?" asked Leo.

"Come on in, slacker. Enjoy your days off?" asked Sandy.

Shep only snickered. He was dressed in a polo shirt with the county emblem showing, a light jacket and khakis.

"You're a barrel of laughs, WB. But, yeah. What's up, Shep? You look pretty casual today," said Leo.

"Not much, Little Bossman," Shep replied. "I'm just getting marching orders from the Ice Queen."

Little Bossman was Shep's nickname coined for Leo after Shep came to work in the office. It was his combination take on the Little Leo moniker and the fact Leo could technically boss him around. Leo knew it was done with affection, and he actually kind of liked it for some reason. Leo was not so sure that Sandy liked her description as the Ice Queen quite as much, though. She never showed any emotion when referred that way which only served as reinforcement the nickname was appropriate. Leo preferred calling her WB or Worker Bee since she really was such for the office.

"Speaking of work assignments, or marching orders, if you will, did y'all by chance look at the Murphy file sent over from the DA?" asked Leo.

"Yes, but only because I told you I would help. Actually, we were discussing the case. Didn't mean to get ahead of you. Have you looked at the file?" asked Sandy.

"Just got through a few minutes ago. You know I appreciate your help," Leo said to Sandy.

Taking time to look at each of them, Leo continued, "Y'all know how I operate as well as I do, and I totally trust you both. So, I'm guessing the marching orders include setting up meetings with the witnesses, gathering any other missing information and retrieving evidence, right?"

"We're all on the same page, Leo. I'll take care of everything," replied Shep.

"Great, Shep. Since we don't have a trial term for another month, I would like to work as much as we can on this felony for the next couple of weeks. We ought to be able to interview all the witnesses and start trial prep before we have to gear up for our own stuff," said Leo.

"I'm on it and I'll have us a schedule by the end of the day," said Shep. He folded a worn notebook containing his notes and left the office.

Sandy remained behind her desk looking at her colleague intently. Leo took a swig from the coffee mug and realized the liquid was no longer hot. He was not into cold coffee and showed his displeasure with a frown.

"Distracted Leo? Black nectar of the gods not as hot as it should be?" posed Sandy.

"I guess I'm pretty transparent this morning. Unlike you, WB. It's just that I have more on my plate than I've had in a long time. I'll get through it once I've got a master game plan," said Leo.

"Well, why don't you warm up your beverage and sit a spell?"

Leo looked at the small coffee maker Sandy kept on her windowsill. It was a smaller version of the one he had seen in his Uncle Jim's office last week. Pretty disgusting looking, thought Leo. Not wanting to appear inhospitable, he poured some of the brew into his mug and sat down opposite her desk. Leo took a sip and was pleasantly surprised that it tasted pretty good.

"At least you weren't the poster child for frowny faces that time," said Sandy.

Leo couldn't help but smile. "I think this is the first time I've ever partaken of your coffee. I have to admit it's not bad. Why do you make your own and not drink from the office pot? Then you wouldn't have to worry about keeping your space so pristine."

It was Sandy's turn to smile. Slowly it turned into a full grin.

The condition of Sandy's office was a running joke to anyone who had ever been inside. Files were stacked haphazardly in every nook and cranny. Several of the stacks appeared ready to tumble at any minute.

"Your sarcasm doesn't define me, Little Bossman."

Leo started laughing and Sandy joined in. It was what the doctor ordered on a Monday morning. Work was almost not work if you could laugh a little.

They spent the next thirty minutes discussing the Murphy case and agreed they would reserve their judgments until they had more information. Neither of them were the type to rush to judgment, but each was troubled about some aspects of the investigation.

Leo decided to bring up the latest issue that had bothered him all weekend. He knew in his mind and heart that it should not be a problem that he knew the victim's sister, but as a practical matter it could become huge. Leo had resolved to disclose the relationship to the defense although he did not feel it was a conflict of interest to continue his position as special prosecutor.

"Let me change direction for a minute," he began. "I know in my mind how I would answer this question, but I want to get your opinion. I've been wondering if we have a problem handling a case when we personally know a party?" Leo asked.

Sandy did not pause for a second. "You know very well the answer to the question. It happens weekly in this office. We have to treat everyone the same and cannot show favor or affection to either side. As prosecutors we have a much higher standard to follow and are sworn to seek justice above all else. So, who got a DUI this time?"

Leo shook his head to the side while framing his reply. "No, well at least nobody I'm aware of right now."

"Okay, I didn't mean to jump to conclusions. It's just that I get calls all the time about So-in-so's daughter, Miss Good Girl, getting arrested over the weekend. You know, it's all a big mistake, and she's never done anything wrong in her life. Now she's going to lose her job and her sorry-arsed ex won't pay child support and she and the kid will be out on the street if I don't give GG a break in her case. Never mind that she drove through two yards in a neighborhood tearing up a television cable box and a host of shrubs. And to top it off, she blew twice the legal limit on the alco-sensor and flunked all the field sobriety tests miserably," she said without giving Leo a chance to intervene.

"Nothing like that, WB. I'm well aware of that kind of scenario. But let me use your example to illustrate what I'm talking about. Say you are a friend of So-in-So, or a friend of the owner of the property that was damaged. Knowing you like I do, you are going to handle the case the same way you would if you didn't know that friend. Of course, I would too. But, in the hypothetical I'm posing, are you under a duty to disclose that friendship to the defense? Furthermore, if you are under such a duty, does the friendship amount to a conflict of interest the defense could challenge?"

"Since we guys and gals wear the white hats in the our version of the Holy Wars, I always disclose the fact I know someone involved in the case. Based on past conversations, I know you do, too. Because our philosophy is to treat everyone equally, I don't see a conflict arising under your hypo. I would definitely put the defense to task to prove how it might be a conflict. That being said, if I felt so close to the party to the point it might affect my judgment, I would bail. We've all done that before," answered Sandy.

"I agree. I guess I needed a little reinforcement. I'll tell you why I bring it up, said Leo.

Leo then relayed a brief history of the newfound relationship with Mickie Thomas. Sandy listened without questions until Leo finished. She looked pensive.

"So, let me get this straight. You first meet this girl at your grandfather's funeral service. She gives you some memento belonging to him that you say is not germane to the situation. Then you find out she is a beneficiary in his will after finding out you are the executor of the very same will. Next you run into her at your grandfather's farm that, by the way, you are inheriting and is located adjacent to the property she's to get. And, the final coincidence occurs when you discover the same defendant you have been assigned to prosecute murdered her older brother. Really?" Sandy asked.

"Yeah, sounds like a novel plot, doesn't it?"

"It's like some kind of James Redfield story, yeah. What does Dee think about all this?"

Leo thought about the long discussion he and his wife had after the trip to see Uncle Jim and to the farm. It had lasted well past their usual bedtime because Leo made sure everybody enjoyed a grilled steak, baked potatoes with all the trimmings and a cucumber salad before watching the classic movie he had rented from the video store. Mindy had loved "Cool Hand Luke" even though she said she preferred Christian Bale to a young Paul Newman.

As soon as Mindy had gone to her room, Leo got a bottle of pinot noir from their small rack, grabbed a couple of wine glasses and led Dee to their bedroom. It had taken the whole bottle of wine to get Dee caught up with the situation. She was attentive and enthralled by all of it, but especially what Leo told her was contained in the journal. Leo had said he would let her read it soon, but he had put it in a safe place until he got through administering the estate.

Whether the story, the wine, the good food or simply the love they shared with each other caused it, Leo and Dee had made slow love to each other that night. It had been a magical time.

"Uh, earth to Leo. Did I lose you? You did tell Dee, right? Asked Sandy.

"Uh, huh. Sorry. I was just thinking about what you asked me. Yes, I told her and she's pretty much fascinated by all of it," said Leo.

"Can't say that I blame her. To get back to our discussion, I still don't see an inherent conflict. However, I believe the relationship between you and the victim's brother should be disclosed to the defense. Also, I didn't hear you say whether Mickie Thomas knows you have been assigned the case. If she hasn't, I think you need to let her know pretty damned quick, too."

"I agree, Sandy. Speaking of the defense, do you know the assigned public defender? I really don't know a lot of those lawyers except the guy in charge and I understand he doesn't try cases."

"Sam Adams, like the beer. He's a young black guy who was in school the class behind me. I knew him fairly well back then and have run into him on occasions around the courthouse. He's sharp. Sam was on that moot court team that made it to the national competition a few years ago and also made law review. I give him maybe another year before some firm makes him a better offer," said Sandy.

"Yeah, young lawyers with those credentials always move on up in a hurry. Get a little experience, get some exposure on a case with some media attention, and he'll be on his way," replied Leo.

"Yeah, but I do like him. I think you will, too."

"If you do, I'm sure I will, too. As soon as we get an opportunity to meet with our witnesses and see what we have to work with, maybe you can set up a meeting with him. Who knows, he might have some evidence he can share that will help us resolve this mess. I'm afraid with the earlier mistrial and some of the allegations made, we'll have a media circus. I know we don't want that, I just hope he doesn't as well. If he's an upward climber, he may not be all that cooperative and could see this as his chance to build his reputation."

"I think he'll be professional, Leo. You'll see, he's a classy guy. Anyway, I've got a motion hearing at 10:00 that I need to get ready for."

"Sure thing, WB. Good luck with that. I need to get busy myself, so back to my cave. At the risk of being redundant, thanks again."

"No problem, just find me some pens," said Sandy with a smile.

"When this is over, you'll have the most unique one I can find, I promise."

With the meeting over, Leo headed back through the maze to his office. He closed the door and took out Papa's journal. He started flipping pages and re-reading some of the passages. A gnawing sense of purpose was taking over him. Apprehension as well.

Could Leo handle all that was on his plate? He better, he thought.

CHAPTER 20

The next several days until the weekend flew by. Workdays were taken up with meetings. Nights were taken up with family. For Leo, it was necessary to keep those days and nights separated so the focus of resolution could take place. He knew some of the challenges he was currently facing would be easier to solve than others. Leo also knew he would resolve them best if he could keep work and family separate without one imposing on the other.

Although Leo thought of himself as a multitasker, he felt more effective when completing one task at a time. Having to deal with a major case and the administration of Papa's estate simultaneously would be easier if he could set priorities and focus on one or the other. It was a blessing to have Sandy and Shep helping him at work, and it was another to have Tim's assistance with the estate. In the final analysis, it would be up to

Leo to seek the best resolution of both concerns in his life. It looked like his special prosecution would take the lead, at least for now.

The case against Lonnel Murphy had emerged as not quite the slam-dunk Leo had been led to believe. This was not an uncommon occurrence when dealing with transferred files. As Leo had suspected when first reading the file, Detective Fletcher Richards had not been totally forthcoming with some elements of the investigation. Leo had worked with him on enough occasions to know that for all his faults, Richards was still a thorough cop who generally covered all the bases when he worked a case. Because the report contained holes, Leo had wanted to talk to him first.

The meeting with Richards, Sandy and Shep had started off cordially enough but quickly degenerated to something much less. Shep had taken the lead initially by design since he had worked with the detective during his years with the PD. The lawyers knew there was a certain amount of trust between officers that transcended the bonds they had with the police. As soon as Shep started asking questions about details, Richards changed his tone.

"Look, Shep. I know you're too good to still be just a cop, but you know I'm good at what I do," Richards said with dripping sarcasm.

Pausing he continued, "If I didn't put something in the report, I either didn't think it was that important, or maybe it slipped my mind to write it down in the stat 5. You know how it is when a lot of shit's going down at the same time. I guarantee everything's still up here that's relevant to the case," said Richards while pointing to his head.

Leo had tried to tone things down when he intervened during the interview. "Nobody's accusing you of anything, Fletch. Shep's only doing a milder version of a defense lawyer's cross. You've been there plenty of times, so let's play it out.

"Pretend I'm a nasty guy representing Murphy in this case. I start by going over how long you've been a cop. How long you've been writing reports. How important they are. How you're trained to write it all down. How often times cases come to court much later, maybe even years later. How often times you can forget details of a case because of the passage of time and the sheer volume of cases you've worked since then. How you might even mix details of cases up. How you forgot to write something down that you've testified to in court if it was so important then. You've heard all those questions, right?" Leo had asked.

"Sure, but I'm a pro, Berry. I can handle those questions without getting flustered or pissed off. The jury will know the lawyer is trying to bust my balls. All part of the game they play. You guys don't have to do that to me."

"Maybe, Fletch. 'Confidence can be a virtue' as my Papa used to say. He also used to say something about pride coming before a fall. Since this case has fallen in my lap, I aim to be ready. I want to be sure of anything out there that may come up that I don't know about. I'm concerned that you're getting plenty upset with us and we're supposed to be on the same team. I can only imagine what might happen when the other side jumps on you pretty hard. It's really just that simple, Detective," Leo had responded.

Richards had been sullen for the rest of the time in Leo's office. He had given explanations oozing disdain to every question or concern that Leo, Sandy and Shep raised. Leo had found out through other questions that Richards had directed Sullivan to write his report with minimal facts. He had done that because "Sullivan is a kid needing more seasoning."

Richards quickly discounted the homeless witness since he was "just a bum" and he had been "drunk on his ass" when Richards interviewed him on the night of the event. When Leo asked if he knew where to find the witness because Shep had had no luck locating him, Richard's response was "there ain't no apartment numbers on the Ocmulgee where that alkie sleeps."

As a way to try and change Richards' mood, Leo had asked Sandy and Shep to leave the office near the end of the interview. When they were gone, the detective had lit into Leo for bringing other people in. He wanted to know why Leo felt the need for additional help and why they were being so critical of the investigation. All the while during his tirade, Fletcher Richards' face had turned to a crimson shade that had the affect of making Leo think of the Alabama slogan, "Roll Tide." Leo had also thought Richards' would stroke out one of these days if he didn't suffer a major heart attack first.

When Richards had finally stopped long enough to take a gulp of air, Leo took the opportunity to ask personal questions about the detective's friendship with the victim. The change in direction resulted in subduing Richards long enough for Leo to score additional information. Leo found out that Richards and Johnny Thomas were in the same hunting club and shared other interests like fishing, bowling and women.

Leo played on the friendship angle as a way to understand the detective's loss and to find out if Richards would have known why Thomas had been downtown so late the night he died. According to what Janice Hill had told Richards and was not in the report, "Johnny had some business with a bartender when he got off work, so they went to eat and have a few drinks until that happened." The detective also said he was told by Hill the business meeting never occurred which was the reason he was confident there was no connection to the murder.

After it was all said and done, Leo was sure Detective Fletcher Richards knew even more than he was willing to tell. Whether something shady was going on with Johnny Thomas had become a concern in Leo's mind that had to be ruled out before going to court. His team would figure it all out soon, thought Leo.

The interview with Officer Sullivan that was conducted next had only intensified the team's beliefs that Richards was not being completely candid about his connections to Johnny Thomas. Sullivan told them when he first saw Winton Stiles in the alley the night of the shooting, Stiles did appear to have been drinking, but he did not seem heavily intoxicated. Sullivan's recollection was that Stiles had been "much more frightened than drunk." Sullivan had said Stiles wanted to leave before the detectives arrived because "they would make him stay at the station all night" and that all he saw was "the black kid was trying to get away." Sullivan also relayed that Stiles heard them arguing about some money before the shot occurred.

Sandy had asked Sullivan why he did not include those details in his report and he had said, "I reported this to Detective Richards as soon as he arrived, and he told me he would investigate those things and that I didn't need to worry about anything but the bare bones. Detective Richards said he would take care of any statements that were to be collected. He told me I would understand one day when I became a detective."

The last witness Leo and the others had questioned before the weekend was the girlfriend, Janice Hill. Hill was a hairdresser who had been dating Johnny Thomas off and on for a few months prior to his demise. Leo had thought of her looking slightly on the worn side but not unattractive. He had thought a little less make-up and a less severe hairstyle would help.

Hill affirmed that she and Thomas had gone downtown to have some fun on that fateful night. They had a nice late dinner at an upscale restaurant and then went to three nightclubs within walking distance of where they ate. Johnny always seemed to know lots of people wherever they went and there was a lot of talking, laughing and drinking through the night.

Before they left the last club, The Night Light, Johnny disappeared for about 15 minutes. Hill said she was not sure where he went or whom he talked to, but Johnny had told her earlier he needed to take care of a little business before the night was over. She said "she had no idea what that business was and didn't care in the least. I was just having a good time." They left the club shortly thereafter and as they walked down the street Johnny handed her an envelope containing cash and asked her to keep it in her purse for him.

Upon further questioning by Leo, Hill had said there were other people on the street that night, but she did not notice anyone watching them. When they approached the car, they were positioned on their respective sides. As Johnny got in the vehicle, the kid appeared out of nowhere and grabbed her purse while she was opening the passenger door.

The only description she could provide of the guy was "he was dark-skinned, a little taller than me and I'm 5 feet 4 inches tall, short hair wearing a hoodie and those baggie jeans they all wear." Later that night, Detective Richards took her to a lineup where she couldn't say for sure if the kid wearing the hoodie and baggie jeans was the one who robbed her, but the clothes looked the same as the one who did it.

Hill's other revelations ended once and for all the armed robbery count as far as the team was concerned. She confirmed she had never seen the person who took the purse as being armed with a gun or any other weapon. It was at worse a robbery by sudden snatching. Furthermore, they all knew of cases handled in their court as misdemeanors with facts similar to these, so the defense would make a huge deal out of this snafu if an effort was made to secure a conviction for the much more serious felony offense.

Also, Hill acknowledged Johnny had gotten his gun out of the car before chasing the person who stole her purse. Forensics had proven the round that ended Johnny Thomas's life had been fired from that gun. Somehow, Lonnel Murphy had gotten the gun away from Thomas in the alley confrontation, but forensics also showed residue on the hands and arms of both. The fatal shot had been at close range that very well could have come as a result of a struggle over the weapon. A murder conviction, even under the felony murder doctrine, would not be a lock and now could be in real jeopardy.

At the last meeting on Friday before the weekend, Leo, Sandy and Shep had hashed out the week's developments. All of them were troubled. They all wanted to talk to Winton Stiles, assuming he could be found. Shep had been trying off and on during the week, but even after using all his street assets and connections with the PD and Sheriff's Office, it was as if Stiles had vanished. Everybody who knew him including the good folks at the Rescue Mission, Salvation Army and the various food banks claimed they had not seen him in months. The frustration of not being able to locate someone potentially crucial to the administration of justice made Leo mad and sad at the same time. Leo only wanted to know the truth of what happened the night Johnny Thomas died, and he wasn't sure if he ever would.

The team had then decided although Shep would keep looking for Stiles, they had to make an effort to conclude the matter sooner rather than later. Sandy called Sam Adams and set up a meeting with him for the following week. If something could be worked out as a plea, Leo wanted it done before spending a whole lot more time preparing for a case that only looked to get more difficult. If that potential plea resolution also caused more anger and pain for those close to either family, it would be unfortunate collateral damage.

CHAPTER 21

It was another Friday night and parties were happening all over the town. In some of the nicer parts of the city some of his customers were naked in their hot tubs. He could picture them sipping on their favorite cocktails adding to the buzz earlier provided by smoking the primo stuff he made available. They would soon be sloshing the heated water all over the deck as they rutted. He couldn't help the wicked grin that came over him at the thought.

In lesser affluent neighborhoods his customers wouldn't be as fortunate to have hot tubs, but they would improvise in other ways to maximize the effects of the product. Word was out that it was the best aphrodisiac money could buy. That was the beauty of the stuff, different strokes for different folks, but they all loved it. The grin got bigger.

The money he was making was outrageous. And the supply had seemed endless until lately. He knew he would have to stop soon, anyway. He was not going to fall into the trap he had seen others fall into in this business. He went to great lengths not to show how much he had. Greed could be a game killer. So, he lived modestly on his salary and horded everything else until he could make his break. Then he would never work again. Work was too much like work.

He also knew from his other job that the longer this enterprise went on somebody was going to find out his role. If that happened, he would be screwed. Therefore, he protected himself by keeping his distance from most other people. He trusted only a few folks and those were the ones who did all the real work.

It was collection night, so he got busy. There were a few more houses on his route before he would need to go downtown to the two clubs. Those were always the last stop. He wouldn't dally and he wouldn't take chances. Not like Johnny did.

What a crying shame that had been. No, that wouldn't happen to him. He was too smart. After all, who knew more about crime than cops?

Dirty cops were nothing new. Not to him.

CHAPTER 22

Leo was up early for a Saturday morning. No matter, however. He was looking forward to a weekend outing with the family. After a hard workweek, there was nothing better to Leo than spending time with the ones he loved.

As Leo whipped up some pancake batter, he thought about what had led up to the plans for today. Leo had looked at the weather report mid-week, and the forecast for the weekend looked to be ideal. He ran his idea by Dee and Mindy and they were only luke-warm at first.

Mindy had said, "Really, Daddy? A picnic at a country farm? I'm much too urban. I suppose you'll want to trade our guitars for banjos next."

"Urban or urbane?" had asked Leo. He really enjoyed playing word games and checking vocabulary with his advanced daughter.

"Definitely urban. Like Grandma Shelly always says, I'm a city girl. I'm not referring to my degree of sophistication," Mindy had replied. Leo smiled at the snippet of memory.

The final step for his batter required a ripe banana, and he secured the last one from a wire basket on the kitchen counter. Leo removed the brown splotched peel and dropped it in the tall waste can near the sink. He cut the fruit into thin slices and folded them into the mixture.

Now that his pancakes were ready to be cooked, Leo placed a flat griddle on the stove and brought the heat up. He tested the temperature with a couple of small drops of water and knew it was ready as they sizzled into nothing. He picked up the large plastic mixing bowl by the handle and poured four not so perfectly round amounts on the hot pan. In no time they were done with a golden brown color that required only one flip. These steps were repeated twice more so that the platter contained an even dozen minus the one he scarfed down during cooking the last installment.

Leo retrieved fresh strawberries from the fridge and maple syrup from one of the cabinets. He washed several of the plumpest berries and dried them with a paper towel. Since he was starving for some reason and it appeared the girls were taking their time making it to breakfast, he decided to eat before them. He sliced a couple of the deep red strawberries and placed them around four more of the pancakes on his plate. He then added some syrup on top and proceeded to devour the food like a person who hadn't eaten in three days. They were quite tasty and he couldn't help the involuntary grunts he made while eating.

He was just finishing his last bite when Dee entered the kitchen. She was dressed in jeans and an oversized tee shirt. Every hair on her head was in place. It was a casual look, but somehow she always looked upscale.

"I see you didn't wait on me and the diva before eating," she said with a smile.

"Sorry, Wink. I don't know why I was so hungry this morning. Uh, and I ate one extra pancake, too."

"It's a real shame you don't like your own cooking," she said as she picked up one of the pancakes. She took a bite and started stroking her throat as she chewed. It was a sign she thought it good. She affirmed this after she swallowed by saying, "Yum, that's a tasty flapjack."

"One of these days I just might start me a diner. I could call it 'Lil Leo's' and cater to the folks who like simple food prepared with a flair. Just think, that could be the slogan. You and Mindy could wait tables and wear cute outfits. We could give up the rat race and be entrepreneurs," he replied.

Dee continued eating the pancake without comment. Mindy joined the group and heard Leo's pitch.

"First, you want to take us to the country. Out in the sticks, no doubt. Now you want us to wait tables in some greasy spoon? Come on, Dad. You're killing the love," said Mindy.

Leo and Dee started laughing. It was hard to tell sometimes if their daughter was being serious or not. It always made some of her statements even funnier.

"Yummers, pancakes! This almost makes up for us having to go to the country today," said Mindy.

"Yeah," said Dee.

"Look, you two. We'll have fun. It'll be like a mini-family reunion. We don't do this very often, getting together with Grandma Shelly and your uncles. And it's a setting where we all come from if you think about it. We'll have some food, tell some stories and be together. Maybe play some football and some music. Give it a chance is all I'm asking," said Leo.

Dee looked at Mindy who had made her a plate and started eating. Their eyes were communicating as only mothers and daughters could.

Dee walked over to her husband and rubbed her hands on his arms. "We're messing with you. You deserve a good day and we promise to have some fun, too. But, I don't have to play football, right?"

"Not even on my team? You do know I'm the best quarterback in the family," said Leo.

"I know, Babes. And, I do have on my helmet," she said patting her coiffed head. "We'll see, then."

They all laughed at the helmet head comment. It was a running joke in the family that the one thing Dee would have to have on a deserted island was hairspray. She often joked that the only thing that scared her more than bad weather was running out of that aerosol.

After cleaning up the breakfast dishes, Leo loaded the car with cooler containing frozen hamburger patties, hot dogs, bratwurst, beer and soft drinks. Next he placed several reusable canvas shopping bags full of buns, chips, ketchup and mustard. He also grabbed the old football that was kept in the garage storage room and placed it in the trunk. By carefully arranging the items, Leo still had enough room to place his and Mindy's matching acoustic guitars contained in their black cases. Leo's mind kept remembering random thoughts as he performed the tasks.

Over the course of the last week when he wasn't spending time working on the Murphy case, Leo thought more about family in general and Papa specifically. Somehow Leo needed to bring everybody together. What better place than where Papa had lived over 65 years of his life?

First, he would draw his immediate family together. Then, he would extend it to the rest. Leo had a vague vision how to do this if he could make everyone better understand Papa. That would not be an easy task because there were some lingering jealousies with older members of the extended family and because some of the younger members didn't really know Leo Oscar Berry, Sr. He had been the patriarch in name only.

Leo could tell them some details about Papa's life that only he knew. That would be a way to personalize the man. The only problem was whether or not he would have to disclose sources.

Leo would not reveal confidences others had given him. And, the journal could not be totally exposed without Leo betraying his grandfather's trust. Thorny problems, but he had to try.

The other dominant thoughts about Papa centered on the Thomas family and their relationship. Uncle Jim had told Leo some things that were not in the journal and were only rumors that might be difficult to prove. Those secrets would need additional investigation as soon as he got the chance. *First things first*, he thought.

Leo went back into the house and called out, "Head 'em up, move 'em out!"

Since he and Mindy spent a fair amount of time watching old TV programs, she knew the next word and hollered, "Rawhide."

Mindy rounded the corner with Tiki in her arms and grinned at Leo. She said as she passed by headed to the garage, "You know, Rowdy would've been a good name for Tiki."

Tiki turned his head in Mindy's direction as he heard his name mentioned. Leo heard him make a noise that he would swear sounded like, "Huhhhh?" Then the dog grinned with his tongue stuck out.

Even the dog was a comedian.

CHAPTER 23

Leo, Dee, Mindy and Tiki made the drive to the farm in record time. As they went, Leo told them the rattlesnake story. He had never told anyone about that memory for some reason, not even to his parents. Maybe it was because it was so unpleasant. Maybe because it was so personal. Maybe because he had put it out of his mind until Papa's funeral. Whatever the reason, he felt it was now the time to share. They were fascinated. Even Tiki seemed to listen raptly. He finished the story just as they pulled up in front of the house. Leo put the car in park and turned it off.

"I thought I'd tell y'all that story to help you see why I want to have a get-together with the family at Papa's place. I've never thought of myself as a country boy just like y'all don't think of yourselves as country girls. But really, I learned a lot about life out here when I was a kid. Papa always called such things life lessons. I want to try to pass those on to you, Dino."

"You do, Daddy. Mom, too. Now please, tell me I won't see a big snake out here today!"

"Yeah," chimed in Dee.

"I doubt it. But, Papa would say 'Always be on the lookout for snakes in the grass.'"

"Tiki will be your protector just like Rusty was for me," said Leo. "Won't you Tiki?"

Tiki started shaking his head up and down. All three of them laughed at the antic.

Leo popped open the trunk and started unloading the car. Dee and Mindy helped him place everything on the front porch. He pulled the keys out of the right front pocket of his Levi's and unlocked the door. They all grabbed a handful of the supplies he had earlier packed and went to the kitchen. When it was all stowed away, Dee and Mindy followed him to the back deck. All of them admired the view and the two girls had to admit it was scenic.

"I think this deck will be the perfect place for us to throw a little family party today, don't y'all?" asked Leo.

Dee had walked over to the large modern aluminum grill that was located on the farthermost corner of the deck. "Wow, I don't remember seeing this before," she said.

"Yeah, it's fairly new. I'm pretty sure that Uncle Jim installed it right before Papa's health started going downhill. Thought it would be more convenient. Papa always preferred cooking on the old brick pit that used to be out there," Leo said while pointing to an area under a large oak.

"After Grandma passed away, he would cook a whole hog on that thing and invite all the family over. Best barbeque I ever had was cooked out there. We would pick pieces off before the hog was even taken off the grate. I guess the old pit finally crumbled down from lack of use and was hauled off."

Dee looked at Leo and thought she detected a trace of sadness in his voice. Mindy momentarily stopped her observation of the landscape and looked at Leo as well.

"Are you okay, Leo?" Dee asked.

"Yeah, I'm fine. One of the things I discovered by coming out here last week was how many memories came flooding back just by looking around this place. Some of it has changed, no doubt. Like that grill, like this deck. All the fields used to have things growing in them. Chickens would be clucking and roosters crowing. Of course, it's not growing season now, but Papa didn't run the farm in recent years like when I was a kid. I've given it some thought, and I think subconsciously that's one of the reasons I stopped coming out here so much after I got to be a teenager. It seemed to be dying a slow death, and I didn't want to see it."

Mindy walked over to Leo and gave him a hug. She was followed by Dee who joined in.

"Do you know whut, chicken butt?" asked Mindy.

"Whut?" chimed Leo and Dee in unison.

"I just remembered something. Even though I never liked coming out here very much, I must've been feeding off Daddy's vibes and feeling a little sad the last time I remember being here. Big Papa brought me a glass of lemonade and told me it was a cool smile on a hot day. It made me smile, too," said Mindy as she stepped away from the group hug.

"Big Papa took me over to the pond, and we fed some ducks with a bag of stale bread. It was the same thing I did with Granddaddy when I was just a little girl. Big Papa was trying to make me feel better, but I kept thinking about Granddaddy and it only made me sadder. Now I remember how sad he was that day. Big Papa was remembering Granddaddy, too."

Just as Leo thought they might all start crying over those memories, they all heard the unmistakable voice of Leo's brother, Dennis. "Let's get this party started!"

Dennis, otherwise known as Denny, was carrying his youngest boy everyone called D-Bo and followed by his wife Les carrying their slightly older son, Bryan. All were smiling as they came onto the deck. Hugs and handshakes followed.

Within a minute, they heard their brother Eddie and his family coming through the house. Eddie's slightly gravelly voice was teasing his shy daughter, Rebecca, who was the same age as Denny's son, Bryan. His equally timid wife, Deb, was holding her hand as they joined the rest on the deck. Their older daughter, Deana, followed them and had her ears plugged listening to the latest tunes. More hugs followed.

Another round of greetings began as the youngest brother, Tommy, and their mother Shelly arrived as well. Tommy, who was recently divorced, had picked up Shelly and brought her to the gathering. His young daughter, Christy, was not with him.

The next few minutes were taken up by good-natured ribbing between the brothers that always followed whenever the Berrys were together as a group. It usually centered around who was the best looking of the brothers although the competition could be over anything.

"I think everybody arriving at the same time for something must be a first for this family," said Leo after the initial hellos were done. He directed the barb at his youngest brother.

"Well, I ain't never been into time, big brother," said Tommy.

"They call that 'island time' down in the Caribbean," replied Leo. "You'd fit right in down there. I must admit we loved it when we made that trip to Jamaica last year. I could easily get into a more laid back time zone. Even Mama would like it if she didn't have to fly to get there."

"No way I'm ever getting on a plane! I'll just enjoy my pool. I'm perfectly comfortable right where I am," said Shelly.

All the family laughed at the familiar retort. Their mother constantly reminded them during conversations that she never intended to move from the modest house they had all lived in growing up. None of them doubted her when it was said.

She continued, "I really like traveling by bus, though. My group has booked a trip to Key West in a couple of weeks. I bet you would like to go back, Leo."

Mindy piped in before Leo could respond, "We all would, Grandma. It's the coolest place I've ever been. But really, a plane is just a bigger bus with wings."

Shelly frowned. "I'll leave flying to you young folks."

"Yeah, we would love to go back, Mama. Maybe next year during spring break we can arrange it. In the meantime maybe Grandma can bring you back a tee shirt, Dino," said Leo.

"Yeah, Grandma! One from Blue Heaven! Please? I can show you on my i-Pad the one I like."

"I'll be happy to, Sugah. Just so long I don't have to look up anything on a computer. Y'all know I don't want to have anything to do with those things," replied Shelly.

They all laughed again at her displeasure over technology. This was another reference all the family heard regularly from their matriarch.

"Okay, Mother. We'll get you a cellphone instead. We've all decided that we're not going to get you that new laptop for Christmas. We thought you might like to take it with you on the Delta flight to the assisted living home, but we can see you're not interested," chimed in Eddie.

"Well, it's okay that y'all want all those cellphones and computers, just don't count me in. I get by fine with my old landline. It's like me, old-fashioned."

Dee chimed in, "Everybody loves you just the way you are. Don't let these boys kid you. We all think you're way cool. I've heard them talking about you as long as I've been a member of this group. They're just boys and don't know how to give compliments. Heck, I still remember when I first met you. You had a gorgeous tan, wearing designer jeans, driving a sports car while rocking out to Bob Seger."

"Hey, I tell everybody that I learned how to cook by watching Mama," said Leo. "And everybody knows she's the best cook around. In fact, we boys all got that from her except for Eddie."

"Yeah, and everybody knows I'm the best cook in the family besides Mama. And remember, the best-looking, too," Denny said.

"You wish," cracked Tommy. "I'm the total package."

"Let's don't beat that dead horse again. Since we've got a little time before checking out this fancy grill, how about we throw around the football? Of course, I'll be the quarterback since I throw the best," said Leo.

The brothers proceeded out of the house to the clearing behind. The area had once been the location of the chicken coop and stretched beyond for at least half the length of a football field. Surrounded by picturesque wooden fencing that led into fields, the pond and the woods to the rear, it was a perfect place to try and relive glory days.

All of the boys had been athletic during high school, and for the next thirty or forty minutes spent their time throwing

Leo's football to each other while reminding themselves of those fun times. While none of them had been big stars on the field, all had participated in the various sports that were in season at the time.

"Go long, Tommy!" hollered Leo.

"Yeah, throw me the bumb," screamed Tommy as he streaked down the way. Eddie and Denny laughed at the reference their father used to rant at the Sunday game on television. They were kids when Daddy once regaled Steve Bartkowski to throw a long pass that he pronounced with the letter u rather than an o.

Denny provided the commentary to the play as Tommy ran and Leo rared back to throw the ball. "The Falcons' quarterback is in the pocket. Billy 'White shoes' Johnson is racing down the right side lines. Time is running out, and the Hail Mary is the last chance for the birds. The ball is in the air, and three defenders are around Johnson. He jumps! I don't believe it! The Falcons have won! Great throw and super catch!"

All the men were laughing as they walked back toward the big shade tree. Up on the deck the women and children were clapping. Their mother called out to them to quit before they got hurt.

Leo and his brothers slumped down on the ground near the tree. It was a cloudless day and although the October weather was a little cooler, all of them had started to work up a sweat.

"That was pretty fun," said Eddie, "but I must be getting old. We used to do this from sunup to sundown and not get tired."

"I'm not even breathing hard," said Denny.

"I know you lyin'," said Tommy while still gulping air.

"Hey, to be in our thirties, we're not bad," panted Leo.

"Still, we ain't kids anymore," replied Eddie.

"Weren't those days great? Not a care in the world. Playin' all day. Kids today don't understand how much fun we had outside. They'd rather be on the computer or watchin' something on TV," said Denny.

"We just have to try and expose them to other ways of enjoying their time. Not that they'll do or enjoy the same things we did. I think it's important for them to at least see us having fun out here today. That's one of the reasons I wanted us to get together," said Leo.

Eddie looked at Leo and replied, "Not a bad reason at all. You said one of the reasons, why else?" he asked.

Leo contemplated his answer for a moment. He wanted to let his brothers in on some of the developments since their grandfather died. How much he should divulge was the big question.

"I've been doing a lot of thinking lately," started Leo. "I guess it began with Papa's death. It seems to me our family has gotten a little detached, and maybe the finality of life has something to do with it. I mean, we stay in touch and certainly any of us would be there to help each other if needed, but it's not regular, if you get my drift."

"I think so, too," said Tommy. "For me, it started when Daddy died. We got together more often before then. Now it's only on Thanksgiving and maybe Christmas."

"I think you're right. We've all got our own lives to deal with and speaking for myself, I put things off thinking I'll have more time next week or next month. Before you know it, it's too late to connect," said Leo.

"Haven't thought about it like that because we run into each other at Mama's from time to time, but I guess it's never everybody at the same time," said Eddie.

"I can't believe Daddy's been gone for six years," said Denny as he shook his head from side to side.

"That's part of what I'm getting at," said Leo. "As I've thought about Papa, I remembered how all of his family, including us when we were kids, would gather over here just about every week. Then Grandma died and things started changing. With every death of a family member, the dynamics changed and maybe it became too painful to continue traditions, whether it was consciously or subconsciously done."

"So, now you think we're repeating history?" asked Denny.

"I think we are. I believe each of us reacted to Daddy's death by retreating into our closer family units. I don't say that's wrong, mind you. I just think we might better cope with the loss by all coming together more often," said Leo.

The brothers looked at each other as they thought about what had been said. Each knew their mother would like such an effort to be made.

"If for no other reason, Mama would be happy if we got together more than once a year," said Denny.

"Alright, we can do that," said Eddie. "Was there something else?"

"Well, I wanted to get with y'all so I could fill everybody in on Papa's will. As y'all know, I've got the responsibility of seeing that Papa's wishes are fulfilled. The will he had drawn provides that all of you get some money, and trusts are also set up for our kids to help with education down the road. I've told y'all about that already. What I haven't said anything about yet is that Papa left me this place. I don't really know why," began Leo.

He paused for a moment before continuing, "I'm more than a little concerned what this might mean to the rest of the Berrys. Quite honestly, I'm not sure what to do about that. However, Papa trusted me enough to figure out how to handle it, so I will do my best."

"Papa always liked you the best," said Eddie. "Everybody else knew that even if you didn't. That's probably why he left you the place. It really doesn't bother me, though. I'm sure Papa had his reasons."

"I can't speak for the rest of them, but I don't have any hard feelings, brother," said Denny. "It's got to be worth some money for sure."

"No probs with me, bro. I'll be glad to get whatever I can out of the deal. I can use some extra cash because of the divorce," said Tommy.

"I appreciate that," Leo said to all of them. "I also wanted to tell y'all a little about Papa you probably didn't know."

Leo then spoke to them about some of the things he had learned through reading the journal and from speaking to Tim Hines and Uncle Jim. Leo felt almost like he was a kid again telling stories to his younger siblings. The only difference now was that the tales Leo was spinning were true to the best of his knowledge.

He started by telling Eddie, Denny and Tommy about their grandfather's experiences during the war including Papa's first love. Leo could tell by the expressions on their faces none of them had ever heard of those things just as he had not before reading of those exploits in the journal. Leo spun the stories without embellishment because they needed none. He went through some of Papa's business dealings and how he developed a lifetime friendship with his lawyer. Leo also told them a little about Gene Thomas and his daughter, Mickie, before stopping to look at his watch.

"Hey, we need to get back to the house and start the grill. I'm getting a little hungry and the girls are probably looking for some backup help with the kids by now. Y'all are probably tired of me flapping my jaws anyway," said Leo.

"You're right about them being ready for some help, but I'm not tired of hearing the stories," said Denny. "You always could tell a good un."

"Yeah, I remember you making up stories about us being trapped in time with dinosaurs and monsters," said Tommy.

"I could eat. Then you can tell some more stories if you want. It'll be like the old days on the front porch when Daddy and the uncles told stuff on each other," said Eddie.

"Maybe so. We all have some pretty funny ones to tell," said Leo.

They all felt good walking back to the house. Like a lot of good memories, Leo hoped these would remain forever.

CHAPTER 24

Dee and Mindy napped in the car on the way back home.
Even Tiki had his head down in Mindy's lap and looked
content from the day's activities. Leo smiled at himself
in the rear view mirror. It had all been what he had hoped for
when thinking about the day ahead of time.

After the cooking, eating and cleanup, everybody had gone
out on the front porch. For the next two hours, they all took
turns rehashing tales of youth. While the stories had been heard
countless times over the years, the laughter could always be
counted on as embellishments made by the tellers only seemed
to be greater than the last time they had been heard.

Denny, who could have been a standup comedian,
especially went to great lengths to describe visual spins of his
episodes. He had all the kids laughing as he told them about the
time in elementary school Leo had demanded the bus driver to,

"Stop the bus, I've got to get out!" because Leo had to use the bathroom. Denny showed them how Leo threw his books in the air and ran at full speed across the yard to their home as he departed the school bus.

More potty humor had followed, as Denny couldn't let the time go by that Eddie had gotten sick with some stomach bug and pretty much smelled up the whole house. Denny had come in from playing outside and said, "Oooh, what stinks?" and Shelly had allowed that, "Eddie's sick." That quote had been immortalized ever since and was applied to anyone who had the misfortune to eat something causing an adverse gaseous reaction.

Not only did he go in to details about childhood events, once Denny got the stage he relayed more recent happenings as well. It seemed that Les became the biggest butt of the jokes as he told about the gyrations she had made when trying to use a rototiller for a backyard garden. Leo had to admit it was funny the way Denny described her unsteadiness running the machinery, and the jarring speech Les used as it pulled her forward through the hardened clay.

He also told of the embarrassing but hilarious memory of the first time Denny had brought Les to Leo's and Dee's home. Leo and Dee had been expecting them, and Dee had cleaned the front glass storm door in expectation of creating a good first impression. When the couple had driven up in the front driveway, Leo and Dee watched in surprise as Les walked into the glass door without realizing it was closed. Denny reenacted the moment in slow motion as everyone including Les howled with laughter.

No family member had been immune from at least one funny episode. Nobody got his or her feelings hurt as a result. They just enjoyed the laughter.

After the comedic moments had ended, Leo had asked for everyone's attention. It had been a chance for Leo to get more serious. He remembered how he began.

"I really hope everybody has been having a good time today. That was the main reason why I wanted us to get together."

Leo had looked around and they were nodding their heads in approval.

"But, I also wanted to talk a little bit about Papa. I think it's important we all think about him today," said Leo.

"Preach on!" said Tommy as he took a swig from a beer.

Everybody looked at Tommy for a moment. Leo hoped his youngest brother was not drinking too much. Loud speech would sometimes provide telltale signs. Such activity could bring the good times to a screeching halt.

"I'm not going to preach, for sure. As everybody knows, I'm not much into that sort of thing. Come to think of it, neither was Papa. I just remembered him telling me one time that God was in here," Leo said pointing to his chest. "And, I think he was right."

"Just a figure of speech," Tommy said with a little less vigor. "Tell us, big bro."

"I know what you mean, Tommy. But, as y'all know, the funeral was on a terrible day. I'm sure that had a lot to do with very few people coming, and I certainly don't blame anybody who didn't. However, because of that, I don't think he really got a proper send off, if that makes sense. So, I thought I would say a few words about what he meant to me and if anybody else wants to, they can as well. Afterward, Dee, Mindy and I are going to drive over to the grave before going back home. If y'all want to come, I think that would be nice," continued Leo.

"I want to start by telling y'all about my first memory of Papa. I've only told a few of you this story, so those who have heard it, please forgive me for being redundant. I didn't even remember it myself until I was at Papa's service. I think it shows a lot about how he was, though."

Leo proceeded to tell the story of the rattlesnake for the benefit of those who had not heard earlier. He continued with some of the other memories. As before, those who had heard Leo's stirring narrative of Papa's wartime efforts were visibly moved. His brothers listened to the stories again to the end without interruption. His mother's eyes glistened with tears, and Leo recognized a look of pride on her face. Dee and Mindy held hands and shared looks at each other as the narrative continued. Even the smaller kids were quiet as Leo spoke. The conclusion of Leo's remarks was poignant as well because they were so personal to him.

"Papa was a private man in many ways. The fact he hid so much of his life from even other members of his family is a mystery. Maybe he thought he would disappoint some of those loved ones. Maybe he was hurt and didn't know how to show it. Papa was not perfect. He lived a long and productive life although he knew disappointments and chose to hide them."

Leo paused for a moment and continued again, "But I know this. He was a hero and not just during the war. He loved his family even if he didn't always know how to say it to them. And, he loved me even though I don't remember him ever saying the words. Papa expressed his love by what he did.

"He taught me things that will stay with me the rest of my life. As y'all know, Papa always called those life lessons that I think we need to pass those on to our kids, too.

"Today, I say in this setting, we just relived a little of the tradition Papa started. I'm convinced he would've approved. He saw fit to leave this place to me for some reason. Right now I'm not exactly sure why, but I'll figure it out. In the meantime, I believe we need to try and find ways to remain as close as I think we've felt here today, and maybe even extend it to others in the Berry clan. For sure, I don't want any hard feelings to come from me being the new owner of this property," said Leo.

Afterward, they all had driven to the cemetery and to the Berry plots. Papa's grave marker had not been set, yet. The freshly dug grave still had a slight mound of dirt higher than those nearby. Dead flowers were strewn on the mound. The weathered headstones next to the grave verified the two adjacent graves were of Grandma and Aunt Ollie. The setting was final and more than a little depressing for all of them.

Some of the family members had bowed their heads in silent prayer. Leo did the same and had prayed that one day all of their spirits would be united in a better place. Others just simply said their goodbyes.

However they had chosen to make closure of the loss, it had been peaceful, thought Leo. No wonder Dee and Mindy now slept as they rode back to their house.

Right before they arrived home Dee opened her eyes and looked at Leo. "You are a credit to the name," she whispered.

"I hope so," he whispered back. "I really hope so."

CHAPTER 25

Another Monday. The weekends always flew by and the weekdays were "slow as pond water backing up a hill," thought Leo as he remembered his law school buddy Jim Bob often saying.

Mondays were the worst, though. There was the fresh batch of paperwork from the various law enforcement agencies to review. Maybe because people had more free time, it seemed folks were apt to get in trouble over the weekend than any other time. Some of the reports he had to read would end up being funny in a way, but most were plain drudgery. They all had to be read and evaluated, though. Like at least 75% of the legal work necessary to do his job well, it was not glamorous.

There were other things about this particular first of the week that bothered Leo as well. Since today was the start of a two-week stretch of motions and non-jury hearings, to be followed by a week of jury trials, Leo thought of only one word-chaos. People pulling at you in every direction. Trying to keep everything straight while maintaining focus. Getting out of whack with the exercise schedule. All the while seeking justice tempered with mercy.

Leo thought about these things as mere consequences resulting from his choice of occupations. He fully understood the pros and cons of public service because he had previously been on the other side. As his mother often said, "There are kick-backs to everything." That was not quite what Leo would have characterized as .such, but he understood what she meant when she said it.

One of the consequences of prosecuting misdemeanors was the sheer number of cases. Because you could hardly ever prepare like you should, you had to be quick on your feet all along the path of handling the cases. Most such offices were understaffed and the lawyers were not paid on the same scale as felony prosecutors further exacerbating the problem. For that reason, many assistants got enough experience to move into a better paying district attorney's office or into a lucrative defense firm. Retention of lawyers was often a problem as a result. Other lawyers who tried to do that for a living got burned out quickly and moved on to something else not related to their degree.

Fortunately for the local office, retention of staff had not been an issue. The Colonel had been able to get the Commission to keep salaries more in line, and everyone enjoyed working for him because of his laid back style of managing. Therefore, the assistants felt a loyalty not often felt in other such offices, and all of them fancied themselves career prosecutors. Leo was no exception.

The chaotic atmosphere today went beyond the norm. The caseload had recently exploded because of changes to several laws made by the legislature, and the courtroom was overflowing. There had to be close to two hundred people crammed inside at 9:00 when court was to begin. Leo couldn't help but think of his recurring nightmare of having to conduct court in the Macon Coliseum by himself.

The immediate solution was to siphon off some of the congregation. Rob, Leo and Sandy decided to ask the judge to allow their retired senior judge to hear some of the cases in the smaller courtroom across the hall. Since Leo was perceived to have the best relationship with both judges, he was tasked to ask their permission. While he was doing that, the other two assistants would attempt to cherry pick cases to be handled by the older judge. Out of respect for both judges and in an effort to hopefully keep appeals down, more complicated cases would be kept in the larger courtroom.

Leo first went to the senior judge's office. Although officially retired, the judge maintained an office in the courthouse. He found Judge Phil Taylor sitting behind his desk reading the newspaper. Leo rapped lightly on the door and the distinguished looking man lowered the paper.

"Good morning, Judge. Did I catch you at a bad time?"

"No, no. Come on in Leo," Judge Taylor said with a smile.

The two had a history that dated back to Leo's law school days. As he had done for every law graduate at Mercer until three years ago, Judge Taylor had taught him the very practical trial practice class. Not only was it the most practical class, it had been the most fun to Leo. As a result, Leo had targeted Judge Taylor as a mentor. Leo often sought his advice and opinions on trial matters after Leo graduated, and it still continued after thirteen years of practice. Anytime Leo had argued a case in his court as a defense lawyer or as a prosecutor, Leo had gone to chambers after the case was completed and asked to be critiqued. Those lessons had been invaluable and made Leo into the trial lawyer he was now.

"Thanks, Judge. I don't have a long time to talk this morning, but I have a favor to ask if you are up for it, and if I can get Judge Williams to agree."

"I figured as much, Leo. I saw the horde milling around this morning as I came in. You want me to hear some cases, right?"

"Can't sneak anything by you, Your Honor. Are you available?"

"I can do whatever you need until 1:00. That is, if what's his name will let me," Judge Taylor said while pointing his thumb in the general direction of Judge Williams' office.

Leo knew there was some tension involved between the judges, but in the final analysis he knew they both wanted the best for the court. Leo supposed anyone in Judge Williams' place would have felt similarly taking over the reigns of an icon like Judge Taylor.

"I think he'll welcome your help this morning, Judge. I just wanted to make sure you're ready if need be."

"Just let me know, Leo. And, thanks. I like helping out."

"Sure thing, Judge. And I appreciate you as always. I'll be back in a minute to let you know."

Leo walked down the hall and found Judge Patrick Williams dressed in his robe and talking to one of the bailiffs while standing in the doorway. All of the bailiffs working for the court were older men long retired from other jobs ranging from firefighter to insurance salesmen. There was one old Marine sergeant/former police officer/former probation officer among the ranks, and he was the one now talking to the judge. His still booming voice could be heard down the hall as Leo approached.

"Yes sir, we've got standing room only. It'll be a challenge just to keep 'em quiet so you can hear the testimony."

Leo could see a frown on the judge's face as he replied, "I don't understand why these calendars can't be managed better. I guess I'll need to work with the commissioners and the legislature to get another full-time judge for the court. Are we ready to start?" asked Judge Williams as Leo joined the conversation.

"We're ready, Judge. We could really use some help today, though. I noticed that Judge Taylor is here. What do you think about asking him to give us a hand? We could limit his cases however you wish," said Leo.

"Another of your schemes, Leo? You do know I figured out some time ago that you're the point man for the Solicitor's Office whenever y'all want something."

The bailiff known as Sarge interrupted, "Little Leo would've been a decent point man in the jungles of Nam when I was there, Judge."

Leo laughed. "Point man. I like it. I would've been proud to serve with you Sarge. However, I'm thankful I wasn't even born then because I'd probably be another old bailiff trying to stay awake. That is, if I lived through the ordeal like you did."

"I'd had your back. Just like now," said Sarge with a big grin. His white teeth gleamed against his dark ebony skin.

"Alright. Keep all the motions to suppress and the cases with controversial legal issues with me. If Judge Taylor can help, that is," he said to Leo with a raised eyebrow.

"I'll make sure he can, and we'll do as instructed, Judge. If you'll give us about ten more minutes we'll be ready to start, and this should help us all get through the day quicker. Thanks, Judge."

Leo had to fight with himself not to run back to Judge Taylor's office. He entered and gave a thumb's up.

"Be ready in ten, Judge." The old judge smirked and nodded his head. Leo made a beeline to the courtroom to let his colleagues know the good news.

Because it had been anticipated Leo would be successful, Rob gave Leo a stack of files to take to Judge Taylor's courtroom. Leo announced to the audience for all of the defendants, counsel and witnesses in those cases to go there and he followed. Rob and Sandy stayed in the larger courtroom and would work in tandem to handle the majority of the cases, but at least now everyone had a seat and the noise had been reduced an octave.

Leo went directly to his side of the bench closest to the jury box and started scanning through the files as soon as he arrived in the courtroom. He had done this many times over the course of his career and knew instinctively which cases would take the most time. Sandy had already loosely arranged the files so that all of the simple contested traffic violations were on top. They were followed by two shoplifting cases that were unrepresented by counsel and a simple battery/family violence case that did have a lawyer on the other side.

Since a lawyer was involved in only one of the cases, Leo would normally call that case first as a courtesy. However, Sandy normally put cases near the bottom of a stack for a reason. Leo quickly glanced through the skinny file looking for clues. There were a couple of her usual unreadable scribbled notes indicating she had met with the victim previously, and the woman wanted the prosecution to go forward. That was important since a high number of family violence cases did not have the luxury of a victim wanting to pursue the charge. Another significant tidbit about the case revealed there were two independent witnesses who had seen the incident forming the basis for the criminal charge. Because the judge was not on the bench yet, Leo approached opposing counsel to get a feel about why the file was a bottom feeder.

Randy Wingate practiced law in a nearby community and from time to time had a client in the State Court. He was somewhat eccentric with a red face indicating he was a drinker and had curly hair worthy of a young girl. Rumors had it that he was constantly on the make and had been involved romantically with at least two of his former clients and a former staff member in his office. Leo had not been particularly impressed with his skills in the past, but Leo had lost cases to attorneys with less.

Wingate was seated beside a guy presumably his client. Leo couldn't help but think the client was a dead ringer for a blonde Freddie Mercury, the late singer for the group, Queen.

"Hey, Randy. Looks like you're the only lawyer with me this morning. Is your case going to take very long?"

"Morning, Leo. Probably not more than about 45 minutes. But, we're not in a rush. You can call us last. I already told Sandy to put us on the bottom," said Wingate.

"Okay, I don't think the ones I have right now should take too long since they're all pro se and most are traffic with one witness for the state. If you and your client want to go down to the snack bar and grab a cup of coffee or something, I'm sure you'll be fine, and I'll cover with the judge," said Leo.

"You're a gentleman, Leo." Wingate looked at his client who nodded. "We'll take you up on that offer. I don't suppose you want to dismiss the case?"

"Sorry, Randy. I'm really not very familiar with the file, and I need to do a review and maybe a quick interview with the witness. Just glancing at the report, it looks like a pretty typical case that I would be unwilling to dismiss at this stage. Before you get back I'll see what I can find out, and I'll let you know if I change my mind."

"Fair enough, Mr. Prosecutor," Wingate said as he and the client got up from their seats and left the courtroom.

Leo walked back to the bench and started flipping through the files. The first three cases were speeding violations made by the same state trooper. When Leo saw the name, he knew from past experience all of the defendants would be using the same defense. Glancing at the clock, Leo asked Sarge to wait a couple of minutes before getting the judge.

Leo picked up the three files and went to the bar separating the courtroom. He called the names of the three persons charged. They all came forward, and Leo addressed them as a group.

"Good morning. My name is Leo Berry, and I'm the prosecutor assigned to handle the cases against you this morning. In case you haven't heard this before, you do not have to speak with me and even though the cases filed against you are minor traffic offenses, you have the right to have a lawyer represent you. If you want one and cannot afford one, I can give you a financial affidavit to fill out so that you can ask the court to appoint one for you. I see in your files that all three of you have signed the "Record of Court" form acknowledging you have had your rights explained to you, and you have all chosen to waive your rights to an attorney and to a jury trial. All of you have indicated you want to plead not guilty to the offense of speeding, and you all want to represent yourselves in a non-jury trial before the presiding judge. Is that right?" asked Leo.

Leo looked at the three people. There were two men and one woman. All appeared to be clean cut without distinguishing features. The two men nodded their agreement, but the woman asked, "Do I need a lawyer?"

"That has to be your choice, Ms. Smith," Leo said looking down at her file so he could address her by name. "Most folks who contest these types of charges choose not to be represented; but as I said, you do have that right. It is unethical for me to make that choice for you, and I don't want you to think I'm trying to influence you in any way."

"I don't really think I need one. I'm forty-eight years old, and this is the first time I've ever been in trouble in my life. I only came to court because I don't think I was going that fast," she said.

One of the men spoke up, "Yeah, me too. I mean, I've gotten a couple of tickets before, and if I had been going that fast, I would've paid it."

"Okay, look. As y'all have seen, we have a huge calendar this morning, and the judge is interested in getting through as quickly as possible. I've reviewed each of your files and see all of you have good driving histories. Congratulations especially to you Ms. Smith, I wish I could say I've never had a ticket," said Leo.

Leo paused for a moment and continued, "While I'm not in a position to totally dismiss your cases this morning, I am willing to reduce the speeds on your tickets so they won't result in any damage to your driving records. That should help with your insurance companies and also reduce the fines as well. That's the best I can offer you at this point, if you're interested. If so, I need to know pretty quickly since the judge is about to take the bench."

Both men immediately accepted the offer. Leo marked the reductions on the citations and called Sarge over to take them to the clerk's office for payment. The woman appeared to be mulling over the offer.

"Your offer seems fair enough, Mr. Berry. I'm curious, though. Did the same trooper who wrote my ticket write the other two? I heard someone point him out this morning while I was in the gallery and they said, 'He'd write his own mama a ticket.'"

Leo tried not to smile, but he couldn't help the hint to one side of his mouth. "You're perceptive, Ms. Smith. I've heard that same thing a time or two. Some might call him aggressive; some may say he's gung-ho about his job. I would classify him as unforgiving when it comes to traffic enforcement. He does not discriminate when he's doing his job. I'm not saying he couldn't have made a mistake when he wrote you a citation. But, I've known him for as long as I've been in this profession, and I do find him honest. Some might say he could use a little more discretion by issuing a few warnings from time to time."

"In that case, Mr. Berry, I'll accept your generous offer," she said smiling. "Thank you."

Leo made the notations on the ticket as Sarge returned. He gave Leo not so subtle thumbs up as he got the file and asked Ms. Smith to go with him to see the clerk. Leo then walked over to the opposite side of the courtroom where several officers were seated and spoke to the trooper.

"Okay, P.J. You can be excused this morning. All of yours decided not to contest."

The hefty trooper raised his left eyebrow and gave an enigmatic look to the prosecutor. "Thanks, I can go home and get some beauty rest now after being on night shift. I trust you didn't reduce 'em too much."

"Only what I'm comfortable with, P.J. I think they all know to slow it down a little now. Go get some sleep so you'll be ready again tonight," said Leo.

Just as Leo turned back toward the bench, he saw another of the ancient bailiffs open the back door. He announced, "All rise!"

Judge Taylor strode into the courtroom with his robe billowing behind. He was an imposing figure as he appeared to jump the stairs leading to the bench and sat in the leather chair facing the audience.

Leo froze in place until the judge could take his seat. He gave a stern look at Leo and asked him, "Are we ready?"

"Yes, Your Honor. The State is ready."

Leo walked without hesitation to his spot at the bench and said in a low voice, "I'm sorry for the slight delay, Judge. I was able to resolve a few cases, though."

"That's alright, let's go. We're burning daylight, Mr. Berry."

For the next hour the remaining cases were called in rapid succession. All of the traffic violations resulted in guilty verdicts by the judge, and the fine amounts varied based on considerations involving drivers' past histories, their demeanor and credibility during their testimonies. Certain officers often were not as effective in presenting their testimony, but the cases during the session all involved seasoned law enforcement leaving the court with an easy choice on whom to believe. Leo had heard the judge say many times, "I will generally believe an officer unless I've been given a good reason not to."

The two shoplifting cases involved cousins who had been charged as co-defendants. They had been observed in Wal-Mart collecting various items in a buggy and then ringing up about half the items while going through the self-checkout line. One of the defendants, La'Shay Jackson, actually admitted her role saying she knew she had not paid for all the items. The other, Questa Jones, claimed she didn't know what her cousin was up to.

"So, Ms. Jones, you've testified you didn't pay any attention to your cousin as she was ringing up the items to be purchased, correct?" asked Leo.

"That's right, I wuz mindin' my own bidness."

"Were you minding your own business when you placed some of the items in the cart?"

"Uh, huh."

"Is that a yes?"

"Uh huh."

The judge interjected, "Please answer the question with yes or no. This recorder may have trouble with your answer otherwise."

"Uh huh, I mean yes."

"And, were you minding your own business when you and your cousin got to the checkout counter?"

Yeah."

"Minding your own business when the two of you were placing items on the belt prior to scanning them?"

"Uh huh, uh yeah."

"So, when your cousin started scanning the items, you didn't notice she was skipping some of them? Not scanning some of the items?"

"That's right. I wuz mindin' my own bidness."

"Well, some of those items were yours, right?"

"Yeah, but I wuz gonna pay her when we got back home for my stuff."

"Because you didn't have any money?"

"Naw. I wuz waitin' on my check to come."

"So let me sum up. You and your cousin were shopping together. You had no money to pay for your stuff. You put several items in the cart you wanted to purchase. You helped place those items on the belt to be checked out. But, you didn't pay any attention to your cousin scanning the items or not scanning some items because you were minding your own business. Is that right?"

"Yeah."

"Would you agree that minding your own business would include seeing that your items were rung up correctly so you could reimburse your cousin later?"

"I guess so."

"Well, you wouldn't want to pay more for your items than they cost, right?"

"I trusted my cousin to get that right."

"Do you still trust your cousin?"

"Uh huh, no reason not to."

"How about the fact that she admitted earlier she did not scan all the items?"

"So what? I wuz just watchin' her. I didn't shoplift nuthin'."

"Then you admit you were watching her not scan some of the items that were intended for your own use?"

"Maybe one or two."

"Thank you, Ms. Jones. That's all for the state, Your Honor," said Leo.

Leo glanced over the top of the bench to see Judge Taylor had already written in "Guilty" on the line provided for the verdict contained on the accusation. The judge was flipping through what looked to be a fairly lengthy criminal history.

"Okay, did you have anything else you wanted to say or any other witnesses to call?" asked the judge.

"Naw."

"Then I find you guilty of the offense of shoplifting, Ms. Jones. I also notice this is your third shoplifting charge, and you've had some other theft convictions as well. Do you have anything to say before I pronounce sentence?" asked the judge.

"You gone do what you gone do. I didn't even take anything out the store, so I don't see how you can find me guilty," said the defendant.

"The statute doesn't require you to take anything out of the store, Ms. Jones. It only requires that you took merchandise with the intent to appropriate it for your own use. I find beyond a reasonable doubt that's just what you did. Looking at your criminal history and considering you have been on probation several times in the past for the same type of offense, it is the Court's ruling that you spend 60 days in jail followed by ten months of probation, and I impose a $500 fine as well," Judge Taylor said.

"You old cracker muthafucka! I cain't pay do no jail time and I cain't pay no fine neitha."

"Alright, that'll be another 20 days contempt added to the 60 days jail. Bailiff, please get her out of here."

As Sarge took hold of the defendant's left arm, she started flailing her other arm and was screaming epithets at him as well. "Get your hands off me, niggah! I'll kick yo' old black ass."

The old Marine showed remarkable restraint and said nothing in response to the tirade. He had little trouble getting her out of the door as the few remaining people in the courtroom buzzed about the events.

It seemed everyone had forgotten that the other defendant was still standing before the judge and had not been sentenced yet. She was noticeably shaking.

Judge Taylor looked down at her and said, "Ms. Jackson, I haven't sentenced you, yet. I see from looking at your history that this is your first offense, and you're only seventeen years old. Do you have anything to say?"

"Yessssirrr," she said as the shaking became more pronounced. "I'm sorry for what I did. I wuz just tryin' to help my cousin. I know I wuz wrong, and I don't want to go to jail. I'm still in school, and I want to make somethin' outta my life."

The old judge's eyes softened slightly. He looked over at Leo and said, "What do you think, Mr. Solicitor?"

"Judge, Ms. Jackson appears remorseful to me. Based on that, the fact she has admitted her role in the offense and taking into account her age, I would recommend she be allowed to do our Youthful Offender Diversion Program. That would give her an opportunity to remove this from her record if she completes it successfully," replied Leo.

Looking back at the young defendant the judge said, "Ms. Jackson, I tend to agree with the prosecutor. I'm willing to give you a chance to keep this off your record if you will agree to complete the program he suggested. It won't be easy, but it's better than jail or being on probation. You'll have to attend mandatory classes and do some community service, and I'll want you to continue going to school as a condition of the program as well. Do you think you can do all those things?"

The girl quit shaking and she looked relieved. "Yes sir, I can. I promise I will."

"All right. I'll impose that sentence then. If you complete the program without any problems, I'll sign an order discharging the case without adjudication of guilt afterward. That will help you later in life when you start looking for a job. Good luck to you. And, stay away from others who don't mind if you get in trouble."

The other bailiff escorted the girl out of the courtroom. Judge Taylor and Leo looked at one another and both slightly nodded. They had worked together long enough so that each knew what the other was thinking. Two defendants, one probably doomed to a life of crime, the other maybe with a chance at having a better life. It was one of the reasons Leo loved his job. Sometimes he felt he could make a difference.

"Okay, what else do we have, Mr. Berry?" the judge asked.

Leo looked down at the remaining file. Randy Wingate's case was all that remained. Glancing at the back of the courtroom, Leo saw the lawyer with his client. On the other side sat two women, one man and a police officer. Leo assumed they were his witnesses.

"I have one case left, Judge. I was hoping I might have a few minutes to talk to my witnesses before I start," said Leo.

"Mr. Berry, I've seen you try hundreds of cases without talking to your witnesses. I see no reason to break at this point. Let's move on. I'm sure you can present the case without too much problem," replied the judge.

The judge was right. It was not an ideal situation, but Leo prided himself on trying cases when he was not as prepared as he would like. Trial purists would be appalled to actually handle trials in such a way, but the reality was that there was absolutely no way to handle the case load Leo had without winging a lot of what he did. Besides, how many variations on the recurring themes could you have?

"Yes, Your Honor. In that case, the state calls for trial the State vs. Chance Willis," Leo spoke to the remaining folks in the courtroom. "Would all those involved in that case please come forward?"

Wingate and his client came to the opposite side of the bench from Leo. The two women Leo had noticed earlier walked slowly to Leo's side along with a police officer who he recognized. The lone male who had been sitting beside the women remained in his seat. Nobody else remained in the courtroom except the two bailiffs.

Leo looked at the three witnesses and asked in a soft voice who the victim was. An overweight female who appeared to be in her early 20's said, " I am, Bonnie Willis." She looked down at her feet after identifying herself.

"So you must be Tricia Downs," Leo said to the other less plump woman. Though she was maybe a size smaller than the victim, she was nevertheless a plus size, thought Leo.

She smiled, her eyes flitted and replied, "At your service."

"I see we also have another witness listed. Is Ricky Downs related to you? Is he here?" asked Leo.

She continued to look at Leo as if she were appraising him. He became slightly unnerved as she said, "Yes, that's him back there." She extended her right arm behind her, and Leo could swear she thrust her ample bosom upward in his direction as she continued. "He said he doesn't want to get involved."

"Well, he doesn't have that option if he witnessed the event that resulted in a crime being charged. Did he witness the assault in this case?" Leo asked.

Downs moved within a foot of Leo and still continued to smile. "He stopped Chance from hitting Bonnie more times than he did," she whispered. Leo could smell too much cheap cologne as his discomfort continued to rise.

Leo glanced over her shoulder to the back of the courtroom. The other male she had identified as her husband got up from his seat and headed toward the door as if to leave.

"Mr. Downs, we need you up here, please," said Leo in an authoritative manner.

The man stopped and ambled to the front. Leo noticed he was wearing a work uniform that had "Ricky" emblazoned above the pocket of his shirt. Immediately Leo thought of him being "a good ole boy." His body language screamed he wished he were anywhere but there.

Just then the judge cleared his throat. "Hmmm, Mr. Berry, is the state ready to proceed?"

"Yes, Your Honor. I apologize for the delay. I was making sure we had all of the state's witnesses here."

For the record, Leo formally asked Wingate did his client wish to plead not guilty and proceed with a non-jury trial that had been scheduled for today. After receiving an affirmative response from the defense lawyer, Leo filled out the accusation and rights form to reflect those choices, signed his name as the prosecutor and handed the forms over to Wingate for him and his client to complete. The completed paperwork was then handed up to the judge who verified the choices on the record.

Leo swore in the witnesses, and Wingate asked that the rule of sequestration be invoked. That rule kept the witnesses from hearing each other's testimony. Sarge escorted the witnesses except for the victim to an adjacent small room as the judge warned the remaining witnesses not to discuss the case among them.

Leo began as soon as the other witnesses were out of earshot. He had his file open and referred to the stat 5 report as he began his direct examination of Bonnie Willis.

"Would you state your name and address?"

"Bonnie Willis. I really don't want to state my address since I'm going through a divorce, and I don't want my husband to know."

"Yes, ma'am. That's understandable. I will ask you to speak a little louder though, so the recorder can pick up all your responses. Is the defendant in this case, Chance Willis, your husband?"

"Yes. But, we're separated."

"Back on May 5, 2012, were you two living together at a location in Lake Wildwood, Bibb County, Georgia?"

"Yes, we were."

"And did something happen during the night time hours on that date and at that location resulting in the Sheriff's Office being called?"

"Yes, sir.""

"Would you please relate to the court what happened causing that response?"

The witness paused before beginning with a tremor in her voice. "Chance had invited some friends over to the house that night. Tricia and Ricky Downs. They got there about 7:00. We kept waiting for Chance to get there before getting started, but he still wasn't there at 8:00."

Leo interrupted, "Y'all were having dinner?"

"Well, we had some snacks ready. It was supposed to be just a little party with them and us. But, like I said, Chance was late. So, we had some buttery nipples and waited on him to get there," she continued.

"I'm sorry, Ms. Willis. What did you say y'all had?" asked Leo.

"Buttery nipples."

"I'm sorry to show my ignorance and I actually hate to ask this question, but what is a buttery nipple?" Leo could feel himself getting a little flushed and was afraid to look at the judge.

"It's a drink, a cocktail."

"Okay, so you and your guests were having drinks and waiting on your husband to get to the house. What happened next?"

"Since Chance was late, I thought I should call him. Sometimes he would work overtime, and I was afraid he forgot we were having company. So, I called his cell. All I got was his voice mail, and I left him a message reminding him we had a party. He still didn't come home, so I called and left another message about 8:30. By that time all of us decided to start without him," she said.

"When you say start without him, what do you mean?" Leo asked, as his uneasiness at not knowing what the answer to the question was.

"Well, uh, we are, or were, members of the Swappers. It's a local club. Club members get together for parties, and we have fun if we like each other," she said and looked down at the floor.

Leo stole a glance at Judge Taylor who looked appalled and mesmerized at the same time. Leo was sure neither had a clue where this was going. He sure wished he could have interviewed the witness before the trial started. As it was going, the story of that night had to get even more bizarre.

"I've never heard of that club. Could you tell us a little more about it?"

"Chance first told me about the club a couple of years ago. I'd never heard of it, either. There's a website where you can check out other couples who belong. We really like hanging out together because everybody likes doing the same things. I mean, we swap recipes, clothes, and all kinds of stuff. If we really like the other people enough, we even swap partners. Just for a night, though. I know it may sound bad to some people, but it's special when you like someone enough to do that. It's exciting and we get to spread love."

The courtroom had gotten eerily silent. One of the old bailiffs quietly licked his lips. Leo had to close his mouth because it had dropped open. *Well, you asked,* he thought.

"Okay, I may have gotten a little sidetracked," said Leo. "I believe you testified that y'all decided to start without your husband because he was late. So, please tell the court what happened next."

The witness no longer seemed nervous or tentative. It was as if she had taken some medication designed to relieve anxiety.

"Tricia and I went upstairs and put on our lingerie. She had brought her favorite pink nightie that I tried on, and she put on my lacy see-through teddy. We were laughing and cutting up because hers was a little tight on me. We eventually went back downstairs, and Ricky made us another buttery nipple. About that time Chance came home," she relayed.

Her expression changed again, and she took a big swallow. She looked at her estranged husband who continued to stare straight ahead without looking back at his wife.

Without prompting the young woman again spoke, "I'm not sure why he was so mad when he came in. He was almost two hours late from the time he said he would be home. I mean, he made the date with Tricia and Ricky. But, he was just so mad. He kept saying, 'Y'all shouldn't start without me.' And, he was calling me bad names, saying I was a slut and a bitch. When I told him not to call me those names, he hit me in the face."

"Before he hit you, had you said anything to him that would have provoked such a response?" asked Leo.

"I just said, 'Hey Baby, where you been? Do you want a drink?' And then he just went off on a rant like I said, and started calling me all kinds of bitches and whores."

"Did he hit you with an open hand or a closed fist?"

"The first time it was a slap with his hand across my face, but it was really hard."

"Then what happened?"

"I guess it was just a reaction, but I slapped him back. Then he started hitting me with both his fists. I don't know how many times he hit me because I fell down, and I think I must've blacked out for a few minutes. All I remember was Tricia wiping my face with a wet towel."

"Did you or someone call the sheriff's office?"

"After I got myself together a little bit, I called. I was afraid Chance might come back and start beating on me again. I've never seen him so mad. In the past when he hit me it was only once or twice, and he would always say he was sorry."

"Objection, Your Honor," said the defense attorney. "My client is not charged with any other offense, and any reference to an alleged prior incident is not relevant and highly prejudicial."

The judge looked at Leo, but said nothing. Leo responded, "Your Honor, as the Court is well aware, prior difficulties between these parties is allowed."

"Denied. Can we move this along Mr. Berry?" said the judge looking first at Wingate and then to Leo.

"Yes sir," said Leo.

"Ms. Willis, how long was it after you called the sheriff's office before someone arrived?"

"Maybe ten minutes."

"And was that Deputy Stone from that office?"

"Yes sir."

"Did you tell him what had happened?"

"Yes, for the most part."

"What do you mean?"

"Well, I didn't tell him about us being swappers. I told him we were having a get together with our friends, and Chance got mad and started hitting me."

"And, what was the reason for not telling the officer about being swappers?"

"A lot of people don't understand our club. I was afraid he wouldn't take that very well. Maybe even think I deserved a beating. I guess I should've told him, but I didn't think it should matter. Nobody deserves to be beat up like that for no reason."

"Did you receive injuries as a result of the attack you've described?"

"Yes, I had a black eye that was swollen shut, and I had a busted lip that I had to get some stitches and some other bruises on my face and oh yeah, a bump on the back of my head where I guess I hit the floor."

"Did someone make some pictures of your injuries?"

"Yeah, Tricia took some with her cell, and I think the deputy took some, too."

Leo had looked through the file and couldn't find any photos. He did find a Sandy scribble indicating she had requested the witnesses to bring pictures if they existed. Leo only hoped one of the other witnesses would have that evidence when he questioned them. This was a recurring problem with presenting cases that were not prepped sufficiently, but certainly not critical to a finding of guilt, if the judge believed the credibility of the witness.

"Okay, did you receive medical treatment for your injuries?"

"Tricia and Ricky took me to the doc in the box near the house. That's where they stitched my lip and gave me something for pain."

"Was the defendant still on the scene when the deputy arrived?"

"No. I'm not sure when he left, but he was not there when I came to."

"So, did you swear out a warrant against the defendant?"

"No. The deputy said he would take care of that. He gave me a card describing victim services and told me I should think about getting a protective order to keep Chance away. I did that and really haven't talked to Chance since. I wasn't even sure he had been arrested until I got a call from the Solicitor's Office about this case."

"Okay, thank you Ms. Willis. Mr. Wingate will probably have some questions for you now," Leo said to the witness.

The judge looked at the other side and asked, "Do you want to cross-examine, counsel?"

"Yes, sir. Thank you."

"Ms. Willis, I'm Randy Wingate and I represent your husband in this case. I have just a few questions. How old are you?"

"Twenty-three."

"How long have you and Chance been married?"

"Three years last month."

"How tall are you?"

"5-4."

"May I ask how much you weigh?"

"You may ask, but I won't tell."

"Would you admit you're overweight?"

"I'm a little heavy."

"You're a good bit heavier than Chance, right?"

"He never complained about that."

"That's not my question. Would you say you weigh at least fifty pounds more than your husband?"

"I guess."

"Judge, if you would allow it, could I ask that the witness stand next to my client so the Court can make a size comparison?" Wingate asked the judge.

"Counsel, I have a clear view of both the witness and the defendant. That won't be necessary. The Court notices the difference in sizes."

Leo studied the defendant as this dialogue occurred. Leo estimated the defendant to be maybe two inches shorter than his own 5'10" frame and probably ten pounds lighter. At the most Leo felt the defendant would tip the scales at 155 pounds. He thought Wingate had made his point since conservatively Leo thought the witness had to be around 210 pounds.

"Yes, Your Honor. I'll move on. Ms. Willis, you admitted on direct examination that you struck Chance, right?"

"I slapped him, but only after he slapped me first."

"You were mad at him, correct?"

"I was upset with him for coming home late, but I wasn't mad about that until I heard where he had been."

"So you were mad at him?"

"After he told me he had been at his girlfriend's house."

"Your Honor, please instruct the witness to answer my questions."

Leo interjected, "Your Honor, she did answer the question, and she's entitled to explain her answer."

The judge looked irritated. "Please just answer the questions that are asked Ms. Willis. Mr. Berry, you may ask her to explain any answers on redirect if you think further explanation is needed. Let's please move this along."

"Yes sir. Okay Ms. Willis, isn't it true that you and Chance have had a rocky marriage?" Wingate continued.

"It wasn't so bad until that night. I mean, we had arguments like any other married couple, but never anything like that."

"In fact, you two sometimes acted out just so you could make up later. Isn't that right?"

"If you're talking about fantasies, yeah, we sometimes acted like we were fighting and then we would make up. But, that was just playing around, you know?"

"No, I don't know. That's why I'm asking you the question. Now, you mentioned earlier Chance had hit you before. Was it during these 'playing around' sessions?" asked Wingate.

"Yes, I mean no. We did play like that sometimes, but he did hit me on other occasions when we were not playing."

"Did you call the police and report those incidents?"

"No, because Chance would always say he was sorry and he would make it up to me. He'd take me out to dinner or buy me a present. I believed he was sorry then."

"When Chance got home he found you wearing a negligee and drinking alcohol while entertaining another couple, right?"

"I was wearing a negligee, and I had a couple of cocktails. Our friends, Tricia and Ricky were there at Chance's invitation."

"Mr. Wingate," interrupted the judge, "This is getting very repetitive and you've made your points. Now, if you have something more or different on the subject, please ask the questions. Otherwise, I don't need to hear any more along the lines you are pursuing."

"I'm sorry, Your Honor. Just a couple of more questions and I'll be through with this witness," Wingate said to the judge.

He turned back to the witness. "Ms. Willis, isn't it true you don't really know how you received your injuries because you had too much to drink and in the scuffle with your husband you fell and got hurt?"

"I fell because Chance knocked me down. I was not drunk!"

"That's all I have of this witness, Your Honor," said Wingate.

The judge looked over at the prosecutor, and Leo could tell he was getting more perturbed by the moment. Judge Taylor's neck had gotten a crimson color that was spreading upward to his face. Leo had seen the signs enough to know he better be quick with the other witnesses.

"We'll call our next witness, Judge. Mr. Bailiff, please get Patricia Downs."

Leo proceeded through the testimony with deliberate speed. This was partly due to the nature of the case, partly to the judge showing displeasure, and partly because Patricia Downs was a person who gave Leo the heebie jeebies. She continued giving looks at Leo that he found unsettling at the least and creepy at the worst.

From a standpoint of a witness, she did verify the key points of the victim's testimony. Additionally, she was able to tell the court what happened regarding Ms. Willis being knocked to the floor.

"Now Ms. Downs, at some point during the confrontation between the defendant and Ms. Willis, did you see Ms. Willis fall to the floor?" asked Leo.

"Yes, after Chance hit her in the face with his fist, Bonnie fell on the floor. It was like a knockout punch in a boxing match," she stated matter-of-factly.

"What happened then?"

"Chance jumped on top of her and started hitting her again. He probably hit her at least five or six times until Ricky pulled him off her. She was out cold for a few minutes before I got her to come to."

Upon further questioning by Leo that was unshaken on cross examination, the witness relayed corroboration of the deputy being called to the scene, the injuries and the treatment since she had been with the victim throughout the time. The witness also characterized the attack as "brutal and unprovoked."

Since the testimony so far seemed more than sufficient to obtain a conviction, Leo decided not to call Ricky Downs as a witness and to keep him available as a rebuttal witness if needed.

Leo called the deputy to verify he had taken the report, documented the evidence and secured a warrant based on the evidence. Leo was pleasantly surprised when the officer produced three pictures of the victim he had made on the scene depicting the battered face. Leo was pretty convinced a conviction was secure at that point. He rested his case subject to rebuttal.

"Do you have any evidence you want to present?" Judge Taylor asked Wingate.

"May we have just a moment to confer?" responded Wingate.

"Please make it quick."

Leo watched Wingate and the defendant talking. He couldn't hear what was being said, but it looked like Chance Willis was not a happy camper. Leo found himself picturing all of the participants swapping around with each other. It was not a pretty sight in his mind. Leo found himself silently thinking, *it's a crazy world!*

Defense counsel finally turned to the bench and announced they would call no witnesses. The judge shook his head slightly up and down and asked, "Arguments?"

Leo looked over at Wingate. Leo knew what he would point out if Wingate chose to argue either self-defense or justification. If Leo had been in Wingate's shoes knowing Judge Taylor as well as he did, he would choose to simply submit it to the court. Judge Taylor was a no-nonsense kind of judge and didn't take kindly to arguments that distorted obvious truth. In Leo's mind that would include what he anticipated Wingate's strategy had been during the short trial. Some sort of justification defense or self-defense may have been successful if there had been no corroboration. So many family violence scenarios were hard to prove because often times it was a "he said, she said" situation. Leo felt strongly that Wingate had simply gambled and lost, and the less said was best for him at this point.

"Your Honor, I know the Court has heard the testimony and can render a fair decision based on the evidence, so I'll submit that without further comment. Thank you, Judge," said Wingate.

The judge looked at Leo. "Yes sir, we agree," responded Leo.

Leo looked over the bench and could see the judge had written guilty on the verdict form. Leo then took a step backward and turned to the victim who had been behind him for the duration of the trial after she had testified. He whispered, "Do you want a stay away order to stay in place?"

"Please. I don't want to ever see him again!" she whispered back to Leo.

The judge first looked at the defendant and then at the victim. His withering stare had been known to make some people pee in their britches.

"In all my years on the bench, I don't think I've ever heard such as I've heard today. I'm not here to judge your lifestyle, though. I'm here only to determine if a criminal offense took place."

"Mr. Willis, there is no way your wife should've received the beating you inflicted on her. It was despicable in my opinion. I find you guilty of the offense of family violence battery. Is there anything you want to say before I pronounce sentence?"

Leo saw the defendant's Adam's apple go up and down before he spoke. "I'm truly sorry I hurt my wife. I just lost it that night. I love her and wish she would take me back," Willis said as he turned and looked at his wife for the first time since the trial began.

"It is not my job to be a marriage counselor," said the judge. "Ms. Willis, do you have anything you want to say before I pronounce sentence?"

"He needs help, Judge. I don't know if putting him in jail will help him. I don't love him like I did, but I don't want to hurt him. I don't think we can be married anymore."

Leo had seen the cycle of violence repeat itself so many times in the past. In a matter of moments, it seemed the victim had gone from never wanting to see the defendant again to I don't think we can be married anymore. Was that an opening of the door?

She continued, "Right now, I want him to stay away from me."

Leo thought maybe she did have a chance to break away. Otherwise, Leo was afraid for her. Some victims never learn, and he hoped she wasn't one of them.

"Mr. Willis, I've looked at your criminal history and see you only have one conviction for DUI. I would normally impose a jail sentence in a case like this, but because you seem contrite, you have no prior family violence arrests, and Ms. Willis has indicated she does not favor any jail time; I'm going to sentence you to twelve months probation with a fine of $1000. I'm also required to make a condition of your probation that you attend a 26 weeks family violence intervention program. If there are any unpaid medical expenses, you will have to make restitution for those. You are also ordered not to have any further contact with Ms. Willis."

The courtroom emptied as Sarge escorted the defendant to the probation office down the hall, and Leo asked the other bailiff to tell the other witnesses they could leave. As Ricky and Patricia Downs walked by Leo, she winked at him behind her husband's back.

Judge Taylor and Leo were alone when the judge said with a smirk, "I think she likes you, Leo."

Leo couldn't help but smile up at the judge who had an amused look on his face. "Well, what can I say, Judge? I do have charm and personality, if I say so myself."

"You're humble, too," deadpanned the judge.

"I do believe that is a candidate for one of the weirdest cases this year. The mental pictures conjured up were almost too much to bear," said Leo.

"Yes, just as you think you've heard everything, something like that comes along," replied the judge. "Look, I've still got a little time before my appointment if you want to check across the hall and see if there's anything else to do. I'll wait right here."

"Thanks, Judge. I'll do that."

Leo hurried to the larger courtroom and was happy to see that the other assistants had whittled down the crowd substantially. Sandy saw Leo walk in and she picked up several more files. She really could read his mind sometimes.

"Can you take a few pleas I've worked out?" she asked.

"No prob. Y'all have really made progress in here," said Leo.

"It's amazing what you can get done when the judge is motivated," she replied.

Leo took the files and the defendants with their lawyers and went back across the hall. Since all the cases had been worked out, the cases were disposed of quickly. All of the parties knew that without being able to reach plea agreements, the court's functions would be severely hampered. Judge Taylor was happy, as was Leo with what had been accomplished.

Leo peeked into the other courtroom when he was finished and could see there were only a few people left. His colleagues had everything under control, so Leo went back to the office.

As he sat down the first thing he noticed was the blinking red light on his telephone indicating at least one voice mail. For some reason it looked foreboding.

CHAPTER 26

"Mr. Berry, this is Agent Ted Springer with the DEA," started the message on the telephone. "Would you please call me when you get out of court? It concerns the case you are prosecuting for the DA. Thank you."

Leo sat in his chair pondering that message as the next one played. "Hey, Leo. It's Mickie. I was hoping we could get together for lunch one day this week. I have something I want to show you. Hope you're having a good day. Call me when you can."

The next message followed and was menacing. "Berry, I hear you're going to offer a plea bargain to that murdering son-of-a-bitch. You're just like the rest of the sorry assholes in the DA's office. You better do what's right."

Leo recognized the detective's voice right away. Even though there was a possibility of a plea in Leo's mind, he had not met with the defense lawyer yet. Leo wondered if there was a leak or if Detective Richards was merely guessing.

Leo always hated hearing the last voice on his machine. "Morning, Leo. Greg Randall with the Macon Telegraph. I'm following up on the Murphy case. I understand it will be coming up for trial soon. I'm trying to get an updated story ready. Please call me."

The scribbled names and numbers on Leo's pad stared back at him. Four messages during his morning in court, and three of them directly related to the Murphy case. The one from Mickie could even be tangentially related since Leo knew he was going to have to tell her soon that he was handling the case. Leo was very concerned how she was going to take that news especially with a result that she may well not like. He was not so sure anymore he should have agreed to prosecute the case, but he hated the idea of backing out now.

It had always been a part of Leo's routine to return messages as soon as possible. Leo knew several lawyers who did not follow the advice that had been given to him by one of his early mentors. Those lawyers were universally disliked and were considered unprofessional at best, incompetent or uncaring at least. Since Leo did not want to be put in any of those categories, he always returned calls even when he really did not want to. He sighed and picked up the phone.

Punching in the number for the DEA agent, Leo was somewhat surprised when it was answered on the first ring. He had expected to go through some bureaucratic exchange.

"This is Springer."

"Agent Springer, Leo Berry returning your call."

"Thanks for doing that so soon. I'm in town today and was hoping I could meet you for a few minutes."

"I should be able to do that this afternoon," said Leo. "You mentioned it concerns a case I'm handling?"

"Let's talk about it in person. I can be there around 3:00 if that works," replied the voice identified as Springer. Leo thought he sounded very professional and reserved as a lot of feds he had met before.

"That works for me, too. I'll be expecting you."

As soon as the short conversation was over, Leo punched Mickie's number. She answered on the fourth ring, and Leo thought initially he had gotten her voice mail. "This is Michelle Thomas."

"Mickie, it's Leo calling you back."

"Oh, hey. The secretary said you might be in court most of the day, so I'm little surprised to hear back this soon."

Leo glanced at his watch and saw it was a little past noon. "Yeah, the staff is instructed to warn callers of late callbacks when we have heavy dockets to deal with. Actually I'm done a lot quicker than I expected. You mentioned lunch, what are you doing today? If you're free, I could meet you in a little while."

"That would be great. Do you mind if we meet close to the hospital? I just got out of class and I'm due to report for my shift at 2:00, and I don't want to be late. My supervisor is a b-bear."

Leo laughed. "Are you sure you wanted to call her a bear? I thought you were about to call her something else."

"I plead the 5th. So, how about the little sandwich place across from the Medical Center, or we could go for soul food at the H&H?" she asked.

"Since I'm not going to run today, let's keep it light. I'll meet you at the Subway at 12:45."

"Great! I can't wait to show you some old pictures I found."

Leo looked at his pad and saw the remaining two notes he had made. He had no intention of calling the detective since he had not been asked to call, and at any rate, Leo was mad at the tone of the message that had been left. With any luck Leo thought he might get the reporter's voice mail as he lifted the phone once more. After all, it was lunch hour for many folks.

Randall's voice greeting was clipped, "Hello, you have reached Greg Randall with the Telegraph. I'm sorry I can't take your call right now, but please leave me a brief message and a phone number. I will call you back as soon as possible."

Leo spoke after the beep, "Hey, Greg. Leo Berry returning your call. You know I can't say very much about a pending case. I can say the case is set next month for trial. Hope you're doing well. Talk to you soon."

Leo had talked with several members of the media over the years while practicing law. He had been extremely wary of some after being misquoted more than once. One bit of advice had been given to Leo by the Colonel after first coming to work for him. "Live by the press, die by the press." Therefore, Leo never called anyone in the media to advise them of any noteworthy nuggets like some lawyers he knew. However, Leo was always respectful to members of the press and realized many were trying to do their jobs of keeping the public informed of current affairs. Leo had a good relationship with Greg Randall for that very reason and wanted to keep it that way within ethical bounds. Otherwise, the press could make you look bad.

Having completed the task of returning calls, Leo looked outside his window overlooking downtown. The sun was shining brightly and the leaves left on the trees were red and gold in the sunlight. It would be a good day for a run, but he had made the lunch date with Mickie. Leo hoped it would give him an opportunity to mend any hard feelings she may have. He really liked the young girl, and felt a kinship because of her connection to Papa.

Leo decided to walk the few blocks to the restaurant rather than drive. It wouldn't be like the usual exercise, but at least he could move some and get the juices flowing. Leo hoped he would be able to run for years to come. However, he was realistic and knew others older than him who had given up the activity due to various injuries, aches and pains. Might as well get used to going slower, he thought.

Mickie was waiting outside underneath the Subway sign when Leo arrived. "I hope I didn't keep you waiting long," he said.

"No, not at all. I just got here myself. I could see you coming. It looked like you were moving pretty fast."

"I was practicing the mall walk. That's what my wife calls it. You know, there are a lot of older people who get their exercise that way. I still prefer running, though."

"Not me. I don't know why people run. Of course, I get plenty of exercise walking around the floor up there," she said while pointing at the hospital.

"It's all about the 'runner's high.' I used to hear runners talk about that, and it sounded like bs to me until I started experiencing it. There is definitely something about getting those endorphins going. Anyway, you appear in great shape and you've got youth on your side. Ready to eat?" asked Leo.

"Thanks for the compliment. Yeah, I'm starving!"

Leo held the door open, and Mickie went in first. The manners taught by his parents were imbedded. He still called older people sir and ma'am, and Leo always opened a door for a female. Mickie smiled at the gesture.

They ordered their food, and Leo paid the cashier. There were a few unoccupied tables outdoors, and they decided to eat there rather than in the more crowded restaurant. For the first few minutes neither spoke as they made a dent in their lunch. Leo thought the turkey sub with all the fresh veggies was tasty. Mickie was wolfing down a meatball sub that looked equally delicious.

Pausing to take a gulp from the cup of sweet tea, Mickie spoke first. "Thanks for meeting me. I've been thinking a lot since we last spoke, and I wanted to apologize."

Leo looked into Mickie's eyes and saw sincerity. "Really, there's nothing for you to apologize for. I can't imagine losing one of my brothers like you did. It was awful for you to have to go through that, I'm sure. I've wanted to talk to you as well. I have some additional information I need to tell you and your other brother. I really didn't make the connection until you told me last time we talked. I feel like I'm the one who needs to offer an apology, as well as my sincere condolences for your loss," said Leo.

Mickie had a puzzled look. "What do you mean about needing to tell me and Pete additional information?"

"Well, maybe I should wait until I have a chance to talk to both of you together," Leo paused. "But, since I feel I know you well enough, I'll let you decide if I should go ahead with some updates on the person charged with Johnny's death."

Mickie continued to look uncertain. "You have updates on the Murphy case?"

"Let me start by saying I had no idea your brother Johnny was the person who was killed until you told me. It's no excuse for me being insensitive, though. I have always believed victims of crime should be treated with respect and as much kindness as humanly possible," said Leo.

He took a sip of Diet Coke through the straw. "A lot of things have happened lately that all seem random but somehow connected. First, Papa died. I loved him, and I feel guilty about not staying as close to him over the last several years. Then I met you at the funeral, and you gave me his most private possession. For him to trust you to give that to me shows how much he must've been close to you. I've read his journal, and it contains remarkable secrets," continued Leo.

Leo took another bite of his sandwich and chewed slowly. Mickie ate some more of hers. They both were lost in thought for a few moments.

After swallowing, Leo began again. "Then I found out Papa made me the executor of his estate. I was really blown away by that. What was even more amazing was he left me the farm. I mean, why me? But, as I've thought about it more, I think I do know why. At least I'm starting to believe there is a plan for me to make it into something special, and I'm going to do my best to make that happen."

"Mr. Leo always believed in you. He told me more than once you understood life more than most," said Mickie.

"Anyway, about the same time I was going through that stuff, I was asked by the DA to handle the prosecution of Lonnel Murphy. You may have been there for the first trial, I don't know. Evidently there was somewhat of a mess that developed causing a recusal of that office. It happens sometimes. I was approached to take over, and I agreed not knowing anything about the victim. In all honesty, I probably would have agreed to take over at that point even if I knew of your connection since I really didn't know you very well. I'm not so sure I would've taken it knowing you a little better now. In fact, if you and your brother want me to get off the case I will." said Leo.

"I was there at the trial. It did get ugly. Since I had never even been in a courtroom, I didn't have anything to compare it to except what you see on TV. I was mad because some people kept trying to make it a racial thing. I'm telling you, Johnny was never racist about anything. I know he wasn't perfect, but he was a good guy. He didn't deserve to die like that," she said and paused. "Although I didn't know you were involved in the case, I can't think of anyone else I'd rather handle it."

"Someone from victim services should have let you and your brother know of the conflict. Maybe I should have as well before now. At any rate, I've been working on the case for a little while, and I feel I need to keep you up with progress reports as they develop. Like I said, I can tell you where we are or wait and talk about the status with you and Pete," said Leo.

While waiting on Mickie's response, Leo ate the last few bites of his sandwich. She appeared to mull it over as she ate the remainder of her lunch.

"If it's all the same to you, I would like to hear whatever information you have, and I'll pass it on to Pete when I can. We haven't been seeing each other as much since Johnny died, and he always is so busy. I can't even keep up with what shift he's been working lately. It might be difficult to set a meeting up with both of us at the same time anyway," said Mickie after finishing the last bite.

For the next fifteen minutes Leo relayed his thoughts on the evidence and the challenges he faced. Leo thought he did a pretty good job at briefing lay people on legal issues in general, but when folks were smarter than average such as Mickie, he was usually a little more technical. She took in all that Leo said and asked smart questions that showed her understanding of legal principles. Mickie looked pensive when Leo was done.

"So to summarize, a murder conviction will be difficult with the best chance requiring you to prove it happened during the course of the defendant committing a felony. Felony murder you called it. You think that may be really hard to do as well, and Murphy could even walk away from that charge. You want to meet with his lawyer and explore a lesser charge like manslaughter. Right?" she asked.

"Pretty much," said Leo.

"If another prosecutor had told me this months ago, I would be royally pissed off. All the weaknesses you've pointed out are something to think about though. And, I really do trust you, Leo. I'll need to talk to Pete. He's been in law enforcement for twenty years and knows a lot more about the law than me. I'll let you know what he thinks."

"Fair enough, Mickie. I always like to get feedback from victims and their families. Please know, however, I have to do what I think is best in the final analysis."

"Okay," Mickie said as she looked at her watch. "Wow, I've got to get to work," she continued as she took a manila envelope from her purse.

"I wish I could spend some more time with you today because I thought you might like to see some old pictures. I'll tell you what, why don't I just let you borrow them for the time being, and I can get them back from you later. Some of them have names and dates written on the back so you can identify who they are. There's even an old one with Mr. Leo and my dad," she said.

"Awesome," said Leo. "I love looking at old pictures. For some reason there are not very many of Papa. I don't know if he was camera shy or what. If you don't mind, I might make a copy or two of some of your pictures."

"Sure, I don't mind at all. I really do have to get to work now. I appreciate the lunch and you filling me in. Now that we've done this, I hope we can do it again soon." Mickie scurried off, and Leo watched as the tiny figure clad in scrubs turned and waved.

Leo opened the envelope and pulled out several photographs. He only scanned the ones of people he didn't recognize but figured they were of members of Mickie's family. One showed a strapping young man in a tan uniform standing by another guy about the same age and of equal build. Leo thought these men must be Mickie's older brothers. The one in the uniform had to be Pete, and the other had to be the deceased Johnny.

The picture of Papa standing by Gene Thomas took Leo aback for a moment. No, Leo didn't remember ever seeing the man, but there was something nagging him. Looking on the back of the photo, Leo saw that someone had written in ink that was now almost faded away, "Leo and Jean, 1971." The spelling of the name was different. French, right?

Leo turned it over and studied the picture. The quality was not the best, but it was revealing. Both figures were about the same size. Papa had on his ever-present hat, and Thomas had hair down to his shoulders. It was the exact same color as Papa's. But, it was the eyes that did it. *Geez,* he thought, *Gene or Jean looks more like Papa than his own kids.*

While still pondering the photograph, the last one in the stack caused him to gasp. There she was in a cracked old black and white shot. She was young and beautiful. On the back written in black cursive french, *"Je t'aime pour toujours. Georgine"* Leo didn't remember much about the French course he took in high school, but he knew what the phrase said. *I love you forever.* And, it couldn't be a coincidence it was signed with the name of Papa's love that he recorded in the journal.

Leo didn't have enough time to sort it out now, however. He had to get back to the office and meet the DEA investigator.

As Papa always said, "Expect the unexpected." Leo could only think how right he was.

CHAPTER 27

Agent Ted Springer was waiting on Leo when he got back to the office. Leo recognized the type immediately even though he had never met the agent seated in the lobby. Well-fitted navy blue suit, starched white shirt, muted tie and polished black shoes covered his lean frame. Some might think the guy exuded arrogance, but Leo thought him as only confident. He was more than likely ex-military with some law enforcement experience in a larger metropolitan city before having been recruited by the feds. Leo really didn't like stereotypes, but he had to admit to himself this guy fit the mold of the others he had met from the federal system.

"Agent Springer, I presume," said Leo as he approached.

Leo stuck out his hand, and the agent responded likewise. "I don't know how you guessed," said Springer. "Please call me

Ted. The term agent somehow seems a negative term to me," he continued with an infectious smile.

"Glad to oblige. Just call me Leo," he said smiling back. "Let's go inside to my plush government office."

Springer laughed at the facetious manner in which Leo emphasized plush. Leo was willing to bet the agent's digs were at least twice as nice.

"Can I get you a cup of coffee or a soft drink?" Leo asked as he shut the door behind them.

"No, thanks. I just had lunch, and I've got to be in Atlanta at 5:30 for another meeting. I don't want to take a chance of getting caught in traffic after having too many liquids, if you know what I mean."

Leo liked this guy more by the minute. Despite his formal appearance, Ted Springer had an easygoing attitude. Looking to be about the same age helped Leo to relate, as well.

"That's how I feel if I'm out on a run, and I had a cup too many," replied Leo. "I understand it will get worse as I get older, so I'm not looking forward to any marathons."

"Eh, you would sweat it out in this climate before you needed to head to the woods. I would hazard a bet you've got some years before you need to worry very much about a weak bladder. I have an eighty-five year old friend who told me the day had come when a good pee was about as good as it gets. I hope that's a ways off for me, too," said Springer.

They both laughed. "So, you wanted to talk to me about the Murphy case?" asked Leo.

"A little, but I don't want you thinking we are trying to butt into your case. I'm really here just sharing a bit of information at this point."

"Well, I must admit I was surprised to hear from the feds. That doesn't happen very often with this job. About the only time I hear from some drug investigator is when they want me to help out some informant in exchange for testimony bringing down some dope dealer. And then it's never a DEA agent who's making the request, it's some local drug unit seeking assistance."

Springer shifted only slightly in his chair, but Leo thought the agent was showing a tad of discomfort over Leo's remarks. What Leo had said was the truth, and if the agent was in Leo's office seeking a favor of some sort, the fish the DEA was trying to land had to be a big catch worthy of mounting on the wall.

"Yeah, I'm aware how that's done. In a previous life I was an undercover officer in south Georgia. It was a lot easier on that level when all I had to do was call up my local prosecutor and ask if he could provide any consideration to a defendant who was willing to help us catch a bigger thief or dealer. Too many levels of bureaucracy with what I do now. That being said, I'm not really here for such a request. At least, not today," said Springer.

"Hey, I didn't mean to imply you were, Ted. As far as I look at it, we all should be on the same team when trying to get lawbreakers off the street. My only caveat is we don't break the rules ourselves while doing that. I think most of us who choose these professions believe that, too. Of course, I've known bad apples in every profession and ours is no exception. Whenever I can help bring some bad egg to justice, it truly makes my day. I bet you feel the same," said Leo.

Springer smiled. "You would win that bet, Leo. I can see why you have a reputation of being a straight-up guy."

"That's good to know. So, what information are you going to share with me, Ted?"

"It concerns Lonnel Murphy's possible connections to a central Georgia illegal drug network. I'm not sure that you're aware about the possible effects such a connection might have on your case."

Leo thought for a moment before responding, "Alright, I don't know anything about Murphy being involved in a drug ring," said Leo, "but it could only involve my case if the victim was involved in the same network, as I see it. Is that what you're saying?"

Springer didn't flinch or shift in his chair before responding. Leo liked that Springer kept eye contact.

"At this point, I can only say it's a possibility. The attorney representing Murphy wants to have a meeting and has contacted the agency. He hinted over the phone Lonnel Murphy had some information about a powerful brand of weed being peddled around middle Georgia. It's supposed to enhance sexual performance. I can tell you there has been an ongoing investigation about such a drug being sold for some time now.

Before Johnny Thomas's death, he was considered a person of interest."

Leo found himself absentmindedly stroking his chin. It was a habit he had developed when he first grew a beard in college. Over the years it had remained whether he had facial hair or not.

"Can you tell me more about Thomas?" Leo asked.

"Since it is a part of an active investigation which does not involve your office, I do not feel at liberty to say a lot more than what I've told you. What I expect is probably what you expect. That is, I'm willing to bet Murphy wants to offer information in exchange for a more favorable disposition in the murder case. I will say this about Johnny Thomas, though. I have not been able to tie him directly to any illegal drug network although he hung around at least one of the other suspects on more than one occasion."

"Okay, I'm thinking out loud now. I will tell you that I also have a meeting later this week with Murphy's lawyer, so I'll wager he's trying to get some leverage through your office before we have our discussion. Not a bad strategy, if he really does have some damaging information about a major drug investigation. I might would do the same thing if I was on the other side," said Leo.

"However, if I were him I would not seek such a deal unless there was a direct relation between the network and the killing. I just don't see Murphy as some major player in such an organization. He's been in jail since the day he was charged unable to make a fairly reasonable bond, and he's represented by the public defender's office. All of that tells me he has no money and belies the notion he's a player in the drug trade," Leo continued.

"Well, I would probably agree with your assessment, Leo. But, if Murphy is desperate enough and afraid of a long prison sentence, maybe he's motivated to give up anything he knows, whether the homicide is connected or not. I tend to think there may be some connection, I'm just unsure at this point. My main purpose for telling you this is as a professional courtesy because I know there is no mention of anything involving drugs in the reports you have. I felt it my obligation to at least let you know this much so you may be prepared for it as a potential issue. If something sufficiently important comes forward as a result of any further discussions, I will let you know," said Springer standing up.

The agent looked at his watch and then stuck out his hand to Leo. Their grip was strong when the two men shook hands.

"It was a real pleasure meeting you, Ted. I appreciate the information, and I will certainly accept whatever help you can give me," said Leo.

Springer looked around Leo's office. His gaze settled on a plaque Leo had received for being the leading hitter in a softball tournament a couple of years ago.

"Sure thing. I can tell you're a team player like me. You might even help out my softball team next year. We can always use another good hitter. See you around the campus," the agent said as he left the prosecutor's office.

CHAPTER 28

Little Leo and Papa were sitting in folding chairs underneath the big tree where Rusty's empty house remained. Crocodile tears flowed from the thirteen-year-old adolescent. He had always thought of the dog as his best friend, and now that friend was gone forever.

Leo thought he shouldn't be crying in front of his grandfather because his daddy had always told him big boys don't cry. Since Papa was his daddy's daddy, Papa had probably taught him that way, too. The thought only made Leo more distraught, and now he openly sobbed.

Papa cleared his throat before speaking. "It's okay to cry, Leo. Sometimes it's the only way to get rid of grief."

Leo looked at Papa and could see those blue eyes were watery. It was the closest to a public display of emotion Leo had ever seen from the strongest man in the world.

"I'm sorry, Papa. I know I'm not supposed to cry."

"I know a lot of people say big boys don't cry, but hear me now, that's bullshit," said Papa. "I've cried plenty of times in my life."

The grandfather pulled out a red bandana from the right rear pocket of his well-worn jeans. He handed it to Leo, and the boy wiped away the tears.

"I've never seen you cry, Papa."

The man looked away to one of the fields and swallowed. With a discreet flick of his index finger, a single tear was dispatched. His eyes were still glistening when he turned back to his grandson and started talking.

"I guess it's a good time as any to talk about life and death. I've seen my share of both. By the time you reach my age, you will, too. Let me ask you somethin', do you believe in God, Leo?" he asked.

"To be honest, Papa, I don't know what I believe. I mean, I go to Sunday school and church, and I read the lessons and listen to my teacher and the preacher, but I just don't know how I feel about all that. Is that wrong?"

"Not in my humble opinion, Leo. I'm goin' tell you how I feel about this old world, but just because I believe it that way, don't make it the gospel. I see all this," he said while looking around the farm, "and it don't make sense to me without some higher power having a say-so in the plan."

He continued, "It has taken me a lifetime to come to my firmest beliefs, Leo. As I have done, you will experience lots of things in life that will help form who you are and what to believe. You're young now, so you haven't had many experiences to draw from. Death, especially when it happens to somebody you love, is one of the most influential experiences of all. Through my experiences with death, I have come to believe there is an essence, or spirit, or whatever you want to call it, that survives when our bodies can no longer make it in this world."

"So, you believe in heaven?"

"You can call it that, if you want. But yes, I believe there is a place where all the spirits return and where we can connect again with one Big Spirit. I think that Big Spirit is what some people call God. I don't know if I can explain it any better than it's a feelin' I have deep inside. Some might call it faith. I call it an overpowerin' feelin' that never goes away. I'll tell you this and you might think it sounds crazy, but I've dreamed of it several times, and when I awoke I had this tinglin' come over me that left me euphoric. Do you know that word?"

"No, sir. I'll look it up in the dictionary when we finish talking," said Leo.

"You're a good boy, Leo. You're smart, and you're goin' to be all right, I promise. You'll figure out what is right as you go along. As long as you live right, you won't go wrong, either.

"Anyway, as I was sayin', the feelin' of euphoria when I dreamed of being with others who have already passed was so compellin' to me that I know that's the way it's goin' to be for me when I'm gone. I get that same feelin' when I see and hear the ocean or lookin' at the mountains or even in the face of a newborn baby."

"So, you believe you'll see Rusty again?" asked Leo.

"Absolutely, I do. It don't mean I won't grieve over him not bein' here with us now, though. So, it's okay to cry over that loss, but knowin' I'll see the old boy again when I leave this old world is enough to get me by," said the grandfather with a smile.

Leo woke up and there was a tingle all over his body. He looked over at the LED display and the time was 4:35. Dee was on her side facing away from him. He snuggled against her and closed his eyes trying to conjure up more of the dream. It wouldn't come back, but it sure had been good while it lasted.

He offered a silent prayer before falling back asleep. *Papa, you and Daddy and Rusty keep the rest of us a place handy because we'll all meet up again one day. I have faith. Thanks, Papa.*

CHAPTER 29

Lonnel Murphy was on the bottom bunk because that's the one he wanted. The dude above him wasn't given a chance to first pick 'cause he was just a punk-ass kid. Never mind the punk was only a year younger than him, Nelly was in the joint on a murder rap and that made him a bad muthafucka in the kid's eyes.

Nelly didn't trust him neither, 'cause evabody done told him to watch the man puttin' a snitch in the cell wid him. Not that he wuz gone talk to anybody he didn't know anyway.

He was feelin' antzy again. His mind wuz workin' hyper speed, man. This wuzn't no place to be and he'd already been here over a year. Some kinda shit had to give soon or he wuz gonna bug, man. He'd already told his lawyah, *Let the feds know I got some serious 411. Don't let the local man know, though. They's part of the problem, and I need a solution.*

He knew it wuzn't nothin' he would do normally. When he decided to take on the thug life, he knew there were consequences if he got caught. But dammit, man! I didn't want to kill that white dude. I wuz just tryin' to get what wuz comin' to me. And, I don't know why he would chase me like that, neither. That money wuz just scratch for him. Shit, man. It wuz just a accident anyway, he thought. Nelly kept runnin' the same old shit around his head and it just wuzn't fair.

The lock on the cell door opened with a loud click and brought Nelly out of his thoughts. A burly guard with a crew cut and bad skin told him to get his ass up 'cause he had a visitor. Nelly walked ahead of the dude and didn't make any quick moves 'cause that could get you hit upside the head, if you didn't watch it.

When Nelly got to the visitation area, he was instructed to sit behind the glass on his side. There sat his mama's brother who got him involved in the life. Uncle Smokey wuz a man he respected. He wuz skrate, man.

They both picked up phones and his uncle asked, "How ya' doin', Nelly?"

"Not so good, Unk. I need to get outta here. I'm feelin' bugshit crazy, man."

"You gotta be patient, Nelly. Your trial's comin' soon and the lawyer says he's got some stuff that can help."

"Yeah, he done told me that same shit, but I don't know Smoke. I'm shook up and scared. I cain't do no life sentence.

Shit, I cain't do twenty years, neither. I'm thinkin' I need to go ahead and play all my cards, man."

"Listen to me, nephew. That's one reason I came today. Word's out you might wanna talk to the man to work a deal. If you thinkin' what I think you thinkin', you better think some more. That way of thinkin' will get you kilt."

"I'm dead in here already, Smoke. You feel me?"

"Look. Just 'cause you know a couple of names of dirty dicks involved in the trade don't guarantee you nuthin'! You better believe me, Nelly. Spreadin' that kind of info is dangerous. These dudes don't play and if they feel threatened by you or me or anybody else, they will use any means necessary to get rid of that threat. If that means you get shived in here or I get hit on the street by a unmarked car just 'cause I'm related to you, or maybe even yo' mama and little sistah's house get burned to the ground with them in it, they will do it. I already know some people who done disappeared for a whole lot less. So, man up, nephew."

"I don't see why I gotta take the fall for this, Smoke. They been shortin' us all along. I done told you I didn't mean to kill that dude! No jury gone ever believe that, though."

"I got it on good authody that the new prosecutor is straight-up. He ain't just after screwin' you over to make a name for hisself. You remember my old buddy Haugabrook that I played ball with back in school?"

Nelly shook his head back and forth before his uncle continued.

"Well, Haugabrook been knowing the guy for awhile and he says that prosecutor helped his boy out when he got all strung out on drugs and started stealin'. Said the guy has been on both sides and knows what's right. I say we need to let yo lawyer meet with this Berry dude and see what he can do. Just give that a chance before doin' anything stupid, okay?"

"Time's up, Murphy," said the guard.

"Just a minute, man," said Nelly in his direction.

The guard frowned as Nelly spoke back into the phone. "All right, Smoke. I'll give it a little while longer. But, I'm tellin' you. I cain't do no long stretch for somethin' that wuzn't my fault."

The two men looked at one another as they hung up the phones. The uncle nodded at the younger man, and he felt profound sadness as his nephew shuffled off in his orange jump suit and matching plastic slippers.

He thought to himself, *Damn kid! It's my fault he's in here. I shoulda protected him and not let him follow me down this road. Now this wheel needs to stop before it's too late. I owe it to him and my sister.*

CHAPTER 30

Leo thought the last three days had sped by like the Road Runner, and he felt like Wiley Coyote trying to catch up. He was chasing while looking out for an Acme anvil to fall on his head. At least it was Thursday and one day closer to the weekend.

Today was supposed to be another busy day just like Monday, Tuesday and Wednesday had been. The hearing to admit Papa's will to probate was set for the morning. There was also the scheduled meeting with Sam Adams to discuss the Murphy case in the afternoon. Two big deals in Leo's life to be discussed in one day weighed on his mind as he shuffled paper on his desk. At least he and the rest of the assistants had worked through the cases set for court next week, and there were now only four defendants left requesting jury trials.

Leo felt relief over getting so many cases resolved the first part of the week. Having been through that process so many times before, Leo was fairly confident most of those remaining would fall by the wayside when pressed toward trial. Truth be known, very few lawyers Leo knew really liked trying cases.

Although it had taken monumental efforts by the office staff to get to the point, he knew most people had little idea how much work had occurred. Leo was now freer to give similar efforts to the other things requiring his attention and hopefully come to satisfactory resolution.

Shep stuck his head in Leo's office as he reviewed the last new file on his desk. The investigator waited until Leo looked up before speaking.

"Whassup, Little Bossman?"

"SOS. Trying to get through yet another ream of reports. Again," replied Leo in mock exasperation.

"Are we still on for the meeting with Murphy's lawyer this afternoon?"

"Yeah, 4:00. If you can be available, hang around. I'd rather you not join us until or if you're needed. I don't want the guy to think we're being heavy-handed."

"Got cha. I'll be down the hall in my cubbyhole if you need me. I need to let you know something, though. My contact in the PD's office told me they found the missing witness," said Shep.

Leo couldn't believe that. In his opinion, there was no better investigator than Shep, and he had been unsuccessful in finding the witness.

"You're kidding me, right? Their investigator did something neither you nor the police have been able to do?"

"All I can say is my buddy over there, you know, Frank Smith who retired from MPD about the same time I did, couldn't help but brag to me he had found him. Can't say with absolute certainty if he was truthing me since this was over a couple of beers after work. I don't think he would b.s. me about something like that. But, we had a friendly wager on finding the guy and he called me to meet for beers. I bet that pompous-ass public defender would crap his britches if he knew Frank and me had such an arrangement," Shep said with a smile.

"So, did Smith tell you anything about where the witness was? Stiles is his name, right?"

"Yeah, Winton Stiles. No, I couldn't get any of the particulars about where he is or what he will say. All Frank would say is it was good for them."

"You sure Frank isn't just trying to play you?" asked Leo.

"Naw, I know all Frank's tells from playing cards with him for the last thirty years. I think Frank feels pretty confident, and to finish the poker analogy, feels like he's holding aces."

Leo found himself stroking his chin. Talking about tells, he needed to get rid of that habit. He dropped his hand.

"Okay, Shep. Thanks for the head's up. Keep at it, and see if you can figure out where Stiles is. If Frank found him, I know you can, too. We really need to talk to the guy. I guess we may find out this afternoon if the defense has him in line. They don't have to tell us, of course, and I bet they won't. At least, not yet. I don't know if I would if I was on the other side. Thinking out loud, it would probably depend on how strong I thought the witness might be for my side. Trial strategy can be tricky."

"I'm on it, Little Bossman. Call if you need me this afternoon."

Leo reared back in his chair and stared at the ceiling. The Murphy case kept getting more interesting and not necessarily in a good way. If the defense did have the missing witness in their corral, Leo suspected it couldn't be a good sign for the prosecution team. Unlike Leo, they were under no legal obligation to let the state know of their potential witnesses unless the witness was an expert or was going to provide an alibi. He had to make sure potential state's witnesses were on the list provided to the defense or risk not being able to call them at trial. The ironic thing about the witness list was that Winton Stiles was listed as a potential witness for the state without Leo not even having the chance to speak to the guy yet. Leo didn't like being blindsided, and this was ripe for such a hit.

After thinking on the issue for a few minutes, Leo walked to Sandy's office. She was alone and doing legal research on her computer. Leo plopped down in a chair without asking and brought her up to speed on the latest development. They were in agreement that they should wait until after their meeting with Sam Adams before plotting any change in strategy. The ball was definitely in the defense's court.

CHAPTER 31

Tim Hines and Leo were led into the chambers of Judge Trey Woodson precisely at 10:00 a.m. It was a comfortable space containing the requisite scales of justice situated in the middle of a conference table that abutted a large desk. The table had seven old-fashioned wooden swivel chairs arranged around the area. A picture of the judge who had served the county before the current one dominated the back wall. His father had served with distinction, and now Judge Woodson was following his footsteps.

Leo felt he was being transported back in time when he entered the office. He knew from his private practice years that 99% of all probate hearings were conducted in judge's chambers although there was a courtroom adjacent to the judge's office if needed. The last time he had been in the chambers was a few years earlier when he had attended a hearing with his mother relating to his daddy's estate.

That had been a sad time in Leo's life since the death had come so suddenly without any expectation of the event. Daddy's first heart attack had been his last and caught all the family off guard. It was a profound moment in time that caused Leo to reevaluate family matters. Now that Papa had died, Leo was experiencing many of those same feelings again. Like Yogi Berra said, *it was like deja vu all over again*, thought Leo.

The juxtaposition of his father's and grandfather's lives and deaths ran through his brain when Judge Woodson rose from behind his desk and walked to the two lawyers. It had been before Judge Woodson's father when Leo was here for his daddy's hearing. Now the hearing was before that judge's son and dealing with Leo's grandfather. There was something almost cosmic about the situation, Leo thought.

Judge Woodson extended his right hand first to Leo and offered sincere condolences. It was a trait Leo wished he had, but always found himself lacking when he encountered others going through the loss of a loved one. The judge then greeted Hines warmly and asked both to have a seat.

"It really is good to see two of my favorite lawyers at one time," the judge said with a smile. "Of course, I see Leo more often since he's here in this rundown building, too."

Leo made a halfhearted effort at a smile, but knew the judge might get on a tear about the condition of the courthouse if he responded in a similar fashion. They had discussed the issue before, and the judge knew Leo agreed the building needed many improvements. Leo was much less vocal about his opinions, however. Those views were left to others with a higher pay grade than he currently had.

Hines either didn't know Judge Woodson was a vocal advocate for the building of a new facility and didn't realize this subject could result in a long delay of the hearing, or didn't care and wanted the judge to know he shared the same opinion.

"Yes, Your Honor. I don't get over to the courthouse nearly as much as I once did," replied Hines. "But, I certainly agree this old building could use a lot of improvements to bring it into the 21st century."

"I still cannot believe the commissioners keep throwing good money after bad in this place. It's completely inadequate for all the courts of this county. It would cost a fortune to bring the place up to code. There are so many security problems, and I'm sure Leo would back me up on this; something bad is bound to happen one day. I'm not blaming that on the sheriff, either. But, there is no way to fix that problem in the current space. Up on Leo's floor for one example, you have defendants, witnesses, jurors, lawyers and even the judge thrown into one space. And, don't get me started about standing water in some parts of my offices when it rains; or how it smells like a sewer coming through the vents; or how little parking there is for our citizens to do their business in the courthouse. It is shameful," Judge Woodson said.

"I would hate to be in their shoes. At least the commission tried to get a SPLOST passed to fund a new facility. I guess the general public chose not believe it was needed. It is unfortunate in my view. Maybe when the economy upturns something more can be done. I do hope nothing bad happens here before then," said Hines.

"Indeed. Sorry, Tim. I know I can get on a rant about this subject at the drop of the hat. We should get down to business since I have another hearing at 10:30," responded the judge.

The judge sat in the chair at the far end of the table. Leo and Hines sat down opposite one another so that Leo was to the judge's right and Hines was to his left. At that moment as if summoned by magic, the clerk came into the room with a file that was handed over to Judge Woodson. She smiled at the lawyers and then left the room.

"Okay, gentlemen. Let's do this. Tim, if you would swear in the witness and present your petition."

The hearing was short and without interruption. Acknowledgments of service on all the heirs-at-law were contained in the file, and since no objections had been filed by any of them, letters testamentary were signed by Judge Woodson that allowed Leo to legally administer the estate under the terms of the will.

Leo and Tim left the office after thanking the judge and stepped into the hallway outside the probate court offices. They had requested several certified copies of the document beforehand. This was done in case they were needed to accomplish any directions in the will. Leo now held them in his hands.

"Thanks for your help, Tim. Since you're a lot more versed in this than me, will you take care of the next steps to transfer property and set up any trusts directed by Papa? I've got enough on my plate at work right now to keep me busy."

"It will be my pleasure, Leo. I wasn't sure how much you wanted me to do along those lines, but it will not be a problem. I have a pretty good handle on all of the assets, and we can get you an updated list in due speed. I'll call you next week after I get an inventory together."

"Great, Tim. Do you have a rough estimate of the value of the estate?"

"Hmm, I'm not sure about some of the real estate holdings, but with his investments and liquid assets I would guess somewhere between three and five million."

Leo whistled softly. "That's more than I thought."

"Big Leo was a shrewd businessman and played everything close to the vest. It may even wind up being more than that. All of the beneficiaries should be well pleased."

Leo thought about a conversation he had with Papa after he was accepted to law school. His grandfather had given him a check for five thousand dollars as a present for graduation from college, and told Leo of the pride felt in the accomplishment.

"The money will certainly help some of the family more than others, I suspect. I just hope it's used wisely. At least a good portion of the assets will go toward funding education of my relatives. The value of education was something he talked to me about as I worked on mine."

Hines shook his head up and down. "In my experience people who come into money unexpectedly fall into two general categories. The first group will rush out and spend recklessly until it's all gone. The second will put it away until they figure out how to use the money to their best advantage. I'm sure the Berrys are no different than every other family and will have some in both groups," he said pausing.

"And yeah, your grandfather was adamant that his estate should be used to ensure as many of his family's futures as possible. He told me on more than one occasion that furthering one's education was a key to success. By no means did he consider it the only key, though. To your grandfather's way of thinking, nothing was more important than hard work. He recognized the value of education and was one of the smartest people I've ever known even if most of his learning came from the school of hard knocks. How about your inheritance? Have you thought about what you might do with the farm?"

Leo looked around the hallway and was a little surprised with the lack of people in the area. It was usually crowded with folks headed into the tax office across the hall from the Probate Court suite.

"I have given it some thought, Tim. I have an idea or two how to make the best use of the property. I'm just not quite ready to pull the trigger. My family recently got together over there and had a great day. In the near future I plan to have a reunion for the extended family at the farm and maybe discuss its future," replied Leo.

"I'm confident you'll make the right decision about the farm. Big Leo was, too. That's why he left you in charge."

"I hope you're right, Tim. The farm is a big part of his legacy and I want to get it right."

Tim stepped closer to Leo and placed his hand on Leo's shoulder. "You'll do fine, Leo."

The two men shared a silent moment in memory of the man who had influenced their lives. Both knew without Leo Berry, Sr. to help shape them, things would have been different in ways unimagined. They also knew he would never be forgotten to them.

CHAPTER 32

Sandy and Leo sat in his office awaiting the arrival of Sam Adams. Leo had thought about the pros and cons of having his colleague attend the meeting with the defense attorney and finally decided it would probably help the other lawyer as much as himself to be at ease. He only knew Adams by reputation and from the few tidbits Sandy had told him about. Leo wanted the meeting to be as pleasant as possible and thought a friendly face could only help in that regard. In the meantime, she was offering advice.

"And try not to stroke your beard so much during the meeting," Sandy said with a smile.

"You don't think it makes me look studious?" asked Leo with a smirk.

They both laughed. Leo did appreciate the gentile reminder about his habit.

As the laughter was subsiding the receptionist brought a tall handsome young African-American to the door of the office. He had an expertly shaped close-cut hairstyle and wore a narrow mustache over a confident smile. To Leo, the man looked remarkably like a younger but taller Billy Dee Williams.

"I hope you two aren't laughing about me," said Adams with a sly grin. "Especially you, Sandy."

Sandy got up from the chair she had occupied and hurried over to the defense lawyer. She got on tiptoes and they hugged with genuine affection. Leo noticed Adams looked a foot taller than the diminutive prosecutor.

As they broke apart Sandy looked up at him and replied, "I promise not to tell any old law school stories on you if you don't on me. You know I know some doozies, lady's man."

"Truce! It's like Vegas, what goes on in law school stays in law school," said Adams with another laugh.

Leo had gotten up from the chair behind his desk as the two other lawyers greeted each other. He now felt a little out of place and wondered to himself if he had made the right decision to include Sandy in the meeting.

Without waiting to be introduced, the defense lawyer headed in Leo's direction with an extended right hand. "You must be Leo Berry. I've heard lots of good things about you, Mr. Prosecutor."

"As I have about you, counselor. It's nice to meet you, Mr. Adams."

"Hey, let's call each other by first names if it's okay with you. We can save the formalities for the courtroom."

"Deal," said Leo as both dropped the longer than average handshake. Leo felt them sizing each other up through their grips.

"Make yourself at home in my humble abode away from my other home," said Leo.

Adams waited for Sandy to sit as Leo shut the door. Leo went back to his chair behind the desk as the defense lawyer took a seat to Sandy's right. Leo couldn't help but notice the man's sport coat and slacks fit his frame impeccably. The term "classy" fit the guy. Looks, style and grace alone would make him a worthy adversary.

"So, what do you say we get right to business. I appreciate you coming over to the office today. I don't know how you feel about it, but I like meeting with the other side and putting everything I can on the table in an effort to resolve cases," began Leo.

"Man, you don't waste time! That's one of the things I heard about you. If that's how you roll, that's cool with me, too."

"One of the things I've heard about you is that you try and disarm your opponent with different methods," replied Leo. "One of those methods is to use the element of surprise whether before or after trial. I understand that strategy, too. I was once on the other side of the desk, and I know there is usually more than one way to help a client. Do you have any surprises for us today, Sam?"

Adams was expressionless at first, but then flashed another engaging smile. "Maybe," was all he said.

"Well, okay. Maybe you'll let us know after we tell you what we think and how we analyze our case," said Sandy.

"There is one preliminary topic I want to bring up before Sandy runs through our analysis, though. We think it is important to tell you that I know a member of our victim's family. She is the sister of the deceased, Johnny Thomas, and lives on property that my grandfather owned and now has been left to me. While I didn't realize there was some connection until after getting the assignment of the Murphy case, and while I don't see a pressing need to seek recusal, Sandy and I felt we should let you know before we get too far down the road," said Leo.

Adams showed outward surprise. He did not comment for a moment.

"I appreciate you being forthcoming with that information, Leo. It says a lot about your professionalism. It would be helpful to me if you would allow me to ask you a question or two," replied the defense lawyer.

"Sure, I'll do my best to answer any concerns you have," said Leo.

"Okay, how long have you known the sister?"

"Just a short time, maybe a few weeks now. I first met her at my grandfather's funeral the end of September."

"And do you feel the fact that you know her or that she had some relationship with your grandfather would bias your handling of the case in any way?"

"I honestly do not. If I did, I would do as I have done in the past when such an issue arose. I would get out of the case and find someone else to handle it. Like our mutual friend and colleague here, Sandy," replied Leo.

"It happens on occasion in our office. I can tell you Leo would never let personal feelings or relationships interfere," interjected Sandy.

Adams sat pondering and looked at both prosecutors before speaking again.

"I'm going to have to think about this in a little more depth before I say for sure, but I'm inclined to think this would not amount to a serious conflict. Of course, if it were to develop into such, I would expect to hear again from you as soon as possible. Otherwise, I would like us to proceed with all due speed. My client is anxious to get on with the process and another delay would no doubt be necessary if yet another conflict arose."

With that disclosure complete Sandy then gave a detailed synopsis of the facts as she and Leo had discussed. They pulled no punches as to the weaknesses they would encounter at trial proving all the elements of the case. Adams listened intently to her recitation without interruption. Leo fought with the urge to stroke his chin. When she finished, the defense lawyer looked first at Leo and then back at his former classmate.

"I just had a flashback to law school. I know I said I wouldn't tell old tales, but I remember an ancient lawyer visiting our trial practice class one day and calling on Sandy to give an analysis of some hypothetical. She did the same that day as she did just then. I can't remember his name now, but I remember how blown away he was with her analysis of the problem. I must admit it is refreshing that you guys acknowledge you have some issues with this case," said Adams.

Sandy spoke up again, "I remember that guy. I think his name was Martin Something or Other. I thought he was calling on me to try and embarrass me since there were only two females in that class. He was an old codger, but he did give some good practical information. Leo and I have talked about this several times since we've worked together and agree a lawyer has to state up front what challenges he faces in proving his case to the fact finder."

"Neither of us believe in pulling tricks on the defense," chimed in Leo. "We try to do the right thing in all cases."

"You know I have to zealously represent my client. But, I also believe in our ethics code. I don't ever want to be known as playing loose with the law," said Adams.

Leo thought he detected unease with the defense lawyer. He decided to press the matter of the missing witness at that moment.

"As Sandy mentioned, we have been unable to locate Winton Stiles. Quite frankly, we're more than a little peeved at what we consider shoddy investigation by the MPD in this case, but particularly with respect to this witness. Our investigator is still working on locating Stiles because his testimony could be vital in this case. He may be the joker in the deck, though. By chance, have you been able to find him?"

The winning smile was no longer in the room. Adams looked at his watch and then at Leo before responding.

"Some might say that is privileged information, but I have never lied to a prosecutor and I don't intend to now. Yes, we have located Mr. Stiles. You should know he is not in good health and probably terminal in the near future. I'm really not sure if he is lucid enough to testify."

Leo found himself stroking his chin when he heard the news. He glanced at Sandy who was doing the same thing. Leo was not sure if she was mocking him, giving him a sign to quit or joining him with the habit. He abruptly stopped and thought before he spoke.

"I have a suggestion. Let's meet with the judge and ask for permission to conduct a video taped deposition. We can do it in the courthouse or another neutral site if need be. I respect your opinion as to whether he is competent to testify, but I think we need to hear what he has to say before making that determination. If necessary, we'll have him evaluated. Doing less than that carries huge risks for your client as well as the sanctity of judicial process. Who knows, Winton Stiles could provide information that will resolve this case once and for all," said Leo.

"Every trial seeks the discovery of the truth," said Adams. "I just don't want my client to suffer from any agreement I make stipulating adverse testimony."

Sandy nodded agreement. "I can draw an order for everyone to look at before meeting with the judge. You'll have the right to cross-examine Stiles as you would any other state's witness. Of course, you'll be free to challenge his credibility and veracity."

The lawyers continued their discussion for another forty-five minutes before Adams again looked at his watch. It looked a lot more expensive than the running watch Leo had on his left arm.

"Before we conclude this meeting, there is just one more question we want to ask. Since you have not asked us what we would be willing to do on a plea bargain, we want to know what you and your client would accept to wrap up this case?" asked Leo.

Adams thought about the question before answering. "I can tell you this. Nelly Murphy has been adamant with me from day one. He told me he did not murder Johnny Thomas nor did he kill him in some heat of passion scenario. I believe him, and therefore we will not enter a plea to either of those charges. I realize there is a possibility that a jury could find him guilty of felony murder, but I think we have pretty good odds that they won't. That being said, our only option would be some theory of involuntary manslaughter. I might be able to sell that, but he would need to be getting out soon. He's getting buggy in that place and he wants out now."

"Okay, at least we know where you are right now. Let's get the deposition of Winton Stiles and we'll talk again. I enjoyed meeting you, Sam. I wish it could be under different circumstances, but that's how we get to know other lawyers a lot of the time, through someone's misfortune," said Leo.

The lawyers stood in unison and said their goodbyes. Leo and Sandy stayed and plotted the next moves. They agreed Sam Adams would be a force to be reckoned with, and one day he would either be on the bench or making lots more money than he did now.

CHAPTER 33

Leo, Dee and Mindy were seated at the dinner table enjoying old-fashioned chicken and rice. It was Dee's mom's recipe except Leo had prepared it using boneless chicken thighs. He had successfully convinced his family over the last few years that those were the tastiest parts of the bird. Leo now used them in practically every chicken dish he made.

"Really delicious, Diddy. I'm glad you didn't make those yucky brussel sprouts to go with the chicken and rice again. They almost made me spew last time."

Leo and Dee snickered at the memory. They were always seeking ways to encourage eating a balanced diet for their daughter. The last time Leo had fixed the chicken and rice, he had prepared some roasted brussel sprouts that took considerable coaxing before Mindy would taste them. When she finally got one in her mouth there was so much gagging it caused Dee to exclaim, "Just spit it out before you throw up!" Thinking discretion was the better part of valor, Leo had stuck with green beans this time around.

"We remember," said Dee. "You said your taste buds had not developed."

"The funny thing is you ate them when you were younger. And, you like cabbage and broccoli which are similar," said Leo.

Mindy looked at them one at a time and replied, "I guess I have discriminating tastes. Besides Dad, you don't like beets and rutabagas even though Mom loves them. Mom doesn't like fish although you love it. So, I can dislike yucky brussel sprouts even though y'all like them. That's logical, right?"

"You'll make a fine lawyer one day," said Leo.

"Not me. I'm going to be a marine biologist. Or, maybe a teacher. Then again, I might change my mind after I get to high school. When did you first know you wanted to be a lawyer?"

Leo spooned out another thigh and a few more green beans. The busy day had made him ravenous. He pondered for a moment before answering.

"I don't know exactly. I remember my parents telling me when I was probably younger than you are now that because I was smart I should be a doctor or a lawyer. I also remember Papa told me I would make a good lawyer. I really got interested in the law while in high school and to think about it now I realize that wasn't very realistic. I was watching old TV shows and movies and being a lawyer seemed cool. I really didn't know very much about the profession at all until I got to law school. I had never even met a lawyer until then."

"So, you really think I would be a fine lawyer?" asked Mindy.

Leo smiled. "I think you'll be a fine marine biologist, teacher, lawyer or anything else you decide to be, Sweetie. You're a smart girl and have plenty of time before making such an important decision. Don't let anyone else make your mind up for you is all I ask."

"Just be the best you can be," chimed in Dee.

Leo watched his daughter as she finished eating. He always was intrigued by her habit of eating one thing on her plate at a time until consumed before eating the other foods.

"I've been meaning to ask you, have you noticed a different car parked near that house on the corner?" asked Dee.

"I don't know that I have, but there always seems to be more cars around that house than anywhere in the neighborhood. I guess since that's the only rental home and no one seems to know anything about the residents, I've grown accustomed to different vehicles being parked there. Why do you ask?" asked Leo.

"It's got a real dark tint on the windows. Looks kinda sinister to me when you can't see if anybody's in the car or not. I tried to see the tag and it was obscured, but I could tell it was not our county," said Dee with a frown.

"I'll be on the lookout and also ask our nosy neighbors on the opposite corner to do the same. It's probably nothing to worry about, but you can never be too careful with all the kids we have living around us."

Mindy interrupted the conversation by asking if she could be excused from the table. She announced there was some pressing homework she needed to get done before one of her favorite television programs came on. When she was out of earshot, Leo changed the conversation.

"Changing the subject, I want to let you know about something that's been on my mind for a couple of days. I met Mickie Thomas for lunch, and she let me borrow some old pictures. I didn't really have the chance to talk to her much about them, but I think they are very revealing," said Leo.

"How so?"

"Well, for one thing, there is a picture of her father, Gene, and Papa together. There is an uncanny resemblance between the two. Gene Thomas looked more like a son than Daddy or his brothers. Also, Mickie's brothers pictures indicate a similar resemblance."

"Are you hinting there may be more of a connection between your grandfather and Gene Thomas other than a business one? You need a lot more proof than a couple of old pictures. Surely you know that, counselor."

"There was one more old picture that provides another hint to a possible connection. Where she got it I can only speculate, but Mickie also provided a picture of Georgine proclaiming her love forever, in French."

"Your grandfather's Georgine? From the journal?"

"I am not positive, but there are too many coincidences otherwise. Unfortunately I didn't have enough time to ask Mickie about the pictures. It's mind boggling and I just haven't had the time to wrap my brain around all of it, yet," said Leo while shaking his head from side to side.

"If it's true, you might have more cousins than you thought," said Dee.

"That has crossed my mind. Anyway, I've got the pictures with me in my briefcase. I wanted you to see them and get your opinion. I'll clean the dishes while you look at them. You'll find my briefcase on the bed and the pictures right on top. I'll join you there in a few."

As Leo stood at the sink rinsing dishes for the dishwasher, he did not notice there was a dark vehicle slowly driving by the house. He also did not know that there was a clean line of sight between his back and the occupants inside the vehicle since the front blinds had been left open. By the time the dishes were loaded and Leo was ready to join Dee, the vehicle was gone without him ever knowing of any potential danger.

CHAPTER 34

Another Friday and another day in court, thought Leo as he drove to the courthouse. It was always a mixed bag of grief and relief for him. On the one hand, it was always busy and many times aggravating. On the other, it could often provide its own form of entertainment, and it meant the weekend loomed with the promise of fun and relaxation. As he had described his job many times before, he was either in court or preparing for court, and given his choice Leo would choose the former.

Leo thought about the night before. He and Dee had studied the old photographs and talked about the possible implications. Because Dee was a lot handier with doing research on the internet, she had volunteered to see what she could find out about Gene Thomas. She had recently been doing some research into her family's genealogy and found some previously unknown facts about her lineage. Leo had welcomed the help and hoped Dee would be able to clear up lingering questions about the mysterious man in Papa's life.

His mind was doing the usual jumping around during the fifteen-minute commute. Here it was late October, and life had been moving at a fever pitch for the last several weeks since Papa had died. The weather was cooling down although the pace of life had been heating up. Maybe a vacation was in order. Mindy would be out of school for a couple of weeks in December. They could do a few days in New York and catch a show or two. They could enjoy the Christmas lights, too. That would be a treat for his two girls. His recent inheritance certainly made it financially possible. Leo decided he would run the idea by Dee over the weekend. Otherwise, it would probably not be possible to have a vacation until spring break or even the summer when Mindy's schooling didn't interfere.

Leo smiled at the thought of another weekend. He would go see his mom tomorrow and maybe go out to the farm afterward. Leo thought it would be a good idea to make an inventory of the furniture and other personal belongings in the house and begin to decide what he should do with the stuff. Very little of the property had been removed as of yet.

Uncle Jim and Aunt Lois had already claimed some of the heirlooms, which had special meaning to them. The items that had been taken were understandable in Leo's mind. Uncle Jim had specifically wanted an old rocker that Papa had used for many years and an old double-barreled shotgun. Aunt Lois wanted the old cookware left in the house, some of which she had learned to cook with, as well as a worn bread bowl that grandma had whipped up batches of biscuits. Both of Papa's surviving children also chose many of the family photographs sitting around the living room. Leo had been somewhat surprised neither of them seemed particularly interested in some of the other furniture that probably qualified as antiques.

Leo wanted all of the extended family to at least have an opportunity to choose an item or two of Papa's property as a memento. It was important that if some object could help keep his memory alive, it should become their possession. He just hoped there were no arguments to come between any of the relatives.

If Leo was going to make a trip out to the farm, he could also try and see Mickie and her brother, too. Leo wanted to return the old pictures to her, and he was anxious to meet Pete as well. He felt Pete would have extra insight into the relationship between Papa and Pete's dad that nobody else would.

It would also be a good chance to let them know of the developments in the Murphy case. He decided to call Mickie after court and see if she and possibly Pete would be able to meet on Saturday afternoon. Leo was hopeful he could become friends with Pete like he had with his sister.

As Leo turned into the county parking lot and began looking for a vacant spot, the Murphy case popped into his head. Trying to find the truth of the case was like trying to find a place to park. It was elusive and confounding.

Just as he saw what might be the answer to the problem of where to put the car, somebody in a Mini Cooper whipped in the spot from the opposite direction. The prestige plate read, XtraSmall. *Stay calm,* he thought. It was the same advice to himself he always tried to remember when driving. Aggression just seemed part of a lot of driver's behaviors, and Leo found it happening to him on more than one occasion.

It was also good advice for the Murphy case. Leo felt the case was getting close to final resolution, but he needed to remain calm. See what might develop from the witness deposition that had been scheduled for the middle of next week. Maybe check with his new contact in the DEA and find out if he had additional information.

Finally, Leo noticed a clear spot of asphalt at the back of the lot and pulled in. He considered himself fortunate not to have to go to the overflow lot a block away and it a good sign for everything to fall in place. Leo literally crossed his fingers as the thought entered his mind.

CHAPTER 35

Friday afternoons were the best time at the office. It really was especially sweet today since the morning had gone much better than expected. Leo and his cohorts had helped dispense speedy justice even though the calendar had consisted of fifteen full pages of all sorts of cases.

He felt hopeful for a few defendants that had been given a second chance by offering them pretrial diversion programs. Those dispositions gave the offenders the opportunity to keep criminal convictions off their records. Young people often did not realize how much that could hurt their chances for gainful employment down the road.

There had been a couple of funny moments to help break the monotony, too. Leo couldn't help but start laughing again as he remembered the guy who was not Hispanic but had asked Leo could he plead no comprende to a traffic violation. It was another example of how folks often did not understand legal terms or how to pronounce them. "Nolo contendere" was a personal favorite of Leo's because he had heard the term mispronounced and misused many times. More than once over the years, he had heard defendants ask for a no contender plea. For some reason, it always made Leo think of Marlon Brando's line from *On the Waterfront,* "I coulda been a contender."

The other laugh-out-loud moment of the morning had occurred when an obviously deranged defendant kept audibly farting in his seat. There were at least three that Leo heard at quiet moments during the court session. Other people had moved away from the guy after the first occurrence. After each one, the defendant would laugh to himself nonstop, and others in the audience would snicker. It didn't get any less crazy when his case was called.

Leo knew the defendant from having had other cases in court for as long as he had been a prosecutor. J.J., as the gaseous defendant was known, had been in and out of the local jail so many times that he ranked in the top ten most arrests.

Defendants with mental problems not unlike J.J.'s were a major source of troublesome issues for the community as it was nationwide. So many ended up in jail because the resources to treat folks with those problems were insufficient. The county jail had become one of the leading de facto mental health centers to treat the afflicted. The costs of the medication alone cost more than a million dollars a year.

Leo remembered the morning exchange with amusement.

"Mr. Jones, how are you feeling today?" began Judge Williams.

"My stomach is upset, Yo' Honah. It mighta been that breakfast burrito I had this mornin'," he replied with a half smile.

"Have you been going to your counseling sessions like we talked about the last time I saw you in court, and taking your meds?"

"I been ovah to the center a few times, but that medicine makes my head feel funny, Jurdge."

The judge looked at Leo who had the file in his hands. "What's Mr. Jones charged with this time?"

Leo had already opened the file and replied, "Criminal trespass at the Corner Convenience Store. It's the same store he has been banned from on several occasions by the owner, the police and the court."

The judge turned his attention back to the defendant. He shook his head and said, "Mr. Jones, what am I going to do with you? You know you're not supposed to go there."

Jones looked agitated. "I wudn't even in that stowah," he replied. "I know I ain't welcome. You gonna do what you gonna do, Jurdge."

Leo looked closely at the defendant. Jones was about the same age as Leo, but looked at least 15 years older. There was something moving in his greasy stringy hair. The clothes he wore were disheveled, and the combination of foul odors coming from the man was disgusting. At least Leo knew if the judge put Jones back in jail, the staff LCSW would see that he was stabilized and put back on his meds. Jones simply would not function as well outside the jail.

"Well, Mr. Jones, you know the drill. Do you want to have a lawyer to represent you?" asked the judge.

"I don't want no state lawyuh. They all work for you and you still gonna do what you want."

"And you understand what you're charged with?"

"I told you I wudn't in the stowah."

"Judge, I'll read from the arresting officer's report. It says Mr. Jones was in the parking lot and harassing customers coming and going inside," said Leo.

Jones glared at Leo with glassy-red eyes and said, "I wudn't harassin' nobody. I only was askin' for some money so I could get sumpin' to eat from the Krystal."

"Mr. Jones, the store premises include its parking lot. Were you in the parking lot?" asked the judge.

"Yeah, Jurdge. I didn't go inside, though."

"Okay then, you've said you don't want a lawyer and you now understand the basis of the charge. So, how do you plead to the charge?" asked Judge Williams.

"I'm guilty of bein' in the parkin' lot, so if that means I'm guilty of criminal trespass, so be it."

"We've been through this process several times before, Mr. Jones. You understand you have the right to contest the charge by pleading not guilty and have either a jury trial or a trial in front of the court without a jury. Is that right?"

"I don't want no trial," Jones said while vigorously shaking his head. Leo stepped back in case something was slung off.

"And you understand this is a misdemeanor which carries the possibility of up to twelve months in jail?"

"Yeah, I know all my rights. Just let me sign and you go ahead and do what you want."

After a few more minutes of going through the defendant's rights with the colloquy being recorded to establish the plea was voluntary, Jones signed the documents. Leo passed the file containing the papers to the judge.

As Leo expected, the judge had decided probation did not have any chance of working. What happened when the judge pronounced a jail sentence was funny and sad at the same time.

"Mr. Jones, I have to conclude because past efforts imposing probation were unsuccessful, the only thing I can do at this point is to order you to serve ninety days in jail."

"You gonna make me serve ninety days for that?"

At the precise moment Jones finished the question, he emitted a loud fart sounding to Leo like a duck quack. The sound was followed by an incredibly bad smell worthy of a sewer.

The courtroom erupted in a cacophony of laughter and groans. One of the bailiffs looked like he would throw up as Sarge stepped forward to escort the defendant from the area.

The judge banged his gavel and demanded order in the court. As the courtroom quieted down, Jones got one more parting shot before being taken out.

"It's the jurdge's fault. He made me shit my britches!"

Leo reared back in his chair and laughed at the memories again. It really was a crazy place to work, he thought.

CHAPTER 36

Leo sat at the desk in Papa's bedroom and systematically went through the drawers. Though he had looked through them once before, Leo was determined to be more precise in his search. He thought if he was going to perform some sort of inventory of the place, it was as good as any place to start.

Leo had a trusty yellow legal pad on top of the old piece of furniture to record anything of value. The first item he had written down was "antique desk in bedroom." The second was the "lamp on top of the desk." Leo wanted both for sentimental reasons since he had spent time there as a child looking up words in Papa's dictionary. He wanted that book as well.

He had dispatched his wife and child to other parts of the house to help with the chore. Leo's instructions were to make a list of items they thought would be useful to other members of the family. He was grateful they were with him and for their willingness to help. Leo's thoughts were the other family members would get first dibs on the property inside the house, and then he would give the remainder to charity or to simply discard as trash if there was no value.

The three of them had gotten to the farm after a stop at his mother's house. It was a cool but clear day, and the house was comfortable inside. With the pleasant working conditions and the extra help, Leo expected the inventory could be completed in plenty of time to go out for dinner afterward.

As Leo opened the last drawer, he made an interesting discovery in a hidden compartment that reinforced what Dee had found on the computer the night before. He and Dee had been seated side by side as she used various search engines for the Thomas surname and saw there were French origins.

Now in black and white, Leo held a copy of a document professing to be the birth certificate of Jean Pitre Thomas. It was written in French. Leo saw the line for Pere was blank. Georgine Thomas was listed as Mere. From what Leo knew of Papa's service time during the war, the date of birth was roughly nine months after his grandfather parachuted into France. It was another hint of the connection Leo had started feeling in his gut after seeing Mickie's pictures.

This document provided even more reason to talk to Mickie and her brother about Leo's suspicions. Maybe one or both of them had other information to confirm that Papa was their grandfather as well. While Leo did not believe Mickie was aware of the possibility, Pete was older and would have been in a position to talk to his father, Jean or Gene, Thomas about his origins.

Leo got up from the chair and walked over to the bookshelves. He pulled the old dictionary from the spot it had held for as long as Leo could remember. There were several good memories of Papa and him looking up words in the book. Leo knew this would be a keepsake for as long as he lived.

He opened the book and the first word Leo's eyes settled on was paradox. Leo smiled to himself. He couldn't help believe Papa was still directing the grandson by pointing out the word. The definition read, "A seemingly contradictory statement that may nonetheless be true."

Leo remembered Papa telling him many times that family came first. If that were true, wouldn't Papa have put Gene Thomas and family at least on the same plane as his other kids? That was assuming that Gene was Papa's son. Of course, Papa may very well not have known he had another son until after he had gotten married to Grandma and had five children with her. What Leo remembered and other family members had said about her, though, could explain the lack of acknowledgment of Gene as a son. She could have simply forbidden Papa from doing so.

It really seemed to Leo that Papa's life was like the saying he had heard from an old English teacher in high school, "An enigma wrapped in a paradox." It was puzzling and contradictory.

Mindy walked into the room interrupting Leo's thoughts. She came to him and wrapped her arms around his midsection.

"You okay, Daddy? You look a little sad."

"Yeah, I'm good, Sweetie. I was just thinking about Papa."

"You really miss him, don't you?"

"Even more than I first realized. He really taught me a lot that I guess I've taken for granted. I never thought about him not being around forever. But, he told me one time that dying was just the beginning to living again. I'm not absolutely sure about that, but I know he was smarter than me, and he wouldn't have said it if he didn't believe it. So, it gives me comfort, too," said Leo.

A breeze caused some wind chimes on the deck to tinkle as Mindy hugged Leo a little harder. Leo patted his daughter's back and took in the moment.

"So, did you get your part of the inventory on paper?" asked Leo.

Mindy backed to arms length and held up her pad. Leo could see she had recorded several items on one side of the sheet and names of relatives on the other side. He shook his head up and down in approval.

"You're a big help. Thank you, Sweetie."

The sound of Tiki barking disrupted Leo's perusal of Mindy's notes. It was the same sound the dog used whenever he encountered strangers.

"Let's go see what the commotion is about," said Leo.

Dee joined them in the front room of the house as Tiki continued announcing someone's arrival. Sure enough a black Ford 150 truck had parked behind the Berry vehicle. The occupants weren't recognizable because of the dark tint of the windshield.

"You two wait here and let me find out who this is," said Leo.

Leo opened the front storm door and exited the house onto the front porch. He called Tiki over and the dog immediately obliged the command. Leo reached down, patted him and said, "Good boy. Sit. Stay."

Leo then waved an open hand toward the truck and both front doors opened. Mickie's grin was infectious as she got out of the passenger side causing Leo to smile in return.

The driver had to be her brother, Pete. He was a few inches taller than Leo and had a well built physique. Even though he was a few years older than Leo, Pete Thomas had a youthful face. The attribute that struck Leo the most was the blue eyes. That, and the absence of a smile.

"Hey, Mickie. It's good to see you again. I'm glad you brought a friend with you," said Leo as he crossed the yard to greet them.

Leo was pleasantly surprised when Mickie gave him a hug. Although he often felt awkward with public displays of affection, Leo had recently found he was getting used to the idea.

She separated from the embrace and said, "Back at 'cha. I want you to meet my brother, Pete."

The two men faced each other for the first time, and Leo stuck out his hand. Pete was slower to raise his, but when he grasped Leo's hand, it was engulfed by the meatiness of the paw of the larger man. *At least he didn't crush it*, thought Leo.

"I'm really glad to meet you, Pete. I'm sorry to say I never got a chance to even though you've lived right next door all these years. I've just recently learned our families go back a ways", said Leo.

Pete nodded slightly and replied, "I guess you could say that. Maybe it's a little surprising we've not met before, but I stay pretty busy and don't socialize very much. I've heard about you, though."

Leo heard the door open and close and turned toward the house. Dee and Mindy were on the front porch looking at the new arrivals. Mindy offered a wave.

"Y'all come in and meet my wife and daughter. I've been telling them about Mickie since I first met her, and they've been looking forward to getting to know her, too."

Mickie was beaming although Pete looked tense. The brother and sister looked about as different as a sunny day on the beach and a snowy day on a mountain.

"Yes, I would love to. "All I'm ever around out here in the sticks are other men," Mickie said as she scrunched her face at Pete and Leo.

"Okay, but we can't stay long. I've got to meet a guy in a little while," said Pete.

The three of them walked up the steps to the porch, and Leo made the introductions. It didn't take but a minute before the females were giggling and had gone into the house. The sounds of their merriment faded as Leo turned again to Pete.

"Would you like something to drink? We've got sodas and beer," said Leo.

"I'm not on duty tonight, so I wouldn't mind a beer."

"Great, I'll join you. Come on in, and we'll go out on the back deck. It'll give us a chance to talk," said Leo.

Pete looked apprehensive as Leo opened the door. Leo wasn't sure if the man was going to enter or not.

"You okay?" asked Leo.

"Yeah, it's just I've been living on the next property all my life except for the two years I was in the service, and I've never been in this house. Seems strange is all," replied Pete.

"Well, it's high time then," said Leo smiling. "Come on and we'll get that beer to celebrate."

With the gentle prodding, the big man entered the house as Leo continued to hold the door open. He waited for Leo to take the lead before going farther inside the house. Leo gave an abbreviated tour and noticed Pete's attention to the details as Leo described points of interest. Upon arrival in the kitchen, Leo opened the refrigerator and looked inside.

"Nothing too fancy, I'm afraid. I do have Budweiser and Heineken Light. What's your pleasure?"

"Bud's fine," replied Pete.

Leo pulled out two bottles with the red label and handed one to Pete. Although Leo would have preferred the other choice, he did not want Pete to have any cause to distrust him. Besides, Leo liked Budweiser even though he didn't drink much beer.

They unscrewed the tops and dispatched them in the plastic garbage can under the sink. After taking a swallow from the beverages, Leo led Pete to the rear deck.

Pete walked to the center of the railing and looked over the landscape. He started at the right corner of the property and gazed slowly to the left. Leo watched the squint exhibited and had a feeling Pete was trying to see his place. Neither man spoke for a moment.

"It's a pretty good view, don't you think?" asked Leo.

"Yeah, I've never seen the area from this perspective."

"It brings back memories every time I look. I had really forgotten a lot of them until Papa died. Do you have any memories of Big Leo?"

Pete kept squinting in the area to the left of the tree line and Leo was not sure if he would answer the question. Leo thought about changing the subject. As Leo thought of a new tact, Pete took a long pull from the beer and turned to look at Leo.

"I've got a few," said Pete with an indeterminable look.

Leo felt uncomfortable. He didn't want Pete to think this was a cross-examination. However, Leo wanted to know as much as he could about all connections that existed between the families. This could very well be the best chance to find out.

"I'm sorry if this sounds like I'm prying, Pete. I certainly don't want you to think I'm giving you the third degree. It's just I've only found out a lot about my grandfather since he died that I never had a clue about. One of those things was that Papa had quite a few business dealings with your father. Another is that y'all lived right next-door, so-to-speak, and rented property from Papa. Therefore, I know there were some links between the families. Now that he's gone, there are very few people left who seem to know what those connections were. I'm hoping they were good. I feel like they must have been at least to some degree since Papa left the property to Mickie," said Leo.

Pete's blue eyes never left Leo's as Leo spoke. They remained locked in that position as Pete responded.

"My first memories as a kid are about Big Leo. I can remember him making me laugh while doing sounds of animals. For some reason, he could always get me cranked off by mooing like a cow."

Pete stopped the grimness of his previous expression and for the first time, Leo saw the traces of a smile. It was Papa like to Leo.

"Me, too," said Leo as he smiled back.

Pete continued, "He came to our house often. Sometimes he would bring Johnny and me a 'surprise' as he would say. I've still got an old compass he gave me. He taught us stuff, too, as we got a little older. Hell, he even taught me how to shoot when I was twelve years old. That made my mama mad."

Pete stopped and took another swallow. "It got more complicated as the years went by. One night, I must've been fourteen or fifteen years old, I heard my parents arguing. It wasn't hard to hear. We lived in a trailer and although it was probably as big as you could buy back then, sound carried. Anyway, I heard Mama tell Daddy that Big Leo could help us build our own house. Then I heard Daddy tell her that he didn't need Big Leo's help. They kept getting louder and louder until I got scared and I finally went to their room. I couldn't understand why they were arguing about Big Leo, so I asked them why. They never would tell me, but after that, I only saw Big Leo maybe two or three times."

Pete looked at the landscape again as Leo thought. Before Leo could respond, Pete spoke again at a lower octave.

"I asked Big Leo one time when I was little if I could go to his house. I can remember him rubbing my head and telling me maybe one day. I even asked Daddy if we could go visit, but all he would say was 'That wouldn't be cool.' I let it go after awhile since I didn't have any control over all that."

Leo watched Pete as they both finished their beers. The bigger man's sculpted shoulders sagged a little after telling of his memories of Papa. Leo's mind was racing as he decided to press on.

"Pete, it sounds to me that you have some of the same memories of Big Leo as I do, at least from a child's way of looking at things. One of the things he did with me and all my cousins was to teach us stuff. Now that he's gone, it's what I remember the most about him. I regret that I didn't spend more time with him as I got older, but it seemed there was always another kid around for him to take under his wing. Perhaps that's how he wanted it," said Leo.

He paused briefly and continued, "As I've reflected on his life, I'm convinced that's what he preferred. Maybe Papa felt he didn't have as much influence on all those he taught as they got older and left the nest. But, he provided lessons that helped those of us who had even small amounts of time with him."

Pete looked hard at Leo. Leo didn't know him well enough to form a lasting opinion, but the lawyer that was always lurking inside told Leo that Pete was angry.

"I felt cheated. It could be as you say, Leo. Maybe you and your cousins did share some of the same experiences as I did, but y'all at least were not cut off like I was. If you stopped seeing the man, it was your choice. I had no choice. Daddy made that clear to me," said Pete.

"I'm sorry, Pete. I had no idea about any of that. I don't want to bring up anything to cause hard feelings. Believe me, my curiosity is no excuse for bad manners, and I apologize for being insensitive. I want us to be friends."

Pete walked over to the table and chairs near the grill. He pulled one of the chairs out from under the table and sat down. Once again he began looking at the landscape. The happy sounds of the girls could still be heard in the quietness of the moment.

"How about one more beer?" finally asked Pete.

"Great minds think alike," replied Leo as he opened the door and went back into the house.

Leo returned to the deck with the cold bottles and handed one to Pete. Leo then took a chair close to him and sat down. For the next few minutes they silently drank.

"Mickie really likes you," Pete finally broke the silence.

"I'm glad because I really like her, too," said Leo.

"In a way I feel more like a parent or maybe an uncle than a brother to her."

"That's understandable. I can't imagine if I had a sibling with such an age difference. She's told me a little about growing up without knowing her parents. That had to be hard on such a little girl. You too, for that matter. I lost my dad a few years ago and I know how that felt."

"All I want is to protect her. Since I've never been too good at finding my own happiness, I can't really help her there. But, I can at least look out for her. She's got a stubborn streak like Mama though, and wants to go her own way," said Pete with a frown.

"Yep, sounds like a parent talking. We all want to go our own way sooner or later, though. My wife and I have to keep reminding ourselves of that," replied Leo with a chuckle.

"Yeah, I guess so. Anyway, I appreciate you getting close to her. Also, keeping us up with the case on Johnny's killer. So, Mickie told me it's coming up for trial soon?"

"Right after Thanksgiving unless we work out something. I'm assuming Mickie has told you about the problems I face.

There's also a witness who may be very important. He's extremely sick and the judge has ordered a video deposition scheduled for next week," said Leo.

"I've been around the court system for almost twenty years now, so I know how it works. For the record, do what you feel is best even if I may not like it," said Pete with a scowl.

"Like I've said to Mickie, I'm going to do my best to see that justice is served. It's what I'm sworn to do and however hokey it might sound to some, I take it as my solemn duty," said Leo before pausing.

"For what it's worth, I'll add this as an observation about that pursuit. The system is not perfect. Like you certainly have in your career, I've seen some bad people who I personally thought were guilty go free," continued Leo.

Leo felt like he was getting on a soapbox, but it was a subject that inflamed his passion. He really did feel like the justice system was the best in the world even with flaws that were exposed too often.

"It is my belief that when that happens, the guilty will answer for it somehow. You can call it final judgment, karma or whatever," said Leo and paused again.

"At least that's how I justify my using plea deals many times."

Pete's blue eyes were staring into Leo's with intensity. Neither man looked away.

"I don't disagree. Justice will be served one way or another," Pete said finally.

"I'll let you and Mickie know as soon as I can. Do you mind if I ask you some questions about your brother, Johnny?" asked Leo.

Pete took a long draw from the beer and looked again at Leo. "What do you want to know?"

"Just some general information like what he did for a living, hobbies, friends, stuff like that. Of course, if you know anything about his trip downtown the night he died, that could be helpful."

"I really don't see what that has to do with the upcoming trial. Just seems you're being nosy to me. Besides, I told the police department I didn't know anything about that night," said Pete.

"Oh, no. What I'm looking for is a way to make the victim into a real person for the jury. I wasn't aware you had talked to detectives."

The big man looked at his watch again. He had already done that several times during the conversation. Leo wondered if Pete really needed to leave soon or if he was merely uncomfortable.

"Leo, I really have enjoyed talking with you, but I do have an appointment I'm going to be late for. Maybe we can get together again soon. I appreciate the beers," Pete said while rising out of the chair.

Leo arose from his chair and extended his hand. Pete's hand once again engulfed Leo's.

"I really appreciate meeting you as well, Pete. I would love to get together again soon. I wish we could have met long ago. There's much more we could talk about when you have more time," replied Leo.

"Maybe so. Look, I don't want to interrupt Mickie's good time," he said as they both heard a new round of laughter inside the house.

"Do you mind giving her a lift to her place?" Pete asked.

"I'll be happy to do that. It does sound like the three of them are getting along well," Leo said with a grin.

Tiki's happy bark could now be heard as well as the laughter. "Mindy must be showing off some dog tricks."

The two men walked back through the house without encountering the girls. Leo escorted Pete to the front porch and watched as he walked to the truck. It was a nice vehicle painted black as midnight. Before Pete opened the driver's door, he once more faced Leo and threw up his right hand. The gesture was made without further words.

Leo stuck his hands in the pockets of his Levi's as the spectral truck disappeared down the road. There was one thing about Pete that stuck out in his mind above everything else, those eyes.

CHAPTER 37

Leo watched in the rear view mirror. Mickey was in the back seat with Mindy and Tiki perfectly perched between the two.

The terrier constantly looked back and forth to whomever was talking while each scratched and petted his wiry coat. Leo doubted the animal would budge if given a choice of being there or being elsewhere with his favorite treat. Tiki's wide grin almost looked photo shopped.

A side-glance at Dee revealed her dimpled smile. Leo silently wished he could bottle the collective positive emotions inside the car. If only everybody could feel that happy, jobs like his would become extinct.

"So, everyone have a good day?" asked Leo.

Everybody responded affirmatively. Even Tiki barked with a clipped "Yep" in dog speak.

After leaving the farm, the group had driven to a local BBQ joint and enjoyed smoked pig with creamy coleslaw and Brunswick stew. With full stomachs, they were now headed to take Mickie home.

Leo reflected on the day as he neared the graveled driveway. It had been good to get the inventory done with the help of Dee and Mindy. Mickie had even lent a hand as the girls got to know one another. Leo had almost sprung the secret he felt certain about, but held back at the last minute not wanting to risk ruining the happiness.

Leo felt he had made some progress by meeting Pete, but the man was still too much of a mystery. He wished he could have spoken longer to Pete because Leo couldn't help but believe Pete held the keys to better understanding.

"Better slow down or you'll go past it," said Mickie.

"Thanks, I can always use another back seat driver to go along with these other two," responded Leo with an exaggerated fake scowl.

"Somebody needs to remind you where to go. Remember the time you kept going in circles in that parking deck?" said Dee.

Leo laughed at the memory of going around and around in the Savannah hotel parking deck. "You have to admit those signs were confusing," said Leo.

"Yeah, J.D," said Dee as she kept laughing.

"Mickie, that's what I call Leo when referring to his Juris Doctor degree and all the good it does him sometimes figuring stuff out," finished Dee.

It was dusk and the passing light played with Leo. He slowed down as he passed Papa's old place and neared the driveway Mickie had described. Leo could understand how someone could easily miss it if not paying close attention.

The sound of gravel crunching underneath the wheels was a little disconcerting to Leo as he made his way in the poor light. He couldn't help but think to himself the scene was suitable for a horror movie. When he finally saw the mobile home with a couple of lights illuminating through lacy curtains, Leo wasn't sure he felt any safer.

"Geez, Mickie! It's spooky in here. Do you ever get scared?" asked Mindy.

"No, really I don't. I've been right here all my life and it's home. Besides, I have Pete just down the way if I need him," said Mickie.

Leo pulled the car right to the front of the dwelling. Mickie opened her small purse and pulled out an oversized shaped M key ring. Leo noticed a whistle and a palm sized can of mace on the ring. He wondered if she really did feel safe.

"Thanks again for a great time. I'm so glad I got to meet y'all. I can't remember the last time I laughed so much. I bet my cheeks are going to be sore tomorrow," said Mickie.

"Me, too!" exclaimed Mindy.

"That makes three of us. I feel like I've got a new little sister," said Dee.

"Or an older one," said Mindy.

Leo smiled as the three girls all got out of the car and hugged. It was amazing the affection was so real in such a short time.

Leo opened his car door and had just closed it when he heard the sound of broken branches. Tiki had a low growl in his throat. Leo looked around to the area where he thought the sound originated, but nothing could be seen in the thick woods. Whatever had made the sounds seemed large to Leo.

The girls stopped talking and also looked. Mindy appeared frightened. Tiki stood rigidly, looking ready to spring.

There was a pregnant pause of silence until Mickie said, "Probably just a deer. I see them all the time."

"Are you sure you're not scared?" asked Leo.

"No, really. Do y'all want to come in?" asked Mickie as she looked at them."

"It's nice of you, Sweetie, but we should be getting back home. We've still got a drive ahead of us," said Dee.

"I totally understand. I hate making that drive, too. Specially at night after a long day."

"Next time we'll get together at our house. You can even stay the night 'cause we've got an extra bedroom, don't we Daddy?" said Mindy.

"Sure, we could do that," said Leo with a smile.

"Yeah, sounds like a plan," chimed in Dee.

Mickie had a wide grin on her face. She hugged each of them one at a time with Leo getting an extra long one last. When she pulled away from him he could see tears in her eyes.

"I can't tell y'all how happy I am right now. I feel almost like a part of the family," said Mickie.

"I think we all agree," said Leo pausing before continuing.

"Alright, we had better go before it really gets dark out here. I'll call you next week with an update on the case."

More hugs followed before Leo, Dee, Mindy and Tiki got back in the car. Mickie entered her home as Leo swung the car into a tight loop flashing his high beams around the wooded area. As the car pulled back down the driveway, Leo saw the front porch light come on.

A few minutes later after the car had gone and the front door light looked like a beacon in the night, a lone camouflaged figure receded back into the woods toward the cabin.

CHAPTER 38

The room was crowded. The center of attention remained in the hospital bed with his head elevated. There were three IV bottles suspended on a metal frame attached to plastic tubing running fluids into the man's veins. A separate machine was attached that gave constant vital signs.

Facing the patient and standing to the left of the bed was Leo. Sandy was sitting slightly to her co-counsel's rear. Defense counsel was standing on the opposite side. At the foot of the bed was stationed a video camera mounted on a tripod. There was a court reporter recording the event. The only other person in the room was an unsmiling woman resembling Nurse Ratched who watched the proceedings in front of the closed door.

Leo glanced back at the court reporter. He knew the guy as the only male court reporter in the circuit, but could not remember the name. Although Leo had never formally met him, the reporter had a reputation as being thorough and fully qualified to handle video depositions. That was especially important to Leo since this was his first as a prosecutor.

"Are you ready, sir?" asked Leo.

The reporter nodded a perfectly coiffed head without speaking. Except for the sounds of the medical equipment, the room was eerily quiet.

Leo looked over at Sam Adams. The defense counsel was dressed smartly in a double-breasted navy sports coat, starched blue shirt and red tie. Tailored tan gabardine pants finished the ensemble. Leo wondered if a professional makeup artist had worked on his face because it looked so perfect. All put together, Adams seemed ready to star on film.

Leo tried to pride himself in dressing professionally, but his own clothes paled in comparison, or so he thought to himself. His clothing fit well and came from a friend's store down the street near the courthouse. It was almost identical in color coordination as Adams' choices, just more conservatively cut. Maybe just a hint more casual, too.

"I'm ready, too, Mr. Berry," said Adams.

Leo cleared his throat and began by speaking into the camera. There were certain preliminary items to be noted.

"Today is November 12, 2012 and we are at the VA Hospital located in Dublin, Georgia. It is 10:05 in the morning. I am special assistant district attorney, Leo Berry III and along with another special assistant district attorney, Sandy Trimble, we represent the state of Georgia. Also present is defense counsel, Sam Adams," said Leo.

"This will be the deposition of Mr. Winton Stiles who is a potential witness in the case of The State vs. Lonnel Murphy. For the record, the state and the defense have agreed to conduct this deposition under these circumstances because Mr. Stiles has serious medical issues which may prevent his presence at trial."

"This deposition shall be used by either or both parties for any purpose allowed by law. Any objections raised by either party during the course of this deposition are reserved for ruling by the court before use at trial. Does that cover our stipulations, Mr. Adams?"

"Yes. At this time let me add that Mr. Stiles was located by the defense who notified the prosecution so this preservation of evidence would be possible," said Adams to the camera before looking over at Leo.

Score a little nick, thought Leo.

"That is correct. Let the state go on record that we appreciate Mr. Adams' efforts in locating Mr. Stiles and his cooperation in this matter," responded Leo looking from the camera to Adams and back.

Leo hoped this proceeding wouldn't turn into a play for the camera. He couldn't help believe that Sam was already doing it, and Leo therefore felt he needed to do the same. He told himself to stop.

Leo then turned to Winton Stiles and briefly studied the man. It was a pitiful sight to behold. The face had the haunted look of someone condemned to die. Almost all hair on the poor man's head was gone except for a few wispy twigs on the sides. The cheeks were sunken and had the appearance of a few days stubble. The eyes were glazed and rummy from sickness and strong medication. They did not look focused on anything in particular. His mouth was slightly open, and Leo wasn't sure if Stiles would even be able to speak out of it. His gown-covered chest was all that could be seen outside of the sheets, and it barely moved as he breathed.

"Mr. Stiles, I'm Leo Berry. Can you hear me okay?"

The witness did not move initially, but then turned his head slightly in Leo's direction. His expression did not change when he finally said, "Yes."

"I know we earlier said what we were here for today, did you hear that?"

"Yes."

"And did you understand?"

"Yes."

"Okay, I'm going to administer an oath. I'm not going to ask you to raise your right hand since you've got that IV, but do you swear or affirm to tell the truth, the whole truth and nothing but the truth, so help you, God?"

Stiles licked his lips and replied, "I'm on my way to see God soon enough, so hell yeah, I'll tell the truth. I've done enough bad in my life and don't need to add anymore to my mess."

The voice that came from the man was surprisingly clear though raspy. Leo couldn't help his growing fascination with Winton Stiles.

"Thank you, Mr. Stiles. Would you please state your name and spell it?" asked Leo.

"Winton Stiles, W-i-n-t-o-n S-t-i-l-e-s."

"How old are you?"

"I look old for my age, but I'm thirty-nine. Don't expect I'll ever see forty."

"Where did you last reside before coming to the hospital?"

Stiles shook his head and said, "Wherever I could find a place at night. I ain't had a residence, as you might say, in the last year."

"So, you're homeless?"

"That's what I said, didn't I?"

"Okay, I'm sorry Mr. Stiles. Can you tell us a little about yourself? Where you're from, family ties, education, background information?"

Stiles looked to the back of the room where the nurse was located. No words were spoken between the two, but she immediately came to his side and held a glass of water as he sipped through a straw. When he finished swallowing, his eyes looked into hers and she placed the glass on a nearby table. She then moved back to the spot she previously held.

"I was born in Kentucky, but I've lived all over the states. My daddy was in the Air Force and got transferred a few times before he ended up in Warner Robins. My mama still lives there, but I ain't got nobody else," Stiles said and paused.

Stiles tried to move himself and grimaced. There was a red button clamped to the sheet that Stiles reached for with his left hand and began pressing with his thumb. Stiles continued after a moment.

"Thank you, Jesus, for morphine. Sorry, where was I? Oh yeah, relaying my glorious past. I never was much good in school, but I finally got out. I figured Daddy had done pretty well in the service and I was ready to get the hell out from him, so I joined the Army. Pissed him off royally. Sorry, I probably shouldn't say that."

"Mr. Stiles, I'm sure neither Mr. Adams nor anyone else here wants to restrict too much what you say. And, some background information about you is helpful to us and others who may eventually hear your testimony. However, maybe we should try to get to the heart of why we're here today. Before I begin my questions about that event that led us here, let me ask you about your current medical condition. Do you mind telling us what you understand about that?" interjected Leo.

"No, I don't mind. I ain't worried about HIPPA even if y'all are," Stiles croaked a laugh.

"I'll tell you about my condition. I've got stage four pancreatic cancer and secondary liver cancer. The crap is spreading and my doctor told me I got no more than four weeks to suffer this shit. I don't want to eat no more and if I could get out of here, I would finish myself with booze and cigs," he continued with another croak.

"I'm very sorry to hear your condition is terminal, Mr. Stiles. I couldn't help but see you self-medicate a while ago and you mentioned morphine. That is powerful pain medication. Are you sure you understand why we're here, and what you are doing today?" asked Leo.

"For the last time man, I know. Thanks for the reminder to use my joystick," he said as he thumbed the button again. Stiles closed his eyes and one corner of his mouth tried to form a smile.

"Alright, please let me know if you get tired or feel the need to stop, Mr. Stiles. I want to direct your attention to the night of the shooting in the alley. Do you remember that?"

"I saw some shootings in alleys when I was in Iraq, but I'm guessing you want to know about the night last year in Macon," said Stiles.

"Can you distinguish between other shootings you may have seen?"

Stiles began coughing and his face turned a different shade of red. The nurse was instantly by his side holding the glass of water. He finally quit his flemy outburst and took a sip. After another knowing look between the two, the nurse took her former station.

"I've seen my share of killing, Mr. Berry. None of it was purdy. Yeah, I can keep them all straight. Just another reason I'm here, I guess."

Leo was feeling uneasy. This guy was off the chain. There was no telling what was going to come out. He felt there was no alternative but to plow ahead.

"So, where exactly were you on the night of the shooting?"

"I was sitting by the dumpster with my sack. Getting my drink on, counselor. Minding my own business. Trying to stay out of people's way. You dig?"

"So, you had been drinking?"

"Man, that's what I do. When I can, that is. It helps me through the night. Sometimes the day, too. I don't mess with anybody and I hope nobody messes with me."

"Would you please tell us what you remember of that night and what you saw?"

The man's eyes appeared to glaze over even more than they had been. Leo wasn't sure if the drugs were inducing such an effect or if Stiles was looking back to the event. When he began speaking again, Stiles' voice was gripping.

"I had gone back to the alley to find a little privacy. Sometimes I drink by myself 'cause I favor my own company and 'cause there are some mean-ass drunks who'll steal from you if they see a chance. That night I had me a virgin bottle of Jim Beam I didn't want to share."

"There were some crates next to the dumpster that suited my ass and that's where I was. I don't know exactly how long I sat there, but I was pretty deep in the bottle when the black kid ran in. It was pretty dark with only one little light shining over a back door to some business or another. I don't think he saw me. He never looked my way at all, but I could see him. He looked scared."

Stiles stopped and looked at the nurse. She responded silently and moved to his side once again. Leo was gaining new respect for her with every act. It was evident she had cared for him some length of time. After drinking some more water, Stiles continued in the same voice.

"The kid's face looked shiny. Like he was sweating. It was warm that night and there he was wearing a sweatshirt. I remember thinking that was stupid."

"In a few seconds the big white dude showed up. At first, I thought he might be an undercover cop trying to arrest the kid. I don't know why, but he just had that look about him. I've seen plenty of cops that have that kinda look."

"Anyway, the big guy started grinning when he saw the kid. He focused on him and then glanced around. I don't think he saw me either. Maybe the garbage can put a shadow on me or something. There was only one way in and out of that alley and the kid was trapped like a rat."

"Now, I don't know whether the dude was meaning to scare him, hurt him or kill him. But, he chambered a round in his gun and walked toward the kid. Neither of them said anything until big dude was right up on him."

"It was tense, man. I couldn't move. Wasn't any place I could've gone 'cause I was trapped, too. It was a buzz killer."

Stiles stopped talking. He retreated into himself, and the room was silent. All that was left was a vacant stare.

Leo had been riveted to Stiles' testimony. Now it seemed Stiles was not going any further.

"Mr. Stiles, maybe it would be easier if I asked you a few questions about what happened. Are you okay with that or can you continue in your own words what you witnessed?" asked Leo.

As quickly as Stiles had gone some other place, he was back. Another grimace masquerading as a smile accompanied his return to the present.

"I can go on. Bad choice of words, buzz killer. That's what I felt at the time, though. I was just minding my own business working on a buzz before those two ended up in my alley."

"So, let's get through this while I still can. Dude was holding the gun on the kid. Dude said, *'You got something that belongs to me and I suggest you give it back right now.'* Kid said, *'Y'all been short changing me.'* Dude said, *'I don't know what you're talking about.'* Kid said, *'The reefer.'* Dude said, *'You've got me mixed up with somebody else. Now give me that money.'* That's when it all went bad," said Stiles with a slight shake of his head.

"I couldn't see exactly how it happened 'cause it was so fast. One second the dude had the gun right in the kid's face, and the next second they're fighting over it. The kid was quick and did some kind of move. Then the gun went off, and the dude fell backwards. The kid was just standing there looking at him for a second and then he ran out of the alley. I wanted to run, too. My buzz was gone, but I wasn't in any shape to run, though. Instead, I just finished my bottle before the cops got there," finished Stiles.

Leo looked around the room. Sam Adams looked almost serene. The nurse still had her scowl working. Sandy had one eyebrow cocked. The court reporter seemed almost bored.

Leo cleared his throat. "Had you ever seen either person who was in the alley that night?"

"No. I didn't know them, had never seen them before."

"Did you have a clear view of the event despite the lack of lighting in the alley?"

"I could see well enough. About the only good part of my body is my eyesight. 20-20 and never needed glasses. Like I said it was dark, but I was close to them even though they didn't see me next to that dumpster."

"Did you hear either of the men say anything else other than what you've testified to already?"

"That's all. I mean the whole thing was over in less than a minute."

"Did you ever see the young black man with a weapon?"

"When the big white guy fell after being shot, I saw the kid with the other dude's gun. How he got it, I don't know."

"And could you tell who fired the shot?"

"No. All I could tell was they were fighting and the gun went off. The kid was holding it afterwards and ran off with it."

"Did you tell any police officers what you had seen?"

"I told the first uniformed officer and then talked later with a detective."

"Did you or either of those officers put that statement in writing?"

"They never asked me to. Never asked me to look at no lineup neither. I guess they figured they didn't need me. That was fine with me 'cause I didn't want to be involved anyway. People end up dead when they do."

"What makes you say that?"

"Come on man! Drug deals gone bad, who cares, right? You go telling cops about some dealer shooting another and soon that dealer going to be looking for you to shut you up."

"I'm going to object to the last question," interrupted Adams.

"We can discuss that later with the court," said Leo.

Leo turned back to Stiles. The man looked ashen, and Leo didn't know how much longer he should go on. Leo stepped back to where Sandy was sitting and they conferred briefly. He then returned to his original place by the bed.

"Just one more question. Other than the reference to reefer made by the young black man, was there anything else that led you to believe the confrontation was related to a possible illegal drug transaction?"

Stiles thought before answering. "No, I guess not. It was just a feeling."

"Thank you, Mr. Stiles. On behalf of the state, I greatly appreciate your testimony today and hope the best for you in the future. Now Mr. Adams may have some questions for you," said Leo.

Adams got a little closer to Stiles and then looked into the camera. He gave a slight nod and began.

"Mr. Stiles, I would like to join Mr. Berry in thanking you for your cooperation in this case. It is very important to the welfare of my client, Lonnel Murphy, and the seeking of justice.

Since Mr. Berry has asked many of the questions we would have asked and we certainly do not want to prolong this process any longer than necessary, I am going to be brief so we can get out of here and let you rest."

Leo watched Adams and continued to be impressed. His adversary was silky smooth and respectful. Adams had a baritone worthy of James Earl Jones and movie star good looks. This man was definitely going places.

"Could you describe the size difference between the two men you saw in the alley?"

"White dude looked to be at least a half foot taller and weighed 60-80 pounds more than the black kid."

"To be clear, the larger man confronted my client, correct?"

"Yeah."

"With gun in hand pointed at my client?"

"Yeah."

"And, my client had no weapon?"

"No, I mean yeah, the kid had no weapon like I already said."

"And, you don't know how the gun was discharged other than it was during a struggle?"

"That's right."

"Could've been an accident, right?"

"Yeah, it could."

"For all you know, the larger man's finger could've pulled the trigger?"

"Yeah, it could have happened that way, I suppose."

"Or, my client could have been trying to defend himself from a much larger person when that person ended up being shot, right?"

"Yeah, the big dude could have killed him on the spot."

"Thank you again, Mr. Stiles. I believe that's all the questions I have," said Adams.

"No redirect for the state, so we will conclude the deposition at this time," said Leo.

The nurse returned to her patient. She gave him some water and then patted him on the shoulder. They both smiled at one another.

The court reporter turned off the equipment and then Leo and Adams both shook Stiles' hand. Leo knew he would probably not see the man again and felt sad at another homeless veteran dying alone.

"Thank you for your service to this country, Mr. Stiles. I truly hope you will find peace," said Leo.

"I hope everybody does," whispered Stiles.

Leo turned and left the room quickly. He brushed tears away before anyone could see.

CHAPTER 39

Leo sat behind his desk staring at the blank computer screen. The Murphy case was swirling in his mind. The deposition had been helpful in some regards, but now Leo was thinking more about his earlier meeting with the DEA agent. The short conversation that Stiles had overheard between Johnny Thomas and Murphy the night Thomas died at least showed a possible illegal drug connection. There was only a hint, however, and no real evidence. Maybe it was a good time to call Ted Springer and see if they could share more information.

Leo looked in the middle top drawer of his desk and found the cardholder he maintained for contacts. Finding the agent's card without trouble, he punched the number using the middle finger of his right hand. Dee always laughed at him for using the digit she called the bird finger for such activities, and he found himself thinking of his wife as the phone began ringing on the other end.

"Springer here," answered the agent on the third ring.

"Hey, Ted. It's Leo Berry. Got a minute?"

"Just a minute, Leo," said Springer as he covered the receiver and said something unintelligible to someone else.

"Hey, Leo. Sorry, you caught me in the middle of a meeting with some folks. Can I help you?"

"If this is a bad time, you can call me back later. I just wanted to let you know I had a deposition today with a witness in the Murphy case, and there was a reference I thought you might be interested in."

"Hmmm, I'll tell you what, Leo. Why don't we meet for a beer after work? It'll be my treat. I've got a little information to share with you, too."

Leo thought about the offer. It just so happened that Dee and Mindy had volunteered to cook dinner tonight, so Leo did not feel the need to hurry home and help. Besides, there was a little sports bar located between work and home, and he could be home in plenty of time.

"Okay, Ted. How about Jock's around 5:30? Will that work for you?" asked Leo.

"Perfect. See you then," said Springer as the line was disconnected.

Leo hung up the phone and leaned back in his chair. He was stroking his chin and staring at the ceiling when Sandy slipped inside the office unannounced.

"I didn't mean to eavesdrop, but I heard you just then. Is that the DEA agent you're meeting?" she asked.

"Snooping around again, WB? You're as quiet as a church mouse. Better watch out or you might hear something you don't want to. But, yeah. I thought I would tell him about the depo and see if I couldn't get a little more out of him while I was at it. Agree?" said Leo.

"I could find out all kind of stuff if I could hear better, Lil' Leo. But, you're right. You should listen to some of the conversations between the secretaries during the day. They can be raunchy and hilarious or petty and mean. As to whether you should meet with Agent Springer, I'm not sure," replied Sandy.

"I'm glad you said it about the secretaries rather than me. I swear, working around a bunch of women is a trip! Anyway, I'm not sure that even if there was some drug angle to the shooting it makes any difference in our analysis of the case. I'm more than a little curious about the possibility though," said Leo.

"That's part of the reason I came to your office. I just got a call from Sam Adams. He wants to meet with us on Wednesday to see if we can work out a deal. Not to be presumptuous, but I told him we would. I can always call him back and tell him something's come up if you have a problem."

"No. You and I have discussed this enough that I'm sure we both agree. Stiles' testimony did nothing to help us. I'm sure your friend Sam feels like he's got us in as good as a position as he's going to have in order to work out a plea deal for his client. By the way, I like Adams. If I were DA, I would push hard as I could to draft him for the team. He's a little flashy, but he's got a great future ahead of him."

"He's sharp, no doubt about it. All right, no need to call him back. Sam said unless otherwise notified he would be here first thing Wednesday morning. I guess we'll see what he's willing to do. I don't guess I have to remind you of the limit tonight. It wouldn't do your career good to get yourself in trouble," said Sandy frowning.

"Not to worry. I'm only having one and then it's to the house for homemade lasagna. My girls have that one on the agenda and I don't want to be late. Besides, I've got a DEA agent to protect me. I'll let you know tomorrow what comes of the meeting."

Sandy gave her usual unreadable look and left. Leo grabbed his stuff and headed for a late workout. There was time for a run and burning a few calories before heading to Jock's.

CHAPTER 40

Jock's was the typical sports bar. There were multiple television sets throughout the establishment including smaller ones located in the built out wooden booths. The HD reception was outstanding, and with the old wood motif it was as if the new age and the old west had merged into the perfect place for men to hang out. Best of all, the beer was cold and the selection was unbeatable.

Set in an old strip mall with at least half the other storefronts vacant, some might think the bar was seedy. However, Jock's was the opposite and had been the catalyst for getting some of the other new businesses back in the area. Leo had been there a few times with his softball buddies after playing in tournaments and liked it.

Leo walked in and let his eyes adjust. The main bar was large and polished with several men seated on heavy stools. He did not see Springer at the bar and was looking around the room trying to locate the agent when he felt someone poke him in the kidneys.

"You ought to watch out where you go, Berry. Somebody might stick something in your back other than a finger."

Leo recognized the voice and without responding turned around swiftly. Before the other man could react, Leo had grabbed the finger and bent it in an uncomfortable angle.

"Sonofabitch! What 'cha doing, Leo? I was kidding, okay?"

"Sorry, Fletch," Leo said while letting go of the detective's digit. "You should watch out who you're kidding with. I still remember enough from that self-defense course I took a couple of years ago."

Detective Richards rubbed his finger with his other hand and looked warily at Leo. For some reason Leo thought of Papa and a word they had shared a long time past. *Inscrutable*. Leo tried to look inscrutable like Papa had been.

"I never knew you were so touchy, Leo. Really, I was only joking around," said Richards.

"And, I'm sorry. I guess I'm remembering a lesson from my grandfather when I was a kid. Always expect the unexpected, and beware of snakes in the grass," replied Leo.

"Well, okay. You can buy me a beer to show how sorry you are for almost breaking my finger," said Richards.

"Alright, Fletch. But, I'm meeting someone here and I don't have time to socialize."

Richards followed Leo to the bar. A young curly headed bartender resembling one of the Brady Bunch boys came over and took the orders. Richards slouched down on one of the stools, but Leo remained standing. As soon as the beverages were brought, Leo paid and threw down a two-dollar tip.

"Thanks, Berry. Here's mud in your eye. Why don't you at least sit down until your friend gets here?" asked Richards as he swigged.

Leo had already turned away from the detective and was again surveying the other patrons. Springer had not arrived, but Leo recognized a few other customers. He nodded to some guys he knew from the open league where they competed. He also saw a friend who he had played a round of golf with a few months ago. The last group he saw sitting in a corner booth consisted of three other detectives.

Leo turned halfway around so he was facing Richards, but could also see the doorway. He really wanted to get home within the hour and hoped Springer would arrive soon. Leo didn't want to spend his time talking with Richards since he was still sore about the quality of the Murphy investigation and the veiled threats the detective had made.

"No offense Fletch, but I need to get home soon. I'm just meeting a friend for a quick beer and I can't stay. By the way, are those some of your coworkers in the corner?"

"I understand if your little woman won't let you out of the house. That's why I'm in between wives at the minute," said Richards with a sneer.

The detective took another hefty swallow of the beer. When he set the mug down, there remained little more than an ounce of the amber liquid. Leo had not even had a sip of his.

"Yeah, that's some of the other swine waiting on me to join them," Richards added as his cheeks puffed out like suppressing a belch.

"Fletch, I know you probably don't care for my advice, but you really ought to be careful drinking so fast. You've been on the job for a long time and had plenty of occasion to see what it can do to people," Leo said.

"You're right, Berry. I don't care for your advice. My advice to you is to live your life and I'll live mine."

Richards downed the remainder of his beer and motioned to the bartender. Another frosty mug appeared instantly, and Richards took another long pull. Leo finally took a first sip and savored the taste of the locally crafted beer. The detective would easily be on his third one by the time Leo finished his at the rate they were drinking.

"You mind if I ask you something personal, Fletch?"

"Nah, go ahead. I'll answer it or I won't."

"I know you were friends with Johnny Thomas. I was wondering how y'all became buddies," said Leo.

Richards kept his hand on the mug, but at least quit drinking. He turned and looked at Leo through red-rimmed eyes.

"We both drove for the same trucking company a couple of years before I joined the force. That's when we first met. Johnny was happy-go-lucky. Do anything for a friend without complaining. Loved to hunt and fish just like me. Had us some good times before that little shit killed him. I should've taken care of him that night," said Richards.

Leo wasn't sure if the detective was talking about taking care of Johnny Thomas or Lonnel Murphy. Richards finished his second beer and motioned again for the bartender. When the third beer was brought the detective ordered a shot of tequila as well.

"The rumor is you're going to let Murphy go. Is that right, Berry?" asked Richards.

Leo looked at Richards who sat staring at the shot. It occurred to Leo that the detective was not the man he first met when he started practicing law. This man was an out-of-shape, alcoholic, cynical version of his former self.

"I don't know where you get your information, Fletch. Nothing has been worked out, yet. I'll tell you if and when a plea deal is decided. I'll say this, though. The case is far from open and shut like I was led to believe when I agreed to handle it. Part of the reason is the way the investigation was conducted. Now I understand that could be due to your being close friends with Johnny Thomas. And, I'm truly sorry for that loss. I've recently met other members of his family and they miss him, too. But at the risk of repeating what I've said before, I will handle the case the best way I know how. I have to be fair and not base my decisions on emotions. The young Fletcher Richards I knew would know that, too."

Before the detective could respond, Leo saw the front door open and Springer stepped in. He scanned the room and Leo waved at him. The agent walked over and joined Leo and Richards. Leo introduced the two men who appeared to be appraising each other.

"Let me order you something Ted, and we'll get a seat over there," said Leo pointing to a corner booth facing the door.

As Leo and Springer waited for the bartender to return with the order, Richards downed the shot and reached in his front pocket. The detective removed a full money clip, took out a twenty and threw it on the bar.

"See you around, Leo. Good meeting you, Agent Springer," Richards grunted as he left his stool and headed toward the table where his fellow detectives sat.

"Pleasant guy," said Springer.

"Papa always told me I shouldn't be facetious," replied Leo.

Leo and Springer laughed as they grabbed their mugs and walked to the booth earlier pointed out. They sat down and turned the volume down on the TV that was showing a rerun of an old basketball game.

"Thanks for saving me from finishing my beer with Fletch. He's on his third one, by the way, not counting the shot he just downed. I'm afraid the guy has a problem," said Leo.

"No doubt. Thanks for meeting me. I've never been here, but it looks cool," replied Springer.

"Yeah, I like it. I don't go to bars much, but this one is convenient to home and my softball team comes here on occasion."

"I know you want to get home soon. So, you've got some info for me?"

"Really, I don't know that it's very much or even if it's helpful to your investigation. I'm second-guessing why I even called you now. Anyway, I was at a deposition earlier today and interviewed a witness in the homicide case I'm handling. He testified that he overheard the defendant make a reference about reefer. That at least implies Lonnel Murphy was involved in some way selling marijuana and that he believed Johnny Thomas had cheated him in some fashion. In that conversation, Thomas never made any statement that would implicate him and unfortunately he died shortly thereafter. I would've never even thought to call you about this if you had not told me Murphy was wanting to talk to you."

Springer furrowed his brow. Both men took a sip of their beers.

"I never did talk to Murphy, by the way. Murphy's lawyer let me know his client had changed his mind before I had a chance to talk to him," replied Springer.

"I've been wondering whether he backed out. Since the lawyer never approached me about it, I figured Murphy either got scared or didn't think becoming a rat would help him," said Leo.

"I appreciate you sharing the tidbit. It does corroborate other intel I have about Murphy being involved as a low level dealer. I'm afraid it doesn't help me much otherwise, however."

"If you don't mind telling me, how is your investigation going?" asked Leo.

"Confidentially, it's not going anywhere. We're at a dead end. All of a sudden it's like the operation stopped. We have an informant who has told us there is no more of the good stuff to be found. My boss has let me know to shut down in two weeks unless we can come up with new leads," said Springer.

Raucous laughter erupted from the table where Richards and his cohorts sat. Leo and Springer looked over at them, but none of them looked back. An idea suddenly came to Leo.

"I remember you mentioning Johnny Thomas as being a person of interest and that it was because of some of the people he hung out with," said Leo.

"Yeah, none of that really panned out," said Springer.

"By chance, were any of those people cops that Thomas hung out with?" asked Leo.

Springer's eyes narrowed slightly. He answered, "Why do you ask?"

"It would explain some things. Like, a major illegal drug operation would benefit from having friends in law enforcement. Help keep the business informed if the heat was being turned up. Especially if the feds were called in. I'm thinking dirty local cops might be a prime reason for an outside agency being asked to investigate. All speculation, of course," said Leo.

"You're good, Leo. It wouldn't be the first time the DEA was asked to look into possible connections like you are speculating on," he replied.

Leo watched Springer as he spoke. The guy was a real professional and would do nothing to betray his mission. Leo guessed Springer would not give away too much, but if Leo could articulate good assumptions, the agent might confirm suspicions.

"So, have you eliminated a certain detective with a penchant for drinking too much and laughing too loudly as a suspect in such a hypothetical investigation?" asked Leo.

Springer glanced at his watch and took another sip. Leo's eyes never left Springer's face.

"As I said, Leo, you're good. The best I can say is no comment."

Leo couldn't help but grin. He knew that was as far as he could expect to go now. Leo held up his half-full mug.

"Then I'll propose a toast, Agent Springer. To justice."

Springer held up his mug, smiled as well and said, "For all."

Neither man brought up the subject again. The two of them talked about other things for the next fifteen minutes, finished their drinks and occasionally watched the group of detectives.

CHAPTER 41

Pete Thomas got up from his bed and went to his kitchen. Insomnia was an affliction he couldn't shake lately. No matter how tired he felt, a full night's sleep had not been in the cards dealt him since the death of his brother over a year ago.

The big man knew the main problem was that he felt responsible for the killing of Johnny. Guilt was a powerful emotion in the equation, and Thomas knew if he was going to get past the inner turmoil, he somehow had to come to terms with the feelings. Recognizing the problem was easy; trying to deal with it was not.

Maybe it would be easier if he could drink away the guilt or take some kind of pill to make it all disappear, but Pete Thomas would not fall into that kind of a trap. He had seen the affects of that kind of thinking many times over and knew it would only make the problem worse if he tried that route. Johnny's friend Fletch was a prime example of that approach.

There were other things on his mind as well, so Pete couldn't totally blame the sleeplessness over his brother's loss. He had knowledge that others did not possess. Some may suspect, but Pete knew for sure.

Leo Berry the third seemed to be a decent guy. Pete thought under other circumstances they might even be friends. Mickie sure thought a lot of him and his family. Maybe he could trust Leo with some of the information. He had always thought he would share with his sister when she got older, but with every passing year Pete didn't really see the point. Secrets were best kept that way the more he thought about it.

His life could have been so different. Pete remembered his parents and their approach to living. They were so much in love, something he had never experienced. Now that Pete was forty, he didn't expect to ever feel that emotion. It made him angry and sad at the same time. Any women he had ever been involved with just didn't fit his standard, whatever that was. He had not even had so much as a date since Johnny died and that was just messed up.

Why couldn't he be more like Mom and Dad? Loving, carefree hippie types wanting nothing more than to live off the land and to raise their kids. At least their values included letting him and his brother to go their own way. That independence had taken Pete in a totally different direction although Johnny had retained more of their style of living. Little Mickie didn't even remember them. At least she had the influence of their mother's sister during her formative years that helped Mickie to be a caring person.

Pete got a glass of water and walked out on his front porch. The November night was chilly and a cool breeze caused his bare skin to prickle. No sounds could be heard, and it felt like the entire world was asleep but him. He looked up and no moon or stars were visible. The darkness enveloped him as if he had fallen into a black hole.

Was this how death felt? The absence of light had a strange calming effect on his emotions.

At that moment an epiphany occurred, and Pete came to a decision. He was not too old to have a life that mattered. He just needed to make amends for some past mistakes before it was too late.

His sudden clarity came from a word Big Leo taught him as a child. Redemption.

CHAPTER *42*

Leo was up early. He was sitting in his recliner reading Papa's journal. Having read it several times now, he was still surprised when he came across entries that were more illuminating than the first time they were consumed by his hungry eyes. Leo was constantly amazed by the depth and quality of his grandfather's revelations despite him being self-educated. It just proved what Leo already knew. Being smart did not necessarily require formal education.

Some of the entries were so crystal clear that Leo had no difficulty visualizing Papa going through the described event. This was especially true of the wartime experiences. However, other entries were sometimes vague and harder to interpret as to their significance. That was how Leo felt when Papa talked about Gene Thomas. Leo wondered if his grandfather did this sort of distinction consciously.

Leo flipped to a particular passage and read silently.

Gene proposed a joint venture involving the use of hydroponics. I didn't like the idea at first, but he was persistent. He thought that it was the future of farming. He intended to educate his two sons in the techniques and have them join the project as partners. I had spent some time with both of the boys when they were younger and liked them. That ultimately sealed the deal.

Since that was the only mention of such a venture, Leo would ask Pete about it the next time they met. Surely there was some reason for Papa to write down the reference.

Leo then found another entry with a similar theme. It was contained in a reference talking about his daddy, uncles and aunts.

I have loved all my children, but I don't know how well I expressed it. It probably was one of my biggest failures in life.

My greatest times were when I could teach them something. It was most gratifying when I saw my offspring discover some lesson that would benefit their lives. I never tried to control them or their creativity, though.

If Gene Thomas was Papa's first-born child as Leo strongly suspected, was this referring to him as well? Absolutely, thought Leo.

Without warning a flashback occurred. Leo was transported to Papa's old Ford. They were coming back from checking on some rental property, but Leo couldn't remember the significance. They were alone in the vehicle, and Leo felt a special closeness because Papa had asked him to come along.

They talked about habits. How some were good and others were bad. Like moving your body every day was a good habit to develop because an active body was a healthy body. Smoking was a bad habit because you brought something into your body that altered what was natural. Papa urged Leo to dwell on the good habits and stay away from the bad ones if he wanted to live a long time.

Alone in the highway was a beat-up pickup truck. Outside the wreck was a disheveled young black woman holding a baby. Papa pulled up behind vehicle and coasted to a stop.

Papa got out of his car and approached the stranded truck. Leo stayed inside with his window down. He had no trouble hearing the conversation.

"Hey there. You havin' some trouble?"

"Yes suh. This old truck quit on me. I'm tryin' to get down to the bus station."

"Where you goin'?

"Tryin' to get to Albany. That's where my folks live."

"That's a cute baby you got. Boy or girl?"

"Girl, named Misty. Cause she was born on a misty mornin'"

"I like that. You gotta man?"

"I did. But he's mean. I got to get away before he hurts the baby. The truck's his. He's goin' to be lookin' for me real soon."

"I could give y'all a ride, if you want."

"Yes suh. If in you don' mind, I would be obliged."

Papa helped the woman and baby get into his old car. There was a timeworn suitcase and another bag holding the baby stuff. Nothing else was transferred. Papa took care of it.

Leo watched the scene with curiosity. He remained quiet as the woman got in the back seat with her baby. She looked to be an older teenager. He noticed a discolored whelp under her right eye that was bloodshot.

"You got money for bus fare?" Papa asked.

"I think I got enough. I hope so anyway."

They drove in silence for the next few minutes. Leo tried to watch the young woman in the back without being intrusive. It was a failed effort because the woman kept giving looks he was too young to read.

"This is my grandson, Leo," said Papa. "Named after his daddy and me."

Leo gave a nod and tried not to stare. His mouth felt dry as a corn shuck baking in the boiling sun.

The woman/girl looked into Leo's eyes. He was lost. Wouldn't it have been easier to just keep going without stopping? This was a complete stranger Papa was helping. What if her husband found out?

"What happened to your eye?" Leo finally asked.

"Baby daddy got mad at me 'cause Misty was cryin'. She couldn't help it 'cause she got the colic."

Leo couldn't believe somebody would get mad about something like that. It made no sense. He had never heard about a man hitting a woman before.

"That's not right to hit a woman," said Leo.

Papa looked over at his grandson and smiled. He then glanced in the rear view mirror and saw that the woman had started crying.

"You okay back there? Is there anything I can do?" asked Papa.

"I'm just glad you helpin' me and Misty. I ain't never had somebody like you do something like that. Thank you, mistuh."

"You're welcome, young lady. If you don't mind a word of advice from an old man, I say don't look back. It's probably goin' to get a little harder before it gets better tryin' to raise your baby without the daddy, but you've taken a big first step today," said Papa before pausing.

"We can't control all the bad things that we go through in our lives. There are some we can control, though. It's like what Little Leo and me were been discussin' before pickin' you up. Gettin' rid of bad habits and findin' good ones to take their place puts you more in control of your life. If you truly learn from this experience, it won't happen to you and Misty again. Sorry, I don't mean to sound like I'm preachin'. Just part of my nature, I guess," Papa finished.

They rode in silence for the next few miles. Leo watched the countryside out of his window. The more he thought about what his grandfather said, Leo realized that Papa was the smartest man he knew. Leo secretly hoped one day to be like him.

The baby was content in her mother's arms. She had a little smile hidden behind a pacifier in her mouth. The mother looked down on her and felt hope.

For the rest of the journey, Papa and the mother, who said her name was Annie, spoke quietly about her plans to go back to her hometown. Leo listened intently and rarely commented.

They arrived at the bus station, and Papa took the suitcase inside while Leo carried the baby's bag. They followed Annie to the ticket window as she asked about the tickets. When the agent told the price, Papa took out his wallet and paid.

Annie's bus was on schedule and was ready to leave in thirty minutes. She asked Leo to hold Misty while she hugged Papa. The baby opened her eyes and looked at Leo. She spit out her Binky and cooed at the young teen. Leo smiled back.

Leo looked over at Papa and the mother. He saw Papa slip some money into her hand. The young mother who couldn't be much older than Leo hugged Papa again.

"Good luck to you and Misty," said Leo before mother and child climbed aboard.

"You, too, Leo. You're lucky to have a granddaddy like him," she said.

As the bus left the station, Annie waved from her window seat. Papa and Leo did the same and then walked back to the car.

They drove back to the farm, and Leo remembered what Annie said. He did feel lucky.

"You know what, Papa?"

"What's that, Leo?"

"I hope one day I can help people like Annie and Misty."

"I would bet on it if I was a bettin' man. You get things a lot of young people don't. Help others to help yourself is a good lesson for today."

Leo closed the journal and remained in his easy chair. He thought maybe that's when Little Leo had started on the path of becoming a lawyer. Helping people was what he loved more than anything in his chosen profession. And, it all began when Papa stopped and picked up a helpless mother and baby.

Tiki had appeared and was staring at Leo. The dog was sitting up on his haunches while moving his front paws up and down reminiscent of a praying mantis. Leo spoke in Tiki's made-up voice.

"Want to go for a walk before breakfast?" asked Tiki.

"Okay, get your leash," answered Leo.

The dog answered by running to the front door. Leo followed and petted Tiki before fastening the leash. Good habits.

CHAPTER 43

The morning had been fairly typical. Never-ending reports to read, charging decisions to be made, phone calls from disgruntled defendants or other whiny folks wanting something left Leo needing his daily run. He knew some things were coming to a head, and he wanted the calmness that came from exercise to help him through.

As his body settled into the rhythm of music from the mp3 player plugged in his ears, Leo found his usual pace and headed toward the cemetery. It was a good place to run without the concerns of traffic. The rolling hills and the scenic views were peaceful and worked in tandem with the sounds of Alan Parsons to produce almost euphoric feelings.

Sometimes there were other joggers in the area who shared the camaraderie found on lunchtime runs. Typically, there were mourners or sightseers walking around checking some of the more famous tombs. However, today was a little chilly and overcast which could have accounted for the lack of other people in the old cemetery by the river.

Leo didn't notice the lack of other people as his feet led him deeper into the graveyard. He also didn't notice there was an unmarked car following his progress some distance away.

If Leo had noticed either the lack of other folks or the sinister look of the car creeping behind, there would have been little he could do. He was isolated and vulnerable.

The car shortened the distance between it and Leo. When it was no more than fifty feet away, the engine revved and the car shot forward like a two-ton missile.

Up ahead, Leo may not have heard the racing engine had not the song that had been playing through his head ended at precisely the same moment. A split second probably saved his life.

He was startled, but reacted in the only way he could. As the car bore down on him, Leo dove out of the roadway and rolled forty feet down an embankment as the car sped by.

Leo lay unmoving afraid to check for possible injuries. He had never broken a bone in his life and was unsure what it would feel like. Adrenaline coursed through his body, and he was even more afraid that whoever had just tried to run him over might try to finish the job.

Leo could not see any car up top from his vantage point. He sat up and did a quick inspection of his body. Other than a bleeding scratch on his left leg, he found no other injuries. Leo was relieved and stood up. He might be sore later, but now he felt fine and knew he needed to move and find help.

Calculating he was about a mile from the main entrance, Leo began going in the opposite direction than he had been. Rather than staying on the narrow road that ran through the cemetery, he ran at an angle over and around graves.

He had lost his mp3 player during the fall, and Leo listened carefully for the sounds of vehicles. Leo ran as fast as he could and felt his heart pounding in his chest. His mind raced as fast as his heart.

Leo knew people had gotten mad at him before. It was a hazard of the trade for lawyers, especially those who are paid to try and get bad people behind bars. He had stared into the eyes of several whose looks could have killed.

But, Leo had also been threatened when he was in private practice. There had been a nasty divorce case in which Leo had represented the wife. The husband was taken to the cleaners in court as he should have been, and he had promised to hurt Leo one day. That had been years ago, but Leo remembered the guy as he ran through the cemetery. Yeah, the man who had terrorized his wife was crazy enough to do something like run over Leo.

Somebody had followed him for sure. Who? Did somebody know his running routine? It certainly was no secret.

Leo told himself he had become too complacent. From now on he promised to be more aware of his surroundings. It was a lesson Papa had taught him many years before, but evidently he had forgotten because his life was so perfect.

As Leo neared the entrance road, he spotted a couple of other runners. He sprinted toward them waving his hands over his head so they would stop.

"What's wrong? Are you okay?" one of the runners asked.

Leo panted while trying to talk. After a few moments of holding his laced fingers on the top of his head and slowing his breathing, he was able to respond.

"Somebody just tried to run me over in a car. Have you seen a car leave the cemetery?"

"No, but we just got here. Are you hurt?"

"I've got a scratch and maybe a bump or bruise. I think I'm fine. Just rattled right now."

"I've got my cell phone in my fanny pack. You want me to call the police?"

Leo thought about it. There was very little he could report. He didn't get a good look at the vehicle and couldn't even describe anything other than it was a dark sedan. There was absolutely nothing he could report about the driver. He was certain the car would be long gone from the area by now.

"I appreciate the offer, but I am unable to give much description as to the car and nothing about the driver. I have several friends on the force, so I'll call and report the incident later. I don't want to get tied up here right now.

The two runners looked at each other and shrugged. After a few pleasantries they ran off, and Leo headed back to the health club.

Leo scanned constantly for dark sedans, but the ones he saw were not menacing. He suddenly remembered Dee asking him about one in their neighborhood causing him to shudder. Was there a connection?

He needed some protection. It was time for him to start carrying his gun.

CHAPTER 44

The afternoon was a blur. After showering and changing back into his work clothes, Leo hurried back to the office.

He called Shep's extension and asked the investigator for help.

Shep called his former captain at the police department and set up a meeting. Leo, Shep, the captain and another detective met in the police headquarters for over an hour. Leo told them everything he could about the incident.

The major thrust of the questions the police had for Leo concerned those individuals who might have had a reason to cause harm. Leo gave a few names of defendants he had prosecuted over the last few years. He also mentioned the name of the defendant in the divorce case several years past. However, Leo cautioned them he had not felt threatened by any of the people in recent times.

As an afterthought, Leo said the only time recently anyone had come close to saying anything of a threatening nature had come in the form of a voice mail from Detective Fletcher Richards. The officers had given each other looks of displeasure. The captain had wanted to know why Leo had not reported such behavior.

Leo had responded he had known Richards as long as he had been practicing law and that he had not taken the message as anything other than the detective blowing off steam. Leo reiterated he could think of no real threats from anyone in recent memory.

The result of the meeting was a promise by the captain to look closely into the possible suspects Leo had brought up. He also promised to have the precinct commander to heighten patrol in Leo's neighborhood.

Leo had left work early and called Dee to let her know he was going to pick up Mindy from school. Dee had seemed stressed over some project she needed to finish and was grateful for Leo's unexpected help with their daughter.

Mindy had entertained Leo with her tales of school and adolescent crushes. Leo had wished she could stay as innocent as she was at that moment, but knew teenage angst lay ahead in wait.

When Leo and Mindy had gotten home, they had changed into more comfortable clothes. Leo got into his favorite worn Levi's and Mindy into baggy sweats. They had watched an old rerun of Saturday Night Live on TV for a little while, a routine they did whenever possible. Leo loved it when his daughter sat beside him on the comfy sofa. Her laughter at Chevy Chase's land shark routine was infectious. Leo knew such moments were fleeting and took on even deeper meaning after the failed attempt at doing him harm.

Shortly before Dee was scheduled to come home, Mindy retreated to her room to do some homework, and Leo went to the kitchen to prepare dinner. He knew Dee was going to be upset about the close call and wished he didn't have to tell her. Leo knew she would worry, but safety required knowledge and preparation.

Dinner had been delicious. Although Leo had not felt much like eating when he started, the smells brought out the hunger as the food had cooked. The grilled chicken breasts were tangy and creamy from the Italian dressing and goat cheese Leo had used on top. The asparagus had been brushed with virgin olive oil and was super fresh. The potatoes au gratin had been the perfect accompaniment and provided comfort.

Leo had waited until the table was cleared and Mindy had gone back to her room before broaching the subject with his wife. Now, as he lay in the bed hearing Dee's soft snoring, he replayed the conversation in his head.

"Wink, I need to tell you something."

"What is it? Anytime you start a conversation with 'needing to tell me something' it is rarely good news."

"While I was jogging today, somebody tried to run over me in a car. I'm fine, but it was scary."

"Oh my God!" Dee said as she embraced him with all her might.

They had held each other in a fierce hug until Leo eased her away with both his hands. He continued to hold her upper arms and looked into her eyes.

"It's okay, I promise. I reported it to the police and they're going to look into it. I don't want you to worry."

"Don't worry? Are you kidding me, Leo? Was it on purpose? Are you sure it wasn't some idiot who doesn't know how to drive? They're all over the road. A few days ago a kid almost hit me while she was texting. You know I've told you about running in traffic! Especially with that music blaring in your ears. I can't stand the thought of you being hit by a car. Maybe you need to get on a treadmill and forget running on the streets." Dee fretted.

"Honey, you know I'm careful when I'm running. I've been doing it how many years now? Twelve to fifteen at least. Evidently, the car followed me into the cemetery and came up behind me when the driver saw an opportunity where no one else was around. You know I always run facing traffic, but those roads are narrow and I've never even come close to an incident over there."

Dee grabbed Leo again and started crying. He rubbed and patted her back as the sobs continued for several minutes.

"I don't know what I would do without you, Leo. I love you so much. Mindy loves you so much. Your mama loves you so much. Everybody does! I don't know why anybody would want to hurt you."

"Well, maybe not everybody loves me," Leo mumbled more to himself than to his wife.

"Leo, you've got to be careful. I don't want to be a widowed single mother, you hear me!"

Afterward they had made love and Dee fell asleep. Now Leo was alone with his thoughts. What had been fear now was turning into anger. It was dangerous to think in those terms, but he was pissed. Leo had always thought angry people didn't think clearly, and he needed to stay focused. He had too many responsibilities for someone to jeopardize his life and his family's welfare.

He got out of the bed and went to his closet. Leo could barely make out the locked box hidden under a stack of tee shirts received from countless road races. Opening it with a key from a hook behind his neckties, Leo saw the old prized possession from his past. It was the S&W.38 revolver Papa had given Leo when he turned eighteen. It might be old, but it was in superb condition. And, Leo knew how to use it well and use it properly. Papa had made sure of it.

CHAPTER 45

Sam Adams had a grim look on his face when he entered Leo's office. Leo had a similar look remaining from the previous day's event. Only Sandy was in a light mood for the scheduled meeting to discuss a possible plea bargain for Lonnel Murphy. She glanced at one and then the other man.

"You guys need to lighten up a little bit. Who peed on you two's cornflakes?" asked Sandy.

"I don't know if you heard the news," began Adams with a scowl.

"What news are you talking about?" said Sandy.

"I'm talking about somebody attacked my client in the jail. He's in critical condition," responded Adams.

Leo couldn't believe his ears. His first thought was whether there was some link between the attack on him and the one on Murphy.

"Why don't you sit down and I'll get you a cup of coffee," said Sandy. "I know how you like it, and I'll be right back."

Adams sat down in a chair across from Leo. He was more casually dressed than Leo had seen him in the past, but Sam Adams was one of those people who always was put together fashion wise, thought Leo. They sat together in silence until Sandy came back with a steaming mug. Adams nodded appreciation. She sat down beside the defense lawyer, and they exchanged silent concerns.

"Do you know the details of what happened?" Leo finally asked.

"Not exactly. Deputies at the Law Enforcement Center told me there was a fight between two groups of young black inmates. They suspect it was gang related. My client was hit in the head with something and was knocked to the ground and kicked several times. They are reviewing video recordings to try and determine who is responsible, but I was told it is difficult to see who did what."

"I'm sorry, Sam. It's not the first time there has been that type of fight in the jail. I know the Sheriff has been trying to take steps to stop that kind of violence, but those groups are hard to contain when they're determined to address some perceived wrong between them," said Leo.

"Yeah, I know. I feel bad for young people who ought to know better. It's why I chose this path I'm on. I really want to help as many of those kids as I can. I'm thankful I had parents who stayed after my butt when I was growing up. You know,

'There but for the grace of God go I,' said Adams as he sipped his coffee.

"I worry there may be a whole lost generation if they don't wake up and smell the coffee. Pardon the bad pun," said Leo.

All three lost themselves to their own thoughts for a minute while drinking their coffee. The fact was all of them thought alike on the subject.

"Well, I don't even know if we should discuss the possible resolution of your client's case until we find out more about his condition. Probably not appropriate under the circumstances," interjected Sandy.

"I agree it's probably a good idea," said Adams. "I plan to go to the hospital later today and see how he's doing. I've been in touch with his uncle and he'll keep me informed. When I find out something, I'll let you know."

"Okay. We'll hope for the best," said Leo.

Adams got up to leave, but stopped at the doorway. He swallowed something invisible.

"You know the really sad part of this whole thing is I believe Nelly Murphy is innocent. I mean not completely innocent of everything he's charged with, because he's old enough to be responsible for his actions. He never should have taken that money. But, I'll never believe he wanted to hurt Johnny Thomas, and for sure not cause his death. I've talked to him and tried to counsel him many times now. He's just a dumb kid who has made stupid decisions. Now it haunts me that I could've tried harder to get him out of jail sooner. I feel like it's my fault," said Adams.

He turned and left the office before Leo and Sandy could respond. All Leo could think about was karma. Some times it was good, and some times it was bad.

CHAPTER 46

Smokey Green was a nervous man. He was the only black guy in the dark room with three burly white guys he could see.

At least two of them were cops. Dirty cops. Mean dirty cops. There was also somebody behind the three he couldn't see. Must be the boss. Smokey knew he could disappear if they found out he was wearing a wireless mike for the feds. He wasn't sure if that DEA man would show up on time if these guys found it inside his shirt.

They trusted him, though. When he had first started working with these mean dirty cops, they had checked him out. At least, that's what they told him. They had come to him, he didn't go to them. And, they knew everything about him. Knew he had sold dope before. Knew he needed money to pay off some bills. Some gambling debts were past due. Knew he was an ex-con who couldn't find a job. Knew he would jump at a chance to make some real money. And it had been nice for a while. Smokey had made more money than he ever had. He wished he hadn't spent it all.

Smokey had never done anything like ratting somebody out. Lately it had become his only option, though. He hadn't been able to turn over any weed in a few weeks. These men in the dark room had warned him about an investigation and to lay low. His source for the good weed everybody wanted had dried up. He was feeling desperate.

Then that agent Springer had showed up and told Smokey he had some information about Smokey selling drugs again. Smokey got the impression that Springer didn't play, neither. Said he knew one more conviction would mean Smokey was going away for good. Springer was a man of his word, or so he said, and would take care of Smokey if he could deliver the source.

Smokey had to trust Springer. Trust. Hard to do. Especially in this line of work. His sister's boy Nelly had trusted Smokey and that didn't turn out so well. Now he might be dying in a hospital room. The whole mess was a big shit ball and Smokey felt like a dung beetle rolling it around.

One thing about being caught between the devil and the deep blue sea, you have to make a choice, he thought. For the first time in his life, Smokey had chosen to try and do the right thing. It was the least he could now do for his nephew.

"So, how's it going, Smoke?" asked Detective Fletcher Richards.

"Not so good, man. I ain't got no money and I need some bad. My nephew's in ruff shape, too, and the doctor says he'll prolly have brain damage if'n he live," said Smokey.

Richards lit a cigarette. He inhaled and the ash burned bright in the dark room. He then exhaled a huge plume of smoke in Smokey's direction.

"Yeah, I heard the little punk went and got his head busted. Bet you feel like shit about it," said Richards.

Smokey felt a brief flash of anger, but contained it. He knew the detective had a hard on for his nephew and would probably kill Nelly if he had the chance.

"I do. He's just a kid. I never should've brought him in."

"Yeah, I'll leave that alone for now. So, why did you want a meeting?" asked Richards.

"Like I said, man. I need some scratch. I can turn whatevuh you can get me real quick. Evuhbody on the skreet wantin' the good stuff."

"Come here a minute," said Richards.

Smokey felt like his feet were cemented to the floor. With great effort he shuffled in front of the detective. Richards stepped even closer so that his belly touched Smokey's chest. Smokey could smell alcohol on the man's breath over the acrid odor of the cigarette.

"You seem a little nervous, Smokey. Got anything on you?"

Richards suddenly tore open the shirt Smokey was wearing and started feeling around the black man's chest and back.

Smokey shivered involuntarily and then stepped backward as Richards took away his cold paw.

"You think I'm crazy, man! Hell yeah, I'm nervous! Wouldn't you be if the sit-yee-ation was the opposite? Supposin' you were in a dark room wid a bunch of big bruthas? Don't you expect you'd be nervous?"

Richards started laughing so hard his ample stomach bounced like a basketball. This was followed by a coughing fit that left the detective red-faced even in the dim light.

Smokey attempted to close his shirt and hoped the hidden microphone was still attached where Springer placed it. He had promised Smokey that it was the latest technology and almost impossible to detect. He had also promised Smokey that agents would be nearby and enter if imminent danger arose. Since no one had busted into the room, Smokey decided everything must be all right.

"So, can I get any mo stuff, man? I need to start earnin' real soon," said Smokey.

"We got a little problem right now. The feds are nosing around number one. Number two, we are low on supply. Not even sure if our source is still in business. We are planning on reaching out real soon. Should know something in a couple of days. It'll be premium price, though," said Richards.

"You guys know you can count on me, right? I'll hustle that shit and we can make mo money quick. Just let me in, man," said Smokey.

"We'll be in touch. Now get your black ass out of here and keep your eyes open and your mouth shut. And Smoke, don't even think about trying to fuck me over. Dig?"

"I gotcha, man. Just let me in and I'll treat ya right."

Smokey's knees were quivering as he turned to leave. He tried to be cool as he reached the door. He thought any second would be his last as he felt the cool night air bathe his face. It was all he could do not to high step down the street away from the abandoned building.

Two blocks away he got in the dark car that held Springer and two other agents. At least he was alive, but he was still shaking.

CHAPTER 47

With the Murphy case now on at least temporary hold, Leo turned his attention to other matters. First, he called Tim Hines and had a lengthy telephone conversation about the estate. Leo found out that all of the bequests were in the process of being carried out. Everything should be completed by the end of the month.

Fortunately, none of the heirs had fought about anything major. Leo knew this was the exception rather than the rule. It seemed that just about every time Leo had handled those kinds of issues when in private practice, there had been all kinds of fights and hard feelings between family members. Everyone had heard horror stories about families squabbling over money. Leo thought this had to be due in part to Papa's teachings over the course of his life. Also, it didn't hurt that there had been a clause in the will cutting out a beneficiary if the document was challenged.

Leo and Hines also discussed Leo's plans for Papa's farm, and Leo was excited that his lawyer had made headway into the plans he had for the property. If it worked out like Leo hoped, his grandfather's legacy would stand for years and if any redemption was necessary, as Papa had thought, it would certainly be sufficient in Leo's eyes.

Next, Leo called Mickie and left a message on her cell phone that he had some news to share with her and Pete. He asked if they could meet and discuss the latest developments about the case. Leo also said he wanted to return the pictures she had let him borrow and talk about them as well.

Leo then worked awhile at his desk, but his heart was not in it. He had to admit to himself the near death experience had affected him in ways never thought about before. Sure, he had experienced life and death. The birth of his daughter had been a wonderful example of the former. The death of his daddy and more recently the passing of Papa represented the grief of the latter.

The fact was a different point of reference for Leo. He thought of the other times in his life when he had felt close to losing his own life and compared them to the feelings of the most recent event.

The first had occurred when Leo was a kid and thought he could swim better than he really could. Leo had swum with Daddy out to a wooden float in the middle of the VFW Lake.

Leo had wanted to stay on the float for a while and was left behind only after promising not to try and swim back to shore without someone watching him. The temptation to prove his prowess was too strong, and Leo had jumped in and started swimming back when he thought no one was watching.

Panic had struck Leo about halfway back to shore when he developed a cramp in his side. He was going down for the third time and had only been able to cry out a feeble attempt for help when a teenaged girl pulled him up from underneath the dark water.

Leo's second close call was when he was a teen and held a job in a grocery store. An armed gunman had entered the store at closing time and was suspicious from the start. Dressed in a long dark coat, floppy hat and sunglasses in the middle of the night, the man didn't look like a shopper. Sure enough, he wasn't and had stuck a pistol in Leo's side while demanding money from the cashier. Leo could still remember looking down at the silver revolver and seeing the hammer pulled back. Thankfully the robbery didn't result in him or anyone else being shot, but the fear Leo had felt that he could die had never gone away.

In retrospect, Leo thought how all the events had played out in slow motion. Every time had been fearful. Every time he had thought about loved ones even as the event transpired. Every time the proverbial life passed before his eyes. Yet, every time he lived through it. Was there some reason?

It all seemed so random, but somehow planned. Leo's skin felt like a prickly pear as the concepts passed through him. He closed his eyes and could imagine being a part of a parallel universe where the physical and spiritual were one. A place where he could see and speak to those so important in his life but no longer present in this world. Was it real or imagination?

Leo was lost in a trance. Daydream?

He walked across the field of young corn and could see Papa and Rusty in the distance. Leo broke into a run and tried to catch up. As hard as his legs churned, he could get no closer. Papa turned around and waved. Rusty's tail could be seen wagging, and he started silently barking his familiar tones.

Leo wanted to talk to them and tell them how much he loved them both, but the words wouldn't form. Then Leo realized words were not necessary and communication was possible without speaking. All he had to do was think it and it was said. Similarly, if he listened he could hear.

Papa! I need to talk to you.

In time, Leo. You've still got things to do, son.

But, I need to tell you something.

Don't worry so much, I know. I love you, too.

A persistent knocking broke the connection. Leo opened his eyes and saw Sandy standing at his doorway. She looked at him with concern.

"Are you okay?"

"Yeah, I'm just resting my eyes."

"You're not a good liar, Leo. You probably need to take a couple of days off and treat that post traumatic stress syndrome," said Sandy while raising her eyebrow.

"Thanksgiving is coming up and I can wait til then. Let me ask you something since you were a psychology major, WB. Do you think we can communicate with the dead?" asked Leo.

"I swear, Leo. I don't know how you can change a conversation so quickly. I'm telling you, you're suffering from almost getting killed yesterday whether you believe it or not. You ought to take a couple of days and just chill."

"Just answer my question and I'll think about it."

"Well, I'm not sure, but I think maybe it's possible. Now, let me do what some therapists I know do. Flip the question so that now you tell me what you think," said Sandy.

Leo smiled. One of the things he liked about his colleague was that she often took some of the same tactics as Leo tried to do.

"I say, yes. I think that it is possible to communicate with those who have passed over. Not in a conventional sort of way, though. I'm not saying I'm some kind of medium or I believe in Ouija boards or anything like that, but I believe that lately I have had some contact with my granddaddy. I have found comfort in that contact, too. A really peaceful feeling comes over me and somehow I know everything will be all right. So, does that make me deranged or in need of professional help?"

"No, and I didn't mean to imply that you needed help."

"Fair enough. Now did you have a reason for interrupting my peaceful interlude?"

"There you go again, changing the subject," she said and paused.

"Yeah, I've got a status update from Sam on Lonnel Murphy. It's not good. Looks like he's brain dead. The family is deciding what to do even as we speak. Sam said his mother intends to donate his organs."

Leo shook his head. Such a waste. He could only hope some good would come from the bad. The donated organs could be life saving for others. It was a noble idea and redemptive, too.

"You know, I think I'll take your advice and take off the rest of the day. I've got enough time to ride out to the farm and take in a little nature," he said.

"Good answer, Leo. Just take it easy."

"Thanks, Sandy. Sounds like a plan."

Sandy left his office and Leo grabbed the folder with the old pictures. He reached into the right top drawer of his desk and got the .38 he had brought with him to work that morning. It was in a brown suede clip-on holster that fit easily on his belt beneath his sports coat. Leo adjusted the holster to an inconspicuous spot. No one even noticed the hidden weapon as he left.

CHAPTER 48

Before Leo left the parking lot he called Dee. The familiar voice was cheerful as she said she was unavailable and instructed the caller to leave a message. Leo couldn't help thinking of his mother's lament over the way everyone was so tied to technology these days. It was true that no one in his generation much less his daughter's could get by without cell phones and the Internet. As it was necessary to let his wife know his plans for the afternoon though, Leo attempted to sound upbeat and promised to be home in time for dinner.

Leo laid the telephone down on the passenger seat and cranked up the car. Just as he was about to put it in gear, the phone rang. Leo did not recognize the number registering on the screen, but answered on the second ring.

"Leo Berry."

"Hey, Leo. It's Pete Thomas. I heard from Mickie that you wanted to meet with us."

"Oh, hey Pete. I'm glad you called. Yeah, I would like to see y'all today if you have time. In fact, I'm headed over to the farm right now if you're available."

"This afternoon works for me, but I'm afraid Mickie is tied up at work. Why don't you come by my place before going to the farm? Just drive by Mickie's trailer and I'll leave my gate open. You'll go through a wooded area before getting there. Okay?"

"Sure, I can do that, Pete. It'll probably take me about forty-five minutes to get there."

"See you then, Leo," Pete said as he disconnected.

It was a short conversation and Leo thought it a little odd Pete had suggested meeting at his place. At least it would be private and provide an opportunity for Leo to talk openly, though.

Leo put the car in drive and jacked up the radio. He always listened to one of six preset satellite channels. Most of his favorites were rock based although he liked one that was acoustic and one that had soul music from the 60's and 70's. If a song came on that Leo didn't really care for, he would change to another channel until he found something that would cause him to sing along. He had long ago discovered he liked older music than most of the stuff being churned out today. Leo was very thankful his parents had listened to the same music when he was a kid and it remained important to him. Before leaving the parking lot, he was already singing along with Otis Redding making him happy.

The day was cloudy and cool. As Leo drove, he thought of similar days when everybody in the family called him Little Leo. For years the time around Thanksgiving had been centered on Papa and the rest of the Berry clan. Although a big turkey dinner would always be a part of the celebration, Leo remembered there was fresh pork sausage because Papa, Daddy and his uncles would butcher a couple of hogs during the cold snap. It was brutal to watch, but the meat was delicious.

Leo thought about the first time he witnessed a hog being killed. Uncle Jim walked calmly to the pen with the rifle pointed downward as the trusting animal came close. It seemed nonchalant the way his uncle brought up the barrel and fired a single shot into the hog's brain. The animal was dead before it hit the ground.

He wanted to turn his head and not watch. But, he couldn't. If Daddy saw him flinch Leo was afraid he might think he was a baby and make him go inside the house. Leo watched as all the men hoisted the hog onto a wooden trailer hitched to Papa's tractor and then returned to the pen to harvest another one.

Leo's older cousin, Hank, begged Uncle Jim to let him shoot the next hog. What followed became a nightmare for awhile in Leo's life. Not as bad as the rattlesnake incident had been, but significant for a long while in the boy's life.

Hank took aim, but when he fired the rifle, the bullet went into the snout rather than the upper forehead. The hog immediately began squealing and running around frantically. Uncle Jim began cursing as he, Daddy and the rest jumped into the pen. It took all of them manhandling the hog before it could be finally killed with the use of a heavy hammer.

The hog was hoisted onto the trailer along with the first one and driven to an area where the animals were gutted and cleaned. This was accomplished with the aid of a wooden platform resembling a gallows and a large metal tub containing water heated by a wood fire.

All the men worked together with razor sharp utensils to get the meat ready for packaging before the day turned warmer. Their white aprons where soon bloody. Breath plumes danced in the cold air as Papa and his grown sons' tandem efforts progressed through the late November morning.

Later in the day after the carcasses were butchered, hams hung in the smokehouse. Unusable parts of the hogs were in galvanized silver wash pots to be taken into the woods for scavengers to feed upon. Grandma and the other women were busy making sausage and wrapping other cuts to divide among the family.

Leo walked around the pen containing other hogs eating dried corn and slop. He cringed when he realized that one day these animals would meet a similar fate. Little Leo wanted to cry over their future.

Papa came up behind Leo without the boy knowing it. His freshly scrubbed calloused hand tussled Leo's hair. Leo looked up into Papa's blue eyes and his grandfather smiled.

"Well, Leo. Did you learn anything today?" asked Papa.

"I guess so, Papa. I know we eat meat everyday, but I've never thought about how we get it. I was thinking that these pigs are going to have to die, too. And, the chickens in Grandma's pen. And, those cows in the field down the road. It makes me sad."

As his grandfather did on other occasions when he talked to Leo, he knelt down so he was eye to eye with his grandson. His weathered face never changed as he spoke, but Leo felt compassion in the voice.

"It's all a part of a grand plan, Leo. I don't pretend to understand it all, but those animals are part of it. They serve a purpose that helps us live. If you think about it, the plants we grow do the same thing. Maybe it doesn't look the same when we harvest them, but their lives provide us nourishment as well. We're not killin' just to be killin' because that is wrong, Leo."

"I don't think I could ever kill anything, Papa."

Big Leo smiled again at Little Leo. He then looked into the distance and didn't respond to his grandson for a long moment. When he looked back at Leo, Papa had a different look in his eyes that the boy did not understand at the time.

"I've discovered we all have to do some things in life we may not want to do. I'll pray to the Great Spirit that you're never faced with havin' to kill something, Leo. But, I'm goin' to say this and hope you always remember. If anything or anybody ever means you harm and you feel you've got to protect yourself or anybody else needin' your help, don't feel bad if you have to kill. In the meantime, maybe you aren't cut out to take place in this ritual every year. It's okay."

Leo had not thought about that day since childhood. That had been probably thirty years ago, but the memory had been revived during a car ride to the farm. Was there some reason?

CHAPTER 49

Leo slowed the car as he passed the farm. Everything looked the same and in order. It would be looking different soon enough if the plans he had fell into place. A fitting tribute to Papa was what Leo wanted.

Down the road he drove until Leo saw the Thomas mailbox. The tires on the Camry crunched the gravel as it turned onto the long driveway and continued past Mickie's trailer. Leo glanced at the residence, but her car was not present. Now that this property was hers, Leo wondered if she would want to build a house.

Leo stopped the vehicle as he came upon the entranceway to Pete's place. There was a thick stand of woods and the driveway was nothing more than a path barely wide enough for his car to pass without being scratched by thick underbrush and overhanging limbs. Leo felt a sudden urge not to travel down the path, but he longed to have a heart to heart conversation with Pete and had told him he was on the way.

Leo crept along the path and thought of being swallowed by the forest. Finally he came to a gate stretching across the way. It had been swung open which allowed Leo to drive through without trouble. He could not help but question the need for such security way out here in the middle of nowhere.

When Leo emerged from the wooded area he felt as if he had found an oasis in the desert. There was a rustic cabin and an impeccably landscaped yard complete with an old well that was pleasing to the eye. He saw several colorful birdhouses mounted on trees. Parked right in front of the cabin was Pete's customized black pickup truck, and Leo noticed how it gleamed even in the muted light. The total effect was surprising and not what Leo would have expected.

Leo got out of the car with his file in hand and walked toward the cabin. Just as he neared the front porch, Pete came from around the right side of the house. He was dressed in jeans and a faded chambray shirt with the tails out past his waist. Well-worn work boots completed the ensemble. Leo in his dress slacks, starched shirt, sport coat, tie and loafers felt out of place.

"Welcome to maison Thomas," said Pete with a mock French accent.

"Thanks, Pete. I didn't know you spoke French. This looks pretty cool. I don't know what I expected when I started down your driveway, but it wasn't this. Did you do all this yourself?" asked Leo.

Pete smiled and walked to Leo. They shook hands and Leo smiled back.

"Let's just say I know a few French words that I learned from my father. Mainly curses because that's about all he used the language for when I was a kid. Yeah, I did all this with a little help from my brother and sister. It ain't much, but it's home."

"Well, I'm impressed. I've never been very handy, so I could never accomplish something like this," replied Leo.

"Thanks. I guess you could say landscaping is a hobby of mine. You should see it in the spring when the grass is green and the azaleas are in bloom." Pete said before pausing.

His facial expression changed slightly. Sadness, maybe regret, thought Leo.

"Johnny and I did it for awhile to make money when we were younger. I've even thought about doing it full-time when I leave law enforcement. Work on my farmer tan all the time. I still have a few of my regulars that I do stuff for. We came up with the name Lawn Dawgs way back when and I have a magnetic sign I stick on the side of my truck when I do that work."

"Well, you can count on me as a customer if you decide to make a career change. My wife and I hate yard work," said Leo.

"I guess that means you won't be working in the fields next door when it's time for planting," said Pete.

"You can count on that, Pete. I don't think I got any of Papa's genes. Actually, I don't think any of my close kinfolks retained that desire. At least, I'm not aware of any."

Pete's face did not betray any thoughts. Instead he changed subjects.

"That file have something I'd be interested in?" asked Pete.

"I think so, but I wanted to give you the latest news on the Murphy case first."

"Okay, why don't you come inside and I'll get us something to drink."

Pete went up the few steps to the porch with Leo right behind. They entered the residence and Leo was as equally impressed with the inside of the cabin as he was with the exterior. The openness of the space had the effect of making the cabin seem much larger than Leo had originally thought.

His attention was drawn to the stone fireplace with a substantial wooden mantel. Sitting atop the mantel was a painting of a beautiful young woman. Leo recognized the face at once. It was the same as the picture in the file he held. Georgine, Papa's first love, was the focal point of the room.

Leo had never described anyone as such, but this woman was enchanting. Leo was not aware how long he stared at the painting. He only knew that he was lost in Georgine's eyes when Pete said something that Leo didn't understand. Leo turned toward Pete who stood at the refrigerator across the cabin.

"Did you hear me? I've got soft drinks, beer, and bottled water. I've also got the coffee pot ready to brew, too. What would you like?" asked Pete.

"Uh, if it's no trouble, I wouldn't mind a cup of coffee with cream, no sugar," replied Leo.

Pete flicked a switch and the rich smell of a Colombian blend soon filled the cabin. Leo turned back to the picture and stepped closer. He was not well versed in art, but the portrait was captivating oil on canvas rendering.

After a couple of minutes Pete walked over to where Leo stood. He held out a steaming mug that Leo accepted. The taste was exquisite as it smelled.

"Why don't you sit down and we'll talk awhile, Leo."

Leo sat down on one end of a comfortable overstuffed couch and set his coffee down on a coaster located on a nearby table. Pete took a seat in a large recliner opposite the couch.

"I see you've been admiring the portrait. My brother actually painted that. He was a talented guy in a lot of ways," said Pete.

"I've never understood how anyone can paint or do anything else artistic. I guess you're either born with those genes or not. Did he leave behind other works?"

"A few. Mickie has them at her place. Johnny never stuck with anything very long. It was like once he did something well, he went on to something else. He was a restless soul, kinda like our daddy."

"The picture is of your grandmother, right? I've seen that same pose in an old black and white photo that Mickie let me see. In fact, I have the picture in this file folder."

Pete took a long sip of coffee while looking at Leo over the mug. A pregnant pause followed as he set the cup down.

"Leo, I'm going to be completely honest with you. The subject of my family's history and how it became entwined with Big Leo has always been a huge thorn in my side. In some ways it was even more of one for my brother. I've only started getting past some of it since Johnny's and Big Leo's deaths. I could never get many straight answers from my parents, and the complete truth died when they did. I'll tell you what I know though, if you start first and tell me what you know."

It was Leo's turn to take a gulp from the mug. Truth. What did he know and what was speculation?

"Okay, Pete. You're a smart guy and I wish I had gotten to know you when we were kids. You're a little older, and I bet you would have been my favorite cousin. That's one conclusion I've come to since Papa's death," said Leo pausing.

"The beautiful girl in the painting is Georgine Thomas who reminds me of Mickie, by the way. I think the cheekbones and mouth cause me to say that. Papa met Georgine during the Normandy invasion. I know that because Papa's journal says so. For whatever reason, the journal was left to me and as far as I know, nobody else has ever seen the contents."

Leo almost felt like he was giving a closing argument before a jury of one. He had thought this through more than once and was determined to get a verdict that spoke the truth. It was what he did in every trial he had ever handled.

"Papa saved Georgine's life the day he met her. In one very brief happy and sad moment of time, they fell in love. They lost their innocence together, and then they were tragically separated in a world gone crazy.

"That one act of love would haunt Papa the rest of his life. He never found her although he looked with determination after the war was over. She vanished like a dream.

"He came back home and made a new life for himself. By all appearances, Leo Berry, Sr. was a success in that life. He met my grandmother and they had raised their kids."

Leo got up from his seat and began to pace back and forth. It was a nervous habit that he often fought against when in a trial.

"Years went by and then your father, Gene Thomas, showed up here. Much to the dismay of my grandmother and possibly other members of the family, Papa became close to him. I believe that was because Gene produced a birth certificate showing he was the son of Georgine Thomas.

"Now I don't know if or why Papa ever acknowledged this to anyone because the journal does not specifically say, but I also believe with all my heart that Papa was the father of your father. A strong case can be made in that regard based simply on appearances. Old pictures of Papa and your father are quite compelling. I note that you have some of the same characteristics, too.

"However, for whatever the reason, Gene Thomas remained an outsider to everyone else in the family except to Papa.

"In Papa's own way, he attempted to make it up to his first-born by going in business with him. As I've thought about this, I realized that your daddy was more like Papa than any of his other kids. All the rest wanted to leave the farm as quickly as they could. Gene Thomas chose farming as a living."

Leo stopped and walked over to the table. He picked up the mug that now contained a tepid reminder of the hot liquid it once was. Leo drained it before setting the empty container back down. He glanced at Pete who had a blank stare into the fireplace.

"Shall I continue? Am I making sense?" asked Leo.

Pete turned his head back to Leo. He opened his mouth, but nothing came out.

"I'll go on then until you tell me to stop," said Leo.

"Based on other conversations we've had, I've come to another conclusion respecting family history. That is, the failure to claim Gene Thomas as Papa's son caused problems in your family. I certainly do not have your total perspective and I would have to bend to your opinions and observations to change my conclusion," Leo said looking into Pete's eyes.

"It all came to a head the night your parents died in the fire. Here I have to depend a lot on speculation and limited information that was provided to me by my uncle. That's due to Papa not writing much about the event in his journal. I really think he meant to, but I think it must have been too painful.

"I know Papa was there that night. I know you and Johnny were not because y'all were in the service. Mickie was there but too young to remember what happened. My Uncle Jim came to the scene and found Papa holding her as the home was engulfed in flames. According to my uncle, Papa was in total shock and kept saying, 'I should've done more. It's my fault.' Whatever he meant, Papa never told Uncle Jim. As far as I know, nobody else knows anything else about that night."

"Stop, Leo."

Pete got up from his chair and walked slowly across the room. His normally rigid form was slumped like he carried a heavy load on his back. Leo followed wanting to finish his thoughts, but did not out of respect.

The larger man stopped at the kitchen sink and picked up a glass out of a wire rack. He filled the glass with water from the faucet and drank half of it. Pete then opened a cabinet and took out a bottle of aspirin. He popped two in his mouth and drank the remainder of the water. After placing the glass in the sink, he went to the nearby table and sat down heavily.

Leo sat at the end of the table to Pete's left. Although not directly across from Pete, Leo observed and remained silent. The pain behind Pete's eyes was noticeable.

"I've said it before. You're a smart guy, Leo. I wish it could have all been different, too," Pete finally said.

"Do you want to talk about it?" asked Leo.

"I'm going to try, but let me do this my way, okay? I don't want to feel like I'm on the witness stand or that I'm talking to a psychiatrist."

"Okay, Pete. I know I have a tendency to make some people think that way, and I need to work on not doing that."

"I've been bottled up about it for a long time. I'm just coming to terms with my feelings. Guilt. Anger. Jealousy. All of those emotions have affected me and made me who I am. At least who I was, because I want to change. I need to change. I don't want to end up like Daddy and Mama and Johnny. So, I think I need to tell somebody about me, and it looks like maybe you've been elected."

Leo nodded more to himself than to Pete. People had often confided to him over his lifetime and he wasn't sure why. Leo hoped it was because he was a good listener as well being trustworthy with others' most private thoughts.

"What you've said today is pretty spot on, Leo. Daddy and Mama did argue about Big Leo. Johnny and I heard them several times when we were little and it scared us. Not because the fights were violent, but because most of the time they agreed about everything. If I asked Daddy about the arguments, he would only say, 'It's complicated.' Mama would say, 'Ask your daddy.' So, it was frustrating. I don't think they ever understood how left out Johnny and I felt. It only got worse when we couldn't see Big Leo anymore."

"As time went on Daddy did tell me and Johnny some about his past. He said he was born in France, but was raised in

Canada by a couple of distant relatives who treated him as their own. He never knew they weren't his parents until he was grown and they told him the truth. His birth mother was Georgine Thomas who died giving birth to him. His father was a soldier from Georgia named Leo Berry. At least that's what Daddy said they told him Georgine had said. You're the lawyer, but I call that triple hearsay. Certainly it was not the best evidence.

"Anyway, Daddy told us he was able to find Big Leo with the help of the VA and decided to come down south to meet him. I guess it must have been a shock to Big Leo and his wife, but I never understood why Daddy couldn't be seen as his son. My reaction was the same as Mama's had been, Daddy should have the name and be a part of the family. But, Daddy never seemed bitter and seemed to accept the relationship as it evolved."

Pete stopped talking and looked across the cabin to the portrait. He sighed and began again.

"I can't describe why or how my feelings changed toward Big Leo after Daddy finally told me he was my granddaddy. He had never done anything to me when I saw him except to be kind, so I had those good memories. But, I started to resent him and that resentment came close to being hate after my parents' death.

"What you've told me today is the most I've ever heard about what happened, and I'm still unsure of the cause. I've studied the incident report that was made by the Sheriff's office and it is vague. It lists Big Leo as the only witness and his statement says he heard an explosion from the kitchen area as he was talking to Daddy outside. According to the statement, both of them ran inside with Daddy going toward the fire and Big Leo running to the baby's room. Big Leo said he grabbed Mickie and ran outside as the trailer filled with flames and smoke. He claimed he called for my parents, but they never answered."

Pete's eyes had become red-rimmed, but tears did not fall. His mouth quivered slightly as he hung his head. His voice lowered, and he did not look at Leo when he began again.

"I couldn't believe it when my lieutenant told me and Johnny we had a pass to go home for my parents' funeral. Johnny and I had joined the Army at the same time, and we were in training at Fort Benning. I guess we were somewhat lucky we weren't overseas or somewhere else not as close to home.

"Not many people came, but Big Leo was there. He tried to talk to Johnny, and me but we wouldn't let him. It was all I could do not to hit him. I told him in no uncertain terms I didn't want anything to do with him ever again. I can still see the hurt look in his eyes, and it made me feel good at the time."

Pete looked up at Leo again.

"I know now I hurt myself as much as I did him. I've got a bucket full of regrets because the man was trying to help. Maybe he didn't do things like I wish he had, but family secrets were too strong. Damned family secrets! I'm tired of them, Leo."

Leo cleared his throat. The emotions conveyed gnawed at him, but he knew there was only so much he could understand because he had not lived through the memories Pete had. That was the thing about sympathy that could be tricky.

"I can only say in deepest sincerity I am sorry, Pete. I know I can't possibly understand what you and your family lived through. As much as I can though, I want to try and make it up. I can't speak for all of the Berrys, but as far as I'm concerned, you and Mickie are members of the family. I believe that's what Papa would want and it's what I want, too," said Leo.

At that moment the front door swung open. Three men walked in. Leo wondered why in the hell Fletcher Richards was here.

CHAPTER 50

"Well, well. Look who dropped in for a visit," exclaimed Richards.

Leo looked at the detective and then back at Pete. Pete's eyes narrowed as his stare was directed at Richards. All three intruders carried automatics in their hands.

"What the hell you mean coming into my house uninvited?" said Pete.

"You know we're old friends, Pete. I used to come over with Johnny all the time back in the day," Richards said through a sly grin.

"Johnny's been dead over a year, Fletcher. And, you were friends with him, not me," replied Pete.

Richards' eyes were squinted, glassy marbles. His face was flushed, and Leo noticed that he rubbed his shoulder constantly with his free hand as he spoke.

"A brother of a friend is a friend as well. At least that's how I've always looked at it," said Richards.

Pete stood up with his hands clinched into meaty fists. His imposing figure caused all three men to raise their weapons and point them at Pete.

"I suggest you sit back down where you were, Pete. I've got a few things to discuss with you and since the prosecutor is here, I've also got some things to talk with him about, too. Both of you keep your hands where we can see them. I sure wouldn't want to think that either of you would cause us any harm," said Richards.

Pete hesitated for a moment and then sat down. One of the men with Richards crossed the room to where Pete and Leo sat. Leo smelled the odor of cigarettes and sweat coming from the beefy body of the man as he first patted down Pete. From under the chambray shirt the man pulled out a Glock that Pete must have been carrying. Leo had not noticed before that there was a concealed weapon. He thought about his own .38 attached to his belt and its location. Leo hoped if the man checked him it would go undiscovered since Leo had it hung toward the back of his right hip.

"Now, that's a man always prepared for the unexpected. Johnny always said that about you, Pete," said Richards.

Pete glared at Richards as the man conducting the search put the confiscated gun in his coat pocket. Cig breath then walked around the table to Leo, reached into his sports coat and felt down his rib cage. Then he patted Leo's hips. Leo held his breath as the man's hand went right past the area where the revolver rested.

"And that's a man never prepared for danger," said Richards as the accomplice raised a hand signifying nothing had been found.

"What are you doing, Fletch?" Leo asked.

"Securing the scene, Leo. Don't worry so much. We'll talk in a few minutes. By the way, I heard you took a nasty little fall the other day," he said with a sneer.

"Not nearly as bad as the one you're going to take, Fletch. If I were you, I'd make myself scarce as fast as I could."

The detective started massaging his shoulder again. He did not look well to Leo.

"In due time, Leo," said Richards and then turned towards Pete.

"Now, Pete. I got a few questions for you. First, do you know what happened to the contents of the storage shed?"

Pete looked ready to explode. His fists were still clinched on the table in front of him. Leo knew he would have to act quickly if things got out of hand.

"What storage shed are you talking about? There are storage sheds all over this county. If you haven't noticed there are hundreds if not thousands of the damned things," Pete hissed.

"Don't be a wise-ass, Pete. You know there's only one I care about. The one Johnny kept under lock and key. The one I also had a key to. The one when I just checked is now empty."

Richards looked over at Leo and grinned. He was enjoying the torment too much thought Leo. The gun he held was pointed toward the floor of the cabin, but there was no way Leo could get to his first before Richards and the others would have clear shots at Leo and Pete.

"Believe it or not, Fletch, I was not my brother's keeper," said Pete.

Richards glanced back at Pete maintaining the same wolfish grin. The grin became more of a grimace as he started rubbing his shoulder once again.

"How well I know that, Pete. I also know you didn't exactly approve of my friendship with Johnny," said Richards.

"When did it all go wrong, Fletch? How did you turn into what you are now? I should've stopped all of it long ago, but I let Johnny down and you led him down the wrong path," said Pete.

Richards started laughing until he started coughing. It was a rattle that sounded as if parts of the lung were being torn loose. When he stopped every eye was on him.

"That's real funny, Pete. You are a sanctimonious prick. Don't tell me you never tried the killer weed your daddy originated all those years ago. I can tell by your look that you didn't know I knew that, right? Well, Johnny told me lots of little secrets about your family. That's because he trusted me, and because I treated him more like a brother than you did," said Richards with a sneer.

Richards turned back to Leo. With any luck, Leo could see the big man have a fatal heart attack.

"Yeah, Berry. I know some of your secrets, too. Like you and Pete and cute little Mickie are cousins. Johnny, too before that little shit killed him. Johnny told me all about Big Leo's kin years ago although his brother here didn't want to tell anybody. You know what I think? I think it's fucked up just like you not wanting to do the right thing in the case. No matter, now," said Richards.

Richards' face had turned a scarlet color. Smoke would be coming from his ears if he were a cartoon character.

"Yeah, since I know all these secrets I guess I must be a part of the family. Families stick together, right? So, Pete, what happened to the rest of the stash Johnny and me had?" asked Richards.

A calmness had come over Pete that made Leo think of Papa. Leo tried to channel the same attitude by slowing his breathing.

"I'm going to tell you what I know, Fletch, and then you can do what you want. Maybe you and Johnny were closer than we were. I take responsibility for that, and I wish I could go back and change it. I've learned that you can't live in the past. If you do, you have no present and you have no future.

"In a way, I'm grateful for the friendship you and Johnny had. You were there for him and helped him in ways I didn't. I knew you guys were having fun and I admit I was a little jealous, but I felt like someone had to be the grownup and that was me since I was the oldest.

"There's not much that goes on in the county that I don't know, so I knew Johnny was experimenting with some seeds he found that belonged to our daddy. When it first started, he said it was only for him and a few friends. He promised me to never sell the stuff.

"We both knew that Daddy was a free spirit, and I saw a little of that same streak in Johnny. Maybe that's why I didn't do more to stop him. I'll tell you this, I still miss that man and he's been gone more than twenty years now.

"Daddy used to tell us that one day marijuana would be legal, and he would produce the best product in the whole country. We would all be rich and wouldn't have to break the law to do it. Until then he only wanted to cultivate enough so he could experiment and improve what would be his brand. We helped him and used hydroponics and other technology to develop it."

Pete stopped talking and looked at Leo. Even in the dangerous setting, Leo was riveted to the new revelations.

"My granddaddy, who was known to Leo as Papa, provided the financing for those experiments. Of course, Daddy didn't tell him what we were doing. At least, not that part. We were using the techniques to grow a lot of different crops, and they were working well, too. My specialty was tomatoes," Pete said with a sad smile.

"It all came to a screeching halt when our granddaddy found out what was going on. Big Leo and Daddy had a huge argument about it, and Daddy stopped. He put the seeds away in a safe place and soon after that he died without ever seeing his dreams come true.

"So, fast forward until a couple of years ago. I started hearing about some new weed being produced around these parts. The first chance I got I asked Johnny what he knew about it and he gave me the line about experimenting. He said he had the same dream as Daddy and started pointing out how attitudes in some parts of the country had changed.

"Maybe I was blind, maybe distracted by working long hours with the county and trying to maintain my side lawn business. Maybe I took off my safety goggles because I trusted that Johnny wouldn't do anything to put himself in jeopardy. Whatever the reason, I didn't take steps to protect him from harm's way.

"Evidently you convinced him to take his experiment to the next level, Fletch. That's on you.

"Then Johnny died. I've been struggling since. I've felt every emotion, but guilt is the worst. Finally, I came to the conclusion that to atone for that guilt, I needed to seek redemption. Ironically enough, I remembered learning that word when I was a kid. My granddaddy, and I'm starting to think of him that way because of Leo, taught me about it."

Pete paused and looked around the room. No one had moved a muscle since he had started his monologue.

"Redemption. The only way I could think to find it was to take away the source that led to Johnny's death. I won't lie, Fletch. For awhile I thought of taking you out since in my tortured brain I felt it was your fault for taking Johnny's dream and perverting it somehow. The more I thought about it, I realized it centered on the plant that has caused so much pain in my family. So, I did what I felt I had to do to find my redemption. I looked everywhere I could think of and found the stash. I emptied the shed and burned everything in a fire out back," Pete said.

"You did what! That was mine! My ticket out of this shitty place! You had no right to do that, Pete," screamed Richards.

"I had every right, Fletch. I turned my back way too long before Johnny died. You know better, too. We've both been on the job almost twenty years, and we can't pick and choose the laws we enforce. I know the feds have been sniffing around the county, and it was only a matter of time before you would be caught. You ought to be grateful," replied Pete.

"You're just like your pantywaist cousin sitting there. All high and mighty and thinking you're better and smarter than everybody else. Nothing like the man your brother was. Yeah, I had to convince him we could make some money, but Johnny understood all right. He knew we would make more in a night than you do in a month. Johnny was a dreamer like me," said Richards.

"Not all dreams are good," said Pete.

The two men who were with Richards started to appear uncomfortable. They were whispering to each other behind the detective and had retreated closer to the front of the cabin. Richards walked to their location and turned away from Pete and Leo to address them. Leo saw an opportunity to ease his right hand off the table. He quickly pulled the revolver from the holster and laid it in his lap out of sight. He then placed the hand back on the table.

Pete watched Leo and gave a slight shake of the head. Pete mouthed silently, *not yet.*

Leo felt the men were trying to decide what to do with him and Pete. If they were going to resort to deadly force, Leo wanted to be in a position to at least put up a fight. Surprise was Leo's greatest ally, and the .38 was not near enough without that element. Time had started to slow down, and his senses tingled.

Richards turned back to face Pete and Leo. The grim appearances of the two men behind the detective only heightened Leo's awareness.

"Give me Pete's gun," Richards said.

The man who had originally taken the Glock from Pete fished in his coat pocket and held it out to Richards. Richards then placed his weapon in its holster and hefted Pete's gun.

Walking back closer to the table, Richards placed himself in a straight line between the other two men and Pete and Leo. Leo felt a slight advantage and formulated his plan.

Richards was looking at Pete when he started talking again.

"I'm sorry you couldn't have been a better brother, Pete. Of course, you've been eaten up with grief since Johnny died. It will be easy for folks to understand how upset you were when your cousin showed up at your house. So upset you lost your cool and killed him right here. Then you realized what you did and couldn't stand yourself, so you shot yourself in the head, too. Tragic how these family squabbles end up sometimes, don't you think?"

"You've lost your mind, Fletch. It's going to be bad for you," said Pete.

Those last words of Pete came out super slow. Richards chambered a round still looking at Pete as Leo pulled out his pistol. By the time Richards turned to point the weapon, Leo fired a single shot into the detective's head. Richards dropped on the wooden floor like a sack of Vidalia onions on a shipping crate.

Pete flipped the large wooden table on its side and ducked behind with the dropping of the dead detective. The other two men were stunned, but then started firing rapidly in the direction of the table. Little did they know the table had been hewn from wood that could repel their efforts.

Leo jumped behind the table, but not before getting nicked by a splinter that struck him in the forehead. He felt the warm blood stream down his face, but there was no pain associated with the wound.

He watched in amazement as Pete reached down around his ankle and removed a small automatic pistol. Pete then chambered a round and looked at his cousin.

Part of Leo was mortified by the actions just taken. Part of him was plain scared from the prospect of dying.

The two men stopped shooting, and Leo had no idea how many times they had fired their weapons. The sound had been deafening in the small cabin and his ears were still ringing. Pete took a position on one end of the overturned table, and Leo got on the other end.

"Listen up, guys! Y'all better get out while the gettin's good. Slide your weapons on the floor away from you and assume the position on your stomachs. It's your last chance!" shouted Pete.

Leo peeked around his side of the table. Remarkably, the two men were standing exposed in the same position near the front door as before. Smoke and the smell of cordite hung in the room. They had their guns pointed toward the table and didn't act like they intended to comply with Pete's request. That was confirmed when a barrage of shots were made at Leo's end of the table.

As Leo ducked behind the table again, he saw Pete roll past his side of the barrier one rotation with his arms extended in front of him. Once again time slowed down and Leo saw Pete fire several shots in the direction of the men. He only heard one shot fired back in Pete's direction. Then all shooting stopped and groans became the only sounds. And the sirens in the distance.

CHAPTER 51

A few weeks passed, and life was getting back to a reasonable sense of normalcy. At least that's how Leo looked at things as he sat in the middle of organized mayhem otherwise known as Christmas at the Berry home.

Leo loved the scene. While he held a seat in one of the leather chairs of his mother's home, all around him was laughter, love and life.

All of his brothers were in attendance along with their wives and kids. Even Tommy's ex was there with their young daughter. It was if all was forgiven between them for this one time of the year.

There were all the usual traditions to be observed after dinner. Exchanging gifts and reliving the holidays through the memories of Leo and his brothers would result in additional hoots and howls.

Now there was the food. Adults and kids alike sat stuffing themselves with all of Mama's delicacies. Everyone had their favorites, and Shelly Berry always endeavored to see that each had something they loved to eat. It was decadent, but nobody complained.

The choices were spread in the kitchen and covered every eye on the stove, spot in the oven and square inch on the counter tops. There was turkey and dressing, chicken and dumplings, baked ham, butter beans, black-eyed peas, creamed corn, squash casserole, macaroni and cheese, candied sweet potatoes, deviled eggs and biscuits. Gallons of sweet tea were set out to wash it down. All fresh and all homemade. Shelly would have it no other way and would accept no help in preparing the food.

The family helped themselves by fixing their own servings onto heavyweight paper platters. There were seats available for them, some at the big table in the dining room, others at individual folding TV tables and a few sitting at the bar.

When the meal was completed, Leo knew he would also be forced to indulge in some serious sugar overload. Not that anyone held a gun on him to make him eat dessert; they were just so good no one could resist no matter how many calories had just been consumed. There were at least two from-scratch cakes Leo saw when he first arrived. One was Italian Cream Cake and the other one was German Chocolate. There were also pecan and egg custard pies in the fridge as well as other freshly baked nut-finger cookies, brownies and fruitcake cookies in a Tupperware® container on the bar.

Leo had just about finished his first platter of food as he surveyed the room watching his relatives enjoy theirs. Eddie was spearing a plump dumpling. Denny was scooping up butter beans. Tommy was inhaling forkfuls of dressing. And, there at the table with center of attention status, sat their newly discovered cousins enjoying all of it for the first time.

Shelly sat at the head of the table as the matriarch of the bunch. Pete sat to the right and Mickie sat to the left of her. All three were talking quietly and sharing compliments as well as the delicious food. Dee sat beside Mickie who had made that request of her before sitting. Occasionally, they would all laugh at something one of them said.

Leo smiled to himself despite the frightening memories of the day in Pete's cabin. The day came cascading back as he absentmindedly chewed on a slab of ham.

His ears were ringing, but he heard the PA clearly when the sirens stopped in front of the residence. Leo recognized the voice that identified himself as a member of the DEA ordering everyone inside to drop their weapons.

Leo tentatively peeked around the heavy table and saw both gunmen immobile on the floor. One was moaning. The other was quiet and still.

Glancing to his right, Leo saw Pete lying on his stomach with his hands extended in front of him. His gun was not in his hand. Pete's face was to the side away from Leo. He was not moving and a pool of blood had formed to his left side. Leo thought he heard gurgling sounds over the other noises in his ears.

Leo stood and hollered to the people outside who he was and that the scene was clear. He dropped his pistol and ran to Pete.

As Leo dropped to a knee beside Pete, several men entered the residence with their weapons drawn. Ted Springer was in the lead and holstered his handgun only after kicking exposed weapons from the two gunmen out of the way. He then aided Leo and his cousin who was having trouble breathing.

The next several hours became a blur, as medical attention was necessary for Pete and Leo. Pete's wound had been much more serious as a bullet had entered his side and collapsed a lung. Leo's minor head injury, while bloody, had only required a few stitches.

Springer and other members of local law enforcement then interviewed Leo. During the process, Leo learned that the agent had been tailing Richards, which afforded him the opportunity to promptly arrive after the gunfire began. The two men with Richards were both dead, one on the scene and the other dying in the ambulance on the way to the hospital.

After Pete was pronounced out of danger, his account of the confrontation corroborated Leo's statement effectively bringing the matter to an end. There was no one left to add or contradict their stories.

Since then, the two cousins had become reluctant heroes in the public eye. They had been hailed for their taking down of dirty cops. Neither wanted the attention, which only fed the media to seek them out to an even greater degree. Their bosses and colleagues treated them with even more respect. Leo only wanted to get back to his previous life and for everyone to quit asking him about the scar on his forehead. Maybe he could when the GBI finished their investigation that had been requested as a precaution by the local police.

The reverie around him brought Leo out of his daydream. His brothers were giving Tommy grief for the second platter of food he had brought back into the den. If anything, it was bigger than the first helping he had scarfed down.

"I don't know if that TV tray will hold all the weight," said Denny.

"I don't know if the commode will hold it all in the morning," said Eddie laughing.

"Y'all just need to worry about your own Jethro plates," said Tommy in response.

"Hey, Mama. Do you mind if I get Tommy one of those serving spoons so he can shovel that load into his mouth better?" asked Denny.

"Leo, would you tell your brother to leave me alone while I try to get nourishment?" whined Tommy in a mock little boy voice.

Laughter was all over the room. This was the stuff of memories.

"Hey, y'all remember the time Leo fixed that monster platter of food and spilled all of it on the floor as he yelled 'supper time.' said Denny.

Everyone including Leo laughed again. That really had been embarrassing at the time. Messy, too.

Leo swallowed the last bit of ham and slowly stood up. He rubbed his belly and then picked up his tea glass with his left hand and a spoon in the right. While clearing his throat, Leo began tapping the spoon on the glass to get everyone's attention.

"Listen up. I've got something to say before I make a belated toast," said Leo.

The noise subsided and all eyes were on Leo. He looked each person directly in the eye for a moment and smiled as he did. It was an opportunity to show his affection toward them individually before making announcements to the whole group.

"As you all know, this has been a year marked with sadness and joy. Now that it's coming to an end in a few days, I think we should all be thankful for our blessings.

"On the top of that list for me is this family. I love you all. That includes our newest members, Pete and Mickie.

Both cousins smiled and raised their glasses in salutes. Pete still had a sling and was more awkward in his acknowledgement.

"To the glue who holds this family together and who 'could make a turd taste good' according to my wife, all I can say is Mama rocks," continued Leo.

They all laughed at Dee's often quoted reference to Shelly's culinary expertise.

"Now, I don't want to get too sentimental about all this, but I believe it's important for us to remember these moments and good times together. I know I don't want to think about it, but I also know one day these times won't be anything but a memory. All good things have got to come to an end. That's why we have the video camera set up in the corner recording. I'm betting that the day will come when we'll enjoy seeing it again.

"With the new year will come new challenges. As Papa used to say, 'Expect the unexpected.' I have a whole new respect for that sentiment, but I look forward to the future while we live in the present."

The room was quiet as Leo paused. They knew what he meant.

"So, I want to propose a toast. Maybe I should've done it before we got started with this feast to be more appropriate and timely, but sometimes we Berrys tend to do things backasswards."

There were a couple of snickers from the kids A couple of the grownups nodded their heads in agreement.

"If you will join me in raising your glasses, here's to the common ancestor whose blood runs through our veins and has helped shaped so many lives. Leo Oscar Berry, Sr., you did well, sir!"

And the rest of the family joined in cheers.

CHAPTER 52

Leo sat at his desk in the study. Tiki was curled up and snoring on the floor beside him. The girls had gone to bed.

It had been the best Christmas Leo could remember. Maybe cheating death twice in a short span of time caused that. Maybe it was knowing there was love all around. Whatever the cause, he felt alive and at peace.

Now he was trying to unwind before joining Dee in their bed. As he had done many times since inheriting the journal, Leo took out the worn book and flipped through it.

Papa had trusted him with it. The thought of that trust had been almost overwhelming at first. Now it made Leo proud and content in a way he had not known possible.

Leo had a feeling the book would continue to be important in his life. Not only were there gems provoking thought throughout the writing, there were references that made him remember things since forgotten or hidden in the recesses of his mind. The life lessons Papa preached in his own way were all there between those tattered covers.

Leo spontaneously picked up his Cross pen off the desk and flipped over to the blank page after Papa's last entry. After a moment he began to write.

Dear Papa,

Thank you for trusting me with your journal. Thank you also for all you did for me when you were in this world. Somehow I think you are still looking out for me, and I thank you most of all for that.

You led a remarkable life. I didn't completely understand until I read your book. I wish I could have fully known you better in life, but I'm happy that I do now.

I know you felt guilty about the son and grandchildren who you never acknowledged publicly. I know this even though you didn't say it in those words. I know it because of the torment you expressed in feeling responsible for death, and feeling you needed redemption.

I don't know that I believe you needed any redemption. You did what you thought best under the circumstances you faced. However, because you asked me to help you find forgiveness, I have done what I could to do just that.

I've done everything you directed with your estate. Because of your generosity everyone in the family will benefit.

I've brought your grandchildren, Pete and Mickie, into the family. They are legacies you can be proud of.

In my mind the best way to show how much you cared for your family and for others is to leave your love for others to share. To do that, I have taken steps to see your prize possession made into a shining example of seeking knowledge.

The farm will become a new high school campus for your home county. I have transferred the property on condition the school will be named after you. I can't think of a more fitting name for someone who advocated teaching and learning.

One last thing before I close. Being the watchdog for this journal has instilled one more lesson you've taught that I intend to follow.

I have bought a journal for myself. I plan to make my first entry as I finish this letter to you.

Love always, Leo

The End

22791131R00249

Made in the USA
Charleston, SC
03 October 2013